I0700105

ENDORSEMENTS

"Rich Adams has very neatly merged a wonderful view of West Point just before the Civil War with the national turmoil of that time, and in the process shown the impact of that turmoil on individuals from all sections of our country. Well done! My heartiest congratulations!

—Dave R. Palmer, Lieutenant General, U.S. Army (Ret.), former superintendent of West Point, historian, Distinguished Graduate of West Point, and author of *The Summons of the Trumpet, The Way of the Fox, and George Washington and Benedict Arnold.*

"…All of my life I have appreciated the privilege of developing great friendships…united behind America's freedom and liberty. But it was not always this way. During the Civil War, such friendships were ripped apart due to cadets' Southern or Northern home places. There was a "parting" of the ways, which led to fighting and killing one another. Thanks to the great work of Rich Adams in *The Parting*, such a terrible period in America's history is presented in a most profound and riveting fashion. There is a truth on these pages we can all benefit from. A great read."

—Hal Moore, Lieutenant General, U.S. Army (Ret.), Distinguished Graduate of West Point, and co-author of *We Were Soldiers Once…And Young.*

"In this wonderful book, Rich Adams tells a powerful and poignant story about West Point and West Pointers on the cusp of the Civil War. Using the Academy and its cadets as a microcosm, he presents a moving portrayal of the passions released when our young nation began to tear itself apart, right up to the first major battle, when classmates and best friends faced each other across Bull Run. A "must read" for every fan of historical fiction as well as for Civil War buffs in general. Brilliant. Stunning."

> —Tom Carhart, West Point Class of 1966 and
> author of *Lost Triumph* and *Sacred Ties.*

"*The Parting* is a very fine achievement! Rich Adams handles his complicated plot expertly, especially the shifting time settings. I especially like the tone and general balance to the military in his love story with Clara."

> —Max Byrd, author of historical novels
> *Jefferson, Jackson,* and *Grant.*

"With its roots in extensive historical research, Rich Adams's *The Parting* brings alive the terrible tragedy of the Civil War and the tearing apart of West Point's Class of 1861, as its members chose to fight either for their state or for the nation. It also instructs us on the remarkable traditions of the United States Military Academy, the raising of leaders of character who, from their insouciance, always emerge dedicated and disciplined, ready to meet their country's greatest challenges on fields of battle."

> —Montgomery C. Meigs, General U.S. Army, (Ret.); former commander U.S. Army Europe; and after retirement, director of the Joint IED (Improvised Explosive Device) Defeat Organization; West Point graduate; and great, great, great nephew of Major General Montgomery C. Meigs, West Point Class of 1836 and quartermaster general of the Union Army during the Civil War.

"*The Parting* is an authentic period-piece story and a gift for the ages to the Long Gray Line, and to all who embrace America's rich and sometimes heartbreaking history."

> —Thomas B. Dyer III, president of the West Point Class of 1967, Distinguished Graduate of West Point, and chairman emeritus of the West Point Association of Graduates.

"*The Parting* is a captivating story about how the officers and cadets of West Point, especially those from the cotton and border states, confronted profound and divisive national political issues on the eve of the Civil War. The resolution of these issues would guide their allegiance in the national crisis. Having entered West Point from Tuscaloosa, Alabama, only a century later, I identified on the most personal level with the main character, John Pelham, native son of Alabama, who during the Civil War would be lauded as 'Gallant Pelham' by many, including Generals Robert E. Lee and J. E. B. Stuart."

> —John S. Caldwell, Jr., Lieutenant General U.S. Army, (Ret.).

—Adapted from the oil painting, Encampment on the Plain, by William Guy Wall, 1862, courtesy of the personal art collection of Thomas Petrie, West Point Class of 1967—

THE PARTING

A STORY OF WEST POINT
ON THE EVE OF THE CIVIL WAR

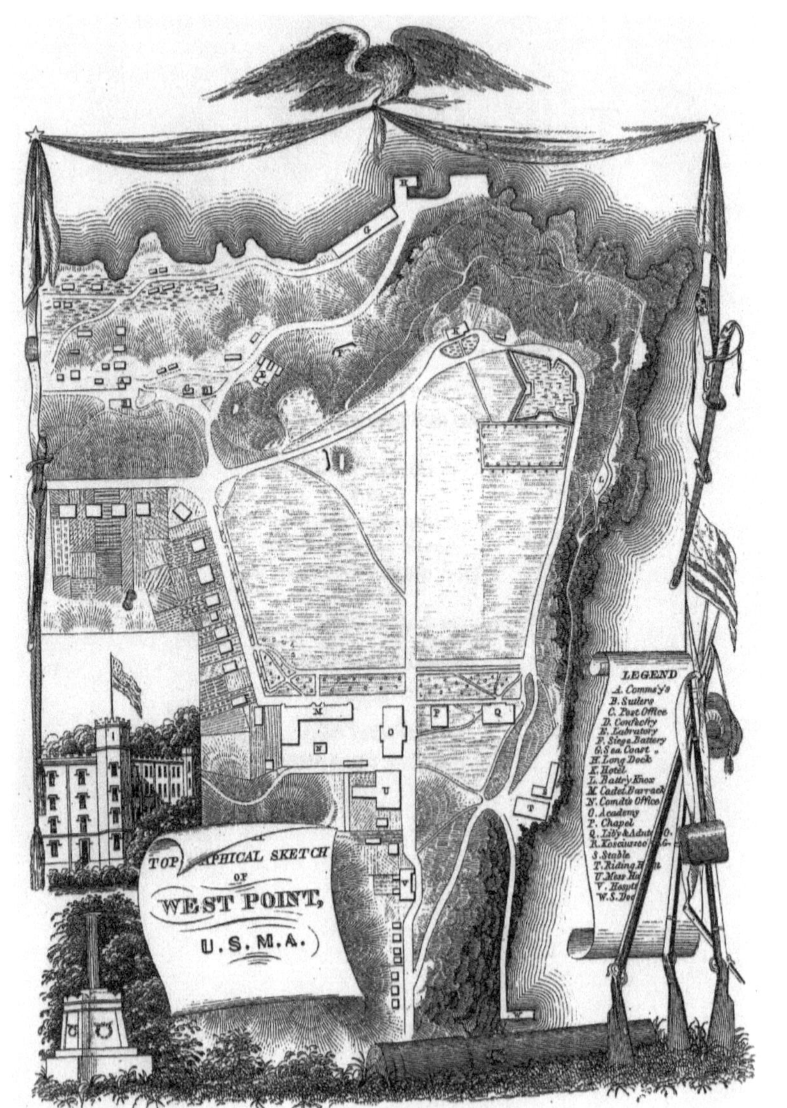

TOPOGRAPHICAL SKETCH
OF
WEST POINT,
U.S.M.A.
LEGEND
A. Comm'y's
B. Sutlers
C. Post Office
D. Confectry
E. Labratory
F. Siege Battery
G. Sea Coast
H. Long Dock
K. Hotel
L. Battry Knox
M. Cadet Barrack
N. Comdt's Office
O. Academy
P. Chapel
Q. Liby & Adjts O.
R. Kosciusco's G.
S. Stable
T. Riding Room
U. Mess Hall
V. Hospt
W. S. Dock

THE PARTING

A STORY OF WEST POINT ON THE EVE OF THE CIVIL WAR

Richard Barlow Adams
United States Military Academy
at West Point, Class of 1967

To Debbie, the love of my life

About This Edition

This Second Edition of *The Parting* includes, at the end of the book, photographs of selected story characters and images of West Point, circa 1860. It also reflects minor revisions and celebrates the American foundational belief that *We hold these truths to be self-evident, that all men are created equal, that they are endowed by their Creator with certain unalienable rights, that among these are life, liberty, and the pursuit of happiness.* The Declaration of Independence, 1776.

God, in his infinite grace, intends the full benefits of his kingdom here and in the hereafter for all who are created in his image. Slavery and its near kin, prejudice, discrimination, bigotry, racism, and intolerance, have existed throughout history. They are human conditions. Millions continue to be bound by some form of slavery, often without allusion to race, color, or creed.

Despite the reality of our non-utopian world, we Americans are becoming, by degrees, a better people, a better nation, and, by extension, the world a better place. *The Parting* enters upon this "becoming process" during America's most defining time in history.

Richard Barlow Adams

FOREWORD

When the author, Rich Adams, was a cadet, I returned to West Point to teach in the Department of Social Science. One of the courses I taught was the National Security Seminar. In it, we touched on the self-determination of nations—specifically how, through the years, the self-determination process influenced the fashioning of national policy. At the end of 1860, when South Carolina became the first of many states to secede from the Union, the nation was torn by starkly contrasting visions of what path our country's national policy should follow.

The Parting is a story that brings American history to life and, in the process, makes you think, smile, and sometimes weep. While the subtitle alludes to this being a story about West Point on the eve of the Civil War, it turns out to be much more. The deft interplay between the three days before the First Battle of Bull Run and the events of the preceding year at West Point is surrounded by a broader treatment of American history and enriched by the infusion of seemingly unrelated facts and events. From the outset, the story is charged with tension between the hope for peace and the reality of war. Fast-moving, vivid, and gripping, *The Parting* is, at its heart, a story of a "band of brothers." Formed at West Point among the Class of 1861, it fell to these brothers to decide on which side of Bull Run to make their stand. This powerful and touching saga is written in a way that draws in readers who have never seen—nor indeed known of—West Point, in no less a compelling way than it does graduates of the Military Academy.

The author's factual account of West Point at the beginning of the war is compelling. His attention to detail, vivid dialogue that captures the temper of the times, as well as his crisp portrayal of key personalities—including the legendary tavern keeper, Benny Havens—will capture both the imagination and the sentiment of every reader.

The author's adherence to documented relationships between actual cadets—some quite famous and some not so, but all significant to the plot—heightens the flow and flavor of the tale.

I applaud Rich Adams for taking on this ambitious project. His careful study and prodigious research have produced a fascinating and artfully crafted novel. In the process, it honors West Point and those who served as their consciences led them during an enormously wrenching period of our nation's history.

> Peter M. Dawkins—First Captain of the West Point Corps of Cadets; President of the Class of 1959; football captain and Heisman Trophy winner; Rhodes Scholar; Airborne Infantry field commander; decorated combat veteran; White House Fellow; Brigadier General, U.S. Army (Ret.); and Distinguished Graduate of West Point.

MAIN STORY CHARACTERS

West Point Class of 1861 (later, the Class of May 1861):
John Pelham, Alabama
Henry du Pont, Delaware
Nathaniel (Nate) Chambliss, Tennessee
Edmund (Ned) Kirby, New York
Thomas Rosser, Texas
Emory Upton, New York
Charles (Chas) Patterson, Arkansas
Henry Walter (Walter) Kingsbury, Connecticut
Adelbert Ames, Maine
Charles Hazlett, Ohio

West Point Class of 1862 (later, the Class of June 1861):
George Armstrong Custer, Ohio
Patrick O'Rorke, New York
Charles Ball, Alabama

West Point Class of 1863 (later, the Class of 1862):
Henry Farley, South Carolina

West Point Class of 1865 (later, the Class of 1864):
Daniel McElheny, Ohio

West Point Military Leadership:
Superintendents:
    Colonel Richard Delafield, Class of 1818
    Colonel Pierre Beauregard, Class of 1838
    Colonel Alexander Bowman, Class of 1825

Commandants of Cadets:
    Lieutenant Colonel William Hardee, Georgia, Class of 1838
    Lieutenant Colonel John Reynolds, Pennsylvania, Class of 1841
Other Military Staff:
    Lieutenant Fitzhugh Lee, Class of 1856, Tactical Officer, D Company
    Antoni Lorentz, Sword Master

West Point Academic Staff:
    Dennis Mahan, Class of 1824, Dean of the Academic Board, Professor of Engineering and Military Science
    William Bartlett, Class of 1826, Professor of Natural and Experimental Philosophy (Physics)
    Albert Church, Class of 1828, Professor of Mathematics
    Robert Weir, Professor of Drawing
    Henry Kendrick, Class of 1835, Professor of Chemistry, Mineralogy, and Geology
    Hyacinth Agnel, Professor of French
    John French, Reverend and Professor of English and Ethics
    Lieutenant Oliver O. Howard, Class of 1854, Assistant Professor of Mathematics
    Captain John Kelton, Class of 1851, Librarian

Clermont College:
    Clara Bolton, Philadelphia, Pennsylvania
    Ellie Lawson, Long Island, New York
    Carol Hill, Jackson, Mississippi
    Alice Paine, Boston, Massachusetts
    Jessica Danford, Clarksburg, Virginia
    Rebecca Astor, Concord, Rhode Island
    Miss Frampton, Assistant Dean and Chaperone
    Mrs. Wigglesworth, Chaperone

Other girls attending cadet hops:
    Eva Taylor
    Becky Thompson

Other Story Characters:

Jefferson Davis, Senator of Mississippi, later President of the
Confederacy, Class of 1828
James Ewell Brown (Jeb) Stuart, Virginia, Commanding General,
Cavalry of Northern Virginia, Class of 1854
Benny Havens (tavern and landing owner; wife Letitia)
Corporal Louis Bentz (longtime Corps bugler; dog, Hanzi)
James, head of service—Superintendent's Quarters
The Pelham family; Dr. Atkinson Pelham, John Pelham's father
Willie, Pelham family slave patriarch
Samuel, John Pelham's boyhood companion
Butch Jansonne, Pelham family overseer
Southern fire-eaters: Senator Louis Wigfall, Texas; Representative
William Miles, South Carolina
Major Robert Anderson, Kentucky, Class of 1825, Member of the
Davis Commission (Summer 1860) and Commander of Fort
Sumter
Albert Edward, Prince of Wales, son of Queen Victoria and Prince
Albert

PREFACE

Fewer than fifty miles north of New York City sits arguably the most beautiful college campus in America, the United States Military Academy, better known as West Point. Visitors who approach the gray castellated cadet barracks and academic buildings from the south see on their right eighteen black granite markers overlooking the majestic Hudson River and the distant Highland hills. The markers measure two feet by four feet and weigh five thousand pounds. Upon their polished faces is inscribed a history—unique, defining, and terrible. This is Reconciliation Plaza, the largest memorial complex at the nation's oldest military academy, a gift from the West Point Class of 1961 to commemorate its own and the members of the West Point Classes of May and June 1861.

The Parting is a story based in fact that enters the Victorian world of West Point during the period from August 1860 through the First Battle of Bull Run (Manassas) fought on July 21, 1861, and is told against the backdrop of slavery, states' rights, the Democratic and Republican Parties, the fire-eaters of the South, the abolitionists of the North, the election of Abraham Lincoln, the secession of Southern states, the election of Jefferson Davis, the resignations of Southern cadets and officers from West Point, the posturings intended to avoid war, and the surrender of Fort Sumter that dashed all hopes for peace.

Chapter One

Thursday, July 18, 1861

Winchester, Virginia

Three Days before the First Battle of Bull Run

In the haziness of dawn common to Shenandoah Valley summer mornings, Lieutenant John Pelham scanned the horizon from behind the battery of four old smoothbore six-pounder artillery pieces. All were aimed, as they had been for a month, to the northeast, at the eighteen thousand Union troops commanded by General Robert Patterson. As part of General Joseph Johnston's Army of the Shenandoah, which numbered twelve thousand, Pelham's mission was Johnston's mission, to deny Union movement toward Richmond where the Confederacy had just moved its capital and where Provisional President Jefferson Davis was still scrambling to put his government in place. As acting commander of the Alburtis Battery, Pelham was providing direct support for Colonel Francis Bartow's brigade. His second in command, and the only other officer in the battery, was Jason Findley, a militia second lieutenant who a month earlier had been teaching math in a school in Lynchburg.

Pelham stood nearly six feet and eyed the gunner at the second of his four artillery pieces. "All right, Corporal Summers, the target is yours."

"You heard the lieutenant," growled the corporal at the five members of his motley gun crew. "You best perform, or I'll be kicking your ass to midnight."

Pelham turned to the other gun crews. "You know what I expect. I want to know what this crew could have done better or faster."

1

The other crews understood well—that when it was their turn, they would receive no quarter.

For a month, Pelham had drilled his green troops with and without live ammunition. At the direction of those higher up, the live ammunition was reserved for real targets. Pelham understood the rationale, but he saw benefit only in tangible results, the hitting and missing of targets, and tended to manufacture live targets where others saw none. Corporal Summers' crew fixed on such a target—a granite outcrop on a distant hillside.

Summers barked the commands to load and fire, and the gun muzzle flashed red. Every eye watching the enemy rock saw it explode in gray smoke, just as a hard-riding courier approached from nearby Winchester. The courier reined his horse and struggled to catch his breath.

"Easy, soldier," Pelham said, his voice calm.

"Lieutenant, sir. Your presence is desired at a meeting at General Johnston's headquarters."

Pelham smiled at the man's polite phrasing of a direct order.

"As soon as you can make it, sir!" The rider jerked the reins and galloped off.

Moments later, the thunder of many horses preceded the Confederate Black Horse Cavalry's return from the northeast. Its lead rider wore a cavalier hat flying a black ostrich plume. The man, Colonel James Ewell Brown Stuart, West Point Class of 1854, and known as Jeb, carried himself high in the saddle.

Pelham mounted a caisson wagon and waved his hat to draw Stuart's attention.

Stuart saw him and trotted up, touching his hat. "'Morning, John."

"'Morning, Colonel." Pelham saluted the man five years his senior. "General Johnston has called a meeting, sir. Even I am to attend, so I'm sure he'll be expecting you."

"And I'll have news for him," said the man with a red beard who touched his hat a second time and dashed off.

Sensing deployment, Pelham ordered Findley to prepare the battery and limber the guns—attach them to chest-mounted carriages drawn by six-horse teams. Similarly, caisson wagons overloaded with solid shot and canister rounds would be readied.

Johnston's headquarters was the Winchester courthouse, and by the time Pelham entered the main courtroom, it was full of officers, all bearing high rank. After a few minutes, Johnston's aide-de-camp entered and announced the general's arrival. The assembled officers snapped to attention. Johnston, bearing a trim mustache, goatee, and thinning hair, returned the salutes with a nod and gestured for everyone to take a seat. He stood before the magistrate's bench, holding two telegrams.

"Colonel Stuart, what have you to report?"

"Favorable news, General. Union forces have pulled back to Harpers Ferry, and there is evidence that they intend no offense. Rumor is Patterson has overestimated our strength and sees himself on the defense. Icing on the cake, his army is dissolving. With each day, more of his ninety-day conscripts called up by Lincoln in April are deciding on home-cooked meals."

The room filled with laughter.

"Ah, God is indeed good," said Johnston, thrusting one of the dispatches above his head. "This is from President Jeff Davis. It was sent early this morning and asks that I consider moving the army with all speed to Manassas Junction to reinforce General Beauregard's twenty thousand troops, spread out as they are along Bull Run. As we all know, our good friend Irvin McDowell left Washington on the sixteenth with around thirty-five thousand Union troops. He arrived late yesterday in Centreville, about three miles east of Bull Run.

"This other dispatch is from General Beauregard. Says that one of McDowell's divisions is presently engaging him at Blackburn's Ford over Bull Run." Johnston scanned the faces in the room. "The telegram is an hour old, so I suspect there is more to the story. Anyway, I was wondering if we might want to help our Confederate brothers."

The room rocked with cheers.

Johnston turned to the blackboard behind him, chalked with the relative locations of Washington DC, Richmond, Manassas Junction, Winchester, Ashby Gap, and Piedmont Station. Between them were chalked intervening distances: 10 miles from Winchester southeast to Ashby Gap atop the Blue Ridge; 10 miles from Ashby

Gap south to Piedmont Station; and 34 miles from Piedmont Station east to Manassas Junction.

"We'll be pushing our green troops to the limit. Have them cook three-days rations. We leave at noon, and when we get to Piedmont Station, the infantry will load on trains for Manassas. Artillery and cavalry will travel by road."

Those in the room scribbled notes.

"General Jackson's First Brigade will take the lead, followed in order by the Second, Third, and Fourth Brigades. Tom, can you be ready by noon?"

The man with a full beard and piercing blue-gray eyes nodded. Colonel Francis Bartow, General Barnard Bee, and General Kirby Smith, the other brigade commanders, likewise acknowledged the order of march.

"I am hopeful we can cross the Blue Ridge no later than midnight," Johnston continued. "For the defense of Winchester, we have two thousand local militia. We'll leave some artillery, and we'll leave the sick. Half of Stuart's cavalry will keep Patterson at bay for a day, and then join up with us as soon as they can."

Johnston cleared his throat. "Gentlemen, we must do this quickly or it will be for naught. Worse, McDowell will have better than an even chance to run for Richmond."

The door to the courtroom suddenly flew open. A wide-eyed youth with a pimpled grin held a telegram high above his head. "Sirs, it is my honor as a Confederate soldier to report that them bluecoats what tried to cross Bull Run at Blackburn's Ford, maybe three thousand of 'em, they never saw our side of Bull Run. We whipped 'em—yes, we did! And it was General Longstreet and Colonel Early what did it!"

CHAPTER TWO

ELEVEN MONTHS EARLIER
JACKSONVILLE, ALABAMA

On Sunday, August 12, 1860, following Holy Communion, the organist played "Onward Christian Soldiers," and John Pelham sang with strength and emotion, catching many in the congregation by surprise. Flanked by his parents, Atkinson and Martha Pelham, and six siblings in a pew bearing a brass plate honoring his maternal grandparents, he was different from what any of them remembered.

The Presbyterian Church in Jacksonville, Alabama, was large by southern standards, seating two hundred whites in the main sanctuary and fifty blacks in the balcony. The sanctuary was a showcase, constructed of the finest materials, courtesy of a town and county where cotton was king and faith in Jesus Christ the foundation of life. The sanctuary and balcony were packed to overflowing for the mid-month Sunday service to be followed by a fellowship picnic. Outside the church, the day was already hot and humid. Two dozen black men and boys tended horses and carriages. Many of them sang their own version of the church hymn; others engaged in banter or waited in solemn silence as flies buzzed the grounds in anticipation of the feast.

In the four years he'd been away, Pelham had returned home only once before. He too realized he bore little resemblance to the seventeen-year-old who had journeyed alone to West Point, New York, in 1856 to take the qualifying examinations for entrance into the United States Military Academy. In the time away from Benton County, recently renamed Calhoun County in honor of the former vice president and South Carolinian, his mind, body, and spirit had been much altered by the Academy's discipline, instruction, and rigor that had reduced the Class of 1861 from ninety-three to fifty. He was more than grateful for the unexpected second furlough. The coming year would be his fifth and last at the school some forty miles up the Hudson River from New York City and a thousand miles from Jacksonville.

Pelham struggled to focus on the service, to be honestly reverent. As he sang the last hymn, his mind sifted the spirited debates he'd had with his father the past week over President Buchanan's successor.

He felt a small hand take his and gave it a squeeze. Its owner, Bettie, his only sister, now seventeen and more than a handsome woman, was home from her third year of college in Maysville, Kentucky. Two summers previous, when Pelham was on a longer furlough of two and a half months, he had traveled to Jacksonville by way of Maysville so that the two of them could journey home together. This past week, they had spent nearly every afternoon as companions, riding or walking the plantation, reliving the past, and dreaming the future. She had proven to be quite a horsewoman and had been delightful company, though some of her northern sympathies annoyed him, despite her declarations that she was only teasing. He admonished her that she was too convincing a teaser and should be careful of her powers. In his eyes, she had grown up too quickly and without his presence or permission. He would dearly miss her when he returned to West Point—the place she called Camelot.

Pelham's older brothers, Charles and William, stood on the other side of Bettie, and beyond them the younger Pelhams—Peter, Samuel, and Thomas.

Suddenly the organist hit a wrong key and awoke the congregation, which responded with sideways glances and snickers.

When the music died, Reverend Peter Smith gave the organist a forgiving look and in a booming voice concluded the service. "Now may the Lord God of heaven bless you and keep you, make his face to shine upon you, and give you peace, now and forevermore. Amen."

The congregation waited patiently for their aged leader to shuffle down the aisle to the front vestibule. The newly arrived and much younger Reverend Paul Knox followed. He had been introduced to the congregation only that morning.

As the Pelham clan filed out, each took the relic's weathered hand and received a personal blessing or word of encouragement. When John Pelham approached the man, he gingerly shook his arthritic hand.

The old eyes glistened. "What can I say, John, but that you give me great joy. What a blessing to your family and all of us to have you home these few days. But it's not fair you should leave so soon."

Pelham gently hugged the man whose cleric robes smelled of naphtha. Reverend Smith had always been in the pulpit and had tutored him for the academy entrance exams. The body that had been forever strong from raising barns for parishioners was a shell of its former self. "You, sir, are ever on my mind, as is home. Anyway, just one more year and I'm done, and after giving the country its due, I'll return, and you'll tire of me soon enough."

"Never, lad," the reverend vowed with a laugh that soured to a hacking cough. Recovering, he patted Pelham on the back. "Good luck, my son, and may God bless and protect you in all that lies ahead."

Pelham greeted the new minister, not much older than himself, and descended the church steps, conscious that his blue furlough uniform attracted attention, trimmed as it was with gold buttons down the front. His brother Will said he looked like a peacock in heat. By a sense he did not fully understand, he was aware, as he had been in the sanctuary, of the glances from nearly every young woman in the congregation. The furtive looks beneath fashionable hats and parasols were not unwelcomed.

The aroma of fried chicken teased his nose as he scanned the lawn from beneath the visor of his blue forage cap, not finding who he was looking for. At the bottom of the stairs, a weathered man of some fifty years stepped in front of him. The man, Butch Jansonne, was the family's new overseer.

"Master John, it was good to finally meet you, and I just wanted to wish you a safe trip back to your school."

The man extended his hand and Pelham shook it. "That's kind of you, Mr. Jansonne."

"I trust you found everything in good order, sir?"

"I'm sorry?"

"The plantation?"

"Why—I assume it's fine. I've no reason to think otherwise."

"Aye. Your blacks are a proud bunch, Master Pelham, and they work well when encouraged, but then you know that I'm sure. You have talked to some of them?" Jansonne turned his head, spat tobacco juice, and wiped his mouth on his sleeve.

"I had intended to, especially the man Samuel, but regretfully, no."

Jansonne seemed relieved and offered a faint smile before taking his leave.

Pelham spied his father in conversation with a man beneath a yawning oak tree at the corner of the churchyard. The discussion appeared serious, and he was drawn to it. The man was Judge Abraham J. Walker, a longtime family friend and a member of the Alabama Supreme Court. Pelham didn't recall seeing the judge in church.

"You two appear to be in need of an arbiter," Pelham said, executing a slight bow.

The judge clasped Pelham's hand. "John, this has become a time of contingencies. And your father—the good doctor—and I appear to see a thing differently."

"Abraham, that would be an understatement," Atkinson Pelham said stiffly, his demeanor softening at the approach of his daughter Bettie.

"I'm so sorry to interrupt, Judge Walker." Bettie said, flashing a smile at her brother. "But, Pa, would you meet my classmate Lucy Bains from Anniston? Can you believe she's here? You simply must."

The judge nodded his assent.

Pelham felt his father's touch as he passed by.

The judge, a full-bearded medium-height man of sixty, considered Pelham before speaking. "My, but you've become quite a man, John. Seems like yesterday, your christening." Walker paused. "In your short lifetime, the country's seen a lot of change. Much is afoot, John, and what I was saying to your father is that we Alabamians need to be prepared for an alternative future, should events unfold as they appear they might."

As was his habit when entering upon a subject, the judge pursed his lips, and Pelham prepared for words spent frugally.

"If the election goes badly and Alabama and other Southern states were to exercise their option, to strike out on their own, try something different, a different form of government, and between them a looser federation with less centralized power and greater respect of the individuality and needs of a state, would you favor Alabama joining such a federation?"

"You talked to Father about this, sir?"

"I suggested to your father that there will be mass secessions if Lincoln is elected, though quite frankly he thinks me wrong. And I suppose there is some chance he's right." The judge glanced across the lawn at the older Pelham talking to Bettie's friend. "Your father believes compromise is still the best wisdom, and that it will prevail as it has in the past. And beyond that, he is dead set against secession no matter what the circumstance. He even vowed to stump with Stephen Douglas to fight it."

"And you're wondering my position on the subject?"

"Knowing that would be useful, yes."

Pelham's father had lamented the divisiveness of the Democratic Party that had given the sectional Republican Party its opening, but vehemently claimed the Democrats would reunite before November and undo the botched conventions in Charleston and Baltimore. He believed the split ticket of Stephen Douglas for the North and John Breckinridge for the South would be resolved.

"Then, sir," Pelham said, "I'm afraid it won't please you to know that, at least for the present, Pa and I are of the same mind." The words nearly stuck in Pelham's throat. "The issues are daily in the papers, as well as what you suggest. But, sir, I believe Pa may be right, that Alabama has very much to lose in what you propose. I can't see the real gain, not in basic rights and certainly not in economics." Pelham paused. "Sir, wouldn't you agree there is much risk in what you're suggesting?"

"There is risk in everything, John—everything worthwhile. But our rights as a sovereign state are in perilous jeopardy and have been for some time. As long as we've had a Democrat in the White House, we've had a measure of sympathy for our needs and our peculiar institution."

Pelham nodded. Slavery would always be the sticking point.

"As you say," the judge continued, "we've survived some divisive times through compromise. But the federal government has become a mean thing, continually growing and assuming for itself responsibilities and rights that naturally, by the Constitution, fall to the states. Worse, its decisions invariably favor the North. If our William Yancey had his way, we would already be a sovereign state, flying our own flag."

Pelham remained silent. His father had nothing good to say about Yancey, Alabama's chief fire-eater—the Northern descriptor for a secessionist. His father said that the only time Yancey wasn't preaching secession was when he was sleeping. He made no attempt to hide his disdain for the man and all those he viewed as loose cannons.

"Do you know how onerously we are taxed by tariffs, John, and how unfairly our commerce is managed by the federals? Do you understand how our livelihood, our property institution, and our right to take property into the new territories are at stake?" The judge didn't wait for an answer. "I suppose you do not take the abolitionists seriously?"

Pelham admired the judge's verbal agility.

"No more than I should, sir," he said. "I believe we skew the group out of proportion, that what John Brown did at Harpers Ferry is distorted history. Personally, I think abolitionists make more noise than allies and number but few."

"Perhaps. But Harpers Ferry has had the South looking over its shoulder."

Pelham didn't refute the judge's point. Colonel Robert E. Lee's capture of John Brown in October 1859 had been a significant event. Brown's bloody, but botched, revolt of slaves in Virginia, intended to catalyze the South into a slave rebellion, had failed. His grand vision had unraveled to a last-ditch stand inside the engine house of the Harpers Ferry Federal Armory in northern Virginia, where he, his sons, and a small number of committed slaves held several hostages. One hostage was the father of a fellow West Point cadet, a grandnephew of George Washington. Pelham knew that Lee had sent under the white flag a recent West Point graduate, Lieutenant Jeb Stuart, to negotiate with Brown. After Brown's refusal to surrender and the bloody aftermath, Thomas Jackson, another West Point graduate and a hero of the Mexican War, mobilized cadets from the Virginia Military Institute to provide security for Brown's trial and hanging.

"How many in your class, John? From the Southern states—the Cotton Belt?"

"Perhaps one in three, sir. I do not believe more."

"One in three? A disturbing ratio, don't you think? I'm not saying that the Democrats can't win, but for the life of me, I don't see how. In any event, we can ill afford to lose more seats in the upcoming congressional elections, and they'll be strongly contested. If we lose them, without doubt the next president will be Republican. Worse it will be Lincoln. And with Lincoln, Alabama or South Carolina will bolt and the dam burst."

The judge's bluntness struck Pelham. "Sir, have you ever been to West Point?"

"I have not had the pleasure."

"I assure you it is the noblest of institutions, and bears none of the political rancor of which we speak."

"And that is to its credit, I'm sure. But the thing is—and let me be candid—if Alabama does secede, we're going to need every military advantage we can muster . . . in the event Mr. Lincoln chooses to make an issue of it. More to the point, we'll need a strong officer corps. We'll need every West Pointer we can get."

Pelham let the remark pass.

The judge leaned closer. "I don't need to tell you how important this year is for you, for all of us. And I hear some very good things about your popularity as a cadet and your performance at the Academy. That among your pursuits you are excellent with the blade and the finest horseman at the Academy. All this, of course, is very well, and cavalry is important, but what we'll really need are artillerists, expert artillerists. I encourage you to—"

The commotion of a carriage advancing up the church drive and shouts for Pelham interrupted the judge. He rested a hand on Pelham's shoulder. "Enough, John. You must be on your way, and I don't envy your journey. I simply ask that you think seriously upon what's happening and your role in it."

"Yes, sir, you may depend upon it. I seek only what is best for Alabama."

The judge nodded. "As do I."

As the judge turned to go, Pelham restrained him with a hand. "Sir, may I write you as matters develop?"

The judge brightened. "Of course, John, and you may depend on my immediate reply. And if you will indulge me one last question.

What is the one thing you want more than anything else at this point in your life?"

Pelham's response was immediate. "To graduate from West Point, sir."

The judge smiled. "Of course. Foolish of me to ask."

Pelham made his way to the carriage and found a crowd wanting a speech. Seeing he had no choice, he mounted the church steps and delivered a captivating oration, that home and all who made it so were sacred to him, and that what he was about to conclude at West Point was for them and for Alabama. This earned him a grand applause and the freedom to depart. He descended the steps feeling, oddly, both euphoric and uneasy. While he shook hands and embraced friends, across the church lawn blacks busied themselves arranging tables and benches.

"Don't think I can't still whip you," Charles, the oldest of the Pelhams, said, waving threatening fists and then hugging his brother.

"Not likely," William, the second eldest, said. "But I sure can." Pelham received another hug.

"I'm counting on you both to take care of Ma, Pa, and the family." Pelham then sought out his younger brothers and finally Bettie, who was trying unsuccessfully to be brave.

"We'll have none of that, sis. You take care of yourself and mind the boys in Maysville. They can't be trusted."

His remark made her smile. "John Pelham, how is it you know that? And, anyway, I can take excellent care of myself, thank you. Besides, I'm waiting for you to find me a cadet."

"And I will, but in return, when you're back at school, take all that Yankee rhetoric with a grain of salt."

"I am not becoming a Yankee."

"I didn't say you were. But the Mason-Dixon Line is taking on more significance, and those from the North are of a different persuasion." He winked and kissed her forehead, at which she came undone.

"There, there, sweetheart," Martha Pelham said, consoling her daughter, and then addressing her West Pointer. "John Pelham, promise me you will read your Bible every night and say your prayers."

"I do, and I will, Mother."

"Mother?" Her eyes glistened. "Lord, they've made you a man."

His embrace swallowed up the small woman. "Ma—I love you so much."

Martha Pelham wiped her eyes. "Willie has a jug of fresh water and ham and cheese sandwiches for your lunch." She handed him a muslin-wrapped package. "And this is for later. Some of young Ora's biscuits and Willie's beef jerky."

"It's time, John." Atkinson Pelham said, taking his son's arm and after a few steps stopping. "So soon. A three-week furlough with only a week at home and the rest traveling."

"I know, Pa. I almost wish I hadn't—"

"Nonsense! Nonsense. Having you for even a few days has meant the world to all of us, especially your mother. You will write?"

"Of course, Pa. As often as I can."

"There is so much going on, John, and our new man Jansonne gets the work done—but—" The older Pelham let it drop. "Judge Walker can be quite persuasive, can't he, John?"

"No more than you, Pa. And as promised, I'll abide your opinion— at least for a time. But tell me about Jansonne."

"He's a strict one to be sure," said his father. "But claims it's needful, given the amount of cotton we have to bring in."

"He uses the whip?"

"I can't say that he overuses it, at least not yet."

"Aren't you concerned for runaways, Pa?"

"That is always a possibility, save for one of the Watson slaves, Charlie was his name. You might remember he used to be old man Watson's driver. Anyway, he ran off and got himself killed in Illinois."

"Killed?"

"They said he resisted arrest, and news of that sort has a restraining effect."

"We've a good black family, Pa. We've never had a runaway, nor given cause for it." Pelham wanted to say more, but knew it wasn't his place. And as for old man Watson, he remembered him only too well.

"We just need to get through the next year," his father said, almost as a prayer.

Pelham sensed a change in his father. He looked unusually tired, and Pelham considered for the first time the stress of running a plantation while at the same time minding the health of a county.

"Pa?"

"Yes, son."

"I am going back to the Academy with every intention of finishing the year, getting my diploma, and being commissioned. You know what that means to me. But if it isn't possible, since I won't be of age … I will need your permission to resign."

The elder Pelham smiled and patted him on the back. "No reason to visit that now."

They reached the carriage and its driver.

"Willie, you take good care of our boy."

The slim black man with a head of white wool smiled. "'Course I will, master."

Pelham climbed up beside the driver. "Okay, Willie, take me to West Point."

Willie laughed. "Well, Master John, I can take you as far as the stage." He made a clucking sound that propelled the one-horse carriage past the line of well-wishers and beyond the smell of fried chicken.

Pelham sat tall on the seat, looking back at the figures on the lawn until they disappeared. The carriage moved smartly down the lane and turned onto the main road, Willie whistling his way through a medley of gospel songs.

After a time of reflection, Pelham broke silence. "Willie, how is it you never get older?"

"Lord, Master John, I suppose cuz I's always been old."

"But you'll outlast us all," Pelham said, giving the slave patriarch a gentle nudge. As far back as he could remember, the man had been old. And for most of the man's life, he had either picked cotton or supervised the picking, until his gift with horses was discovered the summer the equine virus swept through the South killing nearly two thousand horses. Willie's root-based cure saved the Pelham steeds. Within a week, Pelham's father had instructed Peter Martin, the previous overseer, that Willie was no longer to work in the field, but in the stables and doing directly for the family.

Continuing, Pelham finally challenged the obnoxious grin on Willie's face the past half mile.

"What are you smiling about, Willie?"

The black man kept grinning.

"Tell me, Willie. What is it?"

"Oh, nothing, Master John. I just happy and proud—proud of you. You gonna make a fine officer, Master John."

"You think so?"

"I knows it."

"Well, maybe I will. And for sure it's been a long time coming. And if it does, you, dear Willie, get all the credit."

Willie's face was radiant. "Ah, Master John, it weren't none of me." Pelham put a hand on the black man's arm. "Willie, next to God and family, you know I love you and Samuel best. And it was you, Willie, who taught me to ride, care for a horse, to fish, and more."

"Oh, Master John."

"And the whole family feels the same, and shame on you if you don't know it better than your name. Pa has always said you're as good, as easy, and as consistent a soul as ever lived, and the glue that holds the place together."

The carriage made good time along the valley road that traversed the Alabama hill country, the air humid and flavored with cut hay and honeysuckle. Cottonwoods, magnolias, and sprawling oaks lined the road. Pelham feverishly stored images of home that would have to last a year: the rolling landscape, the woods, bottomlands, and dark-water creeks; the fields of cotton, wheat, and corn; the laborers in the fields; the houses, barns, and slave shanties; the daily wash hung out to dry; the fences of wood, stone, and wire; the horses, cattle, and hogs grazing dumbly; the cats and dogs lazing in the afternoon sun; and the chickens clucking about as if they owned the world.

A man on horseback approached from the opposite direction. Evidently impressed with Pelham's uniform, the man touched the brim of his hat, and Pelham responded in kind.

After another mile of silence, Pelham cleared his throat. "And Samuel? How is he?"

"Oh, Samuel, that boy is fine, just fine, Master John."

"I had hoped to see him."

"In the field, Master John, got to bring in that cotton. You know that. Your daddy made Samuel the boss black man in the field."

Pelham was well aware of Samuel's promotion. The day before, his father had lauded Samuel's work. Still, it should have been easy for

Samuel to visit the big house either in the early morning or late evening, if only for a few minutes; and Pelham had very much wanted to see him, to know how he was doing, and to mend how they had left things when he had last been home on furlough. He thought of Samuel often and the history they had—and it was always Samuel, never Sam or Sammy. Memories of their time of innocence and fantasy came easy when they had been inseparable from sunup to sundown. Happy times until the day everything changed. The game had changed everything. He had never meant to hurt Samuel, and they had both survived and grown up. He thought of the year before he'd gone to West Point, when his father had entrusted him with a hundred acres of timber land, challenging him to clear and farm the land with a work force of six of the blacks. His father had agreed with the men he'd selected, including Samuel. For ten months they had toiled as one. They felled trees, cut wood, grubbed the land, constructed living quarters, plowed fields, planted corn, and brought in a harvest, all before the fall frost. Through it all, Samuel had worked the hardest.

They crossed the covered bridge at Four Mile Spring, the sun bursting through holes in the tin roof. Pelham reached for his valise and retrieved the ham and cheese sandwiches his mother had given him, handing one to Willie.

"Thank you, Master John."

"Tell me, Willie. How are things on the plantation? Tell me the truth."

"Oh, Master John—"

"Don't sweeten it."

"I suppose we do got some bumps with the new overseer, that's a fact. But I expect that's natural." The old man picked his words like watermelon seeds. "And I expect that's why you ain't seen Samuel. Master Butch ride Samuel pretty hard, he do." Willie forced a smile. "But everything gonna work its way around."

Pelham took a long pull on the jug of water and passed it to the black man.

They continued in silence until they crested a hill that brought Willie to life. "There 'tis, Master John. Blue Mountain." The old man pointed down at a small town in the valley.

They arrived at the stage office a few minutes before four o'clock, the fourteen-mile trip taking three hours. Pelham checked in for the morning stage and directed Willie to the Wilkes Boarding House, a block past the stage office.

"You made good time, Willie. After watering and feeding the horses, you should make it back well before dark."

"And that's good, cuz you know I don't take so good to the dark." The black man spoke with relief in his voice.

"Nothing is going to get you, Willie."

The man smiled and handed Pelham his duffel.

"Thank you, Willie. Thanks for everything." Pelham extended his hand.

Willie grasped Pelham's hand with both of his. "My pleasure, Master John, my pleasure. You take real good care of youself, you hear? All us want you back safe and whole."

"I will, Willie." Pelham gazed into the old man's eyes with the sudden urge to ask him if he had ever wanted to be free.

"Is they something else, Master John?"

Pelham smiled weakly. "No, Willie."

CHAPTER THREE

WEST POINT, NEW YORK

That same Sunday afternoon, the apprentice post courier, Alden Weir, the youngest of sixteen children born to Robert Weir, the Academy's drawing professor, ran as fast as his short, spindly legs could carry him, clutching a sealed envelope. In less than a minute, he covered the distance from post headquarters to the large well-appointed home of the superintendent of the United States Military Academy, currently occupied by its oldest superintendent, Colonel Richard Delafield. Delafield, attired in a regal blue uniform and sporting bushy white chin-curtain whiskers, stood on the wide front veranda waiting to review the Corps of Cadets when they turned out for parade.

"Colonel, sir." The breathless boy handed Delafield the telegram. "For you, sir."

Delafield patted the boy on the head and rendered him a sharp salute. "Thank you very much, Alden."

"Thank you, sir!" The boy raced off in the direction he had come.

Delafield ran a finger around the inside of his collar, frustrated with uniform alterations that never kept pace with his weight.

"Colonel, sir, some ice water?" A distinguished-looking black man in a pressed white topcoat put a tray in front of the superintendent.

"Thank you, James." Delafield drew a pair of thick-lensed wire-rimmed spectacles from his coat pocket. The glasses rendered him fish-eyed but were essential for reading. After digesting the telegram, another from General Winfield Scott, still general-in-chief of the Army, Delafield glanced across the Plain.

"Bad news, sir?" After five years of daily contact, the head of the Delafield's service staff understood the superintendent better than anyone. And whether he wanted to be or not, James was privy to the Delafield's inmost thoughts.

"Dammit, James. How am I to perform my mission when the secretary of treasury won't approve my budgets?"

"Yes, sir."

"Hopefully, Jeff Davis can do us some good."

James nodded at the reference to Jefferson Davis, the senior senator from Mississippi, who the day before had departed for Washington DC after concluding his commission to evaluate the Academy. The commission had included three other members of Congress, along with Major Robert Anderson and two junior officers. The inspection and review of the Academy had lasted a month and had included interviews with cadet officers in the First Class and selected members of the Second Class.

Delafield placed the telegram and his spectacles on the railing and peered across the Plain at the distant encampment. The field of white tents was barely visible through the encircling double row of elms that had been planted only a few years earlier. The city of tents was the annual summer encampment for the Corps of Cadets, this year numbering two hundred and seventy-eight. The cadets ranged in age from sixteen to twenty-six and represented all thirty-three states. Across Jefferson Road from the superintendent's quarters, a steady stream of civilians, including wide-eyed ladies in Victorian dress, approached the array of benches in anticipation of the afternoon parade.

Delafield fixed his gaze on the flag that furled above the crown of trees at the north end of the Plain. When he first laid eyes on the flag as a new cadet in 1814, it bore fifteen stripes and fifteen stars, inconsistent with the eighteen states then in the Union. The flag had not been changed since 1795, there still being disagreement on how to account for Tennessee, Ohio, and Louisiana. Not until 1818, under President Monroe, would the flag bear stripes for the original thirteen colonies and a star for each state. The standard that now waved boasted thirty-three stars, and Delafield wondered how many more would appear when the territories from Mexico were ready. The flag reminded him of

Davis's remark, that government intentions to keep slavery out of the new territories could fuel a fire no one needed.

Where had the time gone, Delafield mused as he surveyed the backs of his hands, his skin wrinkled, liver spotted. It seemed a lifetime ago when he'd graduated first in the Class of 1818. Twenty years of field assignments had followed, and then came his first appointment to West Point as superintendent. Those seven years had been a proud time, when the children were home, a time of fond memories. The idyllic assignment was followed by the Mexican War and more years of field service until, in 1856, he was ordered back to West Point as superintendent for an unprecedented second term.

At first, it had been a source of pride, but the shine of it had long worn off. He had held the Academy's top post for nearly a fifth of its lifetime, having learned that if you design it, you build it. During his career he had architected, constructed, or otherwise had a hand in almost every significant structure at the Academy, including the academic building, the cadet barracks, the library and post headquarters building, the cadet chapel, the ordnance compound, the mess hall, the hospital, the riding hall, and the horse stables.

But now, at age sixty-two, he was numb to the routine of Academy life and the responsibility of caring for, feeding, and evaluating the Corps of Cadets. And to this was added the headache of the little fiefdoms in the academic department and the upkeep of the Academy's physical plant. He was mentally and physically exhausted, tired of the annual inspections by the secretary of war's five-member board of visitors. Its members—congressional delegates, senior military staff, and civilian academics—forayed way beyond their primary purpose of evaluating the cadets in their June examinations. Invariably, the board opened doors and pulled out drawers beyond their assigned scope and challenged what they little understood.

And once again, the board had arrived in late May, inspected the facilities, assessed the curriculum, monitored the faculty's final examinations, applauded outgoing First Classmen, and monitored the examination of civilian-attired, pimple- faced freshmen who would form the next class of plebes. But, as always, he greeted them with politeness and feigned interest in their opinions and recommendations.

After the board's departure, Jefferson Davis and his commission arrived. If it had been headed by anyone other than his gaunt-faced friend, it could have destroyed his summer. But Davis made good on his word that the commission would impose no burden on summer training. Delafield knew that Davis loved West Point, and Davis had often been in a position to do it great service. After seven years of military service and escorting Chief Black Hawk to prison after the Black Hawk War, the young Davis had resigned from the military to prepare for a political career while raising cotton in Mississippi. From 1844 to 1846, he served Mississippi in the United States House of Representatives. At the outbreak of hostilities with Mexico, he resigned from Congress and raised a regiment known as the Mississippi Rifles, which gained considerable renown. After the war, he returned to politics as a U.S. senator from Mississippi and as secretary of war during the term of President Franklin Pierce. Delafield knew Davis was an ardent states' rights man, but not a secessionist. In fact, earlier in the year, Davis had submitted several resolutions in the Senate to salve the clamor of secessionist rhetoric. When last he and Delafield talked, Davis was optimistic, or at least hopeful, that the Union might still be saved.

From the south, along Jefferson Road, Delafield noticed the approaching figure of Dennis Mahan, dean of the academic department and professor of military/civil engineering and military science. Mahan, a thin man, carried his signature worn leather briefcase and mounted the steps without invitation. His face bore a look of gravity, as it always did.

"Dennis," said Delafield.

The waiter poured the dean a glass of water.

"Colonel, sir." Mahan extracted a worn folder from his briefcase. "As requested, documents addressing the issue and illustrating my points."

Delafield nodded as he took the folder. Mahan had finished first in the Class of 1824—as had William Bartlett, professor of natural and experimental philosophy, Class of 1826; and Albert Church, professor of mathematics, Class of 1828. The three of them formed the core of the Academy's intellectual vigor and oversight.

"I'll give it priority, Dennis." Delafield lifted his eyeglass in the direction of the cadet encampment. "Care to stay for the review?"

"I'm quite sure I've seen enough parade reviews, sir. Classes begin in less than two weeks, so, if I could hear back from you—"

"I'll get back to you on the morrow, Dennis. But a question if I may. How long have you been dean of the academic board?"

Mahan paused to think. "I suppose about thirty years, sir. Possibly more."

"And every year at this time you bring me a folder."

"It's my responsibility, Colonel. To steward the curriculum."

"Um," Delafield mused, his glass raised. "To the great defender of our hallowed institution."

After Mahan was gone, Delafield opened the folder, knowing that the contents addressed the matter of the Academy's ethics course. He extracted two documents. The first and thickest was the preliminary report from the Davis Commission, indicating that according to both cadet and officer feedback, the ethics course was unnecessary. The character traits of honor and ethics taught in the course were sufficiently covered and stamped on every other aspect of cadet life, not to mention preached every Sunday. The commission favored, instead, another course in civil engineering or one in the new field of electrics. The second document was the academic board's defense of the course, authored by Mahan.

Delafield slipped the documents back in the folder. He understood his role and the need for peace. He would support Mahan.

He gazed back at the Plain, where two men in army blue approached from the encampment site. He recognized one as Lieutenant Colonel William Hardee, Class of 1838. Hardee was the Academy's commandant of cadets and second in rank to himself. Hardee was in charge of the Academy's tactical department. Delafield couldn't make out the other man at first, but then recognized him as First Lieutenant Fitzhugh Lee, Class of 1856, and the newly assigned tactical officer of Cadet Company D. To Delafield, Hardee struck an imposing figure even at a distance. He was pleased to have the Southerner at his side. In the war with Mexico, serving under Zachary Taylor, Hardee had performed brilliantly, earning two brevets for gallantry. He was a fair but demanding steward of both the Corps of Cadets and the tactical department. His departure, scheduled for October, had been troublesome to Delafield. His replacement had only just been named in the dispatch on the table.

Fitzhugh Lee was also an imposing figure, and the nephew of former superintendent Robert E. Lee, Class of 1829. The younger Lee had already been decorated for gallantry on the frontier, and, in the short month and a half that he had been on post, had become a favorite of the Corps of Cadets.

The thought of Lee's uncle, who had run the Academy from 1852 to 1855, remained a burr to Delafield. Although, he liked the man personally. But history would remember Bob Lee as the consummate leader, the soldier's favorite, and a hero of the Mexican War, while he would be remembered as a builder of buildings and a taciturn taskmaster. That cadets still talked of Lee in the most favorable terms was particularly irksome, as it was Lee who had advanced the idea to increase the Academy curriculum from four years to five beginning in 1855. Since then, it was he, Delafield, who had to live with it and with the cadets who detested the extra year of schooling.

"James, would you pour two more glasses?"

"Of course, sir."

Hardee and Lee arrived, sporting neatly trimmed beards and mustaches, and saluted at the foot of the veranda.

Delafield returned the salutes. "Evening, William. Lieutenant Lee. A hot day for our cadets."

Hardee ascended the stairs, followed by Lee. "For all of us, sir."

James handed the two officers their ice waters.

"Been a continuous stream of hot days," Delafield said. "But not so bad. And another ten days, and you'll be out of your tent lodging and back with the family." Referring to Hardee's large set of quarters adjacent to his own.

"Always good to be in a fine house, sir," Hardee said, "but I truly do enjoy being in the field with the cadets, and the tent living is as easy as it ever will be."

"So, you think a Sunday review is necessary?"

"Trust me, sir. The plebes need more work."

Delafield handed Hardee the telegram.

Hardee's eyes narrowed as he read. "Lieutenant Lee, would you excuse us for a moment?"

"Of course, sir." Lee saluted, descended the steps, and took a position on the lawn.

"Amazing stuff," Delafield said. "First the railroad and now the telegraph, and both so damn fast. They've changed how we live."

"Indeed, sir," Hardee, said, rereading the telegram.

"So, what do you think?" asked Delafield.

"I'm more than disappointed. I thought, surely, Bob Anderson would be my replacement. Davis as much as assured me."

"My recommendation too. Major Anderson's already a legacy here, and the most popular artillery instructor we've ever had. On top of that, he's a gifted administrator and bona fide hero—brevetted three times."

"Does Anderson know?" Hardee asked.

"I should think not. I think this is General Scott's courtesy to me. If I pushed the issue, I expect he would relent. But you read his reason?"

Hardee nodded.

"Apparently our Secretary of War John Floyd—that Virginian—is pulling strings."

"Which is inappropriate," said Hardee.

"Yes. And it is our right not to like it. But our lot to keep silent. What do you make of Scott's recommendation in lieu of Anderson?"

"John Reynolds and I have good history. He was Class of 1841, a plebe in my company when I was a First Classman, and even then, mature for his years. We served under Zachary Taylor in Mexico. As I recall, he was twice brevetted for gallantry. Since then, he's been on the frontier. He'll do well here and leave a good mark, though his brand of discipline is likely different than mine."

"Not so different, I think." Delafield slipped the telegram back inside the envelope.

"Will there be overlap?" asked Hardee.

"I'll send my response first thing in the morning and press the point. I want a seamless transition. Of course, it is not too late for you to extend. I know that would satisfy both Scott and Floyd."

Hardee glanced at the encampment site. "Four years is more than enough, thank you. I need to get back to the troops and to the frontier. Besides, the family is looking forward to a furlough in Georgia."

"Suit yourself, but don't be surprised if you come back as superintendent."

"You would wish that on me?"

Delafield's laughter was cut short by a cadence drumbeat from the military band on the Plain. The lead company of the Corps of Cadets emerged from the encampment, and Hardee and Lee followed Delafield across Jefferson Road to the reviewing stand.

Chapter Four

Monday morning, August 13, Pelham woke late and was the last to board the stage out of Blue Mountain. Before stepping onto the stage, he instinctively scanned the postings for fugitive slaves in the stage office. Attired in a pair of brown cotton pants and a bleached linen shirt, he was altogether indistinguishable from other young men traveling the country. He sat next to an older lady in black attire, who was as wide as she was short and accompanied by a black girl who Pelham took to be in her early teens. Across from him were what he assumed to be two cotton men.

"Anybody mind?" Pelham asked, reaching for a newspaper on the floor of the stage.

"Not at all, son. We've all read it—me twice." The man who spoke offered his hand. "Sidney Banks."

"Much obliged, Mr. Banks. The name's John Pelham."

"Mind me, there's not much in it, Mr. Pelham." Banks gestured at the paper as the stage jerked forward. "How far you going?"

"New York, sir."

Banks raised an eyebrow. "Now that's a trip. What takes you so deep into Yankee land?"

"I school there."

"Do tell?" His eyes narrowed. "What do you think of them?"

"Yankees?"

Banks nodded.

"Not so different, really. Aside from the way they talk, they're pretty much like us, except they seem to take better to the cold and snow."

Banks shuddered. "Don't like snow and don't like Yankees." With that, he tipped his hat over his eyes and despite the jostling of the stage was soon adrift in a light snore.

The second man held a well-worn western novel up close to his eyes. The lady introduced herself as Wilma Hawkins, and explained that she had just buried her husband, one Harry Hawkins who had died of consumption, and she was returning to her family in Indianapolis.

"I'm sorry for your loss, ma'am," Pelham said.

"We'd have been married forty-three years this October," she said tilting her head toward the thin black girl. "This young thing is Rosie. She just turned fourteen. She takes some kind of good care of me."

Pelham leaned forward. "Hi, Rosie."

The girl kept her gaze on the stage floor but returned his greeting with a nod.

"Tell the young man what's going to happen to you, Rosie."

The black girl said nothing.

"She's some kinda shy, that one. When we get home, she's going to get her papers. She'll be free. Yes, she will. That's what's going to happen. My Harry wanted that. Isn't that so, Rosie?"

The girl looked up, her eyes exhibiting more fear than joy.

"Problem is she doesn't quite know what it means yet, to be free and all."

Pelham nodded. "I understand, and you are indeed generous to do this for her."

The man reading the novel peered at Pelham over his book.

"She has no family and is all I got except for my son. His name's Harry too, like his father." She lowered her eyes. "Harry's going west, but before he does, he'll sell our place and give me all but a little of the money and I'll live on that."

The stage driver announced the crossing of a shallow stream. "Anyway," Mrs. Hawkins said, "I think Rosie will take care of me 'til I'm gone. She said she would, and I'll pay her what I can."

"I'm sure she will, ma'am."

The widow smiled before being nearly pitched from her seat when the stage bottomed on a shallow stream.

Pelham was still holding the small package from his mother. "Ma'am, do you mind …?"

The widow patted his arm. "Lord no, son. Smells wonderful, and you got to keep your strength."

Pelham removed the muslin wrapping that contained strips of jerky from Willie's smokehouse and two of young Ora's buttermilk biscuits. He offered the widow lady a biscuit, but she graciously declined, which was well enough, because he was famished. He ate and washed the meal down with the bottle of beer he had purchased in the stage office.

Afterwards, he settled into the paper, soon in agreement with the man, Banks. The publisher was content to keep the same stale issues in the air, his journalism flat and woefully biased.

"Young man." Mrs. Hawkins tapped Pelham's arm. "When we get to the rest stop, would you mind terribly getting us some water? I don't move so well, and don't want to leave the stage if I don't have to."

Pelham smiled. "Yes, ma'am, my pleasure."

"You are too kind. You come from fine family. I know it. I can tell these things."

"You are sweet to think so, ma'am."

"I'm quite sure of it."

After the rest stop, Pelham closed his eyes, hoping to nap, but instead juggled in his mind thoughts political and otherwise. He processed again and again the judge's words, the game being played by the new overseer, what his father and Willie had said, and the disturbing reality that not once had he seen Samuel. All gristle in the chewing part of his mind.

Late in the afternoon, the stage driver hollered, "Talladega, one hour."

Pelham spent the night at the Talladega railhead and the next morning caught the train to Selma, thinking it strange to travel southwest before heading east. In Selma, he caught the train to Montgomery, relieved to finally be heading in the right direction. Everywhere, he saw the same landscape of red earth, cotton fields, and pine trees. The widow lady and her young black were also on the train, and upon arriving in Montgomery, he aided them with their luggage and led them to the station hotel. The next day, he helped them onto the train for Atlanta. Outside of the Atlanta station, the three of them skirted a spirited rally of fire-eaters. That night, Pelham again slept fitfully, waking to another hot, sultry day and breakfasting on steak, eggs, and warm milk.

Returning to the Atlanta train station, he helped Mrs. Hawkins and her young attendant onto the train to Chattanooga, refusing an envelope offered by the widow, but accepting her best wishes. Before the train pulled away, Pelham caught the young black girl staring at him through the open window. He touched the bill of his cap, and she smiled.

Chapter Five

August 15, 1860

Nashville, Tennessee

Nathaniel Rives Chambliss, known as Nate to his West Point classmates, stood conspicuous on the platform, and not because of his height and uniform. It was his Romanesque face and piercing brown eyes. He strolled to the ticket counter and exchanged a nickel for a newspaper, tucked it under his arm, and rejoined his two older brothers at the platform railing.

"You wait until now to tell us," Paul, the older of the two said, more than miffed.

Robert, the other brother, lit a cigarette. "Yeah, Nathaniel, what's that all about?"

At the shriek of a train whistle, heads turned to see the iron snake appear a half mile down the track, its single nostril snorting black smoke.

"Because it's not important and more of a pain than it's worth." Chambliss attempted to conceal the pride he felt having been appointed first captain of the Corps of Cadets for the coming year.

"The hell you say!" Paul said, reaching in his pocket. "You'll be a general one day and run the whole damn army." He pressed something into his brother's palm. "Mom and Dad would have been proud."

Chambliss opened his fingers to see a gold coin the size of a five-dollar gold piece. It bore the family crest on one side and the Union eagle on the other.

"John sent it," said Robert, referring to their eldest brother, an Army colonel stationed in San Antonio.

Chambliss examined the coin. It had been John who backed his appointment to the Academy.

"Dad had it specially minted, Nathaniel," Paul said.

Chambliss remembered little of the father and mother who had died while he was an infant. "But, why me?"

"Apparently, you are the chosen one," Paul said sarcastically.

"All aboard!" reverberated the conductor's voice from a bullhorn. Chambliss slipped the coin inside his pocket, hugged his brothers, and started for the train.

Behind him, Robert barked, "Take it easy on the plebes, brother."

Over his shoulder, Chambliss shot back, "And you two don't forget to write. Your letters mean a lot."

"To a tough guy like you?" quipped Robert.

"Trust me—West Point can be a lonely place."

Chambliss disappeared inside the train and settled down for a trip that would take three days. As the locomotive pulled from the station, he opened the newspaper and read the cover article. He shook his head. John Breckinridge had defined his Democratic platform, and there was no incentive whatsoever for any but a slaver to support him.

Eleutherean Mills, Delaware

Henry Algernon du Pont, President of the Class of 1861 and son of the ardent Whig, Henry du Pont, himself a West Pointer and member of the Class of 1833, was the oldest of nine children. In the only home he had ever known, the massive family estate on the Brandywine River, du Pont determined that he would fully enjoy this meal, one of his last before returning to West Point. In three days, he would depart for New York City and the following morning catch the steamer upriver to the Academy. He was nearly finished with a second helping of baked ham and sweet potatoes and had been careful to save room for the sugar-crusted apple pie that sat on the French buffet.

His question about the family munitions business, the largest in the country, still hung in the air. It seemed odd to him that not a word about the business had been spoken since his arrival. His seven sisters and younger brother appeared to tense when he asked the question.

Furrows formed on the forehead of the elder du Pont. "Henry, it's not been a good year. And I was thinking it best not to burden you. But we've had three accidents, two minor and one major. Seven fatalities. Seven good men. What sparked the explosions, we still don't know—not for sure. I've made changes and nothing more recent has happened. God willing, we're past all that."

Du Pont sensed the doubt in his father's words.

A kitchen helper cleared the table while another arrived with dessert plates. Du Pont's mother nodded to her youngest daughter, six-years-old, who, wide-eyed and with great sense of purpose, disappeared and soon returned carrying the apple pie like a crown to a coronation.

"Thank you, my dear," said the du Pont matriarch. "Henry gets the first piece." Turning to her son and passing him the first piece, she asked, "Do you think you'll still finish first in the class?"

"I suppose," du Pont said matter-of-factly, as though nine years of Latin and a year of prior college made the outcome rather predictable. "I have a pretty good lead on Charlie Cross, and Charlie doesn't seem to want it that bad."

"Do you know where you will go for your first assignment?" his father asked.

"Based on what's happened to the Class of '60, I'll probably end up on the frontier, one of the territories. But where and doing what depends on my branch. I'm thinking Corps of Engineers, but … Any more milk, Mother?"

"And when you've finished your service?" his father pressed.

Du Pont put down his fork and smiled. "After my obligated four years, if the offer is still there, I would be honored to return home and work for you, Father."

The older du Pont beamed. "With me, Henry. Not for me. And tell me. After all we've talked about concerning the election, who is your man?"

"I daresay anyone but Lincoln," asserted the younger Henry with conviction. "Lincoln and all the Black Republicans, I'm quite convinced, are but rascals bent on stirring up a too-full pot of nothing good."

"I thought you might consider John Bell of the new Constitutional Union party. He's as good a man as ever there was." The senior du Pont, who had witnessed his beloved Whig party fall from grace, desired anyone but another Democrat. "For the nation's sake, I think we need change. Certainly, Buchanan has been a disappointment."

The young West Pointer, for the sake of peace nodded, conceding that he would not decide hastily, though it struck him odd that his father, brilliant in every way and a prominent behind-the-scenes political player, was so thoroughly anti-Democrat, when Delaware itself was a slave state. That the family chose not to have slaves did not seem reason enough to repudiate the state's chief party.

Du Pont held out his plate. "Mother, might I have another slice of pie?"

BROWNVILLE, NEW YORK

"Eliza Kirby, that was without doubt the very best meal I ever et!" Garrison Blake made the pronouncement with jocular flair, waving a white linen napkin in surrender and patting his stomach. "And one I wager Edmund will not quickly forget, given what I understand of Academy food. Am I right, Edmund?"

The two young girls at the table waited for their brother's response. "Sadly, sir, you are entirely accurate," said the young man with dark hair and coal black eyes. Edmund, known as Ned to his West Point classmates, liked this widower who spent so much time with his mother, and who had known his father well. He knew his mother would never remarry, that his father could never be replaced. But she needed company, and Garrison Blake provided both excellent company and not a little humor.

"Shall we retire for a brandy and smoke, Edmund? I know that your mother keeps ample and quality supplies of both."

"Certainly, sir." Kirby rose to his feet and kissed his mother lightly on the cheek. Realizing what he had done, he gave her a proper hug.

"So like your father," the stately gray-haired woman whispered. She turned to Blake. "Don't let Edmund take too much of the brandy."

Kirby gave his mother a look and followed Blake into the study, where the older man selected two brandy snifters and poured from a decanter a liquid that appeared gold in the light of the gas table lamp. Blake removed a box of cigars from the desk drawer, offered one to Kirby, and picked one for himself. They both clipped their cigars and fired them with long matches. Given the constraints and abstemious nature of the Academy, Kirby smoked little and consumed alcoholic beverages infrequently. However, on this final night before returning to West Point he would indulge himself.

As they sat savoring the brandy and puffing cigars, Blake shared an anecdote, which did nothing for Kirby, but which made the big man nearly choke with laughter. At the end of the telling, Kirby saw that Blake's glass was empty and offered a refill. Blake nodded appreciatively, gesturing with a plump finger for a slightly larger portion. He then raised his glass in a toast.

"You know, Edmund, your mother is very proud of you and brags about you constantly. Says you are following wonderfully in your father's footsteps, and your grandfather's too. Am I correct?"

"Yes, sir, but that's a mother's job." Kirby's father and grandfather had been career militarists, and both had attained the rank of general. In 1821, his grandfather, Major General Jacob Jennings Brown, for whom Brownville, New York, was named, was the first general to be appointed "Commanding General" of the Army.

"My, I couldn't handle that kind of pressure," the portly man confessed.

"It's not so bad," said Kirby, who had been the Corps' sergeant major the year before, the highest-ranking man in his class, and one of only four cadet captains to be commanding a cadet company in the coming year, despite his being the second youngest in the class.

"Edmund, are you aware that I was part of the coalition that got Lincoln the Republican ticket in New York?"

Kirby expression suggested otherwise.

"And that without New York, Seward would likely have gotten the nod. But with New York, Lincoln is nominated on the third ballot."

Kirby would never have suspected Blake of such handiwork.

"My take on the November election," Blake said, "is that our man, Lincoln, not so much popular as convenient, will win. Not necessarily the people's vote, but the electoral vote.

He stood up and walked to the window and peered into the darkness. "Do you know what that means, Edmund?"

"Sir?" said Kirby.

"That means that those who didn't vote for him will have to accept his victory."

Blake's comment struck Kirby as odd.

"Yet that's not going to happen, is it, Edmund? No. Some of the Southern states have as much as promised that if Lincoln wins, they'll leave the Union. Of course, you know all that. When South Carolina and Georgia walked out of the first Democratic convention, it split the Democrats. A brilliant stroke for our Republicans, as much as handing us the presidency. Indeed, if not for the split, I doubt the Democrats could have lost this one."

Kirby nodded, being of the same opinion.

Blake returned to his seat, his demeanor glum. "But that we win the election is not necessarily all good, Edmund. This secession business is messy and cannot be sanctioned." Blake's placid face turned pinkish. "We cannot allow it. We are sitting on a powder keg and there are firebrands everywhere."

This a side of Blake Kirby had never seen.

"After Brown's raid and the horrors in Kansas," Blake said, "the entire country is just plain angry. Issues are quite literally black or white—no middle ground. Newspapers are disgustingly biased, defending the holiness of one camp and denouncing the hellishness of the other. The Kansas battleground for slave/non-slave election is an unmerited fiasco. Neither side concedes gains to the other. Both sides are guilty of murderous killings. There can be no winner."

Blake took a long pull on his brandy.

"I don't know what the answer is, Edmund. And don't know that anyone does, save our Maker." Blake's face receded on itself as he pressed the snifter against his chin. "Still, the one saving grace is that the South has been preaching and threatening secession for forty years and has yet to make good on it. God willing, it is still rhetoric. God willing, once the election is over, cooler heads will prevail."

Blake pointed a pudgy finger at Kirby. "Mark my words, the Academy is a crucible where what is to come will be played out in miniature. If the broad spectrum of cadets can keep their heads after the election, then perhaps the nation can weather the storm."

Blake drained his brandy. "Edmund, you are a gifted leader and a man of unswerving faith. I cannot urge you strongly enough to do whatever you can to calm the waters. Because if they can't be calmed at the Academy ..." Blake rose heavily to his feet. "I wish your father were still alive."

Blake placed his empty glass on the desk and left the room as Kirby downed the rest of his brandy, welcoming the burn.

Chapter Six

August 15, the train from Atlanta was oversold, and in the thick humidity of summer, the smell of humanity was almost too much for Pelham. Aisles were blocked with suitcases and dogs. Tied to the top of every passenger car were travel trunks, boxes, crates of chickens, and myriad other things. His only salvation was a window seat with a window that worked. The chain of iron chugged through the cool of morning into the heat of day, traversing valleys and trestle bridges, steaming across bottomlands, and climbing hills at speeds as slow as a walk. Fields of cotton eventually gave way to wheat, tobacco, and corn, and the landscapes of pine forests metamorphosed into oaks and maples and the gently rolling hills of Virginia.

After three days of inactivity, the grime of coal smoke, and straining to see through sooted windows, Pelham was done with trains. He longed for a horse, even one of the uninspired nags from the West Point stable. At every stop, he got off, exercised his legs, breathed fresh air, bought a piece of fruit, and found a discarded newspaper to give his mind investment. He wrote letters to his mother and his sister, and a candid letter to his father about the new overseer. When not reading, writing, or napping, he studied fellow passengers and imagined their comings and goings.

When the train finished the four-hundred-mile trip to Richmond, Pelham checked into the Virginian Hotel across from the station. A fortyish man with one well-muscled arm took Pelham's money for room and board and a hot bath. The man caught Pelham staring at his pinned-up shirtsleeve, and without elaborating said, "Buena Vista."

Pelham found the hotel newly renovated, featuring hot and cold water and flush toilets at the end of each floor. In his room, he stripped, grabbed a towel, and headed down the hall. He gave the attendant his bath chit, and an hour later, shaved and much revived, he descended the staircase for supper, picking up a newspaper on the way.

The hotel dining room was elegantly appointed, with cushioned booths along three walls and red velvet privacy curtains between the booths. Wait stations occupied the interior of the room, stacked with glassware, china, silver, and white linens. The headwaiter greeted Pelham with a deferential smile and sat him next to a corner booth, taking his order for a beer.

Pelham sipped his beer as he read the paper's front-page article, a tongue-in-cheek proposition that the needs of both Democrats and Republicans could be amicably met by granting the South its right to property, including slaves, in the new territories. "Slave masters," the writer asserted, "should not be restricted from taking their slaves wherever they wanted. Do not hinder the Southern man from moving to the New Mexico territory or to the Colorado Territory and taking his slaves. It is his right. He, as much as the man from the North, fought for that right. However, once there, what will his slaves do? The land's geography and climate are not conducive to cotton, tobacco, rice, or sugarcane. Unless they can be made to harvest sage and cacti, they will serve little purpose other than to be fed, clothed, and housed." Pelham found the obtuse argument amusing.

A moment later the headwaiter sat two men in the corner booth, honoring them with a bow. "Senator. Congressman. It is very good to see you again. Something to drink?"

"Ale, please," said William Porcher Miles, U.S. congressman from South Carolina as he retrieved papers from a black leather folder.

"I would have thought whiskey," jested Louis Trezevant Wigfall, U.S. senator from Texas.

Both men sported full beards, tailored dark suits, white linen shirts, and dark cravats. The congressman slid a single sheet of paper across the table. "Louis, lobbying will consume us if we're not enterprising. I see a series of dinners paid for by the party with increasingly expanded guest lists, beginning, of course, with those of the Cotton Belt."

"Dinner parties." The senator playfully patted his stomach and took up the list of names.

"And," Miles continued, "state conventions must be planned and all done orderly, with proper form and appearance—every element of propriety."

A black waiter returned with a frothy pitcher of ale, two mugs, and two bowls of peanuts: one roasted, the other boiled.

"And, of course," Miles said, "there are other matters, quite delicate, that will require attention."

"Indeed." The senator murmured as he eyed the list.

"To test the loyalty—or lack of it—of those you see," Miles said. "We'll need a man who can ingratiate himself and discern the truth behind another man's rhetoric."

The senator looked up. "You mean a man who can out drink another man?"

"In a word."

The senator downed his ale as though it were water. "I see mostly Washington-based military men and men of commerce."

"Precisely. Avoiding conflict requires their support, or at least their neutrality."

"I will, of course, serve in any way I can, William."

"And we thank you for it, Louis. We must—" The congressman lowered his voice. "We must convince the majority of Washington of the rightness of secession, that a state indeed has absolute sovereignty and an inherent right to leave the Union if its interests are not otherwise benefited. Nothing more than our forefathers intended and what occasioned our break with Britain. That so many states now form the Union is almost explanation enough as to why interests and needs once similar and mutually beneficial, are now neither similar nor compatible. Rather, we find ourselves in a most unhealthy malaise, which festers the whole."

"A toast to righteousness," said the senator, downing the last of the pitcher. "Now, perhaps a whiskey?"

The congressman nodded, and straightway the senator placed the order.

On the other side of the velvet curtain, what he was hearing captivated Pelham who only pretended to read his newspaper.

A waiter delivered a bottle of whiskey and two shot glasses to the senator and congressman, and then took their dinner orders, as well as Pelham's. All three selected the daily special of T-bone steak, fried potatoes, green beans, and apple pie.

While the congressman nursed his whiskey, the senator poured himself a second double shot. "Still, William, on the main we'll achieve the high ground soon enough, and then the bulwark will not be tested." The senator's voice was decibels louder than before. "I'll stake my fortune on it."

"Louis, please," remonstrated Miles. "Lower your voice."

Pelham caught the edge in the congressman's tone.

"Relax, William, we are among friends. These are our people."

"Don't be naïve. Those of a different persuasion are everywhere."

"Here, I've corked the bottle. Happy?" The senator caught the arm of a passing waiter, handing him the bottle. "Young man, bring us a bottle of French red. Bordeaux, if you have it." Wigfall smiled at the congressman and jested, "My friend, you see a Pinkerton behind every newspaper."

A dusty bottle of fifteen-year-old Pomerol soon appeared, and the head waiter poured a taste for the senator as the food arrived.

Pelham understood well that he was sitting next to two fire-eaters no less vehement than Alabama's William Yancey, and he had heard a word from the senator he hadn't heard before. *Confederacy.* He ordered another beer and inched closer to the privacy curtain.

The meal passed with little conversation, and when it was over, the senator ordered brandies and cigars. When they arrived, the senator announced in a voice for all in the restaurant to hear, "My friends, I should like to propose a toast!"

Pelham heard a fist pound the table on the other side of the curtain and the jingling of silver and crystal.

"For God's sake, Louis. You are inebriated."

"Surely you jest. And if I am, it's from freedom's fruit, not drink." When the animated senator appeared from behind the velvet curtain and faced the waiters' stand, Pelham thought him remarkably erect.

Ambling to the center of the room, the senator, his face beaming, turned a pretty pirouette and held his glass high.

"I propose a toast to the Land of Dixie!"

From Pelham's vantage point, the toast appeared universally embraced.

"My friends, and I know you are," the senator continued in a practiced tone of political oration, "would there be anyone here with the intention to vote for the man Lincoln come November?" His question held no hint of alcohol.

After an awkward silence, a man sitting with four other men stood up and thrust his fist in the air. "I'd sooner kiss the devil!"

The others at the table echoed the same, and then the entire restaurant erupted in hoots and hollers, castigating Lincoln, all Black Republicans, and lauding one great Southern state after another.

"I am indeed among friends," said the senator, smiling. "And I thank you that we are all of one accord!" He downed the last of his brandy and returned to his seat and turned to Miles. "I rest my case."

"By all that is sacred, Louis," Miles said, indignant, "rest more than your case."

Early the next morning, August 16, a dense fog enshrouded Richmond. Pelham, somewhat slow-headed and cottoned-mouthed from the night before, changed into his furlough uniform and boarded the train bound for the nation's capital. The train slipped quietly out of the station as if respectful of the hour, and soon Pelham was asleep, his head pillowed on one of his flannel shirts rolled up against the window.

Unknown to him, the two politicians who had dined next to him the night before were on the train and seated in the First-Class car, forward of the dining car.

"How do you propose we proceed?" Senator Wigfall whispered as he wiped perspiration from his brow.

"Buchanan is key," Congressman Miles said. "A staunch Democrat, but a malleable duck. The bachelor enjoys good parties, and we'll see that he gets them. He'll see himself as the great compromiser and push for reconciliation, and so much the better for us. The rub will be his position on federal installations in the South. I and a few others will keep him occupied and convinced that what he wishes can be and that what the South requires, the acquisition of all forts and arsenals within its borders, can also be."

The senator rubbed his temples and unfolded the sheet of names he had pocketed the evening before. "Well, on the military side, I suppose I should speak first with Floyd. The secretary of war is solid South and will give me his take on the who and the how."

An attendant pushed a cart down the aisle, and the senator wrestled a pitcher of steaming coffee from the man. For the next half hour, the senator and congressman pored over names and constructed a strategy. When the senator could no longer keep his eyes open, the congressman let him drift off to the shuffle of the train.

The smell of bacon roused Pelham from his slumber. The fog was gone, but dense low clouds masked the sun. He made his way to the dining car, and a waiter escorted him inside, where the senator and congressman were already seated.

Miles took notice of Pelham's uniform. "Citadel?"

"No, sir. West Point."

"Impressive. What year?"

"Class of '61, sir. This is my final year."

"You look relieved. Where's home?"

"Alexandria, Alabama, sir. Near Jacksonville. I'm returning from furlough."

"Northeast Alabama?"

"Yes, sir, we have a plantation there."

"Great state, Alabama, and you have a fine man in William Yancey." Miles extended his hand. "I'm Congressman William Miles of South Carolina, and this is Senator Louis Wigfall of Texas, though formerly of South Carolina. Would you care to join us, cadet …?"

"Pelham, sir. John Pelham. I … I shouldn't intrude, sir."

"Nonsense. We insist."

"Then, I'd be honored, sir."

The senator's face was pallid, but with effort he managed to extend a hand.

Pelham shook it and drew up a chair.

The congressman signaled for the waiter. "Anything you want, son. It's on us. And you certainly deserve it."

Pelham made no pretense of refusing and ordered coffee and enough food for two. They engaged in small talk until breakfast was served.

The senator talked into his coffee. "Mr. Pelham, my friend won't tell you, but before entering Congress, he was the most popular mayor Charleston ever had."

The congressman waved off the remark. "This is an unexpected pleasure, John. To meet one of our young lions. You West Pointers area special breed."

Pelham cut a piece of smoked Virginia ham. "Thank you, sir. I realize I am very fortunate."

"Though I suppose, now, with what's going on, it is a difficult time. You must find it a challenge to stay focused." The congressman comment was more a question. "Would you mind sharing your take on the political climate at the Academy?"

Pelham expected the question. "Sir, most of us embrace an attitude of laissez-faire, respecting one another, whatever our opinions."

The congressman nodded. "A fitting response between gentlemen, though I suspect you cannot ignore what is afoot."

"No, sir. And I believe we are as aware of the issues as we can be. I think my classmate Henry du Pont put it best, saying none of us is another's puppet, but rather free thinkers who reflect the views of an entire nation. And as large a country as we are we hold many views. To my mind, we have agreed to disagree. And besides, we are kept rather busy from reveille to taps all year long, which alone keeps the place civil."

"Your classmate is of the Delaware du Ponts?" the senator asked.

Pelham was surprised by the question. "Yes, sir."

The senator glanced at the congressman. "I know the man's father and his munitions company. He has been before my committee. Quite large government contracts, they have."

Pelham reached for another piece of toast.

"Then your classmate, du Pont, must be a Republican."

"Henry? I should think not."

"Really? His father is, or was, a staunch Whig. And … I would have thought otherwise."

"Sir, I'm quite sure he and his father differ on politics."

"You know him that well?"

"We are best friends."

"What are your own feelings about the election?"

"I am bred Democrat, but not optimistic about the election."

"Because the Black Republicans will win?" The senator buttered a piece of toast. "But is that so bad?"

"Sir?"

"A Republican victory might be celebrated by more than Republicans, son."

At this, the congressman shot the senator a stern look.

Ignoring him, the senator continued. "And the Academy as a whole, what would their position be on the election?"

"We are vastly Democrats, sir," Pelham said, peeling a boiled egg and applying to it generous pinches of salt and pepper. "But with two candidates vying for the post … I am sure you, sir, can speak much better to that."

The congressman nodded. "So, there are no extremists at the Point?"

Pelham immediately thought of Emory Upton. "One, I think. But I believe him harmless enough."

The senator was suddenly animated, the vast quantities of coffee seemingly doing their job. "What do you think of the Northern preoccupation with our peculiar institution, John?"

"I suppose I don't think of it, sir. It is what it is—in the woof and weave of our fabric. But I'm quite certain most Northerners don't have a bone to pick with it. After all, they benefit from it as much as we do."

"Your family has slaves?"

"Yes, sir."

"Many?"

"Fifty, sir—maybe more."

The congressman cleared his throat. "Senator Wigfall and I are headed back to Washington to do what we and other faithfuls can do to right the wrongs that are severing us from the North; ties that you must know are thread thin. Slavery, of course, is part of it, but not all of it."

The congressman looked at Pelham. "Would you care for anything else, son?"

His mouth full, Pelham returned a sheepish grin and shook his head.

"Some of us are unequivocally convinced that the South and the North are oil and water—that we can no longer be agreeably mixed, that we have inexorably distanced ourselves from one another, and that compromise only further breeds anger and distrust and resolves nothing. Take the Fugitive Slave Act, a federal act to placate the South. It was passed on the moral grounds of safeguarding our property, pure and simple, but if anything, it has emboldened a sympathizing North to paint us as inhumane and unchristian. And all the while, very few fugitive slaves have been returned to their owners. And I'm not saying we are without sin—we have our faults. But the wrongs committed by the North, which increasingly oppress us, will be sealed in cement if Abraham Lincoln is elected."

The senator leaned across the table. "John, Congressman Miles is prone to sugar coating. What he is saying is that we must not let Lincoln's shiny boot soil our Southern pride. Do you understand my meaning?"

Pelham nodded.

"It takes little imagination," the senator continued, "to see why the blood of our people boils at his effrontery, his intent to steal what we possess and deny us the full blessings of the new territories."

The senator rubbed his temples again. "You've studied the Mexican War?"

"Of course, sir."

"A cousin of mine. Name of Willard Wigfall. He had a wife and two young boys. He answered the patriot's call and fought in the war as a lieutenant. He was gut shot serving under Taylor at Monterrey. Took two days to die, and for what, John? He and thousands of Texas sons sacrificed, and to what benefit?"

Pelham returned a sympathetic nod.

"In the federal government," the senator said, "non-slave states control the House, and now with California a free state they control the Senate. We are defenseless against the will of the North."

A part of Pelham wanted to affirm the senator's argument, but instead he sipped his coffee.

"John, can you imagine what it is like for us to sit in chambers and witness what is taking place? The dismantling of the South?"

Pelham wiped his mouth and folded his napkin.

"It has come to this," the senator continued. "The South is no longer an equal to the North. We are a minority within the Union, a voice ignored and powerless to safeguard itself. Such a voice is no voice.

Mark my words, if Lincoln is inaugurated and the South remains in the Union, it will be reduced to servitude."

Pelham shifted uncomfortably in his seat.

Sensing Pelham's unease, the congressman interjected, "Louis, I believe we've beat the drum enough. John, life at the Academy must be quite an experience. Would you care to share some of what you've been through?"

Pelham jumped at the invitation. He recounted anecdotes from his plebe year and about the rigors and stress of academic life, and soon had the senator and congressman in stitches. The meal ended on a positive note, with the congressman paying for breakfast and handing Pelham a cigar.

"Again, John, we want to thank you. You've made our trip most pleasant."

"Sirs, I am very much in your debt, and I feel like I've been in the presence of—"

With a slicing hand motion, the senator cut him off. "I'm not sure we want to know what you've been in the presence of."

The three of them had a good laugh.

"Seriously, sir," Pelham said. "You and Congressman Miles have my utmost respect. I fear yours is a largely thankless job. And whatever we face, my hope and prayer will be that good comes from it."

The senator smiled broadly and extended his hand. "Count yourself lucky that you are a soldier and soon to be an officer."

"I do, sir."

The congressman offered his hand as well. "Best of luck in your final year, John. I hope we have the pleasure of meeting again."

"I would like that very much, sir."

Returning to his car and seat, Pelham found the train's plume of smoke on the other side of the car and quickly raised the window. The meal and coffee made him light-headed. He breathed deep the country air. Settling back in his seat, he found himself considering William Yancey in a different light. If he was anything like the senator and the congressman, was that really such a bad thing? Even the fire- eaters of South Carolina and Virginia might not be as irrational as his father had painted them.

Ten miles after Manassas Junction, the train sat on the track for several hours while a bridge trestle underwent repairs.

When the train finally stopped in Washington DC, the two politicians approached Pelham on the platform and before bidding him a gracious farewell suggested a hotel for the night. Finding the hotel, Pelham again slept fitfully before falling into a deep slumber. He awoke too late to catch the morning train. As a result, he spent the day seeing the sights of Washington DC, including the one-hundred-and- fifty-foot stump of the unfinished Washington Monument. He also saw the mural painted by West Point's drawing professor, Robert Weir, in the rotunda of the unfinished capitol building. While touring the capitol building, he remembered John Meigs, a Fourth Classman and friend in his cadet company, and the highest-ranking man in his class. The man's father, Colonel Montgomery Meigs, Class of 1836, was the supervising engineer for the construction of the capitol extension and new dome. He found the colonel in his office, and the two conversed an hour over a cup of coffee.

After a sound night's sleep and an early knock on the door by a member of the hotel staff, Pelham boarded the train for Baltimore and Philadelphia. On the morning of the nineteenth, he boarded a final train that snaked east and eventually crossed the sea grass of the Jersey flats, beyond which he disembarked from Newark on a ferry to New York City.

Chapter Seven

Puffs of white clouds in a lazy blue sky looked down on the majestic Hudson River whose origin was Essex County, New York, three hundred miles to the north. The dark wide ribbon of water divided the rolling landscape of greens, yellows, and browns. The cliff faces of the west bank gleamed bright in the sun, and the valley that bore the river's name stretched northward to the Catskill Mountains and beyond. Maritime vessels and barges of every description crowded the river, traveling north and south, tipping their hats with horns, whistles, and bells, as ferries labored against strong currents from one side of the river to the other.

Pelham checked his pocket watch. It was nine o'clock and the *Lovely Lady*, a newly commissioned paddlewheel steamer, was en route from the city harbor to destinations as far north as Newburgh, ten miles beyond West Point. The steamer had already made one stop, and the mid-August sun had climbed high enough for temperatures to be warmer than anyone desired, sending passengers to the top deck in search of cooling breezes. Patrons talked loudly over the sounds of steam boilers and churn of the boat's massive paddlewheel. In the crowd, near the middle of the boat, John Pelham, Henry du Pont, and Nate Chambliss stood together, each in his furlough uniform.

"That's hard to believe, John," du Pont said after hearing Pelham's account of his encounter with the senator and congressman. "And I'm not sure you were supposed to hear those things."

"Why not?" Chambliss said, his eyes shut and his face to the sun. "What is he or any of us going to do with it?"

The previous night in the city had been a highlight for the three of them, Chambliss particularly happy to have time with du Pont, who would be Corps quartermaster on his battalion staff. The evening passed quickly, the friends sharing furlough stories and taking in a burlesque show after supper. That morning, anticipating Academy mess hall food, they drank coffee and consumed steak, eggs, and biscuits until they could stomach no more.

Chambliss gazed about the deck. "So, Henry, shall either of us find love in the waning days of summer encampment?"

"I fear not enough time, Nate," Du Pont said, sneezing as he often did from perennial hay fever. "Female companionship, other than my sisters, I greatly missed during furlough. Not much to pick from on the Brandywine."

Chambliss eyed Pelham. "But old John here, he doesn't care. He's got that brunette from Cornwall."

Pelham produced a sad face. "Nay, sir. You are mistaken. I must report that I am no longer in Joanna Furman's plans."

"And pray tell, why?"

"Expectations."

"Regarding?"

"Marriage."

"She would have been quite the catch, John," Chambliss offered. "And we all must be caught eventually."

"Mayhaps," Pelham conceded. "But she pressed me, and I could not mislead her. To my mind, a man must know himself, test himself, before settling down. And I am not there, yet."

"You can't be serious," said Du Pont.

Chambliss said nothing, his attention drawn to a gaggle of girls in stately dress at the bow of the boat.

"Mind you," Pelham said with a wink, "I'll continue to be sociable. For I am a gentleman, or soon will be by act of Congress, and a gentleman must attend to the ladies."

"Which is no problem for you," du Pont said, irritation in his voice. "You, being on the Hop Committee, enjoy a distinct and unfair advantage."

"Now, Henry, don't tell me the uniform isn't enough," Pelham said, removing his furlough hat and breathing deep the river air. "What a glorious day, my friends. Can it really be that we are finally near the end of our suffering, that we will actually graduate and leave our rockbound highland prison?"

"Did you hear that, Nate?" du Pont said. "I claim honor violation. For if any of us loves the place, it's John."

Chambliss remained focused on the bow of the boat.

"All the same," Pelham said. "We are now First Classmen, and our suffering will be minimal."

Chambliss turned at Pelham's comment. "Why would you think that, John? We're a far cry from graduated and face one hell of a year."

"Not with my lauded friend at the helm," Pelham, said his tone patronizing.

"You think I'll show concession?"

"To your friends," said Pelham.

"Not a chance—least of all you. I'll be the horse's ass."

Du Pont grinned. "Nate is right. Justice must be blind."

"So that's the way it's going to be? Going to be a horse's ass? And that's the thanks I get for letting you to be my friend?"

Chambliss punched Pelham in the shoulder.

"I suppose I am to salute you," Pelham said, his eye on the shore.

"That would be nice."

A young black man in a white jacket approached with a tray of ice waters. Du Pont handed out the ice waters and raised his glass. "A toast to the Class of 1861."

The three clinked glasses.

"A class whose fate is at the polls," du Pont added.

"Ah, ah, Henry. We agreed, no politics," said Chambliss, reminding du Pont of the moratorium they pledged the night before. That not a word of it until back at the Academy. It had been the only topic the night before. Though all Democrats, they were for different reasons, which precipitated much debate.

A small boy skidded into du Pont. "Excuse me, sir."

The boy turned to Pelham and held up a folded piece of paper and announced in a high pitch, "Sir, I was told to give this to you."

Pelham took the piece of paper.

"It is from one of the ladies, sir," the boy said, pointing to the bow of the boat.

Pelham, Chambliss, and du Pont eyed the bow of the boat, Pelham extracting a nickel from his pocket.

"Thank you very much, sir." The jubilant boy turned on his heels and disappeared into the crowd.

Pelham unfolded the scented note.

"Out with it," du Pont demanded.

Pelham smiled and cleared his throat. "'Dear, sirs. We are traveling to the United States Military Academy to lodge at the West Point Hotel and wondered if you were cadets.'"

"Nate, there is a God," exclaimed du Pont. "But why does John get the note?"

Pelham spied one of the girls, dressed in light blue, waving a gloved hand above her head. He instinctively touched the bill of his hat. "Friends, perhaps I can do us some good."

Chambliss patted Pelham on the back. "You, John, are a shallow fellow, unworthy of the fairer sex—but nevertheless our only hope."

"Merely your servant."

"On your way, lad," Du Pont said with a shove.

"Patience, Henry." Pelham straightened his forage cap, then slipped through the crowd toward the bow of the boat. There, a group of six young women stood in neck-to-deck full Victorian attire, each deftly shielding her face from the sun with an artfully crafted parasol. Instinctively, he ranked them, finding none deficient on the exterior. As best he could tell they aged from late teens to early twenties.

"Ladies, please, allow me to introduce myself. John Pelham is my name, and I wish to respond in the affirmative to this note written with such a lovely hand. We are indeed cadets at West Point. We're all returning from furlough and are most delighted to know that you will be joining us."

The girl dressed in light blue, in Pelham's estimation the prettiest, stepped forward. Her face radiant and tanned, framed by flowing ash blond curls and inset with large emerald eyes, she extended her hand. "Sir, the note is from my hand, and my name is Clara Bolton. My friends and I are from Clermont College on Long Island, and we are very pleased to make your acquaintance. Was it, Cadet Pelham?"

"Yes, ma'am. At your service."

The woman's confident manner impressed Pelham. Taking her hand, he made a sweeping bow which tickled the other girls.

"Don't mind them, Cadet Pelham," Clara said apologetically. "They're not used to a real gentleman. Let me introduce you to my roommate, Ellie Lawson." An attractive brunette stepped forward and extended her hand. "Ellie is our only native Long Islander."

Four more girls were introduced: Rebecca Astor, a petite, demure girl from Concord, Rhode Island, with an oval face, button nose, and long blond hair; Carol Hill, a vivacious redhead from Jackson, Mississippi, whose eyes nearly scorched Pelham; Alice Paine, an attractive and poised woman from Boston with black hair and high cheekbones; and Jessica Danford, a tall, curvaceous brunette from Clarksburg, Virginia.

Pelham greeted each girl in the manner he had greeted Clara, and each greeting drew fresh giggles.

After the introductions, Clara said, "We'll be at the hotel for almost a week, and we are so very excited." The joy and energy in her words was spontaneous. "None of us has ever been to West Point. But we hear the best things about the Academy, how nice the cadets are, and of course, the dance parties."

"We call them hops, ma'am."

"That's right, your hops. And isn't there one tonight?"

Pelham hadn't given it thought, but it was Monday, and Monday was a hop night. "Why, yes. And if you are with us for a week, two more after that."

"Isn't that marvelous," declared Clara. "Do you like to dance, Cadet Pelham?"

Pelham grinned, "Of course, ma'am. Very much."

"Then, if you don't think me too bold, may I place you on my card for the first dance?"

Pelham wanted to pinch himself. "It would be my honor and pleasure, ma'am."

Rebecca Astor stepped forward. "And the second dance—may I have it?"

The mother lode, Pelham thought, and before long he was conscripted by all the Clermont girls.

"Where are you from, Cadet Pelham?" Clara asked.

"Alabama, ma'am. Why?"

"That's quite an accent you have."

"I could say the same for yours."

"I, sir, am from Philadelphia, and we don't have accents there." Clara crossed her arms coquettishly, the other girls giggling.

Carol Hill took Pelham's arm. "Sir, I don't think you have an accent."

"That's because you're from Georgia," Clara said effusively.

"Mississippi, dear."

"There's a difference?"

"Right—well." Pelham, more than pleased with himself, glanced at his classmates. "Perhaps I should introduce my friends?"

"Oh, yes! Yes, you must!" Ellie Lawson insisted. But hardly had she spoken when her expression and that of the other girls blanched, and from behind Pelham came a loud, "Ahem."

He turned to face two gray-haired matrons, tented in dark dresses with thin white collars. One was tall, the other short, and both remarkably well fed. They stood arms crossed, staring at Pelham through wire-rimmed glasses.

Clara stepped between Pelham and the two women. "Miss Frampton, Mrs. Wigglesworth, I should like to present Mr. John Pelham. He is a cadet at West Point." Clara turned to Pelham. "Miss Frampton and Mrs. Wigglesworth are our chaperons, and Miss Frampton is our assistant dean."

Miss Frampton, the taller woman, cocked her head with an air of authority.

Pelham caught Clara biting her lip as he clicked his heels and bowed slightly, his greeting eliciting only a perfunctory nod, and not a word or change of expression.

Weighing his options, Pelham chose retreat. "By your leave, ladies. And if I have intruded, I humbly beg pardon. I wish you a most pleasant voyage."

As he walked off, he heard the shrill voice of the assistant dean. "Fifteen minutes, girls. Just fifteen minutes, and look at you, already flirting with total strangers. Be ashamed—be ashamed! Mrs. Wigglesworth, we're going to have our hands full. We'll have to watch them like hawks. And what are you smiling about, Miss Bolton?"

Upon his return to Chambliss and du Pont, Pelham was greeted with downcast faces, the two having witnessed the whole.

Chambliss shook his head. "Beware the elders."

"They are harmless enough," Pelham said, his face morphing from deadpan to Cheshire.

"We're in?" Du Pont said in disbelief.

"We're in, Henry. Three of us and six of them."

"The devil you say," quipped Chambliss.

"But let us be very clear on one thing. The note writer, Clara Bolton—the girl in blue—she's mine—if she'll have me."

"Fair and done," agreed du Pont.

"Of course—first fruits," said Chambliss, grinning. "My dear benefactor, which one for me?"

Pelham eyed Chambliss judiciously. "Horse's-ass?"

Chambliss bowed submissively. "My apologies, sir."

"Accepted. Then, it can only be the girl from Virginia. Jessica Danford. She's as trim a peach as you might desire and nearest your height and homeland."

"And me, John?" du Pont asked. "Which for me?"

"For you, Henry, our esteemed class president. I should think Ellie Lawson, Clara's roommate. A lovely lass from Long Island."

Pelham spent the balance of the trip deep in thought, standing at the railing, his eyes tracing the craggy cliffs, shadowed inlets, and distant heights beyond the western shoreline. His imagination was alive with history. He understood history. It was his greatest teacher, and he was living it. He saw in it the continuity and circling themes of life, and in the Hudson Valley the crucible of American independence.

How often had mused over its history? How it must have been for the would-be nation in 1777, when English general, Sir Henry Clinton, and his fleet of well-armed ships sailed from New York City up the Hudson, making short work of the colonial river defenses on Constitution Island opposite West Point. Clinton's plan was to sail up the Hudson and link with General John Burgoyne, whose mission was to forge south from Lake Champlain. Had he done so, the aspiring nation would have been cleaved in two, defeated piecemeal, and once again brought to heel. But Burgoyne had failed in the north, defeated at Saratoga, and had surrendered to General Horatio Gates, emboldening the young republic, and forcing Clinton to abandon his Hudson prizes and return to New York City to winter in.

The steamer approached Verplanck's Point, and Pelham sought out the buttress and ruins of Stony Point, where in 1779 General Anthony Wayne had led troops up the steep embankment to recapture what the British had held for two long years. Pelham imagined himself in the pre-dawn attack, scaling the steeps and surprising the British asleep in their quarters. In minutes, the half- naked mercenaries capitulated, and the battle was over. The threat to West Point, scant miles to the north, was eliminated.

For Pelham, the War of Independence was his war. He had adopted it, reading about it much more than required by the Academy. He claimed as his own the few victories and many defeats, the extraordinary hardships, and the insurmountable odds of beating the greatest army and navy on earth. His study of the colonial campaigns had placed him in Washington's mind. He embraced for himself the frustrations of the slow but inexorable transformation of ill-equipped and poorly trained militia into an army that would persist until France committed herself and British home landers wearied of the investment.

In his four years at West Point, Pelham had come to know what Washington fully understood—that the jut of land and the right-angle turn in the river that gave the place its name was the most defensible ground along the river's entire length. Washington had been brilliant to choose the Polish engineer Thaddeus Kosciusko to construct its defenses and father the new country's Corps of Engineers. In the late winter of 1778, Kosciusko had constructed water-level firing batteries and covering redoubts, and when the ice was gone stretched a massive boom and chain across the river to Constitution Island. The chain's links weighed a hundred pounds and were forged of two-inch square iron bar. He had engineered the parapeted fort on the Point's broad plain, which would initially bear the name Fort Arnold, for the once heralded Benedict Arnold. Farther west on much higher ground, a second fort would be constructed, named for Colonel Rufus Putnam.

Pelham understood well that fortress West Point was impregnable to sea and land attack, but not to treason. When the namesake of the fortress, General Arnold, took command of it in 1780, his pride was much wounded from lack of recognition and what he perceived to be inferior assignments. To Arnold's credit, his decisive attack on British defenses at Saratoga, during which he was severely wounded, had been key to the colonial victory and the defeat of Burgoyne. In his eyes, he had been marginalized for his efforts. Abetting his wounded pride was the death of his first wife and subsequent marriage to a prominent Tory's daughter. To salve his wounds and line his pockets, he bargained through Major John André of the British Army to betray Fortress West Point to the British for the sum of twenty thousand pounds and a general's commission in the British army. General Clinton had but to sail his ships up the Hudson to make good on Arnold's invitation. But God had intervened, of that Pelham was sure. Hours before the deed was to be executed, Major André, by all accounts a noble man, was apprehended by colonial militia, who found on his person condemning papers. He was not in uniform and summarily paid the penalty of a spy, while the forewarned traitor fled West Point to a British ship less than an hour before the arrival of General Washington, en route to make a routine inspection of West Point and unaware of Arnold's treasonous act.

What impressed Pelham more than all else in his study of the war was how circumstance raised up individuals to accomplish unique and extraordinary feats—people like Washington, John Adams, Alexander Hamilton, the Marquis de Lafayette, Thomas Jefferson, Nathanael Greene, Henry Knox, Israel and Rufus Putnam, Christopher Tappan, New York's George Clinton, Betsy Ross, and the Stillwell sisters. By the end of his Third-Class year, his initial enchantment with the nation's founders was much tempered. The demigods had taken on flesh and descended from pedestals to instruct him on their weaknesses as well as strengths, convincing him that the country's survival beyond gestation could only be attributed to the merciful hand of providence.

Still, the war had been won, and he was immensely proud of a grandfather who had fought alongside Washington, and for himself to be a son of the first and only democratic nation in the world—a nation that in its infancy would sit at a global table of monarchies and embarrass itself in commerce and international relations; a nation that would fight another war with Britain before finally flexing the muscle that would make it a world power.

Of all the demigods, Pelham esteemed Washington most, and embraced his concern for the fledging nation's failure to provide for the common defense. After the Revolutionary War, the nation had disbanded its army, sending home all but a few soldiers. Of the less than one hundred professional soldiers that comprised the army, fifty-five were stationed at West Point. Washington argued vehemently for a standing army of significantly greater number and for a national military academy to train its officer corps—and that such an academy be located at West Point, a recommendation shared by John Adams, Alexander Hamilton, and precious few others.

Not until 1802 would President Thomas Jefferson, an earlier opponent of what he perceived to be an elitist military school, establish the United States Military Academy at West Point.

Pelham breathed deep the air off the Hudson, his heart beating faster as the steamer passed Bear Mountain and Anthony's Nose. His mind drifted back four years to his first trip to West Point on the sloop *Oranje*. His mother, paranoid over the explosion and burning of the *Henry Clay*, made him swear not to book a steamer, saying he was too young to die.

Pelham sensed that the most significant chapter in his life was coming to an end, the cadetship that would claim a quarter of his life. But the thought evaporated with the sight of Buttermilk Falls, the small cloister of civilization south of the Academy. On the crest of the bluff was the five-story Cozzens Hotel, and from it his gaze dropped down the steep granite escarpment to the shoreline, where he spied a small dock, and next to the dock the two-story structure that was Benny Havens' Landing.

Chapter Eight

Beyond the crest of the bluff, Pelham could make out the nearest structures that made up the military school. After depositing passengers at the landing for the Cozzens Hotel, the steamer blew its whistle twice, signaling its approach to the Academy's South Dock. As the vessel drew near, Pelham made out figures on the road that descended two hundred feet from the bluff down the steep incline to the water's edge.

Two boats were moored at the dock, and two more anchored nearby. The narrow shore was stacked high with shipping crates, bales, barrels, stacks of wagon wheels, and various iron stock and mechanical implements. The dock swarmed with the activity of a dozen shirtless longshoremen. On the lower deck of the *Lovely Lady*, the crew made ready and tossed heavy ropes to hands on shore. The boat secure, the crew dropped the gangway, and Pelham, Chambliss, and du Pont were first to disembark. It was Pelham who spied the welcoming committee.

"Well toast my buns, boys. Look who's here to greet us."

On the dock in dress gray uniforms stood Ned Kirby and Charles Patterson.

"You're the last of the class to return," Kirby shouted.

Patterson, a medium-height man from Arkansas with handsome features, piercing green eyes, and wearing the three gold stripes of a lieutenant on his uniform, handed Pelham a cigar.

Pelham sniffed the cigar and bit off the tip.

Patterson lit the cigar and through teeth clenching a well-worn pipe observed, "Our final year in the womb, John."

"Let's you and I enjoy it, Chas," said Pelham.

"No doubt we will, my gallant friend."

Pelham threw an arm around Ned Kirby. "Did you get some smokes from your mother?"

"Half a box, John," said Kirby with a wink.

Pelham scanned the upper deck of the steamer for the Clermont girls, and as he did, two more cadets snuck up behind him.

"Good thing you laggards showed up," announced a swarthy man in a gruff tone. "Hadn't been for Walter, I'd have reported you absent without leave."

Pelham spun around to face Tom Rosser, the tallest man in the class and his roommate for the past three years. "Your best and only friend, Tom? Surely not you ugly dog. Let me look at you." Pelham was genuinely happy to see Rosser who championed no stripes on his uniform. "You've kept the house pretty?"

"You'll find accommodations unchanged." The swarthy, dark-haired and dark-eyed Texan took Pelham's valise.

"Walter," Chambliss exclaimed to the man with Rosser. The man was Henry Walter Kingsbury, a lieutenant and the Corps adjutant.

"Expected you yesterday, Nate." The tall Connecticut man grinned through a face full of freckles.

"The trains run when they run, Walter. I trust the Corps is whole?"

"But without its leader," said Kingsbury, taking Chambliss's bag. "Jefferson Davis and the commission are gone, and I think we got the message across on the mess hall. Not that it will do any good. I talked at length with Major Anderson. He's impressive—would make a great commandant, even superintendent."

Chambliss was only half listening. He too was scanning the upper deck of the steamer.

"But the plebes are starting to come around. A few incidents in the last two parades and some hazing problems. The usual."

"Political issues?" Chambliss asked.

"Camps are forming, but no fights."

Chambliss nodded. "When's my first formation?"

"Evening parade."

Pelham stood nose to nose with Kingsbury. "Okay, mister mouthpiece, let's hear it."

Kingsbury gave him a look. "Here?"

"And now," insisted Pelham.

Kingsbury drew in a deep breath and, as if calling the Corps of Cadets to attention, boomed across the Hudson, "Battalion attention!"

Every head on the dock and steamer turned. After a brief hesitation, Pelham gave Kingsbury an equivocal gesture. "Not bad."

"Then we're off?"

"A moment, Walter." Pelham again trained his eyes on the top deck of the boat. The two chaperones and all the Clermont girls except Clara Bolton looked down on them. Carol Hill waved a handkerchief until collared by Frampton.

"Someone you know?" Patterson asked.

"Girls we met on the boat."

"No, I mean her." Patterson pointed to an open doorway on the lower deck. Clara Bolton held up a sheet of paper with the words *See You Tonight*. Pelham grinned and touched the bill of his hat. The next instant, a nervous deckhand rushed Clara inside.

A horn sounded, and the steamer pushed away for its next stop, the Academy's North Dock where the West Point Hotel omnibus would pick up the Clermont contingent.

"I'm liking this," Patterson said, stroking his chin.

"You like anything in a skirt," said Pelham.

"No, I mean it. She's really cute."

"Don't even think about it."

"Come on, John. 'Fair is foul, and foul is fair.'"

"What the hell does that mean? Besides, she's a woman of breeding. Definitely not your type."

Patterson pulled Pelham's forage cap down over his eyes. "You consummate bastard."

Pelham adjusted his cap. "Premature, dear Shakespeare. For she hath friends."

"Really? Then, begging your pardon. I meant, you consummate bastard, *sir.*"

"That's better."

The seven friends strode briskly up the inclined cinder road, passing the Academy's mammoth riding hall, where all but Pelham and Rosser harbored painful memories. They proceeded past the stables, approaching the level of the Plain and the east side of the two-story building that housed the Academy library and post headquarters. Before cresting the Plain, each of them extinguished his prohibited tobacco product.

The familiar sounds of summer training greeted Pelham. Stern voices directing marching units, fifes and drums, the thunder of horses, the percussion of muskets, and the thunderous retorts of shore guns aimed at Crow Nest far to the north.

"Lieutenant Lee wants to see you," Kirby told Pelham. "Any idea what it's all about?" As commander of D Company, Kirby wanted to know everything that was going on, especially when it involved the company tactical officer wanting to see one of his men.

"Possibly, Ned. But let me not say yet."

They stood at the southeast corner of the Plain. The flat expanse of land was a half-mile square and, in many ways, defined the Academy. To the east and north, the Plain fell precipitously to the river's edge, while L-shaped Jefferson Road bordered the south and west.

"Moratorium over," du Pont declared, handing Pelham a newspaper, and pointing to the headline on the front page: "Republicans Virtually Assured Presidency."

Pelham made short work of the article. "It's *Harper's Weekly*, Henry. What do you expect?"

Kingsbury put a hand on du Pont's shoulder. "Upton's been asking about you."

"Upton?"

"He wanted to know when you'd be back."

"Why?"

Kingsbury shrugged and jogged off in the direction of Kirby, Patterson, and Rosser, already heading back to the cadet encampment site. Pelham, Chambliss, and du Pont made their way to post headquarters to sign in from furlough.

After signing in, Pelham told du Pont he was going to linger in the library for a while. After du Pont and Chambliss were gone, he took the stairs to the second floor and the hexagonal battlement tower at the northwest corner of the building. Floor to ceiling leaded- glass windows and a landscape mural across the ceiling gave the room an old-world look. This was one of the two havens he had at the Academy.

Several of the windows were cranked open for ventilation, and he stood at one, looking north over the Plain. The smell of horse and sulfur were sweet to his nose, bringing to mind the time he, Tom Rosser, and Chas Patterson arrived on June 2, 1856, among the ninety-three bright-eyed seekers of glory who would take two weeks of qualifying examinations for entry with the Class of 1861. He could still see some of their faces—faces that held the hopes and fears he had harbored. They all had such grand dreams, and in the evenings talked of glory, fighting Indians, and becoming generals.

It was then that he and Rosser became fast friends. Having both been raised in cotton country, they tried to out boast each other on how much cotton they grew and how far they hauled it, Rosser claiming victory with a forty-mile trip to the gin. Day after day, gray-haired professors taught, asked questions, and posed problems mathematical and otherwise to prepare them for examinations administered by the stoic board of visitors. He remembered the evening before the names of those who would enter the Class of 1861 were to be announced. Convinced at first that he had tested well, by midnight he was convinced otherwise, forfeiting an entire night's sleep. The next morning, he listened as the names were read aloud. They included Nate Chambliss, Walter Kingsbury, Ned Kirby, Chas Patterson, Henry du Pont, Tom Rosser, Emory Upton—and his own.

He felt afresh the pain of not hearing the names of already good friends, of seeing their downcast tear-stained faces, seeing them quietly packing bags and boarding the steamer home. He remembered how, soon enough; he had wished he'd been one of them. He was unprepared for plebe year, for the lowly estate through which he had to pass, through which every graduate had to pass. It was the toughest and longest year of his life, seeming to have no end. But end it did, and when it was over, an exhilaration that eclipsed any he had had, or could imagine, suffused him. The relentless hazing by upperclassmen, the unending stream of plebe duties, the grueling academic schedule that claimed another twenty souls in the January academic board vendetta, and the absence of personal time—they all bore the sweet, sweet fruit of June. The feared, almost godlike upperclassmen extended their hands in sincere friendship; professors nodded approving heads. The intense pride of surviving plebe year was his. But most remarkable was the transformation and amalgamation of a class that he had witnessed through the long year. The man of silver suffered and succeeded no more, nor less than the man of pewter, their fates ordained by a system that granted neither distinction nor concession. The wide spectrum of personalities, beliefs, strengths, and weaknesses had become the Class of 1861, a class of uncommon mettle, whose motto would be "Faithful to Death." And now, more than ever, he embraced the strength of that bond.

Pelham studied the scene in front of him, the western third of the Plain alive with marching drill. Eight-man squads of plebes responded to commands from upperclassmen, their movements giving the appearance of indecision, first turning right, then left, then reversing direction, and then executing a series of complex movements that unexpectedly produced a straight line which then marched off in a new direction. In the center of the Plain, upperclassmen on horseback advanced in groups of five and ten, first in a trot and then in a cloud-raising gallop, sabers drawn, ready to clip heads off target dummies. In the eastern foreground, the polished brass barrels of the West Point battery gleamed in the sun, as sections of cadets conducted mock firing drills. Beyond the artillery pieces, cadets armed with muskets shot at targets raised at the crest of the bluff. At the north end of the flat Plain stood its only blemish, the fifteen-foot-deep depression known as Executioner's Hollow.

Beyond the marksmanship range stood the cadet summer encampment, and northwest of the encampment, on the edge of the bluff, the West Point Hotel, where Clara and friends were checking in. North and east of the encampment site were the eroded breastworks of what had been Fort Arnold, but now Fort Clinton.

Pelham turned his gaze to the northwest, to the successive layers of steep verdant hills, over which he and his classmates had hiked for days on end with weapons and full packs during plebe summer. On a promontory, he could make out the stone wall around Fort Putnam. Taking in the countryside and sweep of the Hudson River, he was convinced the Academy could not rest on more beautiful ground.

As he left the building, Pelham spotted the familiar figure of a man in army blue and with a bugle approaching from the direction of the encampment. Behind the smallish man, a dog trailed at his heels.

Pelham grinned, "Old Bentz, my dearest nemesis!" He clasped the hand of Corporal Louis Bentz, whose leathered face also bore a grin.

"Mr. Pelham, I have not seen you about."

"I am just now back from furlough, and I see you and Hanzi are no worse for wear."

The bugler's dog nudged Pelham's leg and raised a paw. Pelham bent down and shook it, and then rubbed the dog's head.

"So, this is your final year, Mr. Pelham."

"It is, and at long last," said Pelham.

"For my money, the years pass too quickly."

"Rubbish. You and Hanzi are eternal."

"But summer encampments are growing old, sir. I spend all my time going back and forth, back and forth."

"You are amazing, Bentz. How many years now?"

The Corps bugler rubbed his chin. "I don't know. Here at West Point, maybe twenty-five, maybe more. I lose track."

"Twenty-five years of destroying our sleep." Pelham placed a hand on the man's shoulder.

"It's a job, sir."

"And of course, you realize what you've done to yourself. You cannot retire. We'll not stand for it."

"Then I'll die blowing reveille."

"That might be acceptable."

The two laughed, and Bentz departed.

Pelham whistled a cadence song as he approached the sentry post at the southwest corner of the encampment and responded to the guard's challenge with the password provided at post headquarters. He found the encampment a bustle of activity and turning down D Company's main street saw Rosser chewing out a plebe.

Chapter Nine

With a clear and majestic view of the Hudson River, the three-story West Point Hotel dominated the north end of the Plain from a nest of elm and oak trees and a flowered landscape. Northwest of the hotel loomed Butter Mountain that people in the area wanted renamed Storm King Mountain, since the behemoth curried bad weather and blotted out the sun in the late afternoon, dropping temperatures ten degrees.

The hotel was its own world, the only public lodging and dining facility on academy grounds, its only competition being the larger and quieter Cozzens Hotel in Buttermilk Falls, a mile and a half to the south.

The hotel walls were masonry stone and brick, covered with a cream-colored stucco. Its interior featured rich woods, polished brass, and crystal chandeliers. Its broad veranda, skirting all but the east side of the hotel, provided panoramic views of cadets training on the Plain and packets and white sails tacking back and forth across the Hudson. On the fresh cropped lawn and in the intoxicating light and warmth of summer afternoons, not a few guests pretended at Rip Van Winkle.

The imposing rock formation of Constitution Island, the northern anchoring point for the Great Chain during the Revolution War, commanded the opposite shore. On the island's sparsely treed surface lived the Warner family, whose daughter Anna had recently penned the hymn *Jesus Loves Me*. She and her sister, Susan, still crossed the river to the North Dock every Sunday to teach Sunday School to cadets and the post children.

Twenty miles upriver, framed by the highland hills, was the town of Newburgh; and thirty miles beyond it, the Catskill Mountains showed themselves only on the clearest of days.

The hotel, boasting eighty guest rooms, was a living thing, steadily expanding since its initial construction in 1829. For over three decades, it had played host to countless travelers, to the board of visitors, to purveyors of every kind of Academy business, and to dignitaries not otherwise accommodated in the superintendent's quarters.

But to the young men in gray, the hotel served a much more vital function. It was the abode of hundreds of young women who made the pilgrimage between early June and late August to give meaning to life. For a quarter of a century, West Point had been without peer as the venue for established and aspiring young ladies to meet the country's most eligible bachelors. To attend a cadet hop was a thing dreamed of and schemed over by mothers in the business of placing daughters. Every Monday, Wednesday, and Friday night, the hotel's first floor was transformed into a place of color, sound, and enchantment, where hearts were stirred, romance blossomed, and pledges were made and sometimes kept.

"And here are your room keys, ma'am." The desk clerk pushed four sets of keys across the counter to the Clermont assistant dean. Miss Frampton made a clucking sound as she snatched up the keys and waddled to the parlor.

"All right, ladies, I have your room keys. Mrs. Wigglesworth and I will be in room 207. Please remember that, room 207. Rebecca and Alice?"

Rebecca Astor stepped forward. "Room 305."

Taking the key, Rebecca and Alice Paine ascended the hotel staircase.

"Clara and Ellen?"

"If you please, ma'am," Carol Hill attempted a straight face. "I believe they are on the back veranda taking fresh air."

Frampton's eyes narrowed. "Taking fresh air? Mrs. Wigglesworth."

With upturned nose, Mrs. Wigglesworth took the key from the assistant dean and shuffled down the hall and out the back door, where she found Clara and Ellie sitting on a porch swing facing the river.

"Clara," she declared, "I'll thank you and Ellen not to leave the group without letting us know your intentions. You are our responsibility, and that is our rule. Here is your room key. A bellboy will bring up your luggage." She glanced at her watch. "You have precious little time to settle yourselves and rest before we meet in the parlor at five-fifteen. Is that clear?"

"Yes, ma'am, perfectly. And thank you, Mrs. Wigglesworth."

The pudgy chaperone eyed Clara suspiciously.

Alone again, the two girls giggled. "Ellie, is this not the most exquisite place on earth? I mean, just look at it." Clara swept her hand across the turn in the river.

"It's quite wonderful—more than I could have dreamed of." Ellie closed her eyes and drew in a deep breath. "I can't wait for tonight, to dance with Cadet Pelham and his handsome friends. Do you suppose I'll meet someone special?"

"Ellie, sweet dear, there are a lot of very fine fish in this delightful pond."

"And I'll dance with all of them but be satisfied with just one."

"Ellie, you're the catch, not them." Clara jumped to her feet. "Come, let's see our room!"

Clara inserted the key and opened the door to room 315. It was small but contained a fine double bed with a quilted comforter and overstuffed pillows, a large armoire, a vanity with mirror and cushioned stool, and a washstand with a porcelain basin and a pitcher already filled with lemon water. A bowl of fruit and a vase of fresh flowers sat on a small dresser. The room's one window was large and open to a cooling breeze that passed through the room and out the transom over the hall door.

Clara stood at the window. "My God, Ellie, look! We have positively the best view in the entire hotel. See the river? It's huge! And can you believe the mountains? And just look at the boats. I can't count the number of sails."

Ellie stood beside Clara, and together they breathed the scented air and ogled the landscape.

"See those children?" Clara pointed to a natural amphitheater fifty yards west of the hotel. A woman was lecturing a group of young girls and boys seated on a long bench.

"Class in the open air. How wonderful is that?" With an impish look, Ellie directed Clara's attention toward the bluff. "You know what's down there, don't you?"

"You mean the dock where we landed?"

"No, silly, next to the dock. Actually, you can't see it, but—" She dug in her reticule and produced a small pamphlet bearing the Academy crest. Thumbing through it, she found what she was looking for. "Read this."

Clara read. "Chain Battery Walk?"

"But everyone calls it Flirtation Walk!"

Clara's eyes widened. "Do you suppose we'll get to see it?"

"Well, you can't go by yourself. You have to be escorted by a cadet."

Clara and Ellie exchanged knowing looks and burst out laughing.

"Just magical," Clara exclaimed, plopping down on the vanity chair and tossing her bonnet on the bed. She untied her shoes and rubbed her feet. "You know, Charles Dickens was right about this place. I read that he and his wife lodged in this very hotel for two nights in 1842, just before they returned to England—maybe in this very room, Ellie!"

Ellie squealed.

"It's in his book, *American Notes*. I do love his books."

"Everyone does." Ellie proceeded to cut an apple into quarters. "But from what I remember, his book didn't do very well, at least here in the States."

"Well, he wasn't much impressed with us, was he? His expectations too high, I think. He likely thought the world's only democracy would somehow be perfect. Still, I believe he was only being candid about what he saw, about our working conditions—and slavery."

Ellie nodded and handed Clara a slice of apple. "He was very much anti-slavery, but then he was English, and the English abolished the horrid business long ago."

"Actually, Ellie, I don't think it was until 1834 that they forbade it in the whole empire. Anyway, I hope our expectations aren't too high."

They both giggled again.

"Did Dickens talk to the cadets?" Ellie asked.

"I don't know, though I don't think so. At least, I don't think it's mentioned in his book."

"I should think the cadets would have enjoyed him immensely."

A knock on the door sent Clara scrambling for her shoes.

Ellie opened the door to a towheaded boy in his early teens, swimming in an oversized hotel staff uniform. The boy announced himself as Joseph and deposited four suitcases and as many hat boxes at the foot of the bed. Then he nervously delivered a rehearsed speech on what they should know about the hotel, from the dining hours to the location of bath and privy facilities at the ends of the hall, to how it was best to bathe or shower early in the day when there was still hot water.

"You are a dear, Joe, but I have a question." Clara gave the boy an innocent look. "Are cadets permitted to call on female guests at the hotel?"

"Oh no, ma'am, I don't think so. Not unless they get permission from way high up."

"Really?" Clara let her disappointment show.

"But they can always call on the veranda, or on the grounds," he quickly added.

Clara brightened and winked at Ellie. "Thank you, Joe." She searched her purse and found a nickel.

"Thank you, ma'am. But that's not necessary."

"But deserved. And, Joe, do you work here every day?"

"Nearly, ma'am. During the summers and the long Christmas holiday. When I'm not in school, I work weekdays and Saturday mornings."

"That's reassuring, Joe. There's no telling when we might need some help."

"Yes, ma'am. I'm your man. I'm always at the bell stand."

After Joseph was gone, Clara turned to Ellie and squeezed her hand. "Ellie, you are my best friend, and this is going to be the best week of our lives."

In room 207, Miss Frampton sat in front of the vanity mirror. She felt haggard, and the mirror showed it. This was the third time she had escorted Clermont girls to West Point, and the memories of prior trips were having their effect.

"We'll not want to let them out of our sight, these girls. Not for an instant You'd think they never saw a man, the way they gawked at those cadets on the boat. Imagine when they see the entire Corps!"

Mrs. Wigglesworth hung another dress in the armoire. "The transformation is indeed puzzling, for they certainly don't act that way around Long Island boys."

"We'll work in shifts and separately if needed and give them very short leash. I want them to enjoy themselves, but I don't want them in trouble. Until convinced otherwise, and I have yet to be, I don't trust these young men. They may be cadets and model citizens, but they are men all the same."

"Indeed, ma'am." Mrs. Wigglesworth sighed. "I can't say this hasn't already been more than I bargained for." Wigglesworth had raised two girls and a boy, and her youngest girl had graduated from Clermont four years earlier and had been in the last group escorted to West Point by Frampton, which was the reason she had volunteered to chaperon. Also, she had never seen the Academy.

"Still," Wigglesworth said, "it's only for a week, and when it's over we'll have them back in school and under books and homework. By the way, putting the girls on the third floor was a brilliant idea. We can guard the stairwells if need be."

"Count them, dear," said Frampton. "There are three stairwells. Anyway, at night the cadets are pretty much in their cage. They can get a great many demerits if they are caught not being where they should be." Frampton stood at the window, observing the intricate movements of a group of mounted cadets training on the Plain. "Still, the male libido is a fearful thing, capable of more than we want to know."

Chapter Ten

In less than an hour, Pelham was again immersed in the regimen of summer encampment. The camp, barely a hundred yards southeast of the hotel, had not changed its configuration in twenty years, except for the welcomed growth of shade trees around its perimeter. For nine months of the year, it was inhabited only by skeleton posts and crossbars made of wood to which tents were secured for the three months of summer. In June after final examinations, the upper classes abandoned the barracks with bedding, uniforms, arms, and accoutrements, and raised the white tents of their summer home. The new plebe class, initially housed in the barracks, would not join them until after entry examinations.

The encampment measured five hundred and fifty feet east to west, two hundred and fifty feet north to south, and was unevenly divided into four sectors.

The western sector was a narrow parcel of land dedicated solely to the camp guard. The area contained five guard tents, an area for inspection of the guard, and an area for the stacking of muskets when not in use for guard duty.

East of the guard sector, the second sector consisted of the parade ground. It was in this sector that the Corps daily assembled for meal formations, inspections, and abbreviated parades. Between the guard and parade field sectors was a well manicured, tree-lined walk, with benches from which visitors could view the encampment parade field and a tent in which visitors could call upon cadets during inclement weather. From the north end of the walk, a cinder path extended to the hotel.

East of the parade ground, the third and largest sector, the cadet bivouac area, consisted of eight parallel rows of white tents, in which two to four cadets were quartered. Two rows of tents faced inward to form each of the four company streets—Company A to the north, Companies B, C, and D to the south. At the east end of each company street were tents for cadet officers.

East of the cadet bivouac area, the fourth sector of the encampment included the field command tents for company tactical officers and a large field headquarters tent for the commandant of cadets, Lieutenant Colonel Hardee. The balance of the fourth sector contained Henry du Pont's Corps quartermaster tent at the east end of A Company, Walter Kingsbury's Corps adjutant tent at the east end of D Company, and several smaller tents for drum boy orderlies, boot blacks, and varnishers.

A visitor inspecting the bivouac area would have thought every tent the same, its arrangement precisely duplicated, from the stacks of neatly folded bedding; to the configuration of washbowls, shaving gear, and assorted other items; to the ordering within footlockers of books, socks, handkerchiefs, underwear, and white gloves. Uniforms hung from a bar strung between the front and rear tent poles. The uniforms consisted of full-dress gray jackets, gray trousers, white trousers, utility drill jackets, reinforced utility trousers for riding horses, and light linen uniforms for summer training.

The purpose of summer encampment was threefold: to immerse cadets in every form of military training; to indoctrinate and assimilate the new class of plebes, instilling in them the discipline that would define them as West Point graduates; and to provide leadership opportunities for upperclassmen as they assumed positions of command and staff within the Corps and fulfilled various cadet training assignments.

Throughout the summer, cadet guards were posted twenty-four hours a day at eight sentry huts positioned around the perimeter of the encampment. Cadet guards patrolled the border of the encampment between sentry posts and challenged all persons entering or departing the encampment. The guard detail for each day consisted of twenty-four cadets mustered from all classes. Only the sharpest and most disciplined plebes were allowed to participate in guard duty. Each man on the guard detail served four two-hour guard tours and spent the balance of his time reading, sleeping, or preparing for the next guard mount inspection.

Guard mount inspection was conducted by the officer of the guard, a First Classman. And as soon as he returned, Pelham learned that he was to be officer of the guard the following Monday. The irony of the assignment, given Pelham's past performance, was lost on no one, especially Rosser. Guard mount inspections were universal grief for all those subject to inspection, as they were the breeding ground for demerits, or "skins," for infractions ranging from poorly shined brass to lint in musket barrels, to inadequately polished shoes.

Once guard mount inspection was finished, a Second Classman, the sergeant of the guard, would march the new guard detail around the encampment. At each sentry post, the guard on duty would be formally relieved and fall in at the rear of the guard detail, his place taken by a member of the new guard.

As Pelham slipped into a pair of bright white cotton dress trousers, a plebe in the company street announced mail call. Moments later there was a knock on the tent pole. At the entrance to the tent, a plebe stood straight as a rod with several letters in his left hand and one in his right hand.

"Sir, mail for Mr. Pelham."

Pelham had just lathered his face for a shave and mumbled for Rosser to take the letter. As the plebe turned to leave, Rosser ordered him to halt.

The plebe stopped and executed an about-face. "Sir?"

"Where's my mail, mister?" demanded Rosser.

The plebe's face paled. Plebes were strictly taught to give only one of four answers: yes, sir; no, sir; no excuse, sir; or sir, I do not understand. To do otherwise invited grief. The plebe chose the last option.

"What do you mean, you don't understand?" Rosser growled as Pelham grinned in the mirror.

Not giving the plebe a chance to respond, Rosser bellowed, "Pea brain, next time you bring Mr. Pelham a letter, there better be one for me. Understand?"

"Sir—yes, sir."

"What's your name, plebe?"

"McElheny, sir."

"Where are you from, McElheny?"

"Ohio, sir."

"I'll be watching you, McElheny."

"Yes, sir."

As the plebe raised his right foot to execute an about-face, Rosser said, "I want you to do me a favor, McElheny. You'd like that, wouldn't you?"

The plebe slowly lowered his right foot. "Yes, sir."

"Tell Fannie I want my spyglass back."

The plebe blinked hard and repeated his earlier response.

In the mirror, Pelham saw beads of sweat on McElheny's face.

"You don't know Fannie?"

"No, sir?"

"Do you know who Mr. Custer is?"

"Yes, sir."

"Mr. Custer is Fannie."

"Yes, sir."

"Do you know why he is Fannie?"

"No, sir."

"Because I gave him that name when he showed up at West Point with long curly locks."

"Yes, sir."

"Do you think it a good name?"

"Yes, sir." McElheny blinked, a drop of sweat landing on his shoe.

"So, you'll do that for me? Ask Fannie to return my spyglass?"

"Yes, sir."

"Exactly what will you say to him?"

"Sir, I will say, 'Mr. Fannie, sir. Mr. Rosser would like his spyglass back, sir.'"

"Excellent. Now get out of here!"

McElheny saluted and left to report to the next tent, expecting no better.

Pelham inspected his face in the mirror. "You going to the hop, Tom?"

"I don't know. They are starting to blur. I may be all danced out. I might just catch up on my reading."

A voice with a New England accent rang out from the company street. "John Pelham of Alabama!"

Pelham grinned recognition. "Adelbert Ames of Maine!"

In full dress uniform, with four large gold chevrons on the sleeves of his dress coat, the handsome, round-faced commander of B Company appeared at the entrance to the tent.

"So how was home?" Ames asked.

"Hotter than Hades, but otherwise better than it should have been. You?"

"Fine, but I've been back a week, and, hell, it's no cooler here." The fine-featured Ames narrowed his dark eyes. "Isn't there something you want to tell me, John?"

Pelham wiped the last of the shaving cream from his face. "Tell you?"

"Come on, John, you owe me. Nate says you've got a covey of quail, and I want in."

Pelham threw his towel at Ames. "Then I suggest, my lobster-loving friend, you not be tardy. Be at the hotel at ten to eight."

Ames threw the towel back. "Done."

When Ames was gone, Rosser slipped Pelham's sword from its scabbard, stepped into the company street, and began performing officer sword drill. "I still can't believe you're a lieutenant. I'll never see one of these."

"Given our habits, T o m, my tenure is likely to be short. But until it's over, I'll enjoy not having a musket on my shoulder." Though not a little mystified, Pelham was more than proud of the three gold chevrons on the sleeves of his dress coat. Ladies attending the hops seemed impressed by the distinction. While on furlough, he had never mentioned the promotion, for he was more than convinced that it was a mistake that would be rectified upon his return.

The Corps' eighteen cadet officers were composed of four captains and fourteen lieutenants and were drawn from the First Class. A cadet captain commanded each company. Chambliss, in addition to being the Corps' first captain, commanded A Company. Within each company, three lieutenants led each of three platoons. The Corps' battalion staff included two lieutenants: du Pont, the Corps quartermaster, and Kingsbury, the Corps adjutant.

Rosser swiftly raised the hilt of Pelham's sword to his chin, the blade pointing upward, and then brought his hand sharply down to his side so that the blade pointed at the ground at a forty-five-degree angle. Rosser returned the sword to its scabbard. "I've no problem with a musket, given the less disciplined life we lead."

"And that we do, don't we, Tom?" Pelham said with a laugh. Within the class, he had the most demerits, and Rosser only three less. Demerits above the monthly allowance of ten resulted in punishment tours for all but the First Class, which was one hour of marching in full dress uniform with shouldered musket for each excessive demerit. Now that they were First Classmen, except for the most grievous infractions, excessive demerits would be satisfied by confinement to quarters, one hour of confinement for each demerit.

Pelham and Rosser understood the demerit system better than anyone in the Corps, with the possible exception of Custer, who had the most demerits in the class behind them. Each year, the three of them flirted with the semi-annual limit of one hundred demerits, which, if exceeded, brought mandatory expulsion. But each tested the limit with the knowledge that if they did graduate, their peers would accord them a level of respect not much lower than that given the first captain. That they spent more money resoling shoes worn out by marching was a small price for glory.

Pelham checked himself in the mirror. His shoes were blackened and polished, his white trousers form-fitted his waist, and his black-trimmed and white-collared gray dress coat with three vertical rows of brass buttons freshly brushed. He donned his blue forage cap, with its brightly shined gold wreath and the gold letters USMA across the front, and then announced that he was off to see Lieutenant Lee.

Pelham waited outside Lieutenant Lee's tent until another cadet emerged. He was a Fourth Classman, bearing a defeated look. Pelham entered the tent and approached Lee's desk.

"Sir, Cadet Pelham reporting as ordered."

Lieutenant Lee returned the salute and motioned for Pelham to take a seat. "Welcome back, Mr. Pelham."

"Thank you, sir."

Pelham felt at ease with Lee and admired him. He thought him the kind of leader he wanted to be. Lee was slim and of average height, but by his bearing gave the appearance of being taller. He was a positive person, competent to the extreme, and shrouded with an air of mystery. Pelham found Lee clear in his expectations as tactical officer; and if one met his expectations, he was content to let you live in peace. With Lee, a cadet stood on his merits, and knew where he stood. That Lee was a recent graduate with already so much frontier experience only enhanced his appeal. Rumors of his near fatal confrontation with Comanches fueled speculation among the Corps as to the details. Rumor was that he had fought hand to hand with two Comanche warriors, wanting only to disarm them but forced to kill them. Whatever the truth, Lee was not inclined to visit the subject.

"Your furlough?" Lee asked.

"Too short, sir."

"I expect so. Traveling to and from Alabama could not have left you much time. I trust you considered what we talked about?"

"I have sir, and I would be honored to teach what little I know."

"Don't be modest. You're the finest horseman in your class and the Academy, and there are some Second Classmen in dire need of instruction. Such tutoring—if I may call it that—seems to stick better when it comes from within the Corps and not from a commissioned officer or enlisted man. I was a cadet instructor my First-Class summer."

Pelham was well aware of Lee's prowess on a horse. "Yes, sir. I'm looking forward to it."

"Per your request, I've asked Mr. Rosser to assist you."

Pelham could not hide his delight. "Yes, sir. No one more qualified."

"He'll give you the details. And from the Second Class, I've picked Mr. Custer, as he'll likely take the lead next year—assuming he's still with us."

Pelham managed a straight face. "Yes, sir. He rides very well."

"Then we're agreed." Lee rose to his feet. "I know you need to ready yourself for parade."

When he returned to the tent, Pelham found Rosser shining brass—his breastplate, waist plate, the Corps insignia for his dress hat, and a handful of dress coat buttons laid out on a white handkerchief spread his footlocker.

"Why didn't you tell me?" Pelham demanded.

Rosser looked up. "We should be royally entertained."

"And the schedule?"

"Tomorrow. Again, on Wednesday. A day of rest, and then on Friday. We'll have two sections of eight to ten, an hour each, one at eight and one at ten. The section rosters are in your locker."

Pelham pointed to Rosser's breastplate. "It's not my place—"

"Damn right, it's not." Rosser picked up the breastplate and applied more polish.

In the company street a plebe minute caller announced, "Sir, there are five minutes until parade formation. Uniform is full dress gray over white."

Pelham checked himself in the mirror. "Tell me it's an encampment parade."

"That would be a negative. Hardee wants full blown reviews in front of God and country to settle the plebes."

Pelham perused the hop card Charlie Hazlett had dropped off and considered what Hazlett had said. It would make the evening more complicated.

The plebe minute caller called out again, "Sir, there are four minutes until parade formation."

Pelham fitted a starched white cross belt over his dress coat and positioned the polished breastplate with a white-gloved hand. He fastened the leather sword belt around his waist and wrapped his waist with the red satin sash of a cadet officer.

The minute caller barked out his final call. "Sir, there are two minutes until parade formation."

Pelham fitted the seven-inch tall black dress hat on his head, from the top of which extended a long, thick black feathered plume. Across the front of the hat was a large gold spread-wing eagle positioned atop the castle of the Corps of Engineers. He turned in the small mirror and satisfied with his visage announced, "After you, Tom."

Rosser stepped into the company street, his dress hat with black pompon in one hand and his musket in the other.

CHAPTER ELEVEN

At five-thirty, the Clermont girls sat around a large circular table in the hotel parlor. Clara rolled her eyes at Ellie as Miss Frampton droned on, already five minutes into another lecture on the leches that might inhabit the Corps. Mrs. Wigglesworth was not in attendance, as she was exhausted and napping before her evening assignment. When Frampton finally rested her tongue, she produced a rubbery smile. "Right then, where is that nice young man?"

Joseph appeared out of thin air.

"We will follow this boy to the parade viewing area, and after the parade return directly to the hotel. Is that clear?" Frampton was looking straight at Clara.

Joseph led the Clermont contingent down the hotel lane, past the display of Revolutionary War and Mexican War cannons on Trophy Point, and then around the northwest corner of the Plain to the public seating area. A large crowd had already formed, including patrons of Cozzen's Hotel, and those arriving by road or packet from Cold Springs, Garrison, Cornwall, and resorts upriver. Some were still making their way up from North Dock.

Owing to Joseph's fast gait, the girls quickly distanced themselves from Frampton. En route they gracefully deflected the sun's warm rays with parasols and talked only of the evening hop and cadets. They soon arrived at one of several long benches on the edge of the Plain. The bench was tagged with a reserved sign, which Joseph removed.

"Best seats in the house, ma'ams." Joseph beamed. "Now, if there's nothing else I can do for you, I gots to get back to my duties, ma'ams."

Clara smiled and squeezed his hand. "We'll be fine, Joe. You've been too kind, and thanks for everything. I'll see you tomorrow?"

Joseph blushed red. "Yes, ma'am. Thank you, ma'am."

Miss Frampton finally arrived, winded, and took a position behind the bench.

Ellie searched the Plain. "So where are they? I don't see any cadets."

Just then drums from the regally uniformed West Point band began to beat cadence. In a matter of seconds there was movement from the south side of the cadet encampment.

"Here they come, girls!" Carol Hill declared in a husky voice.

"Miss Hill!" Frampton screeched in a shrill voice.

Martial music from the Academy band replaced the drum beat and pealed across the Plain.

Rebecca Astor and Alice Paine stared with mouths agape and eyes wide. Jessica Danford peered through the group's only eyeglass. "Oh, my gosh! They're beautiful!"

Alice Paine reached for the eyeglass. "Let me see."

Ellie clutched Clara's hand. "I've got goose bumps."

"Me too," Clara admitted.

The Corps of Cadets marched forward led by its battalion staff, with Nate Chambliss in front and, centered two paces behind him, Walter Kingsbury and Henry du Pont.

Chambliss halted the battalion staff directly in front of the reviewing party and fifty feet from the reviewing stand. Colonel Delafield, Lieutenant Colonel Hardee, and two visiting French diplomats stood on the elevated reviewing stand. The five-man color guard formed on the company line fifty feet behind the battalion staff. Then, beginning with A Company, company guides posted forward to assigned positions on the company line, and the four companies formed on the company guides.

The martial music stopped abruptly, the sun's rays reflecting brightly off the dress hats and bayonets of the assembled Corps. To Clara, the cadets appeared as Greek warriors clutching spears.

After a profound silence, Chambliss executed an about-face and bellowed, "Bring your companies to order arms and parade rest!"

The Clermont girls exchanged expectant looks.

"Order!" company commanders barked in unison. "Arms!" On that command, every rifle-bearing cadet executed the five-step drill that brought the butt of his weapon to a spot on the ground next to his right foot.

"Parade, rest!"

Every man's left foot shifted eighteen inches to the left, and every man's left hand was brought crisply to the small of his back.

Ellie pinched Clara. "Do you see him?"

"Who?"

"Clara!"

"I can't see any better than you. They're too far away, and they all look alike."

"They all look handsome," said Ellie. "What's going to happen now?"

"Will you shush? I don't know any more than you do."

Beneath a pastoral sky, Delafield and Hardee critically eyed the Corps' performance. The march-on had been acceptable, though Hardee observed that the spacing between Companies B and C was greater than it should have been.

Chambliss executed another about-face and rendered to the reviewing party a salute with his sword. "Sir, the Corps is formed!"

Delafield returned the salute.

Chambliss turned back to the Corps. "Bring your companies to attention and present arms."

The Corps, as one, executed both commands, and Chambliss again faced the superintendent. Then he, du Pont, and Kingsbury presented arms in a flash of steel blades.

Carol Hill made a swooning sound, eliciting giggles from the other girls.

"I am not amused, Miss Hill," Frampton said in a pitch that could break glass.

Delafield returned the salute and gave the command, "Pass in review."

Chambliss faced the Corps and repeated the command. "Pass in review!"

Company commanders brought their companies to "order arms" and then "right shoulder arms." On Chambliss's cue, the band struck "The French National Defilé," a Corps favorite and a delight to the crowd. Chambliss wheeled the battalion staff and proceeded to a point directly in front of A Company's first platoon. On his command, the platoon stepped off on its left foot in perfect cadence with the battalion staff. The first platoon was followed by the second and third platoons. B Company, with Adelbert Ames at the head, followed A Company, and then came the color guard, C Company, and D Company with Ned Kirby at its lead. As each platoon made the final turn to pass in review, it executed a maneuver that formed two long ranks of twelve cadets, with the challenge, little appreciated by the assembled throng, of maintaining perfect alignment while passing the reviewing party.

At a marker near the reviewing stand, unit commanders gave the order "eyes, right," and heads snapped forty-five degrees toward the reviewing party. On the same command, each officer raised his sword and brought it down sharply at a forty-five-degree angle.

Clara's heart thumped in her chest as the band played and the grim-faced cadets approached and marched before her. Around her, the crowd roared for each platoon. With the passing of each unit, her heart beat faster, and she wondered if she would survive long enough to see Pelham. As companies and platoons marched past the reviewing stand, they continued straight ahead for fifty yards and then executed a left turn toward the encampment.

The color guard passed the reviewing stand, carrying the Stars and Stripes, the army flag, and the colors of the United States Corps of Cadets. On either side of the shoulder-to-shoulder flag bearers, marched a cadet bearing a musket with fixed bayonet. As the national flag passed before the crowd, those in uniform stood at attention and saluted; those not in uniform placed hands over their hearts.

"There he is!" Ellie screamed, after C Company had passed in review, her voice all but drowned out by the crowd noise.

Clara had already spied Pelham in front of D Company's third platoon and shuddered with excitement. She waved impetuously, unable to take her eyes off Pelham.

Ellie suddenly stood up and cheered loudly.

"Miss Lawson," Frampton bristled, "be a lady and sit down!"

At Frampton's voice, Clara checked herself. Frampton was right. Be a lady, she told herself. It was just a parade. She hardly knew the man, John Pelham. It was the martial music—yes. And the crowd, the men in uniform, and their terrible weapons. She wiped perspiration from her brow and took a deep breath. But try as she might, she couldn't take her eyes off Pelham.

Pelham shouted, "Eyes, right!" in a voice that shocked Clara. She swallowed hard, and when his sword slashed through the air, every eye in the platoon looked straight at her. Frozen, she was unable to breathe until the platoon had passed and Pelham had ordered, "Ready, front!"

And then he was gone, followed by the last of his platoon, and just as quickly the martial music ceased, and the parade was over.

"Come, girls, back to the hotel," Frampton said with a perfunctory air. All but Clara and Ellie stood up and dutifully filed off behind the mother hen, their tongues a whir.

Clara and Ellie sat alone on the bench as drummers continued to beat cadence until the last of the Corps disappeared into the distant encampment.

Ellie put a hand on Clara's arm. "Are you alright?"

Clara hid her face beneath her parasol and wiped her eyes with a handkerchief. "Ellie Lawson, you will never speak a word of this to anyone."

Chapter Twelve

Half an hour after the Corps returned from the review, Bentz sounded the call for supper formation. Pelham and the rest of the Corps formed on the parade field, not at all optimistic about the meal that awaited them. The chatter of the four companies came to an end with adjutant Kingsbury's command to come to attention.

When roll call reports were rendered, Kingsbury turned to Chambliss. "Sir, all present or accounted for."

At Chambliss's command, fife and drum began to play, and the battalion staff led the Corps the half mile distance to the mess hall. They marched across Jefferson Road onto South Gate Road, between the Cadet Chapel and the academic building, and onward to the mess hall located south of the academic building.

The mess hall, constructed in 1852, was a large structure made of locally quarried gray granite, with imposing towers and medieval battlements. The main dining room easily contained the entire Corps, and a wing at the south end of the mess hall served as the dining facility for the Academy's academic and tactical departments.

As each platoon approached the steps leading up to the imposing entrance, commanders gave the order, "at ease, march," at which all semblance of order was abandoned.

After releasing his platoon, Pelham joined the Babel scene in the dining hall. The hall measured one hundred and fifty feet long by fifty feet wide, with a ceiling height of twenty-five feet. Large windows ringed the hall, spaced every fifteen feet, and were open for ventilation. Within the hall were three long rows of five tables, and at the north end was a single table for Chambliss, du Pont, Kingsbury, and members of the lower classes from A Company. Each table sat eighteen cadets.

Breakfast was served at seven, the midday meal at one, and supper at seven.

Crossing the mess hall to D Company's area, Pelham brushed up against Emory Upton, standing at the head of an A Company table. "Behaving yourself, Emory?"

The abolitionist almost smiled. "Just challenging only what must be challenged, John."

"I'll take that as a yes." Pelham strode across the dining room until restrained by a hand that belonged to Kingsbury.

"You never mentioned the girls," said Kingsbury.

"You never asked."

"I had to?"

"Sorry, Walter. Supply and demand. But as it happens, Tom isn't going to the hop, so if you're interested …"

"You know I am. And if I may be so bold—neither too thick, nor thin."

"Hotel steps, ten till eight." Pelham slipped Kingsbury a note. "If you wouldn't mind."

Kingsbury, glanced at the note. "My pleasure."

Pelham weaved between the tables to the D Company dining area and assumed a position at the head of a table next to Rosser.

"Battalion, attention!" Kingsbury boomed from the north end of the dining hall, drawing immediate silence from the Corps. "Father God, we thank you for our country, the Academy, and this food, and ask that you to bless us in your service. Amen. Take seats!"

More than two hundred wooden stools scrapped the gray slate floor, and plebes already seasoned in their duties dispensed to upperclassmen beverage preferences of water, milk, tea, or coffee. At the same time, sixteen waiters emerged from the kitchen with huge trays bearing platters of meat, boiled potatoes, and string beans.

"McElheny, bread, please," Pelham said, realizing that he hadn't eaten since breakfast. McElheny, his eyes straight ahead and chin drawn back into his neck, passed the bread platter up the table.

Pelham tore a piece from the loaf and took a bite.

The imposing dining hall was a curious paradox of white linen tablecloths and napkins, sterling silver and bone china, and food that was neither inviting nor sufficient. But whatever else was passed as food, the bread, always fresh for supper, never disappointed.

Standing guard around the hall were solemn portraits of men in uniform and men in suits, soldiers and academicians past and present. And above the short hallway leading to the south wing was a portrait of Colonel Sylvanus Thayer painted by Drawing Professor Robert Weir. Thayer, a former superintendent, was acknowledged by all as the father of the Military Academy for his sweeping contributions.

As would be the case for breakfast, only a few faculty and staff were present for the supper meal. However, for the midday meal, all faculty and staff would be in their seats, as this was the established time for dissemination of information and discussion of matters academic and otherwise.

At opposite ends of the table located at the west end of the wing were places for Colonel Delafield and Professor Mahan. These and the remaining seat assignments at the table were as fixed as reveille and retreat. William Bartlett, professor of natural and experimental philosophy, had a place to the right of Mahan. Albert Church, professor of mathematics, sat to the left of Mahan. Next to Professor Bartlett sat Professor Weir and next to Professor Church, Henry Kendrick, professor of chemistry and geology. Next to professors Weir and Kendrick, and consequently next to Delafield, were places for Hyacinth Agnel, professor of French, and John French, professor of English and ethics, who, as an ordained minister, also served as the post chaplain. Of the faculty, Kendrick, a major brevetted twice for heroism in the war with Mexico, held the highest regular army rank.

At a second table sat active-duty army officers assigned to the Academy to teach. At the head of this table was Lieutenant Oliver Howard, assistant professor of mathematics.

At a third table, Lieutenant Colonel Hardee sat with Lieutenant Lee, the three other cadet company tactical officers, the post adjutant, the post quartermaster, the post engineer, and the master of the sword, Antoni Lorentz.

After another bite of bread, Pelham pointed to the platter in front of Rosser. "What's the mystery meat?"

Rosser sniffed the platter and made a face. "Mutton."

Pelham thought it remarkable and altogether deceptive that boiled mutton could look so much like boiled beef.

At the end of the mess hall, du Pont eyed Kingsbury who was actually eating the mutton.

"Walter, how in all that's holy do you eat that stuff?"

"It's not so bad, Henry, and it's excellent protein." Kingsbury sliced another bite, oblivious to the fat and gristle dominating the cut.

"Protein? You see it as protein when it tastes like—"

"Right, a strong taste. But that's the nature of it. A distinct flavor." Du Pont shook his head in disgust.

"Henry, you've got to rest your senses and eat what's before you. You need your strength."

Du Pont thought of the steak, pork, chicken, vegetables, fruits, cakes, and pies he had consumed on furlough.

A tall wiry man walked up behind him. "Welcome back, Henry." The man's voice was low, just a whisper, and terse.

Du Pont didn't bother to turn around. "Emory."

"I didn't think you would stoop so low, Henry."

Du Pont turned to face Emory Upton. "What is that supposed to mean?"

Upton gave Chambliss and Kingsbury a pasty smile. "I think you know exactly what it means. You surprised me, Henry. I would have expected loyalty from our class president."

"Drop the riddles, Emory," Du Pont said, not in a whisper.

Upton raised his hands submissively and departed.

Kingsbury, his cheeks full of mutton, gave du Pont a look. "What's with Upton?"

Du Pont shrugged ignorance.

"You okay, Henry?" Kingsbury asked.

"Me? Why?"

"Look at your fork."

Du Pont gagged at the gristled mutton on his fork.

Ten minutes into the meal, waiters appeared from the kitchen with bowls of bread pudding, a dessert staple of leftover bread that had been cubed, sugared, and wetted with cream. Pelham noticed amber specks in the pudding and suspected cinnamon, which would preclude the need for Sammy, the molasses syrup in silver pitchers on every table, universally applied to anything that needed sweetening or disguise.

Having made the evening matchups, Pelham's mind was at peace. He had Nate Chambliss with Jessica Danford, Henry du Pont with Ellie Lawson, Chas Patterson with Alice Paine, Adelbert Ames with Rebecca Astor, and Walter Kingsbury with Carol Hill. Of course, the matchups were only initial introductions, a chance for a foothold.

A single chair scrapped the mess hall floor, and Kingsbury rose and stood at the small lectern beside the battalion staff table. "Attention to orders!" he bellowed as he sorted through a handful of notes.

"There will be a meeting of the Ring Committee at the battalion staff table immediately after supper. The Yearbook Committee will meet Thursday evening after supper in the academic lecture hall. And Lieutenant Howard's bible study will meet at Trophy Point Friday morning immediately after breakfast."

When Kingsbury paused, Pelham thought he had forgotten, but Kingsbury was only clearing his throat. "And the meeting of the Dialectic Society originally scheduled for tonight has been postponed until tomorrow evening after supper in the First-Class Club."

Pelham, president of the Dialectic Society, breathed a sigh of relief.

After the meal, Kingsbury boomed, "Corps dismissed!" and the hall exploded in a rustle of stools as members of the Corps returned individually and in clusters to the encampment.

Outside the mess hall, a tall Second Classman came up alongside Pelham and Rosser. "My lieges!"

"Fannie." Pelham slapped George Custer on the back. "Are you ready to train up your classmates?"

"More than ready—and ready to get out of Dutch with the tactical department."

"Funny, Tom and I were thinking the same thing. Going to the hop?"

"Nope. I'm not taking any chances between now and tomorrow."

Rosser tousled Custer's hair. "Now don't overthink this, Fannie. Eyes not on you might be on us. And where's my spyglass?"

Behind them, du Pont, chairman of the Ring Committee, raced out of the mess hall, intending to be the first to meet Pelham at the hotel.

Chapter Thirteen

Half an hour before the hop, Clara sat rigid in front of the vanity in a pair of white pantaloons and a white cotton half-slip. The face in the mirror was screwed up in pain.

"Tighter," Clara insisted, exhaling more air. "It has to be tighter, Ellie."

Neither girl was by any measure overweight, and their feminine lines accented all the right places. But in Victorian tradition, even the slimmest of figures had to be further compressed.

Ellie pressed her foot against Clara's back and with one final tug, cinched the last of the corset.

"The inquisition is not over!" Clara gasped.

Side by side, they stared in the mirror at cleavage and hips that would excite a dead man.

"Now the bird cage," Clara said, her face filled with expectation as she and Ellie reached for hoopskirts, substructures that would make them look like dinner bells. Layers of petticoats followed, and finally a dress that all but covered their cleavage.

The two brushed their hair and applied final makeup.

"I almost feel sorry for them, don't you?" Ellie said, rubbing her cheek with a final touch of rouge. She pursed her lips and cast a practiced glance over her shoulder in the mirror. Then she leaned forward and ever so slightly squeezed her arms against her breasts. Pleased with the results, she giggled. "Yes, I do pity them."

Clara laughed and again took over the vanity.

A minute later came a knock on the door.

"Come in," Clara said without hesitation.

In the vanity mirror she saw in the doorway a girl her own age, her face bearing a panicked expression. She wasn't a Clermont colleauge, but Clara remembered seeing her in the lobby. Even then, she had been striking, and even more so now being fully dressed for the night's hop.

"Forgive me, you must," the girl said. "I'm so sorry to intrude, but my hairbrush exploded. Well, not quite. I dropped it and the glass handle shattered. And my roommate only uses combs. Can you believe it?"

Clara smiled, intrigued by the girl's southern accent, and amazed at her speed of tongue.

"But where are my manners. My name is Eva Taylor, and I was hoping—no—praying you might lend me a brush. I mean, when you're finished."

"Of course, dear. I'm Clara Bolton, and this is my dear friend, Ellie Lawson. Please, come in." Clara stood up and handed Eva her hairbrush. "The vanity's yours. Where are you from?"

"You are a dear, and Kentucky is my home." Eva applied long strokes to shimmering black hair.

"You came all the way from Kentucky?"

"My sister, Becky—she married a cadet, David Jones. He's in the Army now—a captain, I believe. Anyway, she said I needed to come to West Point and meet some cadets, and so here I am. Finally. I've been promising to come for the longest time. I was visiting family in New York City until yesterday."

"Did you come to find a husband?" Ellie asked.

"Ellie!" chided Clara.

"Well, truthfully, I've got all the offers I need back home. But…" A beguiling expression crossed Eva's face. "Becky seems so happy with her David, and she gets to move around, see the country and all. I would love that. So, I thought …" Her expression a coy smile. "What's the harm in a little window shopping?"

Laughter filled the room.

"You two have been so kind," Eva said, returning the hairbrush. "Thank you so very much. It was Clara Bolton and Ellie Lawson?"

Clara nodded, smiling, and Ellie extended her hand.

"Aren't you two the dearest things. See you girls on the dance floor."

Chapter Fourteen

Fifteen minutes before the hop, Pelham was alone at the base of the hotel staircase. A breeze off the Hudson tickled his ear, and the braided scent of roses, lilacs, and honeysuckle amused his nose. The evening was more pleasant than he had expected, the air less humid, and the temperature no more than seventy degrees. He knew that in two hours it would drop another ten degrees. Under the light of a gas lamp, he glanced at the hop card and reviewed the program. Engraved on the cover of the tasseled dance card was a scene of the Plain, with the encampment in the foreground and the hotel and river beyond. Inside were printed the evening's twenty-four dances, which included eleven Waltzes, three Gallops, three Lancers, two Deux Temps, one Trois Temps, one Polka, two Redowas, and one Polka Redowa. All the selections pleased him. Adjacent to each dance entry was a space for the card bearer to enter the name of a partner. Pelham smiled, knowing the intrigue and romance that would play out over the next few hours.

Ned Kirby with Becky Thompson on his arm approached Pelham. "'Evening, John."

"'Evening, Becky. Ned." Pelham bowed slightly.

"Congratulations on the teaching assignment. I thought Lee wanted a bite of you," said Kirby.

"He might yet," Pelham said.

"I understand some Clermont girls are here," Becky said with an expectant look. "Mother went to Clermont. She says it's a wonderful school, John."

Pelham nodded. In his opinion, Becky Thompson was the prettiest of the Thompson girls, with a fine figure, blond hair, and perfect teeth, but at eighteen, too young for him.

As Kirby led Becky up the stairs, she batted her blue eyes over her shoulder and whispered, "I'll save you a dance, John."

Pelham smiled and tapped the railing with his fingers. Three weeks absence had left him with little more than a week of his final encampment. For him, summer encampment was the best part of the year. He often reflected on his first encampment, after surviving entrance exams and entering the Corps as a plebe. He hadn't known how to dance or that there were so many ways to dance. Few in the class had, and none had understood the protocols of the ballroom or gentlemanship, the social graces of being an officer. He still carried the image of Mr. Flambeaux, the plebe dancing instructor, ranting like a drill sergeant, but managing over the slow cooking fire of plebe year to transform boys with only left feet into men of poise and grace. By the end of the year, he had been schooled in every dance that might surface at a hop, and during the year had partnered with Rosser, du Pont, and Kirby, learning quickly to avoid Rosser's feet. The next encampment, Flambeaux's good work was affirmed when he danced with a live female, and at the end of the dance found her all smiles and without injury.

"You look lost," said a man with a southern drawl.

"Hey, Charlie," Pelham said, shaking Charlie Ball's hand. A fellow Alabamian, Ball was a Second Classman and close friend, although unlike Pelham, he played the Academy game well and was the odds-on favorite to be first captain in the coming year.

"John, I still can't believe you traveled all the way home and back in three weeks."

Pelham smiled. "I don't recommend it."

"Wish me luck," Ball said, touching the bill of his cap. "There's a northern belle inside waiting for me."

Du Pont was the first to arrive, though less than a minute ahead of Nate Chambliss, Chas Patterson, Adelbert Ames, and Walter Kingsbury. Like Pelham, they each sported a gray dress coat, white trousers, blue forage cap, the red satin waist sash of a cadet officer, and white gloves.

The appearance of another man drained the color from Pelham's face.

"Hey, roommate … guys," Rosser said, glancing at the sky. "Another glorious night."

Rosser sensed Pelham's discomfort. "I'll fend for myself, John."

From the hotel veranda, a voice called down, "Mr. Pelham?"

Pelham looked up to see Clara Bolton surrounded by her friends. "Why, Miss Bolton, ladies, what lovely sights you are."

Clara flicked open her fan. "And aren't you the handsomest of men."

Pelham led his troop up the stairs, while Rosser remained on the lawn.

"Shall we meet one another?" Pelham said.

"Please," Clara said, stepping back and organizing her friends in a semi-circle.

Quickly and masterfully, Pelham made the introductions. As he did, Clara slipped back inside the hotel, past two short figures hiding in the shadows, and emerged with Eva Taylor in hand.

"That tall handsome man on the lawn," Clara said. "Is he one of your friends, Mr. Pelham?"

Pelham didn't mask his surprise. "Him. Why … yes."

Rosser, stood straight as a pole and executed an overdone bow. "Do you suppose he would like to meet my friend, Eva Taylor?"

"Indeed. He is Tom Rosser, my roommate and a consummate gentleman from the State of Texas."

Patterson couldn't suppress a snicker. Rosser mounted the veranda in two steps.

The matches made, Pelham took Clara's gloved hand, saying in a voice only she could hear, "It appeared you enjoyed today's review."

Clara blushed. "You saw me?"

"I'm a soldier. I'm supposed to see everything."

In the shadows of the entrance, Miss Frampton whispered something to Mrs. Wigglesworth.

Pelham suggested that the matches mingle, and while Alice Clausen was getting the correct spelling of the first captain's name and Rosser was introducing himself to Carol Hill, Walter Kingsbury approached Eva Taylor.

"Miss Taylor, forgive my boldness, but may I request the favor of a dance?"

Eva smiled easily, checked her card, and offered Kingsbury the seventh dance.

"You honor me, ma'am, and …" Kingsbury hesitated, glancing at Rosser, still occupied. "If I might be even more bold, have you given away your last dance?"

Eva studied the Corps adjutant with curiosity and decided in his favor.

"Your servant," Kingsbury said, touching his cap and retreating.

Clara pulled Pelham aside. "Cadet Pelham, you have acquitted yourself most admirably."

"Not me, but we. For without your Miss Taylor—" He gave Clara a dubious look. "I daresay, had I shown up with yet another friend, you would have manufactured yet another match."

Clara laughed. "I can't thank you enough for what you have done. You have made us all feel so much at home. I am going to take so many special memories from this week. I just know it."

"I hope you feel the same at the end of your stay, but now I must confess something."

His pronouncement caught Clara off guard.

"Alas," he said, "I was informed by Charlie Hazlett that I'm floor manager for the second half of the hop. I suppose the penalty for being gone three weeks."

"What does that mean?" Clara asked.

"Once I'm on duty, I'm prohibited from dancing or otherwise enjoying myself. Rather, I must mingle, make sure everyone is having a good time, settle partner disputes, check the punch bowl. That sort of thing."

"So, we shall have just one dance?"

"Have you committed for the twelfth?"

She opened her card, holding it so he couldn't peek, and made an entry. "Now I have."

"Excellent." Pelham lowered his voice, confounding the two women in the shadows. "May I suggest that later in the evening, if you find yourself in need of fresh air, that you'll want an escort on the veranda? That happens to fall within my assigned duties."

"Fresh air?" Clara said with a straight face. "Well, I am usually a woman of great stamina. But tonight, I very well might need some fresh air."

"Yes, ma'am," Pelham said.

"Cadet Pelham, will you get a great many demerits if you call me Clara?"

"No, ma'am—I mean, Clara."

"Much better. And will I get a great many demerits if I call you John?"

Pelham smiled.

"John, I am so looking forward to this whole week."

The paired young ladies and West Point cadets continued to converse, and soon the girls, not wanting to show favoritism, had entered the names of all seven cadets on their hop cards.

Charlie Hazlett, the night's head hop manager and Pelham's close friend, stuck his head out of the door. "We're about to begin, mates."

Pelham offered Clara his arm.

The main dining room had been cleared, so that it had every appearance of a ballroom. Hazlett, short, handsome, with dark hair and deep blue eyes, rang the dance bell that signaled the start of the evening and then raised a hand to the expectant crowd.

"Welcome one and all to tonight's hop. Let's hear it for the band, for if they are encouraged, they will indeed play better."

Laughter filled the room as the ladies clapped gloved hands, producing little effect. In contrast, the cadets stomped their feet on the wood floor, whistled, and loosed catcalls, drawing smiles from the fourteen uniformed members of the dance band.

"Thank you, ladies and gentlemen. Our first dance is a waltz by Johann Strauss. Enjoy your evening!"

Hardly had Hazlett finished, when Pelham slipped Clara past Patterson and Alice Paine onto the dance floor. Seconds later, the floor was packed as the bandleader's baton twitched to life.

Clara expressed unveiled surprise. "You, John Pelham, are an excellent dancer."

"You make me so, my lady. Though I should confess that instruction in dancing is a requisite here."

"A requisite?"

"The belief is that officers must be gentlemen, and gentlemen must be able to lead on the dance floor as well as on the battlefield." Pelham scanned the room, his gaze resting on the refreshment table. "I see your Miss Frampton is well positioned."

Clara glanced at the punch bowl table. "Always."

"She looks like a fun person," Pelham quipped.

"Just tending her flock," Clara said. "And over there—" She nodded in the direction of the dining room entrance. "is Mrs. Wigglesworth. We're trapped, John."

Pelham noticed du Pont gracefully leading Ellie Lawson around the dance floor. The two smiling and talking. Soon the mother instinct in him confirmed that all the matches were off to a good start.

In the meter and pulse of the waltz, the ladies in their elegant long dresses seemed without feet, floating across the floor at the slightest pressure from white gloved hands at their waists, all the while maintaining Victorian distance from their partners.

Too soon the first dance was over, followed by applause and more foot stomping.

Eva Taylor, with Rosser towering beside her, touched Clara's arm. "And don't you two make a fine couple."

Clara glanced at Pelham, who appeared not to have heard.

As Pelham escorted Clara off the floor, he gently squeezed her hand. "Thank you, my lady. I would not have thought that Quakers cottoned to dancing."

"Cottoned?"

Pelham smiled. "Never mind."

"You flatter me, John, but get me for a Lancers and you might change your mind."

"Doubtful, my lady."

"Miss Bolton?" Chas Patterson's Arkansas accent was unmistakable.

"Mr. Patterson." Clara extended her hand.

"Ma'am, please call me Chas." Patterson led Clara onto the dance floor.

Pelham was already across the room offering his arm to Carol Hill. "Miss Hill, my southern neighbor and kindred spirit."

"Indeed, Cadet Pelham, in the thick of these vulgar Yankees, we must stick together. And do call me, Carol."

The two squeezed onto the already packed dance floor as men lined up one side and ladies on the other for a Lancers Quadrille.

The magic of the evening continued to build with music, movement, and gaiety claiming hostage all in attendance. Hearts on both sides of the battlefield planned strategies, and as the evening wore on gallons of iced punch were downed from ridiculously small glass cups.

By the time Pelham approached Clara for the thirteenth dance, her face, like that of every girl in the room, had been re-powdered and her hands reclad in fresh gloves.

"You are flushed, my lady," Pelham said, offering Clara his arm.

"And you are shiny," Clara said, drawing a scented handkerchief from her sleeve and wiping his brow, letting her fingers linger on his cheek.

"Thank goodness for another waltz," she added. "And do be gentle, for I think I shall really need that fresh air."

They were again swallowed up on the dance floor.

"Enjoying yourself?" Pelham asked.

"Oh, John, how could I not! And to think, you do this three times a week, three months a year. Do you realize how lucky you are?"

"Lest you forget, my lady, there are twelve months in a year, and for nine months the hotel is empty of any reason to come to it. We are veritable monks. I have but Rosser to look at—can you imagine that?" He twirled her easily, and as he did confirmed that the two chaperons were still at their posts. "Will you be able to elude your guards?"

"Leave that to me, John, and don't think ill of them, for they only to keep us lambs safe from wolves. Be there wolves here, John?" Clara said, batting her eyes.

"Nary a one," Pelham said with a straight face.

"Yes, I believe you could be a bad boy given half a chance." She squeezed his hand. "Give me fifteen minutes. I'll meet you at the reception desk."

Pelham stood alone with his back against the lobby counter, snapping to attention each time someone exited the ballroom. Ned Kirby and a giddy Becky Thompson suddenly emerged.

"Waiting for someone?" Kirby said, giving Pelham a knowing look.

"Just resting," Pelham said, then raising a finger. "Ned, a moment, please—"

The two huddled for half a minute, and then Pelham winked at Becky. "You had a good time tonight, young lady. I was watching you. And you are putting the visiting competition to shame. Old Ned here better keep an eye on you."

"You hear that, Ned?" said Becky, kissing Pelham on the cheek. Kirby whisked the youngest Thompson through the front door.

"So quickly into another girl's arms?" said Clara, leaning against the hallway wall.

"You can't trust men," said Pelham. "I see you got by the trolls."

"Diversionary tactics. Isn't that what you call it? Ellie drew their attention. So, just where is this fresh air?"

Pelham led Clara onto the veranda, where they encountered Lieutenant Lee and another officer smoking cigars.

Lee touched his hat. "Mr. Pelham. Ma'am."

Pelham saluted Lee and the other officer. "Lieutenant Lee, sir, may I introduce to you Miss Clara Bolton."

Clara extended her hand.

"Lieutenant Lee is my company tactical officer, Clara."

Lee clicked his heels. "A very good evening to you, Miss Bolton. Mr. Pelham, please pass on my compliments to the orchestra. They are more than usually superb tonight." Lee turned to Clara. "Ma'am, you are in the company of a real gentleman."

"Thank you, sir. I can see that."

"Miss Bolton has requested some fresh air, sir," Pelham said, his tone officious.

"Yes, a number of the ladies seem to be in need of it tonight. Must be stuffy in there. I believe you'll find the air freshest on the river side of the hotel, Mr. Pelham."

"Yes, sir, I'll trust your judgment."

Though not alone on the back veranda, Pelham and Clara enjoyed a measure of privacy in the darkness. Flickering lights on the two banks of the river and the glow from the town of Newburgh beneath a starry sky gave the Hudson an air of enchantment. A breeze off the river sent a sudden chill down Clara's back. Sensing it, Pelham put his arm around her shoulder.

"A button for your thoughts."

"I thought it was a penny," said Clara.

Pelham took her hand and pressed something into it. "It's one of my brass uniform buttons with the Academy crest. A keepsake for your visit."

"John, you shouldn't have. Thank you, and I will treasure it always." She slipped the button inside her silk purse. "Shall I tell you what is on my mind?"

"Only if you are having a good time."

"That, you must know." Clara's smile was wasted in the darkness. "Tell me about your home, John."

"Now that could take a while."

"Please, I want to know."

"Well, for me, home is everything. We have a cotton plantation in northeast Alabama—near Jacksonville."

"And your family?"

"Pa runs the plantation and serves as the county doctor."

"He does both?"

"And has for years."

"How does he find the time?"

"I don't know. And I can't count the times I had to drive the buggy so he could mend a bone or deliver a baby in the middle of the night, only to see him up bright and early the next morning, managing the plantation."

"You love him, don't you?"

"I do. He's the hardest working man I've ever known and a just man, though he could apply the belt with the best." Pelham's smile was wasted in the darkness.

"You were a naughty boy, then?"

"I was a Pelham. I had to keep up with Charlie and William."

"Your brothers?"

"And mentors. For good or ill."

Clara inquired about the rest of Pelham's family, with particular interest in his mother, and the discussion leading to his grandmother. He talked at length about both, until he realized the time. "I'm sorry. I'm rambling, and I can't imagine how many of the lads inside have been looking for Clara Bolton."

"You have a dear family, John. A large family is so wonderful, and to live in the same place all your life is special."

"So, it's only you?" Pelham asked.

"I have a brother, Harry. But he's eight years older and more like an uncle. He practices law in Newark. Father is a doctor, like yours, but teaches now at the University of Pennsylvania. Mother—" Clara's voice suddenly quavered. "—my mother is gone. She died when I was fourteen, after we moved to Penn."

Pelham drew Clara close. "I'm so sorry,"

"A form of consumption. But now she is in heaven with the angels. And all is perfect for her."

"I understand Penn is a beautiful campus. Do you get snow there?"

"A little," Clara said. "Your friend, Henry du Pont ... he's nice and a fine dancer."

"Henry? Oh yes, he's the best."

"We had time to talk. And I inquired about you."

"You did?"

"I asked him if you had someone special in your life—a particular lady friend."

Pelham was grateful for the darkness. "And what did Henry say?"

"That you had a good many friends, and that some were indeed girls, but that there was no one in particular now."

Pelham relaxed.

"He said that this very day when we all came up the river, you vowed not to get serious with a woman for many years. I think he said, until you knew yourself—or something like that."

Pelham fumbled for a response.

Clara was surprisingly cheerful. "I just wanted you to know that I feel the same way. Honestly. I, too, must avoid a serious relationship. I have my goals and can't afford to complicate my life. I can't be distracted from my studies."

Pelham wasn't certain whether to be relieved or wounded.

Clara drew herself up to him. "John, that is not to say I don't like you. For I do, very much, and hope you like me." She met his eyes. "In fact, I want to be with you as much as I can this whole glorious week."

"Of course," Pelham said, unsure what she meant.

"So, I propose we become the dearest of friends, John." She expressed the proposal with childlike enthusiasm. "Unlike you, I have not one friend who is also a boy. And it would give me great joy if you would be my one true friend who is a boy."

"A boy?" said Pelham.

"A man." Clara giggled. "Will you, John?"

The more he digested the thought, the more agreeable it tasted. "Clara Bolton, I would consider it a great honor be your friend who is also a boy."

Clara kissed Pelham lightly on his cheek, an affection he did not expect, and squeezed his hand. "You have made me very happy, John. We shall have the grandest time." She kissed him on the other cheek. "Now, maybe we've had enough fresh air?"

For Pelham, the rest of the evening passed slowly as he played the floor host. When not otherwise engaged, he found himself searching the dance floor for Clara, always finding her smiling and with someone else. Twice she had caught him looking and flashed him a generous smile.

At the end of the hop, following the last dance, he approached her. "You, my lady, have broken more hearts than the Academy allows and still have two hops to go. The Corps will be decimated by the time you leave."

"You silly. I've had an incredible time, John. You better not have duty Wednesday night."

He smiled. "I don't, and …" He leaned forward. "If you would like, there is the possibility that I could call on you tomorrow afternoon."

Her eyes grew large. "Oh, could you, John?"

"Would you like to see the campus?"

"I would love to!"

"I'll know more in the morning and get word to you."

"There's a young bellboy, Joseph. He is a dear. Ask for him. I'm in room 315." She placed a hand on his arm. "John, you have to make this happen."

Ellie Lawson approached them, her face flush. "Hello, John. I so enjoyed dancing with you, and thanks for introducing me to Henry.

He is tremendous fun." She turned to Clara. "Come on, girl, we've got to go, or Miss Frampton will lock us in our rooms tomorrow."

Quickly, the Clermont girls disappeared from the ballroom, and Pelham made his way to the punch bowl, joined there by du Pont. "I saw you talking with Ellie, John. She's special. Did she happen to say anything about me?"

Pelham studied the man who had complicated his life. "As a matter of fact, she did, Henry."

"Really? What was it?"

"She said that you were … fun."

"Fun?"

Pelham nodded. "Fun."

"What the hell does that mean?"

Pelham shrugged, and du Pont walked off deflated. Pelham poured himself another warm punch—the ice long melted—and spied Rosser and Patterson across the room. He waved them over.

"Chas, my man, how are you and Miss Alice Paine doing?"

"Shall I compare her to a summer's day?"

"She would be more lovely and more temperate?"

"Exactly, John."

"And, Tom, how about you and Miss Taylor?"

Rosser's expression was shock.

"What? You don't like her?"

"Miss Taylor … John, I think the girl sees something in Kingsbury."

"Say it isn't true, roommate. It cannot be that a southern belle prefers a Connecticut Yankee?"

"I know … incredible. But Cathy Hill—"

"Carol," interrupted Pelham.

"Right. She couldn't take her eyes off me."

"And she speaks our language, Tom."

"Exactly."

Pelham motioned for the three of them to huddle, confirming they were out of earshot. "Enough of the fairer sex, my friends. We've respects to pay."

Patterson looked at him, "Respects?"

From the look on his face, Rosser knew well what Pelham meant. "No, John."

"No? How can you say that?" Pelham's hands were on his hips. "Isn't it past time we visited our friend?"

The light went on for Patterson. "Benny?"

Pelham nodded with a grin.

Rosser rolled his eyes. "Not from encampment, John. There are too many guards. Wait until we get back to the barracks."

"We don't pay respects when it's convenient. We pay respects when we've reason."

"And just what's the reason?"

Pelham grinned again. "Making it this far."

"But remember last time?"

"That was a fluke."

"We were nearly caught!"

"But weren't, were we? Chas is in. Right, Chas?"

"Definitely," Patterson said.

"And so is Ned," said Pelham.

Rosser raised an eyebrow. "Kirby's in?"

"He gave me the nod earlier. But, Tom, we'll understand if you're not up to it."

The sting of the gauntlet was enough. "When?"

"Tomorrow night after taps."

Chapter Fifteen

Choosing not to attend the hop, Emory Upton, who for all his eccentricity was acknowledged by his classmates, even du Pont, as the class genius, labored under candlelight in the cadet encampment, penning a response to Sarah, his favorite sister and most faithful correspondent. As always, her letter, which had arrived that afternoon, boosted his spirits and commitment, but for the first time urged caution.

She counseled specifically against exhibiting too ardent a stand for precipitously unslaving the country. She was as passionate an abolitionist as he was. But she reasoned that while Lincoln might be elected easily enough, the Republicans would need time, even years, to see their desired end realized. Its very electability depended upon millions of voters who, while staunchly anti-Democrat, for sundry reasons had no interest whatsoever in unseating slavery. She reminded him that for the vast majority of the needed votes, the central issue was not slavery, but the federal government, tariffs, the sovereignty of states, and the grievances of Southern states regarding the new territories.

"Unconverted intentions are worthless," he wrote her. "Unless Lincoln changes his position, the black man will never be free." However, even after writing this, he acknowledged that the man must first be elected before he could cross the Rubicon. He thanked her for the family news, which had filled three pages of her letter, and he included something she could share with each family member, which included parents and eight siblings.

Upton sealed the letter in an envelope and standing at the entrance to his tent called out into the darkness, "Mr. Saunders."

Seconds later an A Company plebe appeared.

"You will ensure this letter gets into tomorrow's mail, Mr. Saunders." Upton's tone was polite but firm, and with the plebe's departure his thoughts turned to Henry du Pont. There was no reason to let the matter fester.

Hearing the bell that announced the end of the hop, he regretted missing it.

Stowing his writing materials, Upton stepped out into the star-studded night and stretched his limbs. A thousand orbs shimmered in the blackness above the Highland Hills.

He breathed deep the cool night air and lifted his hands to heaven, praying silently. *Father God, your will be done in my life and in the life of our nation. Grant me and those around me wisdom and mercy. Forgive my imperfections. Help me to forgive others and to guard my tongue. Father, especially help me to forgive those who dismiss the truth. And, above all, Father, keep me resolute.*

Unconsciously, Upton rubbed the four-inch scar on his cheek inflicted by the South Carolinian, Wade Hampton Gibbes the year before. A constant reminder of his temper and that he needed to think before acting. What had happened to Alexander Hamilton could have been his fate. He had believed that Gibbes sullied his name and honor with rumors of his sleeping with a black woman while at Oberlin College. He had been so enraged he challenged the First Classman to a duel that took place that very evening in the cadet barracks. Not only did he find Gibbes the better swordsman, but that Gibbes was likely not the one who spread the rumor.

That Gibbes had shown him mercy, Upton credited not in the least to Gibbes, but to God's providential grace. He had shared the episode with his Oberlin mentor, the evangelist Charles Finney, expecting sympathy, even support for his actions. But to the contrary, Finney expressed disappointment, declaring that violence reconciled nothing.

Chapter Sixteen

Tuesday morning, August 21, Pelham awoke to the retort of a single cannon and old Bentz bugling first call and reveille. The disturbance was made complete by two overly eager drum orderlies. At the same time, two hundred yards to the northwest, the nation's flag was raised. The rest of the day would be similarly ordered when Bentz sounded assembly, mess call, drill call, tattoo, call to quarters, and taps. At six o'clock, five o'clock in the late fall and winter, Bentz would sound retreat and the flag would be lowered.

After the Corps returned from breakfast, Pelham paid Lieutenant Lee a visit. He left the tactical officer's tent in fine spirits, heading directly for the hotel. In the lobby, he found the boy Clara had described.

"Joseph?" Pelham asked.

"Yes, sir."

"Would you be so kind as to give this note to Miss Clara Bolton? I believe she is in room 315." He handed the boy the note and a nickel.

"Oh, yes sir, you can depend on it, sir. And thank you, sir."

Shortly after ten o'clock, Pelham was on the Plain, perched on his sorrel mount and awaiting the second section of Second Classmen, who were on probationary status for deficiency in horsemanship. The first section had come and gone, clearly proving why they needed additional instruction. Satisfactory completion of the remedial instruction would require completion of a three-jump obstacle course and delivery of a deathblow to a target dummy at the end of the run, all within the space of a minute and while exhibiting competent control of a horse.

From the direction of the stables, Rosser and Custer approached with eight Second Classmen in riding apparel and armed with dragoon sabers.

The section formed around Pelham.

"Before you is the obstacle course," Pelham said, wasting no time. He nodded in the direction of the linear course, three hundred yards long and consisting of a jump of three feet, a second jump of four feet, a third jump of three feet, and then a flat run of seventy-five yards leading to a straw-filled dummy.

"You need to be confident," Pelham said. "The course is no different from what you faced in the spring. Some of you ran it well enough, but too slow. Others ran it swift enough, but not well, which is to say not in control."

Some in the group focused on Pelham, while others stared anxiously at the course. All knew that if they failed the obstacle course, they would be dismissed from the Academy.

"So, why don't we warm up a bit, get the legs loose, get used to whatever gallant steed the army has issued you today? Mr. Rosser, would you be so kind as to lead the way?"

Rosser rendered a casual salute and hollered over his shoulder, "All right. Follow my gait and don't run up my ass."

Rosser led the section in a sequence of trots, canters, and gallops around the Plain, returning to Pelham.

Pelham forced a smile. "Yes, we are a bit rusty, aren't we? Some of you are out of balance, too far forward or back. Some of you are fighting the natural rhythm of your horse. Either will cost you speed and poise points. And, yes, the army wants you to look good in the saddle."

Several in the class snickered.

"Okay, once again. This time with Mr. Custer in the lead."

When the section returned, Pelham admitted to some improvement and, with that, led the section at a trot to the obstacle course.

"Before we start, let's break it down so we take chance out of the equation. A horse is neither dumb nor stupid, not even these glue nags. A horse is intuitive, it can read its rider—sense whether he lacks confidence. If the horse senses fear, you'll literally be along for the ride, like a flea on a dog. The key, then, is to manage your fears and project confidence." Pelham spoke with easy authority. "The other key is balance. You have to move and flex responsively with the horse and remain centered when you jump." He turned to his assistants. "Mr. Rosser and Mr. Custer will demonstrate."

Rosser, followed by Custer, separated by less than ten yards, accelerated to a gallop. They executed the jumps and stuck the red heart of the target dummy with ease and grace as the class looked on.

Upon their return, Pelham announced, "Forty-five seconds. Not bad." Turning to the Second Classmen, he smiled. "I know what you're thinking. You weren't reared to ride, you haven't enjoyed your time in the riding hall, and you've spent more time under the horse than on it."

More snickers.

"We've all been there, and it's the same with every class. But that will change. And of course, it must. You are in the Army, and your career depends on your ability to ride. You must ride well and over rough terrain, through timber fall, across battlefields. And it certainly wouldn't do for your troops to see you timid on a horse. And riding this course is simple. Finish in a minute or less, tag the dummy, and stay balanced. That's all we want. Do it and you're free to leave. Any questions?"

"Sir, you make it sound easy," said Andrew Collins of B Company, speaking for the otherwise catatonic section.

"It is, Mr. Collins," Pelham said. "Mr. Rosser, call out each runner. I'll be positioned at the four-foot jump. Mr. Custer will keep time at the finish line."

Once in position, Pelham signaled Rosser.

"Mr. Collins, you're up," announced Rosser.

When Custer's arm dropped, Collins and his horse lurched forward. He began well and cleared each of the three jumps with acceptable form and speed. However, he fumbled for his saber, barely nicking the dummy's shoulder.

The next rider was Ron Williams from D Company. After executing the first jump, Williams made the mistake of pulling back on the reins as his horse approached the four-foot jump. The horse reared, depositing Williams in a heap.

Pelham looked down on Williams. "You okay, Ron?"

Williams jumped to his feet and brushed the dust from his riding pants, his face red with embarrassment. "Sure, John—I mean, sir."

Pelham wasn't used to being called sir. "You've got to trust your horse, Ron. He's made that jump a thousand times, so let him take the lead. You're fortunate the ground is still soft. It will be brick hard this afternoon."

"Yes, sir."

Custer trotted up with William's horse.

"Thanks, Fannie," Williams said, then returning to the section.

Of the remaining six riders, all but one failed the course because of time, poise, or deficient contact with the dummy.

Pelham assembled the class, making a great show of Jason Lott of B Company, the only cadet to pass the obstacle course. "See, it can be done! Let's hear it for Mr. Lott who is now free to go about his business."

Approbation, muted with envy, attended Lott's departure for the stables.

Pelham canvassed the seven remaining members of the section, their faces long and defeated, and offered a conciliatory smile. "You've two more sessions to pass the obstacle course. Pass the course and you join Mr. Lott."

Pelham sensed their fear. "Who was the finest horseman ever to ride at West Point?"

Without hesitation and with a straight face, Collins piped, "John Pelham, sir. Everyone knows that."

The rest of the section and Rosser guffawed. Custer quipped, "Collins, your nose has a distinct color to it."

"I believe it was Grant, sir," Ron Williams volunteered.

"Very good, Mr. Williams. Ulysses S. Grant, Class of 1843. Grant jumped a horse a height of six feet inside the riding hall and could ride anything with four legs. And why could he do it?" Pelham paused. "Because he grew up in the saddle, that's why. But we don't expect you to imitate Grant or us. You just need to pass the obstacle course—the same one we've all had to pass. And you have the ability. I've seen it. Okay, we're done for today. And I'll wager that before the end of the third day, all of you will have passed the course. And Mr. Rosser knows I can't afford to lose a wager."

From behind the section, Custer cleared his throat. "If it's all the same to you, John, I'll take that wager." Custer produced a Liberty Head five-dollar gold piece and flashed it for all to see.

Back in the encampment, Emory Upton marched the short distance to the quartermaster tent and found du Pont at his desk.

"I want to know why, Henry?" Upton demanded.

Du Pont put down his pen. "What' s crawled up your ass, Emory?"

"Don't play ignorant with me, Henry."

Upton's face flushed red. "Last week, I was officer of the guard and reported to the Commandant's tent for my guard briefing."

Du Pont sat passively in his chair.

"He wasn't there, Henry. And neither was his orderly. There were papers scattered on the floor, so I picked them up."

"Your point, if you will?"

"One of them was a record of communication signed by you."

Du Pont stiffened in his chair. "You read a confidential memo?"

"Dammit, Henry, you harpooned me!"

"I did no such thing, Emory."

"You deny what you said?"

"Lieutenant Colonel Hardee asked me a direct question, Emory. I had no option but to answer."

"You said I was extreme, Henry. That's not true."

Du Pont couldn't resist a wry smile. "Not true? Hardee asks me who has radical views in the Corps, and you're telling me you're not in the mix? The only self-avowed abolitionist in the Corps? If you were of the closet time, I might have let it slide. But Emory, you're not, and you know it."

"I have a right to my opinions. Same as you."

"Emory, you almost lost an eye to Wade Gibbes."

"It was a point of honor, Henry."

"What do you want from me, Emory? An apology?

"I am not an extremist, Henry."

"Okay, maybe I could have picked a better word. But, if you read my memo, which was a clear violation of confidentiality and a five-demerit offense, you would have seen that you weren't the only one mentioned."

Upton shook his head, unappeased.

"I think we are done here, Emory."

After washing up for the midday meal, Pelham and Rosser fell in for the march to the mess hall. On the mess hall steps, Walter Kingsbury pulled Pelham aside. "I'm in love, John."

"Again?"

"No, I mean it this time. Do you think Tom holds a grudge?"

"He's shattered, Walter. Tell me more."

"It's crazy. I can't get the girl out of my mind. Eva Taylor is in every thought I think, every breath I breathe."

"I hope you write that down?"

"It's embarrassing, John."

"It's demeaning."

"I'm serious."

"The adjutant is smitten."

"She's of the Zachary Taylor clan. The president was her uncle. She remembers visiting the White House."

"I'm impressed."

"Her father is assistant commissary general for the army, and the best part is that her sister is married to a West Pointer. So, she knows what's coming."

"My friend, I smell a fully cooked goose."

"And a distraught bird, I am. She leaves Saturday—and Sunday I die. My heart broken." Kingsbury wrung his hands.

Pelham placed a consoling hand on his shoulder. "Then I suggest you make the most of life before Sunday."

Chapter Seventeen

At two forty-five, Pelham approached the hotel expecting to find Clara waiting on the veranda, but instead saw only two bearded gentlemen taking coffee and enjoying a pipe.

"Cadet Pelham." A voice behind him attempted sternness.

Pelham spun around to see Clara in a floral gown, peeking out from behind a large elm tree, her face radiant.

"Aren't you the sneak?" said Pelham, offering his arm.

Clara sprang forward and took it. "What are we to do, John?"

"What I promised."

"Oh, I can't wait." She opened her parasol and gave him a curious look. "How is it you can be with me, when I see so many of your colleagues still training?"

Pelham smiled. "Colleagues? I've never thought of them that way. But in answer to your question, it's my compensation for being a cadet instructor. I am teaching horsemanship this week, and in return I get Tuesday and Thursday afternoons off from two-thirty to five."

"You clever man!" said Clara, squeezing his arm.

They walked a short distance to a curious circling of large iron links supported on short posts. "A necklace for a giant?" Clara said with amusement.

"Part of the great chain that stretched from West Point to Constitution Island over there. During the Revolutionary War, it was intended to keep British ships from sailing north of West Point."

Clara ran her hand over one of the large links. "Did it work?"

"The British never tried it."

"And what about those?" She pointed to a row of cannons she had seen on the way to yesterday's parade.

"Spoils from the Revolutionary War, the War of 1812, and the Mexican War." Pelham motioned toward the bluff. "Before we get started, I want to show you one of my favorite spots."

He led her to a cast iron bench that overlooked the Hudson. A cluster of large elm trees shaded it. From the bench, one could see the entire valley and the river alive with sloops, schooners, ketches, and dinghies.

The sound of horses announced the hotel omnibus coming up from the North Dock.

Clara sat on the bench. "Look at all the birds. If only I had some bread." She patted the bench. "Come sit with me."

Pelham scanned the Plain for a uniform, and seeing none, obliged her.

"So beautiful," Clara said, her eyes on the Hudson.

Pelham nodded, and the two sat quietly enjoying the moment. Soon, squirrels appeared in number, scampering from tree to tree; birds joining them, stabbing the ground for worms.

"Is it true that cadets are not to hold hands with a lady friend except at a hop?" Clara asked, sliding her hand over to Pelham who squeezed it.

"We have a good many rules, my lady."

She pointed to a small gothic house nearby, its steeply gabled roof boasting extensive filigree trim. "That is absolutely the cutest gingerbread house I've ever seen."

"That's the Simpson House, our confectionary—where we leave our teeth." Pelham said. "Come. There is much to see."

He led Clara past Executioner's Hollow, the localized depression in the Plain, remarking that he was not personally aware that anyone had actually been executed there. They crossed Jefferson Road and walked slowly past the quarters of the commandant, the superintendent, and Professor Mahan. Pelham gave detailed histories and anecdotes for each.

"The gardens behind the houses are quite impressive," Clara said. "And the flower beds are beautiful."

"The flowers are for show. The gardens are functional, providing vegetables of every kind and fodder for livestock."

"I did notice a lot of chickens and a cow."

"And sometimes a chicken wanders off never to be seen again," Pelham said with a look of innocence.

She wagged a finger. "You are a bad boy, aren't you? But I will say, you are an excellent guide who keeps me wanting more."

"Trust me, four years in this place and you could do the same." He directed her attention to the house adjacent to Mahan's quarters. "That is the Thompson house, a Corps favorite. You remember Becky, the girl with Ned Kirby?"

"The one who kissed you?" Clara said with a judging glance.

"Becky is the granddaughter of Mr. and Mrs. Alexander Thompson. Her family has been on post since 1806, and in that particular house since 1838. Her grandfather was the Academy's military storekeeper. He passed away prematurely in 1809, but his widow and three daughters were allowed to stay on post for serving it. In the early days the Academy had no organized dining facility, and the cadets boarded with local families, the Thompsons being one of them. Now that we have a mess hall, those with a high grade point are invited to take meals at the Thompsons. The widow Thompson is advanced in years but still does a great meal. Kirby got to know Becky when he was invited to dine. Henry du Pont takes meals there every chance he gets."

"I can see that she and the family are quite special to you." Clara closed her parasol when they reached the shadow of a behemoth four-story Tudor-Gothic structure. "What, pray tell, is this?"

"That, my lady, is the cadet barracks, my prison for nine months of the year."

Pelham described in detail the configuration and organization of the barracks as they continued east on Jefferson Road.

"And this?" Clara asked, pointing to a long, massive three-story building next to the barracks.

"That is the academic building, where I suffer most," Pelham said, producing a pitiable face. "I take most of my classes in it, and soon, after but another week and a half when you're back at Clermont, I will return to its bowels and grow pale and pink inside it."

"Yours is a difficult curriculum?" Clara asked.

"So, we are told. We lose between thirty to forty cadets each year, mostly plebes, and not many of us are at a loss for brains."

"And you—you are a good student?"

"Well, I have yet to be invited to the Thompsons," Pelham said. "I'm in the middle third of the class. Actually, the bottom of the middle third. But I retain what I learn and learn what I think is important. The rest—I just get by."

"And your favorite subjects?"

Pelham smiled again. "Same as any college man. Cavalry, artillery, infantry, fencing, ordnance, doctoring horses."

"Don't be silly. Isn't West Point an engineering school?"

"The best in the country," Pelham said with pride. "And I find the engineering subjects quite interesting. There will be a lot of them this year, and I can see their application once my four years of service are up."

"You'll not make the army a career?"

"I'm not planning on it. But it's a free education. In fact, I'm paid to be here, though not much. As a Southern boy, my dream is to run a plantation—my own. After defending the frontier and safeguarding the sagebrush, I'll make room for somebody else in this army."

"So that you can be a farmer?"

"You cut me, my lady. I'll be more than a farmer."

"I'm sure you will," Clara said without conviction.

As they crossed South Gate Road, Pelham pointed down the street to the mess hall beyond the academic building, describing it.

"Why is it called a mess hall?"9

"The post surgeon and his assistant surgeon quarter in the building with their families, and the hospital attendants quarters in the basement."

"Have you spent time in the hospital?"

"Very little—until this past year when I got kicked royally by a horse." He raised his pant leg to reveal a not-so-faint purple and yellow bruise on his shin. "I was in bed for four days."

"You poor baby. May I?" She stooped down and inspected his leg. "You're lucky the tibia wasn't fractured, or worse."

"You know about tibias?"

Clara smiled as she rose to her feet, gazing with interest at the building on the other side of the road. It was unlike any other on the campus, possessing arched stained-glass windows and a balustrade roofline, incongruent with the other Academy architecture. "Your church?"

"Yes. The Cadet Chapel. It's Greek revival or something, and every Sunday we are in it. Whether we believe or not."

"Excuse me?"

"Relax, my lady. I mean that after Sunday morning inspection, church attendance is mandatory for every cadet. Al Mordecai, as devout a Jew as there is, frequently sits next to me. The Catholics are marched to services in Buttermilk Falls, south of post."

"You believe, don't you, John?"

"What do you think?"

"I hope with all my heart you do."

"Then you'd be right, my lady."

Clara smiled. "Can we go inside?"

"If you wish." He glanced about, and then led her up the stone steps, past the portico of four Doric columns and through the massive entryway. As he removed his forage cap, Clara crossed herself.

"You are a Catholic Quaker?"

Ignoring him, she proceeded down the center aisle.

Pelham followed, indifferent to the fact that he had broken every rule in the Academy book by taking an unchaperoned woman inside an Academy building.

"This sanctuary is beautiful, John." Her eyes devoured the church interior: the worn gray slate floor, the massive dark mahogany pews, the eighteen-foot Corinthian wood columns, the downward facing cannons embedded in white plaster walls, the ornate wood and marble altar, and the large mural high on the somewhat concave wall behind the altar.

She stared at the mural on the concave wall. "That is an exceptional piece of artwork."

"It's called *Peace and War*," Pelham said. "Painted by our own Professor Weir. He heads up the drawing department. The mural is eleven feet by twenty-two feet, and you can see that the curved surface gives it a sort of three-dimensional look."

"It really does," Clara said.

"Professor Weir is internationally recognized and has a painting in the U.S. capitol."

Clara proceeded down the aisle to inspect the mural in more detail. The painting consisted of an altar framed against a starry sky. On the left side of the altar, Peace, in the form of a woman clad in white, held an olive branch; in her other hand she held a Bible. War, on the other side, was a Roman soldier with his hand on the hilt of a sword. The two faced away from each other. On the face of the altar were the words, RIGHTEOUSNESS EXALTETH A NATION, BUT SIN IS A REPROACH TO ANY PEOPLE, PROV. XIV.

"What symbolism and depth for a school that instructs men on soldiering. It truly is a masterpiece."

"You have studied art?" Pelham asked.

"We study everything—a little. They want us well rounded," she said with a prissy face, and then continued to look about the chapel. Embedded in the floor and on the walls were a number of black shields and bronze placards.

Pelham answered her question before she could ask. "We memorialize everything here."

Clara smiled and gestured to the balcony above the entrance to the sanctuary. "Can we go up?"

"Anywhere you like." Pelham led her up the curved wooden staircase. The balcony greeted them with more pews and more plaques.

"Surely this man isn't still alive?" Clara pointed to a plaque that was like the others but bore only the inscriptions *Major General* and *Born 1740*. There being no name or date of death.

"That was," Pelham said, "or I suppose is for Benedict Arnold."

"The traitor?"

"The same—the thought being that traitors are nameless and live forever in dishonor."

Clara surprised Pelham by slipping into a pew and drawing him in close to her. She folded her hands, closed her eyes, and bowed her head in prayer. Pelham stared at her a long moment before closing his eyes and attempting to pray. As they sat in silence, he found his senses fully engaged—the smell of her perfume, her softness against him. He cracked open an eye and took in the color and smoothness of her skin, the tiny brown mole on the nape of her neck, and the fineness of her blond hair.

"What are we praying for?" he asked, breaking the silence.

She uttered an audible Amen. "For you, my friend. My dearest new friend who is a man. Not a boy."

"For me?"

Clara kissed Pelham lightly on the cheek. "I prayed that God would grant you a noble life. For you are indeed a good and noble man. You are my knight. And I have never known a knight before—."

She hesitated, studying his face. "Am I distracting you?"

"Distracting me?"

"By kissing you on the cheek. I don't mean to—"

"No, no. Not at all." Pelham fumbled. "There's no reason that friends can't express affection for each other. A kiss on the cheek … I'm sure friends do that."

"Of course, they do," Clara said, beaming and kissing his other cheek.

Pelham cleared his throat. "We best be off. I want you to see the Academy's showcase before we head back."

"Lead on, dear knight!"

East of the chapel lay the Tudor-Gothic building that housed the Academy library and post headquarters, a monolith structure of steel gray granite and reddish-brown sandstone.

Clara studied the building's exterior and its three towers, and then pointed to the middle tower that boasted a rounded cupola.

"That is our planetarium," Pelham explained.

"Can we go inside?"

"Perhaps. Let me check."

In a minute he was back with the report that they could, and once inside, described the building's layout, that the east side of the building housed one of the finest libraries in the country, and the west side, the post headquarters and the offices for the superintendent and his staff. When he mentioned that the second floor was home to the Department of Natural and Experimental Philosophy lecture hall with all its displays, Clara was giddy to see it.

They ascended the stairs, and once in the lecture hall strolled between the various physics displays and new inventions. Pelham attempted to describe them to her satisfaction, but soon realized he was no match for her questions.

"You've a most curious mind for a woman," he said.

She gave him a look. "Does that door lead to the planetarium?"

"It does. Would you like to see some stars?"

"Can we?"

Once inside and seated and after allowing their eyes to adjust to the darkness, the heavens exploded above and around them, and again Pelham was aware of her femininity. Her gentle breathing and her hand resting harmlessly on his thigh made him thankful for the darkness and her inquisitive mind. He answered her questions with all he knew about the major constellations and their importance to navigation, and how cadets spent a great deal of time using instruments to glean from the stars where they were and where they were going.

When they returned to the ground floor, Clara asked if she could see the library. Once inside, she exclaimed, "Oh my gosh, John! So many books and stacked so high."

Fifteen feet above them and circling a portion of the interior wall, a narrow wrought-iron walk accessed books of every description on the ceiling-high shelves. Portraits, large and small, covered much of the room's dark wood paneling.

"Good afternoon, Mr. Pelham," sounded a deep male voice.

Pelham spun round, surprised and disconcerted to see the post librarian, Captain John Kelton in the shadow of his corner desk.

"Captain Kelton, sir. I didn't realize you were here."

"Just out from the stock room, Mr. Pelham. We received a shipment of new books." The librarian's face was unreadable behind his bushy mustache. Pelham knew full well that if Kelton reported him with an unchaperoned woman, he would spend the rest of his life in confinement.

Pelham chose directness and with a casual air introduced Clara. "Captain Kelton guards these books as if they were his children, Clara."

"Especially watchful of you, young man." Kelton produced a ready smile. "Mr. Pelham is a voracious reader."

"I am pleased to know it and not at all surprised to hear it, sir." Clara said, proceeding to inquire as to how many books were in the library, what kinds of books they were, and about the portraits on the wall, especially the portrait above the man's desk.

"That, ma'am, is Sylvanus Thayer," Kelton said with pride.

"An impressive man."

"Indeed, Colonel Thayer was, and is, a quite impressive man, though gone before my time as a cadet. But I think Mr. Pelham will agree that much of what you see of the campus and how the cadets are trained are his doing and his dream. He was superintendent from 1817 to 1833, and had considerable influence on our current superintendent, Colonel Delafield. Thayer might still be here if he hadn't got crosswise with President Andrew Jackson. During Jackson's presidency, cadets dismissed from the Academy because of gross misconduct were easily reinstated if politically connected, and Jackson was one for granting such favors. It infuriated Thayer and flew in the face of what he considered essential order and discipline. Right or wrong, he resigned as superintendent and has never been back to West Point. He currently serves with the Corps of Engineers, though I'm not sure where."

"Sir," Pelham said, making a show of checking his watch. "I want to thank you for your time, but we had better be heading back."

"Of course, Mr. Pelham. I'm pleased you dropped by, and I'm very happy to have met this young lady."

"And I, you, Captain Kelton." Clara extended her hand.

Outside, Pelham resisted the impulse to tell Clara what he had just risked, and since marksmanship was over for the day, he took her on the most direct route along the bluff road to the hotel.

"So, my most interesting lady friend, what is it that you study at Clermont?"

"I'm finishing what is called a preparatory medicine program."

"Excellent. You are to be a nurse?"

"Well, that's the intent of the course—but actually, no. I am going to be a doctor."

Pelham drew back. "A—?"

"A doctor, John."

"A . . . female doctor?"

"I am a woman, yes. Is that a problem?"

"No. No—of course not. I've just never met or even heard of a female doctor."

"Precisely, and I know of only one myself, Elizabeth Blackwell. But someone needs to be next, and why not me?"

"A female doctor." Pelham voiced the words as though trying them on for size.

She stopped abruptly, her arms crossed.

Pelham raised his hands in defense. "I mean . . . it just takes some getting used to. But to your credit, you are clearly intelligent and curious to a fault. From the patient side, I believe you could be at ease with anyone, and you certainly have what I know of a doctor's demeanor. It's just …"

"Just what?"

"You are—don't take me wrong—a rather nice-looking woman. And I am not sure how that would—"

"I can make myself homely if I have to." Clara screwed her face up in a way that made Pelham chuckle.

"Well, it seems you have much in your favor," he said in a conciliatory tone. "Especially with your father being a doctor."

"After Clermont, I will have three, maybe four years of medical training."

"Have you been accepted to a school?"

Clara hesitated. "No. Not yet."

Pelham sensed frustration. "I'm sure it will happen."

"My grades are nearly perfect, John. I will graduate Clermont first in my class." The irritation evident in her voice. "I don't mind the sight of blood, I know the human body, male and female, and I can down a shot of whiskey as well as you can."

Pelham rubbed his chin. "Um. Imminently qualified. And for what it's worth, I would very much like for you to be my doctor."

Clara smiled. "Don't patronize me, young man."

"Here we are," Pelham announced as they reached the foot of the hotel stairs.

"John, I have truly enjoyed this whole afternoon. Just being with you. I feel so at ease with you." Clara hesitated. "I was wondering … Ellie mentioned something about a lovely walk along the river."

Pelham smiled. "You mean, Flirtation Walk?"

Clara waited for him to say more, but he didn't. "Is it pretty this time of year?"

Pelham grinned. "How about you see for yourself. Say Thursday afternoon?"

"Oh, can we, John? I could make us a glorious picnic. What is your favorite dish?"

"I'm not picky. But if you're asking. I love fried chicken, and we never get it in the mess hall."

"You poor baby. Fried chicken it is, and I'll surprise you with a dessert."

Pelham squeezed Clara's hand. "Until tomorrow's hop."

"Actually, I'm going to watch you parade this evening. I'm not going to miss a single one. Thank you again, John, for being such a wonderful friend. And don't eat too much before the picnic."

"That won't be a problem."

Clara glanced about the Plain and kissed Pelham on the cheek.

Chapter Eighteen

Following her afternoon with Pelham, Clara briefed Ellie and the other girls on her tour. They were more envious than pleased, and she didn't blame them. An hour later, at the abbreviated parade on the encampment grounds, she waved without restraint as Pelham led his platoon past the reviewing party and was convinced he had winked at her. Accordingly, she was in a particularly jubilant mood when she and Ellie returned to the hotel. But at the top of the staircase, they were confronted by Miss Frampton.

"Ellen, do you mind if I have a word with Clara?" Ellie

looked at Clara. "No, ma'am. Of course not."

Frampton motioned for Clara to follow and waddled to the corner of the veranda. "You are having a pleasant time here at the Academy, Clara?"

"Yes, ma'am," responded Clara, on her guard.

"Would you mind filling me in on your afternoon?"

"I'm sorry?"

"Your rendezvous with Cadet Pelham."

"Are you referring to my campus tour?"

"Why did you not inform me? You know the rule. You are my responsibility."

"And you are quite right, Miss Frampton. I was remiss, and I am sorry. It was a spur of the moment thing. I just didn't think to tell you."

"Didn't think to tell me," Frampton repeated. "I think you see too much of that Pelham boy."

"Meaning no disrespect, ma'am, but he is hardly a boy."

"I am sure you are quite right," Frampton said, raising an eyebrow. "Clara, I am not singling you out, but your father, when he first brought you to Clermont after your mother passed, God rest her soul, made some things quite clear to me. He wished to be fully satisfied that you would be trained in all things necessary for the proper upbringing of a lady. I pledged to him I would do just that and have personally attempted my best to do so."

"I'm sorry, ma'am. I don't understand your meaning."

The assistant dean drew back, not a little surprised at Clara's tone. "Miss Bolton, Clermont is a finishing school, a true seminary for girls. While we are happy to provide you with a profession appropriate to a lady, our primary goal is to make you a woman of refinement."

"Am I failing to be, ma'am?"

Frampton was momentarily nonplussed. "Your father was insistent that you receive the finest instruction in every aspect of becoming a woman, and that you be able to fit seamlessly into any level of society."

"Fit seamlessly," repeated Clara. "That sounds like Father. Has he complained to you?"

"Of course not," Frampton said. "At least not about that."

"Then what?"

"Well … last week, I received a pointed letter from him seeking an explanation."

"About what?"

"I had written him about your aspirations."

"My aspirations?"

"Of you … your wanting to be a doctor, Clara."

"Did I ever say I wanted to be a doctor?"

"Well, maybe not in so many words, but you did ask to take the anatomy course at Columbia, which is an all-male school."

"And what did Father say?"

"In a word, he did not want me or Clermont making a man out of his daughter."

Clara flushed red. "Miss Frampton, do you doubt my female nature?"

"Of course not, dear. But how can I ignore the perceptions and desires of a parent?"

"You mean a parent who pays the bills."

"I mean a father who is deeply concerned about his daughter. You know that, Clara. In any event, in my response to him, I made it clear that I would not counsel you to pursue any profession that rightly falls in the male domain."

"Miss Frampton, may I ask you a question?"

"Of course you may."

"Have you ever seen a man naked?"

CHAPTER NINETEEN

Before supper, Pelham had an unexpected visit from Emory Upton; and after supper made his way to the tunnel-like sally port that extended through the cadet barracks. He entered the door next to the sally port and climbed the stairs to the First-Class Club, a high-ceilinged room with a long conference table, a few smaller tables for card and board games, a billiard table, and several lounge chairs. The north and south walls were set with large leaded-glass windows. The interior walls bore paintings, etchings, and shelves for books, newspapers, and magazines. The room also served as the meeting place for the Dialectic Society, now entering its thirty-sixth year. Pelham took a seat at the head of the conference table and waited for the rest of the society's eighteen members to arrive. Included in the number were Henry du Pont, Adelbert Ames, Chas Patterson, and Emory Upton.

After a few minutes, the society's sergeant-at-arms, Patrick O'Rorke, signaled to Pelham that all were present, and announced, "This meeting of the Dialectic Society is hereby called to order."

O'Rorke, the oldest member of the Second Class, was tall, slim, freckled, and a brilliant and eloquent man. He was the first Irish cadet to make a real mark at the Academy, ranking just below Charlie Ball in class standing and serving as first sergeant for D Company.

At Pelham's direction, O'Rorke read the minutes of the previous meeting held in May.

"The minutes have been read," Pelham said, looking around the table. "Are there any corrections?"

None were offered.

"Then they'll be filed as read."

"Now," Pelham said, rising to his feet and placing the tips of his fingers on the table. "A point of privilege if I may. Since you have seen fit to place me in this chair."

His remark drew laughter since he had been elected president during the May meeting when he was in the hospital mending from his leg injury. The election was deemed reasonable since he had been vice president the year before.

"I have given considerable thought to what we might do to make a real difference this coming year, a year in which politically so much is at stake for the country and all of us. I've asked myself, should we ignore the issues? Should we play it safe and like we did last year and in years past, settling for simply poking fun at ourselves? Or should we face the enemy head on and give voice to what is on everyone's mind and debate it accordingly?"

"And pray tell," Patterson said, pinching an empty pipe between his teeth, "what is on my mind, John?"

"Whether or not a state has the right to secede from the Union."

Patterson's expletive suggested otherwise.

"Thank you, Chas," said Pelham, unfazed. "But when I reflect upon what a Dialectic Society should be about, I see an opportunity and a responsibility to place squarely before the Corps and anyone else who attends our debate, the arguments for and against this incredibly central and, yes, divisive issue."

In the silence that followed, Emory Upton sat at the opposite end of the table, his face deadpan.

"You don't believe in foreplay, do you, John?" Adelbert Ames said, breaking the ice.

Pelham raised his hands in an appeasing gesture. "I have only made a suggestion. I am not even allowed a vote unless it's to break a tie. I'll go with whatever you decide, and we can certainly pick another topic. My only fear is that we become irrelevant at a time when the Corps needs relevance."

Du Pont, initially off balance with Pelham's candidness, spoke next. "Colonel Delafield will never sanction it, John. He would see us as teasing a hornet's nest—and he would be right."

"Perhaps, but we won't know unless we ask him, will we? I don't mind defending the topic if we are in agreement."

The room was again quiet.

"I understand the hesitancy," Pelham said. "And so, I propose we adjourn early this evening and task ourselves to come up with a debate topic in the form of a one-sentence proposition for our next meeting in September. Mine is just one idea. We'll vote on the topics and decide on our debaters, then schedule the debate sometime in mid-October. Whatever the topic, I'll take it to Delafield to get his stamp on it. If he denies it, I'll offer up our second choice."

Du Pont so moved, and the motion was seconded by Patterson, followed by a mumbling of "ayes."

Pelham glanced at the clock on the wall which showed only ten minutes of elapsed time since the meeting started. "I would entertain a motion to adjourn."

Ames so moved, and the motion was seconded by du Pont and approved by all.

Pelham grinned. "I declare the shortest Dialectic Society meeting in Academy history adjourned."

Chapter Twenty

After camp lights were extinguished at ten o'clock, the cadet officer of the guard made his inspection, starting with A Company and ending with D Company. He walked methodically down each company street, confirming with a lantern that each bed was occupied.

Fifteen minutes after bed check, Pelham whispered to Rosser, "Let's be at it, Tom." Rosser followed him under the canvass flap, past Lieutenant Lee's tent, past the commandant's tent, and past the tents of drum orderlies and boot blacks. They found Kirby and Patterson waiting at the eastern perimeter of the encampment.

They waited for the guard's predictable movement from north to south. When the guard was beyond earshot, Pelham gave a bird call, and then snaked Indian style through the darkness to Thaddeus Kosciusko monument and the safe haven of the river bluff.

Pelham turned around, grinning. "Be we thirsty, lads?"

"Parched," said Kirby.

Patterson made a choking sound.

Rosser said nothing.

"Then we're committed," said Pelham.

In the lead, Pelham proceeded under a full moon, the air decidedly cooler. With the practiced silence of a tactical patrol, they hugged the tree line that bordered the bluff. Barely a hundred yards into the journey, Rosser grabbed Pelham about the waist, and Pelham understood why. He stood looking over the edge of a fifty-foot cliff.

He chastised himself for being distracted as they skirted the ring of gas lampposts encircling the library and post headquarters. At the rear of the building, they descended through moon shadows to South Dock Road.

Try as he might, Pelham couldn't purge Clara Bolton from his mind. She had taken up residence, confusing all that had been in good order. Worse, she had changed the playing field—introduced an unfamiliar game—with rules he didn't understand.

At the switchback in South Dock Road, Pelham took the footpath that ascended to the bluff. Before reaching the crest, he detoured onto a little used trail that bypassed the South Gate guardhouse. Beyond the guardhouse, they scrambled up the embankment to the cinder road leading to Buttermilk Falls.

Patterson slapped Rosser on the back. "You can relax now, Tom."

"Me?" said Rosser. "It's you three risking stripes."

"That's what life is about, Tom," Patterson said. "Risk."

Kirby, with the most at risk, being a four striper, whistled a bright tune, and quickly enough Rosser's mood improved, leading to a pronouncement, "I think I'll start with ale."

"Aye, while the flip is made," said Patterson.

Pelham strode briskly down the dark road, lost in his own thoughts about Clara. He struggled with how to proceed. Her nature was disarmingly transparent and kind, seasoned with endearing sincerity and wit. No pretense or facade within her. And about these things, his heart and mind wrestled.

Is that what you really want, the platonic? It is untried territory and likely to wear thin.

Not so. The platonic affords intimacy a person would never otherwise know, real friendship born of respect and noble intention.

But are you not a man, and is she not a girl easily more attractive and intriguing than any you have ever known? Befriending her with a friend's motive is a slippery slope, and serves what end?

Pelham struggled to shake the conflicting thoughts from his head. However, Clara had made her desire clear enough. At the approach of a rider, he cautioned the others. "To the woods."

After the rider passed, they continued on, as did the debate inside Pelham.

What of her kisses, and the way she touches you? You think her so naive as not to understand your nature, your chemistry? Don't confuse naïveté with genuine affection.

Pelham smiled in the dark. Whatever the temptations, he would bear them.

Ten minutes later, they reached the sleepy village of Buttermilk Falls, and snuck past the nearly dark Cozzen's Hotel, its young ladies and mothers or chaperons readying for another day and another hop. A quarter of a mile beyond it lay the stone steps that led down to the river and the lights below. Approaching their destination, they were spurred to a trot and a swift descent down steep stone steps. At the base of the steps, to their right stood a wood structure, cheerily silhouetted against the river. A candle burning in the second story window evidenced that their friend was at home, and it was safe to enter. Against the landing's small dock, a single sloop lolled in the light chop, an oil lamp behind the mast blinking eerily like a jaundiced eye.

Chapter Twenty-One

The tavern was alive with light and laughter, and the unmistakable sound of Benny Havens.

"I'd say he's got a fair business going," Pelham observed, mounting the porch steps with a finger to his lips and Rosser, Kirby, and Patterson on his heels. He swung open the heavy door and delivered a boisterous, "Benny, we're back!"

Inside the small tavern, three tables of patrons eyed the uniformed intruders.

At the far right of the tavern, behind the bar, a man with rosy cheeks and silver-gray hair threw up his hands. "Well bless my soul, if the prodigals ain't returned!"

Pelham and the others waited for the old man to round the bar and greet them with a proper hug.

"Masters John, Tom, Ned, and Chas. And here I was thinking you'd given up on your old friend." Havens crossed his arms. "And would you be having a thirst?"

"A mighty thirst, Benny," Pelham said, tossing his forage cap on the hearth.

"We're here to celebrate, Benny," proclaimed Rosser. "Start us with ale, Benny. But make us our flip." The Texan produced some silver coins. "And this is for arrears."

"Master Tom, you're an honest man." Havens pocketed the coins. "Rest yourselves and trust me to keep vigil out back."

Pelham and Rosser sat opposite Kirby and Patterson at a table flanked by barreled provisions and a stone fireplace.

Benny returned with four frothy pints of ale. "This is indeed a surprise and a blessing in my old age."

Pelham raised his mug. "Your health, Benny."

The others echoed the same.

"Moreover, to the man who's seen us at our worst," added Rosser with a wink, "and still loves us."

"Pshaw. Let me get the flip going, lads." The Irishman returned to the bar to assemble the ingredients for the beverage for which he was renowned.

Pelham gazed about the tavern as Patterson filled in Rosser and Kirby on the challenge Pelham had given the Dialectic Society.

There was a rustle of chairs, and the four men who Pelham took to be the crew for the sloop settled their bill.

Pelham sipped his ale, his gaze fixed on the old tavern keeper. If ever there was a constant in the world, it was the man behind the bar. Benny Havens was known by all in gray, but only as a true friend to those willing to risk dismissal for his different brand of education. Pelham knew Benny's life story. That the man was born in 1787 in New Windsor, some thirteen miles north of West Point. In 1802, at the age of fifteen, the year the Academy was founded, he was hired by the Academy sutler who ran West Point's general store. While working for the sutler, Benny was expelled from Academy grounds for selling a bottle of rum to a cadet wanting to better enjoy his Christmas. The man went straight to his cups and made a spectacle of himself, and at the encouragement of authorities revealed his source.

Havens glanced up from behind the bar and caught Pelham's eye. He nodded and smiled when Pelham raised his mug.

In the War of 1812, Havens had served as a first lieutenant in a company of volunteers drawn partially from Buttermilk Falls, which at the time boasted barely one hundred souls. His company had been stationed on Long Island and saw no action. But a woman named Letitia Stuyvesant captured his heart and later became his wife. After the war, Havens became a woodcutter and a carpenter, primarily cutting and making hoop poles for barrels. In such capacity, he was allowed back on Academy grounds. He built a small, attractive cottage close to the cadet hospital, and after a time, reverted to his natural calling. In due course, Letitia gave birth to a son and then three very pretty daughters. The daughters all married, one an officer. For many happy years, Benny and Letitia befriended cadets and supplied them with food and drink, though in the earlier years it was more Letitia's buckwheat cakes, roast turkeys, and the like that made them a living, rather than Benny's bartending, though soon and rightly enough it was

Benny's recipe for hot flip that gave him the edge over competing establishments.

The master barman pulled a large brown earthenware pitcher from beneath the counter, a tray of eggs from the cold box, two bottles of ale, a jug of rum, a tin of sugar, and an assortment of spices essential to the making of his flip, a concoction far and away the favorite of most patrons—especially cadets. He deftly cracked eggs over the pitcher and added ingredients measured by sight and feel.

Next came a generous quantity of ale and an ample measure of rum, the whole beat into a frothy mixture. He then extracted a white-hot "flip dog" from the stove and in dramatic fashion plunged the iron into the pitcher. The resulting hiss drew the attention of all present, the aroma of caramel soon wafting through the tavern.

Pelham reflected further upon the thorn in the Academy's paw. In 1825, the nearly sainted Sylvanus Thayer, bent on temperance for the Corps and well aware of the propensity of cadets to visit the Havens' cottage, achieved his aim by convincing Congress to purchase for ten thousand dollars the land upon which the Havens' house stood. As Havens owned the house but not the land, he was paid for the house and ordered to vacate. While an effective measure in the near term, the move interrupted the Havens' business only a short time. The entrepreneur moved his growing family to temporary accommodations in neighboring Buttermilk Falls. In a matter of months, his trade was in full vigor and beyond Academy reach. But it was not until 1843, when Havens purchased property for the landing, that the tavern was built in which Pelham and his friends found themselves.

While Patterson speculated with Kirby and Rosser on the next commandant, Pelham inspected the tavern, tracing with his finger the initials he had carved as a plebe in the tabletop. Now, it had been three months since he and Rosser escaped through the tavern's back door when the duty officer followed up on a report of cadets leaving post.

Had anything been added, had anything been changed?

Pelham surveyed the tavern as if he might be required to sketch it for Professor Weir, who had never been much impressed with his talent. Weir had taught him to see a thing first in its whole, before seeing it in its parts. The tavern was a single room, twenty by forty feet, its length parallel to the shoreline, its wonderfully worn pine plank floor stained by whatever spilled or missed the spittoon. The ceiling was rough mahogany with massive dark ceiling beams, from which stubby whale oil lanterns hung on iron hooks, providing soft, soothing light. Its entrance was bordered on one side by a window, which in the daytime opened to glorious views of the river and the hills beyond. The plastered walls bore a dull yellow-ochre finish, nearly black around the stone fireplace. The thick rough-cut square columns bore hooks for every miscellany.

Pelham registered the line, color, and sense of everything: the tarnished brass lionhead doorknob, the narrow stairs rising to the second floor where Havens and his wife lived, the mahogany bar with stools crafted by Havens himself, the liquors and wines behind the bar, the cork dart board, the cracker barrel in the center of the room, and the collection of unmatched tables, chairs, and benches that made the place a tavern. The walls were alive with paintings, etchings, and sketches, and swords, sabers, and musketry that gave the place the feel of an armory.

"How went your trip, Master Pelham?" Havens shouted from behind the bar.

"A blur, Benny. Too much and too fast."

"I expect so. So little time."

Rosser pointed an accusing cigar at Pelham. "So why would you have us wait so long to visit our friend, John?"

The last of the other patrons settled their accounts, receiving a hearty farewell from Havens.

"Benny," Pelham declared, "you are undoubtedly the most congenial soul in the valley and likely on earth."

"Don't know about that, Master Pelham." Havens' eyes twinkled. "But I do believe a stranger is but a friend I've yet to meet." The tavern keeper's tone turned serious. "These are interesting times, lads."

"T'will resolve itself, Benny," Patterson said easily.

"You think, Master Patterson?" Havens forced a smile. He removed the flip dog and spooned a taste. Removed too soon, the beverage was flat; left too long, it had a burnt flavor. Benny smacked his lips, smiled, and rang the bell above the bar reserved for hot flip.

Patterson drained his ale and fetched his pipe. "Glorious is the here and now. And, oh, how we'll pay for it with sleep."

"Not if we mind and limit ourselves," Pelham said, lighting the cigar Kirby gave him. "But we had to come. Think of what little time remains. When we graduate, Benny and all of this will be a memory. But we are agreed, one flip and we're gone. Right?"

Havens gingerly served the four steaming tankards of hot flip. "This will cure your demons, and certain you'll not find a serving like mine nowhere's else."

Patterson sniffed the beverage and loosed a guttural purr.

"Pure heaven, Benny," Kirby declared, his lip foamed with flip.

The four toasted Havens again, and then each other, then the class, and finally their last year at the Academy.

Patterson stood up. "And it's only right we toast our benefactor, John Pelham, for his Clermont girls."

"Hear, hear," shouted Rosser tousling Pelham's hair.

"And I'll let you know that Miss Alice Paine and I are getting along famously," declared Patterson.

"A poor judge of men, is she?" said Kirby.

Patterson ignored Kirby. "It pains me to say it, John, but I am indeed obliged to you."

"Then pay me back in academics. For it's there I'll need help."

"Not as much as ole Tom," Patterson said, poking Rosser in the ribs. "And just how are things with Miss Taylor?"

"Name change, Chas," Pelham interjected. "Seems Tom prefers the southern lass, Carol Hill."

"What about poor Walter?" Patterson asked.

"I suppose he'll just have to make do with Miss Taylor," Pelham said with a grin.

"And you and Clara?"

"Clara and I are where we need to be, Chas."

"As it should be, for she's the queen of six royal bees."

Letitia Havens descended the staircase. "Hello, boys. What's our topic?"

Benny rounded the bar. "Mum, I believe it's manly passions."

Pelham nearly choked on his flip.

"Though, dear wife, I can't quite recall exactly what it is they are talking about."

Now it was Rosser's turn to choke.

Letitia winked at the young men. "Seems he figured it out a few times."

When the laughter died, Havens asked if he might join them. Pelham drew up another chair. "So, what's new with you, Benny?"

Before he could respond, Patterson was in Benny's face.

"Is it true, Benny, what John says? About the Marquis de Lafayette coming to visit you?"

Pelham shrugged his shoulders. "What can I say Benny? The man is a Thomas."

"Master Chas," Havens remonstrated, "there are likely some things I've said you might rightly question, but as far as that fine Frenchman goes—you know he was adopted by George Washington—he most certainly did pay me a visit. It was …" Havens searched his memory. "1824, I think. When he was making his grand tour of the country that he served so well in our struggle for independence a half century before." Havens eyed Patterson with curiosity. "You're not pulling my leg, Chas? You really don't believe me?"

Patterson assured him he wasn't.

"So, you want to see the nail holes? Give me a minute."

Havens got up and rooted behind the bar, surfacing with a well-polished cherry-wood chest. He unlocked it with the small key that hung about his neck and after some searching retrieved a small polished wooden box. Returning to the table, he placed the box in front of Patterson.

"Go ahead, Master Patterson, open it."

Patterson lifted the lid and found two buttons inside. "May I?"

"By all means," said Havens.

Patterson removed one of the buttons and examined it. "Real gold?"

"It is."

"Fine workmanship."

"I should think so. And that fine French general was the guest of Superintendent Thayer. And I'm sure it was none to Thayer's satisfaction that the general was determined to pay me a visit. Why, I don't know, or how he even knew I breathed the air. But he arrives with others in his company, and I didn't know whether to bow or curtsey. He marches right up to me and asks if I am the one who makes hot flop. I don't correct him, but say I am, and I make him and his friends a very fine batch indeed. From then on, we got on famously, becoming the best of friends. With me, of course, doing most of the talking."

Pelham grinned. "Of course."

"The marquis," Havens said, "enjoyed a good story, no less than you, and laughed better than most men. We had a gay old time. When he finally left, it was after midnight. Before he goes, he gives me them two buttons with his face engraved on them. Made in Connecticut, he said. Then he thanks me and says if ever I get to France, he'll show me around Paris."

Patterson sat dumbfounded.

"Okay, Benny. Okay, I believe you." Patterson placed the button back in the box. "You're incredible, Benny! So, tell me, what did the Marquis look like?"

"What did he look like?" Havens placed his hands on hips and guffawed. "What did he look like? Lord, he looked old. That's what he looked like. By then nearly seventy." Havens thumbed his chest. "And damn if that disease ain't catchy."

When the laughter died, Pelham exhaled a cloud of gray smoke. "Benny, how is it that you, who hardly ever travel farther than New York City, get to regale and endear a Frenchman, an authentic Revolutionary War hero?"

"Don't know about endear'n, Master Pelham. Though, there's something about being a tavern keeper that puts people to ease. I will say that if we're talking heroes, I'd offer up the likes of you. I've seen it so often. You'll leave this place, and come a Mexican War or whatever, you'll prove me right or die trying."

Letitia came up alongside her husband and placed a loving hand on his shoulder.

"I'm just proud I get to know some of you," Havens continued. "Though not as many as I'd like, and glad enough when some of you come back to visit your old friend, like Jeff Davis did recently and Edgar Poe before he passed away too soon before his time."

Pelham nodded, thinking that Davis had probably visited Havens during his commission trip. He could picture the tall wiry senator and the tavern keeper talking through the night, reminiscing about the old days, about the time thirty-five years earlier when cadet Davis was caught in the tavern by a tactical officer and subsequently court-martialed, only to be reinstated by President Jackson. They likely would have joked about that and a later incident when Davis eluded a raid but, in his escape, stepped off a cliff nearly killing himself.

"I'll come back, Benny," Pelham promised. "Davis and Poe won't have a step on me."

The others pledged the same, Rosser adding blithely, "That Poe gives me the creeps."

"He shouldn't, Tom. He had as brilliant a mind as ever graced West Point and possessed a very keen, though dry, sense of humor. God rest his soul. And Poe was beloved by his classmates."

Pelham and the others knew the story, that when Poe arrived at West Point to join the Class of 1834, he had already published his earliest works. He attended West Point to appease his stepfather, who thinking himself rid of the young man proceeded to disown him. Learning of it, Poe decided he wasn't where he needed to be and did all he could to get himself dismissed, including missing formations, skipping classes, and spending evenings with Benny Havens. As a consequence, he and Havens became fast friends. Sylvanus Thayer tried to persuade Poe to stay, but the poet departed the Academy in February of 1831, eight months after his arrival.

After Poe's departure, Havens would talk about the man's admiration for the Corps and his bond with his classmates, pointing to Poe's next published collection of works, entitled *Poems*, with the sentiment on the title page, *To the U.S. Corps of Cadets this volume is respectfully dedicated.*

Pelham knew that Havens had copies of all of Poe's works, and was quick to recite one of his poems, especially "The Raven."

"No, you would have liked him, Master Tom. Believe me," Havens concluded. "He could actually be quite like you at times and delighted the Corps with his satire—always aimed at the leadership."

Rosser laughed. "Then assuredly I would have liked him very much."

"And imagine the fun we had," Havens added. "Each time, him coming in with something new to rattle my nerves."

"Can you imagine living inside that head of his?" Kirby said.

"I'd never get to sleep," said Patterson.

Pelham put a hand on the tavern keeper's arm. "Yours is a long list of friends, Benny."

"Aye, there have been many, Master Pelham. I think of former cadets. Of Grant, Jackson, Sherman, Longstreet, Burnside, Meade, Heath, Sheridan, Pickett, Thomas, and Strong—all of them my boys. And others, of course."

"We know of Grant and Jackson from the Mexican War," Rosser said. "But the others …?"

"Were like you," Havens said. "No different. All of them did what you're doing. They took risks. And for what? Its own reward."

"For flip," Rosser countered, raising his tankard. "'Tis this elixir that courses down my throat that draws me to you, Benny."

"So smooth and soothing, so friendly, fruity, faultless, flawless, this flip of ours." The words fairly flowed off Patterson's tongue.

"But, alas, mine's empty," Rosser said, his tone mournful. "What say you, my friends? Another round?"

"What about going it easy, Tom?" Pelham ribbed his roommate.

"Have we ever?" Rosser replied with a wink.

As Havens prepared a second batch, he shouted from the bar, "You think you know a thing or two, don't you, boys? But I'll bet there is something you don't know. There is one at the Academy who has headed an academic department for more years than I can count, who used to come and visit me. Can you name him?"

The four of them were incredulous and pooled their guesses, with Pelham finally announcing, "Can be none other than Professor Kendrick." Kendrick made his own peach brandy and would occasionally invite cadets to sample his wares, Patterson testifying to its quality and Kendrick's good humor.

"Don't believe I ever had the pleasure of Kendrick's company," Havens said. "So perhaps, a clue. Who is the one man most responsible for the departure of cadets from the Academy?"

The clue gave away the answer. But none could believe it.

Rosser shook his head. "Professor Church?" He had almost been dismissed by the very same professor.

"Aye, Albert Church, your professor of mathematics, Class of 1828. Same class as Jeff Davis, though Church was at the top and Davis near the bottom. But I assure you," Havens said in defense of Church. "His predecessors were just as villainous as he, and I'm sure his successors will be no less. There's just something about math that undoes a man. Church was a good lad, and he and I hit it off pretty well. I expect because mathematics has been a passion for me. Indeed, I used to tutor some of you lads back in the old days."

Pelham knew it. "But Church is so … normal."

"Normal now and no longer an imbiber, I understand. But I remember a different Church, and one night in particular. He and three others came to visit, and they were into a fine time when an informant warned them that they had been discovered absent from the barracks and officers were on the way. Letitia and I hid them as best we could. Church, being a small fellow, we hid in that flour barrel." Havens pointed to a barrel in the corner. "But to no avail, as all four were discovered, and one as white as a ghost."

Pelham's stomach ached from laughing.

"All but Church were court-martialed and dismissed," said Havens. "But the clever Church raised a point with the court officer that I was never quite clear on. But it prevailed, and his fate was settled favorably by President Van Buren."

"You find us amusing, don't you, Benny?" Pelham said, wagging a finger.

"I find you a blessing. I find that you undergo great change during your time here. And after you're gone, your lives are exciting. And Letitia and I live through you as we hear how you spend your lives." Havens turned thoughtful. "And soon the four of you will be gone. Anyway, if we didn't have the likes of you as part of our lives, dropping in at all times of night, I would have retired from this business long ago."

"Now that's a naked lie, Mr. Havens," Letitia declared as she washed dishes.

Havens produced a weak scowl. "What do you know, woman?"

Pelham seized the moment. Rising to his feet, he began to sing, joined by Rosser, Kirby, and Patterson. They sang the first verse of the song penned decades earlier in honor of the tavern keeper, a song sung to the tune of "Wearing O' the Green."

Come fill your glasses, fellows, and stand up in a row
To singing sentimentally we are going for to go.
In the Army there's sobriety, promotion's very slow
So, we'll sing our reminiscences of Benny Havens, Oh!

Oh! Benny Havens, Oh!—Oh! Benny Havens, Oh!
We'll sing our reminiscences of Benny Havens, Oh!

Letitia crossed the room with a brown bound book. "You honor us, boys. It was your Horace Porter of last year's class that presented Benny with his book entitled *West Point Life*. In it are most of the verses that have been penned for my Benny."

Pelham hugged the aged woman. Porter had been a good friend and last year had been the Corps adjutant and president of the Dialectic Society.

As the young men sang two more of the more than sixty versus collectively known as "Benny Havens, Oh," the old man's eyes required drying.

Chapter Twenty-Two

Wednesday morning at precisely five o'clock, Bentz played the first note of reveille, his bugle again punctuated by two energetic drum orderlies. Immediately, the dead arose amid yawns and oaths, the lighting of lamps, and rustled movements across wooden tent floors. In each company street, a plebe announced the minutes remaining until reveille formation, and by the time the two-minute call was made, the last of a stream of dark figures scurried onto the four company streets for the first formation of the day.

The three platoons of D Company stood at attention in front of First Sergeant Paddy O'Rorke.

"Report," O'Rorke said in a tone respectful of the hour.

"First Platoon, all present and accounted for," a man in front of the lead platoon reported.

O'Rorke returned the man's salute.

"Second Platoon, all present and accounted for." O'Rorke returned a second salute.

"Third Platoon, all present, except for Cadets Pelham and Rosser."

Laughter followed by cheers erupted from the three platoons of D Company. O'Rorke executed an about-face and rendered the report to an expressionless Ned Kirby, who in turn rendered the report to the battalion adjutant, Walter Kingsbury.

Minutes later, Kirby flung open the flap to Pelham and Rosser's tent and kicked Pelham's footlocker. Pelham shot up. "What the—"

Rosser peeked out from under his comforter.

"Fine example, boys. You haven't left the tent and already have a skin."

"Morning, Ned," Rosser said with a sheepish look and stretching his arms. "And I thought you worse off than me."

Pelham was more circumspect. "Hell, Tom, why should this year be any different?"

After Kirby departed, Rosser invested himself in mentally counting demerits, announcing, "At this rate we can still graduate."

While the cadets breakfasted in the mess hall, Colonel Delafield sat at a small table that James had set on the veranda of the superintendent's quarters. He finished the last of his morning meal while reading the newspaper and savoring the serenity of solitude. His wife Harriet, along with Professor Weir's wife, had ferried the Hudson to catch the train to New York City for three days of necessary and not so necessary shopping. They would not return until the following day. His disposition was further improved by the thought that this would be his last summer encampment. General Scott had as much as promised him that come January, he could either retire or mark time in a Washington job until the chief of engineers post opened. Either way, in his mind he would be gone from the campus that had become so claustrophobic.

His only wish was that his wife shared his viewpoint, which she didn't. She rather enjoyed the idyllic life and her position as queen of court. Beyond this, clouding his more or less sunny countenance, was the continued hesitancy on the part of Scott to actually name his replacement.

"More coffee, sir?" James asked.

Without waiting for a response, he tipped the silver coffee pot and filled the superintendent's cup.

Delafield put down the newspaper and studied the black man.

James felt the attention. "Sir, is there something?"

"James, in the nearly five years we've been together, you've told me nothing of yourself."

"Sir?"

"I see more of you than my wife, and yet know nothing of you."

"But sir … it is not my place."

The superintendent waved off the remark. "Nonsense, James. Have a seat."

The servant placed the coffee pot on the table and sat stiffly facing the superintendent, his back straight as a board.

"So, tell me of yourself, James."

"Sir, there is not much about me. I was born a slave, and now I am a free man. And I have worked for the government as a house domestic here at the Academy for the past eight years."

"Don't tell me there is not a story there," Delafield insisted.

The black man squirmed in his chair. "Fifteen years ago, sir, I was given my papers after my master died, he being true to his promise to free me."

"A good man, then. And where was that?"

"Brusly, Louisiana, sir. I was born into sugarcane, third generation, and had worked my way from the field to the house."

"That must have been a red-letter day for you, James, getting your freedom."

The house servant's face suggested otherwise as he glanced over his shoulder at the Plain. "Sir, I was very close to a young woman. She had been purchased by my master only months before he died. Her name was Juniper. She was the kindest, sweetest soul I had ever met, and to me the most beautiful woman I ever seen."

Delafield sensed he was unearthing something.

"This woman, sir, was to be the master's new cook, and she and me came to know and understand each other in special ways, both of us working in the house and all. I intended to ask her to be my wife, as much as I could have a wife, and I believe she would have said yes. I even asked permission of the master, and it pleased him to know it."

"Where is your Juniper now?"

"Only God knows, sir. Master died sudden like from his heart." James said. "His son come down from Opelousas to settle the estate. It all happened so fast, sir. The day after he come down, I get my papers and am beyond myself with joy. I go looking for Juniper to tell her—but she is gone."

"Gone?" said Delafield, stunned.

"That morning, sir. Sent away to a plantation near New Orleans to settle a debt." James paused to regain his composure. "I'm sorry, sir, but I never even had a chance to …"

"Go on, James."

"The master's son, he was a good man, but he knew nothing of me and Juniper. When I told him, he said he would do whatever he could to get her back and that I could pay him as I was able. He wrote the new owner to say he'd pay in cash money what the man wanted to settle the debt and to send Juniper back. He told me not to worry, that he would send Juniper to join me in New York City." The servant's eyes filled with tears.

"New York City?"

"It was all arranged by my master before he died. Before noon, I am on a steamer out of Baton Rouge with a small purse of coins and a letter I am to give a family in New York City."

"And you've not seen your Juniper since?"

"Weeks later, a letter come from the master's son. He is so sorry, but the new owner of Juniper has already sold her to a man in Mobile who lost his wife and needed a mammy for his children. I got two more letters from him, but he never did hear from the man in Mobile. The last letter said he could do no more—and that was the end of it, sir."

When James fell silent, Delafield wanted to say something, but could think of nothing.

"I held to hope, sir. For the longest time, I did."

"And that's why you've never married?"

"Hope is a powerful thing, sir—till it's dead. And when it's dead, it leaves such a hole. Anyway, it just don't seem right. Me to marry and all."

Delafield stood up and put a hand on the black man's shoulder. "I am so sorry, James. And I was wrong to put you through this and am sorry for it. I truly wish there was something I could do."

"I don't see how, sir. It's been so many years." The servant's lip started to quiver. "Sir, I can't even remember what Juniper looks like anymore."

The black man rose to his feet and began clearing the table. "Will there be anything else, sir?"

"No, James. And, again, I'm so very sorry."

"Yes, sir. Thank you, sir."

The servant raised the tray to his shoulder and disappeared inside the house. At the same time, an army private appeared at the foot of the stairs with a telegram.

Delafield returned the man's salute and took the telegram. After reading it, he called into the house, "James, good news from Jeff Davis. The Senator says the mess hall fare will improve posthaste, and our boys and the rest of us will get a decent meal. On top of that, we can expect more and better horses within two weeks."

"Oh, yes, sir," James replied weakly from inside the house. "That is indeed good news."

Delafield had hoped for more, but Davis had warned him that federal dollars were scarce and congressional interest in the Academy was, at best, tepid. He reread the last of the telegram, where Davis congratulated him on the state of the Corps and the Academy facilities.

Later that morning, after every man in the first section of remedial instruction had passed the obstacle course, the chagrin on Custer's face turned to delight when roll was called in the second section, and Mr. Collins reported that Mr. Williams was in the hospital with a stomach virus.

"I had nothing to do with it," Custer told Pelham with a toothy grin.

One by one, each man in the second section eventually passed the obstacle course. As they did, they eagerly awaited dismissal. However, before granting them leave, Pelham admonished the section to visit Williams in the hospital and encourage him for Friday. Otherwise, they might never see him again.

For the First Classmen, a refresher surveying class followed the midday meal, and those in D Company sat Indian style in a semicircle at the northwest corner of the Plain. The instructor was a stocky sergeant sporting a fiery red handlebar moustache.

"Gentlemen, the Theodolite instrument is man's greatest invention, affording him the ability to map any topographic feature. With it we can know the world as it really is." The sergeant removed the cover from the instrument and continued in his thick Scottish brogue, "Mr. Patterson, would you be so kind as to set and level the instrument."

Patterson did as instructed, setting up the tripod, affixing the Theodolite, and leveling the instrument with its precision thumbscrews.

The sergeant examined the setup, checked the level, and nodded his approval. He perfunctorily described the component parts of the instruments and how the instrument was to be used. This was all a rehash for them, especially for Pelham who struggled to pay attention. His eyes kept wandering in the direction of the hotel where, even at a distance, he could see activity of interest on the front lawn.

"So then, Mr. Pelham," the instructor said, picking up on Pelham's inattention. "Let's see if you remember how to use the Theodolite. Would you please demonstrate for the class by selecting a target and giving us an azimuth?"

Pelham got to his feet, approached the instrument, and intentionally looked through the wrong end of the scope, drawing laughter from his classmates.

"We are not amused, Mr. Pelham, and have a schedule to keep." The instructor's tone was terse.

Pelham swung the eyepiece toward the hotel and sighted through the aperture at a group of girls huddled by the hotel omnibus. Rosser picked up on it and poked Kirby.

In the magnification of the eyepiece, Pelham saw Clara with her friends. She was talking and gesturing, and suddenly all of the girls were laughing.

"Sergeant," Pelham called out in a loud voice, "azimuth, eighty-one degrees, thirty-six minutes, fifteen seconds."

"Your target, Mr. Pelham?" The sergeant asked after writing down the reading.

"The center of the oak tree, Sergeant."

The non-commissioned officer sighted through the instrument and found that the crosshairs were indeed centered on a tree. He read the angle and compared the measurement with Pelham's reading. He fingered his mustache and grunted. "That will be all, Mr. Pelham. Mr. Kirby, would you care to give us the vertical angle to the top of the Academy flagpole.

Chapter Twenty-Three

Later that day before the parade review and after shining the brass hilt of his sword, Pelham selected a well-used rag to polish his shoes. He was interrupted by a knock on the tent pole and the figure of Emory Upton.

"Emory," Pelham said, spitting on the black polish he had applied to the toe of his shoe. "Have a seat." Pelham pulled the remnant of the old handkerchief tight around his forefinger and rubbed polish into the shoe leather using a light, rapid circular motion.

"I thought the society meeting went well, John," Upton said, his statement more of a question.

"Were we at the same meeting?" Pelham cracked. "I sensed coolness. But regardless, as we agreed, the subject could not have been proffered by you with any hope of acceptance. And I remain in your camp that we should give it voice—both sides of it."

"Who do you see as the debaters?" Upton asked.

"That all depends on how it comes down and whether the topic passes muster with the superintendent. Delafield is a very cautious man."

"John," Upton said, "I would like to debate against secession."

Pelham put his rag down. "And I'd like to be King of France. Be realistic, Emory. Your chances are not good."

Upton said nothing, which surprised Pelham.

"Emory, the society, like the Corps, is heavily Democrat. If the topic is accepted, the group, not I, will select its debaters. And you must know how you are viewed—"

"As an extremist?" said Upton.

"The important thing, is that we may get the forum you want, Emory."

Upton greeted Pelham's reply with a single nod and rose to his feet. "Are you coming to the hop?" Pelham asked.

Upton's face suddenly brightened, and Pelham caught the hint of a smile.

"I believe I will."

"If you do, I'll introduce you to my friend, Clara Bolton."

Upton smiled. "I have heard good things about the young lady."

Much to the joy of the Corps and the regret of visitors, including Clara and her friends, the evening parade was canceled due to a short drizzle that stopped just before supper. After the evening meal, Pelham and Rosser made ready for the hop and ambled the short distance to the hotel. On the way, they talked strategy for the Friday session with Williams since he had been the one most in need of the second session. And having missed it would have his mettle sorely tested.

"Hey, Tex," Carol Hill called down from the veranda.

Rosser bounded up the stairs and presented his arm, and the two of them disappeared inside the hotel.

A second figure appeared on the veranda. "And how was your day, dear knight?"

"My lady, my day was excellent. Most excellent. And yours?"

"They canceled the parade," Clara said, feigning a pout.

For Pelham, the second hop passed all too quickly. He partnered with Clara for six dances, all of them waltzes, the time affording them conversation and a measure of intimacy. The rest of Clara's hop card bore names like Chambliss, Patterson, du Pont, and, courtesy of Pelham, Emory Upton.

As the end of the evening approached, Pelham approached Clara. "Shall we skip the last dance?"

"I'll meet you in the lobby," said Clara.

Moments later they were on the rear veranda, again facing the river.

"So many stars," Clara said. "So beautiful—so very like a dream. One I wish might never end, John."

"I'm pleased you are having a good time, and I see you haven't lost your effect on the Corps. You even got Emory Upton to smile."

"You know, he's a good dancer," she said, adding with a hint of melancholy, "John, I am so happy, but so sad too. Half the week is gone, and we have only one more hop."

Pelham squeezed her shoulders. "I know. The stuff of time is fleeting. But we'll have our picnic."

"And such a picnic it will be," she said, finding her gaiety again. "Promise me you'll have a sailor's appetite?"

"I always do."

For a time, neither spoke but rather gazed out across the Hudson until the final strains of music played out.

Clara turned in Pelham's arms. "John?"

"My lady."

"Cadet Upton … Tell me he is your friend."

"Emory? Yes. He is. Why?"

"He is so easy to talk to. I told him about us."

"About our being friends?"

"Best friends. Do you mind?"

Pelham was glad for the darkness. "Why should I mind?"

"I find him most interesting, but also—"

Pelham couldn't imagine what might be coming.

Clara giggled. "He talks so very fast."

"Yes," Pelham said, relieved. "He does."

"He reminds me of Father. Yes, he is very much like Father."

"My lady, 'tis time I was off," Pelham said, placing a finger on her nose. "Would you bestow your friendship seal upon your humble servant?"

"Of course, you silly."

Instead of her customary peck, she drew Pelham close and pressed her mouth full against each cheek.

"Until tomorrow, dear knight."

Chapter Twenty-Four

Thursday afternoon at two o'clock, Clara, carrying a picnic basket with a red gingham coverlet, glanced nervously over her shoulder as she glided down the back stairs of the hotel. Walking quickly past a stand of well-leafed maples, she found Pelham waiting with a neatly folded blanket tucked under one arm. They exchanged expectant looks, and she kissed him lightly on the cheek, finding the sun warm on his face.

Without a word he led her down a gravel path, over the crest of the bluff, and beyond sight of the hotel. After a few minutes, he asked if he could peek in the basket.

"You'll have to wait, young man," Clara said. "And you already know there's fried chicken. The rest is a surprise. But you can smell." She raised the basket to his nose.

Pelham sniffed and tried to peek, and for the offense had his hand slapped.

"Temptress! What is that on your neck?"

"What?"

"Little red dots?"

"I didn't get them all?" Clara matter-of-factly wetted the finger of her glove and rubbed her neck. "Gone?"

Pelham grinned. "Gone."

"It was Ellie's idea." Clara giggled. "The sneak made me up a sickly face and then had Carol Hill run get Miss Frampton."

Pelham shook his head in amusement.

"When she came, I carried on awful, and she made a big fuss. Said I should rest—that she would procure a tonic."

Pelham helped Clara down a flight of stone steps.

"She came back with castor oil—imagine! Thank God for Ellie. She said I was asleep and shouldn't be wakened, and that she would administer the medicine when I awoke. And so, here I am."

"Your roommate's beauty is exceeded only by her cunning. She and Henry are still a number?"

Clara smiled. "Henry has promise."

Pelham led her down the steepest part of a hillside path, through tree thickets, and around exposed granite faces, until they reached North Dock Road at a point near the river. As they walked down the road, Clara saw letters and numbers cut into the massive granite stone of the hillside.

Anticipating her question, Pelham said, "These are names and dates of battles. Some Revolutionary War and some Mexican War."

Thinking her distracted, he attempted another peek in the basket and suffered the same fate.

"Don't they teach you patience here?" Clara said, shifting the basket to her other arm.

"Oh, but you are a hard lady." Pelham directed her attention to the river's edge, where men were unloading coal from a barge, and other men were loading the coal onto haul wagons.

Soon they arrived at a posted sign in a clearing to the east of the dock. Clara read the fine lettering: *Entry Prohibited to all but Cadets and their Accompanied Guests.* She smiled and squeezed Pelham's arm. "So, this is Flirtation Walk. I am actually here."

"You may be anticipating more than there is." Pelham said, leading her into the wood along a narrow path of crushed stone.

After they had gone but a short distance, Clara said, almost in a whisper, "Such a secluded place. I am glad to have my knight to protect me."

"Your servant," said Pelham.

"Aren't you glad we don't have to play games, John? That we can simply be together, have fun the way real friends do?"

"Best friends," he said, his smile somewhat affected.

"The very best."

She gripped his arm tighter as they walked the twisting path, a cooling breeze rising off the river. Coming to an opening in the trees, she exclaimed, "Oh my gosh, look at all the boats!"

The Hudson was alive with vessels of every variety, including barges and a large whaler.

"Do you sail, John?"

"I can row a bit, but otherwise there is not a nautical bone in my body."

Clara stooped down over a small bush to inspect its tiny white flowers. "I've never seen these before."

"Shadblow," Pelham said. "They normally don't last this long."

"Aren't they the most delicate creatures? They look like edelweiss."

Pelham picked a cluster of the tiny flowers and with a grand gesture presented them to Clara.

"For me?"

"Beautiful flowers for my lady, whose heart exceeds their beauty."

"Thank you, though I suspect you've used that line before." She placed the flowers in a silk handkerchief and tucked them in her basket.

They continued along the winding path, Pelham answering a continuous stream of questions, until Clara suddenly froze mid-step. "Oh! What was that?"

"What was what?" said Pelham.

"You didn't hear it?" She slinked behind him and pointed over his shoulder. "There in the bushes."

"Relax, my lady. It's just a family outing." Pelham directed her attention to an opening in the trees where a doe and two fawns grazed on grass.

"They don't seem much interested in us, do they?" said Clara.

"Trust me, this is home to the king's deer. And we've many birds, squirrels, coons, and possum. And don't faint if we flush some quail."

"Snakes?"

Pelham produced a straight face. "Strictly prohibited."

Clara smiled.

The two of them ambled on, at times close to the river's edge where they heard waves lapping the shore. At times distant, with only the sound of their footsteps and the twitter of birds.

"I feel like we are in some sort of enchanted forest," Clara said, her voice full of wonder. "You come here a lot, don't you, John? I mean— with girls."

Pelham didn't respond.

"Don't say you don't, John Pelham. I bet you have a different girl every week."

"Not every week. But neither am I a monk."

"You are a bad boy," Clara said, playfully pinching his nose.

As they rounded a bend and the path ascended, Pelham stopped and raised a finger to his lips.

"What?" Clara asked. "What is it?"

"Professional courtesy. Let's give them a minute."

Ahead of them, a couple embraced beneath a granite overhang.

"Why—that's Alice Paine and your Mr. Patterson," Clara declared, almost indignant. "I'll stake my life on it."

"I do believe you're right."

"That little sneak. How did she get out?"

Pelham smiled. "I love it. That thing you do with your nose."

"What?"

"Look, they're gone," said Pelham

"Do you think they will kiss again? I mean, down the path, where there is no rock?" Clara flashed a coy look.

"I suppose, if the situation demands," Pelham said with a straight face.

In a moment they too were beneath the overhang, Pelham intending to pass it by. But Clara restrained him.

"So, this is your Kissing Rock?" "It is, my lady."

"I understand there is a legend about it."

"Yes. Though, I don't know that it's true," Pelham said dismissively.

"Tell me."

"Well, it is said that if a cadet and his date do not kiss beneath this rock, the Academy and indeed the entire country will fall into ruin."

Clara affected great emotion. "Oh, dear me. How terrible!"

"But to this day," Pelham said, "thanks be to God, none have failed to do their duty, and the country and the Academy are secure."

"What then are we to do?" Clara asked, batting her eyes.

"We? Well, I must leave that up to you, my lady."

"Well, I won't have the demise of civilization on my conscience. I suppose we must do our duty." Clara put her basket down and positioned herself beneath the rock. Closing her eyes, she tilted her head back and presented her lips. With firmness of purpose, she declared, "Do it."

Pelham wanted so to laugh, but instead leaned forward and kissed Clara lightly on the lips.

Her eyes opened, and she said, "There. It is done, John. We have done our duty and preserved the nation and your school." In an instant, she was several steps up the path. "Where should we picnic?"

Inside Pelham, the game was on. The skirmish lines of heart and mind clearly drawn. "Not far. Just up ahead."

On they walked, up and down and around the steeps of the shoreline, past the point where the great iron chain had once been attached, until Pelham stopped at what he called Gee's Point, the easternmost tip of West Point. An unattended lighthouse and a glorious view of the Hudson and the town of Garrison on the other side awaited them thirty feet below.

"This will be a little tricky, my lady," Pelham said, taking the picnic basket from Clara. He descended the sloped rock face backward, holding Clara's hand and allowing her to brace against him. When they arrived at the water's edge, he spread his wool blanket on the ground and assisted Clara off her feet.

"Oh, John, is this not absolutely the loveliest spot that could possibly be? And look, those people are waving at us!"

Fifty yards offshore, a sloop heeled in the wind. Clara waved at them.

Pelham reclined on his back.

"So," Clara said, "not counting me, how many girls have you brought to this rather magical spot?" She removed her bonnet and undid her bun, allowing her hair to fall about her neck.

"I'm not all that good at math," Pelham said, his eyes closed.

Clara giggled and leaned over him, shaking her hair so that it teased his face. "You are my best friend, aren't you?"

"More so with each minute, my lady."

"Look at me," she said in a gruff tone, holding a rock above his head, an all-too-serious look on her face.

Pelham raised a hand in defense. "Have I offended, my lady?"

"Silly, this is no ordinary rock. This too is a kissing rock. I pronounce it so."

She leaned over and kissed him on one cheek and then the other.

Her breath tickled his nose. "Yes, we are the very best of friends, aren't we? And what we did at Kissing Rock was our duty."

"It was. We had no choice."

She reclined on the blanket beside him. "The sun feels so good, doesn't it, John?" She folded her arms and closed her eyes.

A boat sounded its horn, and Pelham announced, "That would be the Garrison ferry."

"To destroy our peace," Clara said, her eyes still closed.

Pelham turned and gazed upon her, the rising and falling of her bodice.

"That does it, my lady. You are the greatest tease I have ever known. I believe you enjoy my torture. And, frankly, I will not stand for it any longer."

Clara opened her eyes. "You're famished?"

Pelham grinned and tweaked her nose.

"Exactly."

Clara reached for the picnic basket and found what she was looking for. "Close your eyes and open wide."

Pelham obliged, and something of a creamy texture was inserted into his mouth. "By all that is holy, this is like dessert. What is it?"

"It's cheese. French brie. It would go well with wine. Don't you think?"

"You tease, my lady," Pelham said, his eyes still closed. "*Voila!*" said Clara, producing a bottle of red wine.

Pelham stared at the bottle.

"I had it opened at the hotel." She handed him the corked bottle and two small glasses. "Care to do the honors?"

He poured three ounces into each glass and made a toast. "To my truly extraordinary friend, who is also a girl."

Clara clinked his glass. "This is such a special experience for me, John." She clinked his glass again. "To our amazing friendship."

She watched Pelham drain his glass.

"I believe wine is forbidden to you, so I thought—"

"You thought rightly, my angel of mercy." Pelham poured himself another three ounces. "Benny Havens would love you."

"Benny who?"

"It doesn't matter. Have you more of that cheese?" Clara gave Pelham the rest of the small wedge. "Where did you come by this?"

"Your hotel chef. He and I have become fast friends. He gets it from the man who teaches you French."

"Professor Agnel?" Pelham said, impressed.

"Close your eyes again."

Clara placed a plump drumstick against his lips, and he nearly swallowed it whole.

Clara arranged two ceramic plates on the blanket, along with knives and forks, the tin of fried chicken, a bowl of potato salad, and half a pecan pie.

For the next few minutes, Pelham was poor company, rather unceremoniously downing everything Clara placed in front of him.

When he had finished the main course, he asked her if she was going to finish her potato salad.

"Such an appetite, my knight. How is it you are not the fattest of men?" She pushed her plate in his direction. "Save room for pie."

The pie was no challenge, and when there was nothing remaining but the gingham coverlet, Pelham offered Clara the last of the wine, which she graciously declined. "My lady, I am replete and toast you for a most incredible meal. But more importantly, for a most memorable week."

"Hmm. And how am I to take that?"

"In the very best of ways," he said, enjoying the effect of the last of the wine.

Clara smiled, but it soon faded. "John, in two days I'll be on the steamer back to Clermont, and you'll forget me. You will, won't you?"

"You underestimate yourself, my lady."

Clara forced another smile. "I pray you are right."

The two reclined side by side, neither saying anything until Clara rolled onto her side and placed a hand on Pelham's chest, fingering one of his uniform buttons. "We've had so little time, John."

"How much is not important, but how we use it."

"We have had a glorious time, haven't we, John? Tell me more of yourself, more of what it was like to grow up in Alabama."

Pelham laughed. "At this time of year, hot. Really hot." He rolled over, his face inches from Clara's. "And speaking of hot, do you mind if I unbutton my coat? I seem to have expanded."

"Of course not."

As he did, she pressed him. "Tell me more about your family. I still can't get my mind around such a large family."

He smiled and tweaked her nose again, and then described in more or less humorous fashion each member of the family, trying not to repeat what he had already told her.

When he finished, Clara said, "Your family so comes to life in the way you describe them. I should very much like to meet the sister who has six brothers and her sanity. And your grandmother, she was like a second mother to you. Right?"

"She was wonderful." Pelham rolled over on his back. "It's hard to believe she's been gone nine years."

"Southern life is so much about family, isn't it? You pull together for everything, and, I think, differently than we do in the North. Your father is amazing. How he can run a plantation and heal the sick, fix bones, and deliver babies is beyond me!"

"True enough, but I think for us, it is the land that is key. There is very little that we can't provide for ourselves from it, and the money we need to take care of the rest comes from the cotton and the other crops we grow." Pelham pulled at the sleeve of her dress. "You, my lady, may be wearing my cotton."

"Do you like the way I wear it?"

"Very much." Pelham found himself staring at her in a way he had not intended. "Anyway, it might surprise you to know that my father's medical practice doesn't bring in much money. Most patients pay us in eggs, milk, chickens, a side of beef, a hog, preserves, or a promise to do this or that. It is the cotton that brings us cash."

"I'm embarrassed, but does cotton grow on trees?"

Pelham smiled and said it didn't and described the nature of the cotton plant, how it was planted, tended, and harvested, and how much labor was needed. He described the problems of boll weevils and killing frosts and the details of the ginning process. "From the gin, it is shipped north to textile mills."

"All of it?"

"I suppose not all of it, but there are precious few mills in the South. Of course, some of the cotton is shipped in bulk direct to Europe."

"By labor, you mean … Negro workers?"

Pelham sensed her hesitancy.

"Yes."

"Have you many—"

"We have about fifty blacks."

"They are … slaves?"

"They make up our black family, yes."

"John, I don't mean to pry, and if you don't want me to, I won't ask. But I've never met or even seen a slave. The Negroes I know are like you and me—they speak well, have manners, and are intelligent."

"I'm sure they are," said Pelham, thinking of Samuel. "But I believe that blacks in the North make up less than one percent of the population. In the South, it's more like thirty-five percent."

"Your slaves, John, are treated well?"

"What do you think?"

Clara smiled. "I knew they would be."

"To understand the South," Pelham said, "its culture, and life on a plantation, you need to understand how important the Negro is in our society. No less than us whites. I can't picture the South without blacks doing what they do. The black man, woman, and child are extensions of every plantation family. And understand that everybody on the plantation, white or black, works for the common good. It's not a case of whites sitting back and letting blacks do the work."

Clara nodded. "I guess all I know is what I read."

"And you've probably read *Uncle Tom's Cabin*, right?" He took her silence as affirmation. "That book is an affront, Clara, and pure fiction. It paints a very narrow and jaded view." He forced a laugh. "And why wouldn't it? The author is an avowed abolitionist. Its premise is clear, and the book has done more to harm relations between the South and North than anything William Lloyd Garrison has printed."

"But, John, you can't say some of the blacks aren't mistreated."

"If you are suggesting there are bad people in the South, I grant you that, just like there are in the North. Think of those who run textile mills, who have treated many thousands of children worse than slaves."

Clara dropped her eyes.

Pelham squeezed her hand. "Can we declare a truce?"

Clara smiled. "John, you are a wonderfully honorable man, more noble and kind than I could ever hope for in a friend."

"My lady, in truth, you hardly know me."

"I do know you, John," Clara said firmly. "You're a man of faith and high virtue. It's just that slavery is so—" She caught herself.

"Cruel? That's what you were going to say, isn't it? If you could only see your face." Pelham cupped her chin in his hand. "If I wasn't so full, I would eat you up." He sat and gazed across the Hudson. "This river has seen more slave trading than you or I could ever imagine. Every colony had slaves, though your state was quickest to give it up."

She began to massage his back. "A truce then."

But Pelham continued. "Times have changed, Clara, and things are different. The industrial revolution transformed the North, eliminating the need for slaves. But what did the North do with their slaves? Free them? Trust me, precious few were freed. Most were sold south at a nice profit. I've no problem with the right of Northern states to abolish slavery. They are sovereign states and can do as they please. One day Southern states may do so, and should, but that time is I think years away. For now, we are nothing without our blacks."

"I understand, John, I really do. It's just that morally—"

"Morally?" Pelham apologized for interrupting her. "There are nearly four million blacks in the South. They represent our single greatest asset. What comes of us if they are suddenly freed to satisfy someone's sense of morality?"

"The government could pay you for them like England did."

"We are not England, my lady. Our government doesn't have the money to buy decent horses for the Academy."

Clara picked up the gingham coverlet and waved it. "I surrender."

Pelham returned a sheepish look. "My lady, there are a lot of inequities in the world. But slavery has been around for all of history, and not just based on color. And I can tell you that in the South, most Negroes are treated humanly. We know they have souls and are children of God. Owners provide them shelter, clothing, food, medical treatment, all the necessities of life. Some are even paid a stipend to spend on themselves. Believe me, there are very few Simon Legrees."

"How long do your Negroes work each day?" Clara asked.

"It's not just the blacks, my lady. We all work from before sunup to sundown, Sundays off, except for minor chores. Again, it takes everyone on a plantation working together to keep it going. Most days we all go to bed exhausted."

"Then slaves aren't whipped for the littlest thing?"

"There are exceptions, I'm sure, based on the nature of their masters. But whites don't have a corner on laziness. If a black puts in an honest day's work, he should never feel the whip."

"So much for our truce," Clara said.

"It's all right. Yours are good questions."

"Then, if I may, one more. Do you lock them up at night?"

Pelham couldn't resist laughing. "You intend to know it all, don't you? Of course not. A slave who runs away is caught easily enough. But, my lady, please understand that a slave's life isn't what you imagine. They have their own quarters, we respect their privacy, and they have their joys. Come Christmas, most have the entire week off. They celebrate every night and dance till they drop, and Lord, can they dance, and sing too. They enjoy a Christmas feast, no less than our own, and can get passes if they've earned them. If a man has a pass and wants to visit a friend on a neighboring plantation, he can do so."

"You love life in Alabama, don't you?"

"You would too if you visited. A visit would make all the difference. Then you would understand, I think." Pelham noticed the ferry pulling away from Garrison across the river. "The hill country of Alabama is truly beautiful, and the weather … well, it's delightful most of the time. Except when it's not."

Clara laughed.

"Alabama is very special, and it is almost impossible to meet a stranger there. Life is honest. Work is hard, but rewarded, and we know who gives us our daily bread."

Clara responded with an amen, and asked, "Are slaves able to have families?"

"Not under the law, I think, but they do have unions that are respected, have children, and for the most part stay together as families. It seldom benefits an owner to split a family—for obvious reasons. If a family is split, it's normally because an owner has no other choice."

"That would be so sad, John. Tell me, do they go to church, are the Negroes Christian."

"In truth, more so than a lot of white folks. They sing the sweetest gospel songs going to field, working their rows, and coming home at night. Beautiful songs, mostly about the Promised Land."

"Your friend, Emory Upton—he only wants the best for them."

Pelham wondered that Upton had shared his views. "Emory is an abolitionist."

"And I'm so glad you are friends, that you respect each other."

"I'm not so sure how much he respects me, but when he goes on about freeing the slaves, I say nothing more than what I've said to you. How does such a thing happen without destroying the South? And he has yet to give me a rational answer."

"Four million slaves," Clara said, as though finally grasping the enormity of the issue.

"One day it may be so, Clara. Slavery abolished everywhere in the country, even the world. In my heart, I know and believe it should be. But how we get there, I cannot begin to know. What I do know is that slavery in the South is not a question of equity. It just is, and always has been."

Clara switched the subject, asking, "Who was your very best friend growing up?"

"Either Charlie or William, my older brothers."

"Brothers don't count."

"Then, I suppose … Samuel."

"That's one of my favorite Bible names. Tell me about Samuel."

Pelham hesitated. "Samuel is a slave."

"A slave," Clara said in astonishment.

"Samuel and I are the same age, inseparable since I can first remember. At least until we were almost eleven."

"And he was your best friend?"

"That surprises you?"

"Well …"

Pelham explained how Samuel and his mother had come to the Pelham plantation when Samuel was five, how Samuel's mother had died within the year, and how Pelham's grandmother had taken Samuel under her wing.

"Ma still talks about Olivette, Samuel's mother, being the most beautiful high yella woman she had ever seen, but so frail. After she died, Samuel lived until just a few years ago with Bones, the skinniest of our blacks. Bones and his woman had no children. Each day, except Sunday, Samuel would report to Grandmother and would be in her charge until the blacks came in from the fields. Pa resisted what he saw as a breach in the social system, but Grandmother prevailed. As a result, Samuel and I were daily companions, thick as thieves," Pelham said. "And we had the run of the plantation."

"Those were good times?"

"The best. And Grandmother became quite attached to Samuel. She believed from the start that he would one day take over Willie's role."

"Willie?"

Pelham told Clara about the family's black patriarch.

"So, what about Samuel now?"

"He's our field foreman, responsible for all the field workers."

"I think I would like to meet your Samuel."

"And you would like him and be very impressed."

"And you two ruled the plantation?"

"My Pa says we were a handful, from spooking the stock to harassing the field hands. He would tell us to go fishing to keep us out of mischief, and it seemed we fished every day until we were maybe seven. Then it was determined I should start school."

"What was school like?"

"I was taught at home. My grandmother was my teacher."

"Your grandmother?"

"She had done a passable job with Charlie and William, and my mother was still raising Bettie and my younger brothers. So, I started my lessons to read and write and do numbers. In the beginning, Samuel would wait in the parlor for me to finish. When I was done, we would play or go fishing."

A blast from a steamer startled both of them, and soon the steamer's huge bow appeared in the turn of the river.

"Anyway, before long, Samuel was repeating to Grandmother things he'd heard from the other room and doing so with a white accent—I mean, without any slave dialect at all."

"Amazing."

"She thought so, and it was then she decided on what I think she knew wasn't right."

"I'm sorry?"

"She decided that Samuel should sit in on my lessons if we both swore to keep it secret. Which we did."

"And that was a mistake?"

"I didn't think so at the time, and I was glad to have someone else for her to pick on. Anyway, Grandmother never failed to tell Samuel how lucky he was, that while he was learning things that I needed to know to make my way in the white world, he would have no worries when he was grown. All he had to do was whatever the family needed done. And if he did, he would be cared for the rest of his life, and his life would be pleasant enough."

Pelham glanced at the ferry that was halfway across the river.

"She taught the two of us for three and a half years, and Samuel proved to be one smart boy. She told him that he was the smartest black boy she had ever known. After our lessons, when we went out to play, Samuel would want to work out problems instead of play."

"That is so wonderful!" Clara said, not hiding her joy.

"We'd write in the dirt or sometimes on my slate with chalk. But it was safest to write in the dirt, so we could erase the evidence with our feet. One of us would write a word or sentence, and the other would read it and check it for spelling. Samuel was a better speller than I was. We did math problems the same, and I had the edge on him there."

"You weren't afraid of getting caught?"

Pelham smiled. "We weren't afraid of anything."

Clara leaned over and kissed Pelham lightly on the lips. "You were a little stinker, weren't you?"

"I felt Pa's belt often enough," he admitted. "But one day it all changed." There was finality in Pelham's words.

"I don't understand."

"The day we played the game."

"The game?" Clara waited for an explanation, but none came.

Instead, Pelham started buttoning his coat.

Clara began gathering things in the picnic basket. "I wish I had known your grandmother."

"My lady, we must truly be good friends. I've never told anyone what I've just told you."

"You are so sweet to say so." Clara kissed him again.

"My lady, I wish we might never have to leave this place, but if we don't get a move on, I won't get you back in time."

Half an hour later, after a quick peek at Kosciusko's Garden, overgrown and in disrepair, they arrived at the hotel.

At the base of the stairs, Pelham squeezed Clara's hand and gave her a grand bow. "My lady, you have made both me and my stomach exceedingly happy."

Chapter Twenty-Five

From inside the hotel doorway, Clara watched Pelham return to the encampment. When she turned around, she almost knocked the spectacles from Frampton's nose. The two stared at each other until the assistant dean said, "Clara, would you join me for tea in the parlor?"

"Tea?" said Clara.

"Or coffee. Your preference."

Clara followed Frampton into the parlor, where the two sat at a corner table. Frampton ordered, and the waiter returned with a pot of steaming water and an assortment of teas and small biscuits.

"Earl Grey or Darjeeling?" Frampton asked.

"Earl Grey, please," Clara said, more confused than anxious.

"You appear to have survived your illness." Frampton's tone was bland. "Sugar?"

"I—"

"Clara," Frampton interrupted, "you asked me if I had ever seen a man naked."

The assistant dean's words stung Clara. "Miss Frampton, please. I was wrong to say it. You must forgive me."

"When I was your age, perhaps a year younger, I was taken to Europe by my parents. Me, an only child. We spent almost three months, from late spring through most of the summer, visiting close acquaintances of my father, then a renowned art critic. He and mother are now deceased."

"I'm sorry, ma'am," Clara said, wondering at her point.

"It was a glorious time in my life. We visited the most incredible sights and met the most wonderful people in England, France, and Italy. As you might imagine, I saw some of the most exquisite pieces of art Europe had to offer. In Italy, we stayed with the owners of a magnificent chateau near Florence, complete with a small vineyard. My room was a large turret-like space on the third floor, and I thought myself a true princess." Frampton paused. "Anyway, the vineyard was cared for by a young man from the village … Oh, I see you are empty. I'm such a poor hostess."

Frampton refilled Clara's cup with hot water.

"He would remove his shirt as the day got hotter, and his bronze skin would glisten in the sun as he clipped the plants, tilled, and weeded."

Clara sensed she was hearing something Frampton had never shared.

"I watched him, or you might say spied on him, for nearly a week from my bedroom window. He was more than handsome—and a well-muscled man." Frampton cleared her throat. "He knew I was there, I felt certain. And I thought he was ignoring me. But one day he surprised me. As I looked down on him, he suddenly turned and stared straight at me. I felt his eyes. We just stared at each other for a long time. Then he cocked his head and gave me the most charming smile. And I smiled back."

Clara couldn't hide her delight at what she was hearing.

"Then, he went back to his vines."

"No! He didn't!" Clara couldn't hide her disappointment.

"But the next day, I left the house on the pretense that I needed some help moving a piece of furniture, and would he be so kind. Well, he was … more than kind."

Clara found herself giggling. "He spoke English?"

"Not a word. Nor I, Italian."

Clara's pulse quickened.

"But we had that … common language," said Frampton, glancing out the hotel window.

"Miss Frampton, you little vixen."

"It may be hard for you to believe, Clara. But in those days, I was what you would call a looker and considerably more petite than you see me now. Before the trip, in Baltimore, a prospective lawyer seriously courted me. And there were others who called on me, though if I were you, I would want proof of my former self."

With that Frampton produced from her purse a photograph wrapped in silk and handed it to Clara.

"My father had a man by the name of Louis Daguerre take this with his imaging equipment while we were in Paris. His daguerreotype process is now, of course, quite common."

Clara studied the face and the figure of the girl in the image and shook her head. "Miss Frampton, you were indeed a looker. And, of course—"

"No need for that," said Frampton. "Anyway, we were in Italy for almost a month, and the young man—his name was Dino— learned some of my English, and I learned some of his Italian. I don't think a day went by that we didn't see each other . . . all of each other."

Clara gasped at what she was hearing.

"Some days, I would come to him in the vineyard. Other days I would wave for him to join me in the house. And to my knowledge my parents never suspected a thing. But then ..." Frampton's voice trailed off. "It was time for us to leave. It was the hardest day of my life. That morning, we pledged our love to each other."

The sparkle that had shone in Frampton's eyes was gone, and she blew her nose.

"I can't express to you my sense of loss. My parents thought me gravely ill, for I kept nothing down on the trip home. Anyway, I wrote him every week for two months and waited for his first letter."

Frampton forced a smile as if collecting herself.

"Please, tell me," Clara said.

"It never came, Clara." Frampton's voice was not much more than a whisper, her face stoic. "I, of course, clung to the hope that it would. I imagined that he'd been hurt, that he'd joined the army, been in a battle, maybe wounded or worse. I even imagined that my parents were intercepting and destroying his letters, which of course they weren't. It never occurred to me, until my heart was utterly undone, that it was simply over. That we had experienced something temporary, a summer fling."

Frampton managed another smile and reached for Clara's hand. "All this is to say that I have no desire to kill your joy, Clara. I just don't want to see you hurt."

Frampton's words caught Clara no less by surprise than her story had. "But, Miss Frampton, you don't understand. You needn't be concerned for me. You see …" Clara found herself stammering. "Y-you … are q-quite mistaken. We—Cadet Pelham and I, we are not … that way. We are just friends."

"Of course, you are, my dear."

Chapter Twenty-Six

That night, Pelham struggled to sleep, unwilling to admit that Clara Bolton had undone him. He fought the passions that would kill the platonic, at the same time realizing how empty things would play out on their current course. Clara Bolton would soon be gone; her smile, her touch, her light, her joy. All that she freely gave him would be gone. And she was right. Time would pass, and memory would fade. Yet he knew one thing with clarity. She had penetrated his shield. She had walked freely within his inmost world and unearthed Samuel. When sleep finally came, so did a long dormant memory.

He and Samuel lay side by side beneath a lone oak tree in the corner of a field not being worked by the blacks. The tree was perfect for shade. The morning lesson with grandmother had gone easy, and they had just finished lunch. It was the heat of the day, and they were shirtless and barefoot.

He stared vacantly at the gray spidery branches of the oak tree. "I'm bored."

"So, what do you want to do, John?" asked Samuel, his eyes closed.

"Don't matter. Just something different."

"How do you mean different?" Samuel opened an eye and squinted at the rays of sun that diffused through the crown of the tree. "Suppose we could swim. I'm boiled alive."

"No, I mean something we ain't never done."

"John, we are ten years old, almost eleven. Ain't nothing we haven't done."

He thought about it for several minutes and then scrambled to his feet. "I got it, Samuel!"

Samuel didn't answer.

"Wake up, Samuel! I got it. I know what we can do!"

Samuel struggled to his elbows, his eyes bleary. "Huh?"

"You ever want to know what it's like to be somebody else?"

Samuel rubbed his eyes. "I've already been a sheriff, an Indian, a knight, a musketeer, a preacher—"

"That's not what I mean. I mean for real."

"I don't get you."

"Let's you and me switch." He was beside himself with the idea.

"Switch what?"

"You be me."

"You?"

"Yeah, you be white and I be black."

"You want to be black?"

"It's just a game, Samuel. Then I can know what it's like bein' you, and you can know what it's like bein' me." His chest expanded with the thought.

"I don't get it. How do I play white?"

"You make me do stuff."

"What stuff?"

He was ahead of Samuel and pointed to the nearby rows of nearly ripe cotton. "Pick cotton."

"You want to pick cotton?"

"I never tried."

"Believe me, John. You don't want to pick cotton."

"Samuel, it's just a game, but first we need …" He rubbed his chin. "Wait here." A minute later, he returned from nearby Cane Creek with a willow switch. "You got to have a whip."

Samuel looked at the willow branch as if it were a poisonous snake. "Take it, Samuel."

Samuel backed away. "I—I don't want it."

"Just take it, Samuel. It's just a game. Then we can play whatever you want."

Samuel shook his head, but finally took the willow switch.

"I am not going to whip you, John."

"What? It was okay to give me a black eye last week?"

"That was fair and fair, an even fight and you know it."

"Relax, Samuel, this ain't no different. Nothing more than a game." He led Samuel to the edge of the cotton field and began to pick cotton bolls, stuffing them in his pockets. The sun beat down mercilessly, and after only a few minutes, sweat streamed from his chin.

"Whew. You're right, Samuel, this is harder than it looks."

"Don't recall anyone saying it was easy."

He continued to pick until Samuel noticed a plant that still had some bolls on it. "John, you got some left on that one."

He saw his mistake. "Damn, Samuel, you're right. Now you got to whip me."

"What for?"

"Because that's the way it works. I missed that cotton, and you caught me."

"I am not going whip you, John."

He had already prostrated himself on the ground and mumbled into the dirt, "Samuel, it's just a game. Do it."

"I don't like this game, John." Samuel's voice was tremulous.

"Just do it, Samuel. Then we can play something else."

Samuel was silent, motionless.

"Do it, Samuel, this dirt is hot!"

He felt the willow switch graze his back, but just barely. "What was that, Samuel? You got to really do it, or it don't count."

He was surprised by a sharp sting and had to bite his lip to keep quiet. "That's it, Samuel. Four more and we're done."

Samuel raised the switch, but before he could bring it down a second time, a man galloped up on horseback.

"Samuel! You stop that! Stop it, Samuel!" shouted the man.

Samuel dropped the switch and without even a glance at the rider, ran as fast as his spindly legs would carry him in the direction of the plantation house.

The man jerked his horse to a dead stop. "John Pelham, what in God's creation is this all about?"

He scrambled to his feet, his head down. "Nothin', Pa."

"You call this nothing!"

"It was just a game, Pa."

Atkinson Pelham dismounted and shook him by the shoulders. "Did I not just see Samuel, a black boy, whipping you, John? A black boy whipping a white boy?"

"It was part of the game, Pa. He weren't gonna hurt me. He didn't want to do it nohow. It was me that told him he had to."

"You, son? Why would you do that?"

"I don't know, Pa." He looked up at his father. "You gonna give me the belt?"

Later, after he had felt the belt like he'd never felt it before, he lay on his bed in his room. Charlie and William had come to visit and wanted to know what he had done. He lied and said he had spooked cows through the best of the cotton. Come suppertime, when he was told he could come down to eat, he found his grandmother crying in the parlor.

"You get along to supper, John," she said, her eyes averted.

There was a pall over supper, and after they finished eating, his father, took him outside on the porch. "I want you to tell me one more time how this all came about."

He explained the game again, that it was his idea, and that Samuel wanted no part of it.

"Son, do you not know how thoughtless you were? Don't you understand the way it is?" His father grasped him by the shoulders. "You don't ever make light of the relationship between whites and blacks—not ever! You understand me?"

"Yes, sir." He quavered in his father's grip.

"Think what you've done to poor Samuel, how the boy must feel."

"Yes, Pa."

"You hitch up the buggy. I need to get to the Williams house for Miss Beatrice."

"Yes, Pa."

The next day, when he took his lessons with his grandmother, he thought her sick, and he didn't see Samuel all morning. Things had changed.

That afternoon, Willie asked him to come outside on the back porch, and when he got there, Samuel was already sitting at a table.

The black man sat across from them.

"Master John, what do you see on this table?"

He looked at the table. "Nothing, Willie."

"Oh yes, there is. What is it, Samuel?"

"Salt and pepper shakers," Samuel replied in the slave dialect he always used when he wasn't alone with his friend.

"Exactly so, Samuel. Master John, is what is in the two shakers the same?"

"No, sir,"

"Samuel, I ask you the same."

"No'em. One gots salt, de other pepper."

"Exactly so. Master John, why you suppose that both shakers are always on the table?"

"For our food?"

"Exactly so, again. To make the food taste just right. But they are different, salt and pepper, ain't they? Yet being different, they are good together, ain't they?"

Both he and Samuel nodded.

"Master John, are you mad cause Samuel ain't white like you?"

He didn't answer.

"And Samuel, are you mad because you're black and not white?"

Samuel didn't answer either.

"Don't appear to me to be so. You two are having the time of your life." Willie smiled. "And that's a good thing. And both of you know how life is, don't you?"

There was an awkward silence.

"Ain't right for you and me to question how God done set all this up. No, sir. We are each born to be either salt or pepper, or somethin in between. But all us is pleasin in his sight."

Samuel stared blankly at the porch deck.

"Look at me, Samuel. Ain't no easier being salt than pepper. You ever see the good doctor or any of the Pelham family lazin around this place?"

Samuel shook his head.

"The light in the big house is on long after you and me are asleep. Ain't that so? The doctor and Master John's momma got powerful stress over how to make all this keep goin', keep us in food and clothes and everything else. And all them in the Pelham family got to go to school and learn them words and numbers that are such a mystery to me."

Samuel lowered his head.

Willie picked up the saltshaker in his right hand. "The Pelhams are the best salt there is, and I believe that to be a gospel fact." He picked up the peppershaker in his left hand. "And this peppershaker is all us in the colored family, with plenty enough to keep us busy and pleasing to our maker. Ain't he made us special to work the fields, to take that hot sun and work til dark, to put in and take out a crop year after year? Look at me, boy!"

Samuel raised his eyes.

"Ain't no shame being pepper, Samuel. You understand me?"

Samuel nodded weakly.

"Without both the salt and pepper, things around here would fall apart pretty quick. That's a fact."

Willie turned to Pelham. "As for you, Master John. Ain't never going to be easy being salt. So much gonna be on your shoulders, but I expect you know that."

He nodded as if he did.

"Now all that bein said, there is no reason the two of you can't forever be the best of friends as you work out your part in God's plan. You just gotta respect his plan." Willie rose to his feet and reached out to the two boys, taking them in his arms. "Now you go out and play, and don't pick any more of that cotton. It ain't ripe yet."

Chapter Twenty-Seven

Friday morning at breakfast, Nate Chambliss, Adelbert Ames, and Chas Patterson made a point of thanking Pelham for the matches he had made—they had all stuck. Chambliss had taken Jessica Danford on Flirtation Walk twice. Ames had taken Rebecca Astor only once but had an invitation to visit her in the city if he could get leave.

"So how is it with you and Clara?" Patterson asked Pelham as they left the mess hall.

"Couldn't be better, Chas," Pelham lied.

"As it should be, for the man who would be king."

"Just let me graduate, Chas."

An hour later, Pelham, Kirby, Upton, and twelve cadets from junior classes sat on wooden benches in the natural amphitheater below the bluff. Lieutenant Oliver Howard, an 1854 graduate who had experienced a profound conversion while serving in Florida, one that had nearly led him into the ministry, stood before them. He turned to a verse in his large black leather-bound Bible.

"So, what then are we to think when the Apostle Paul says to the Church in Rome, 'For all have sinned and fall short of the Glory of God'?"

"That none, save Christ himself, can live a life without sin," Upton said, his head bowed.

"Do we believe it? In all of history, not one person?"

"I don't see how anyone honest with himself could think otherwise," said Pelham.

"So, you are with us, Mr. Pelham," Howard said, voicing surprise. "I thought you distracted."

"Sorry, sir. And as for sin, God created us in his own image and gave us free will—freedom of choice—and with this freedom, I for one tend to seek my own interests, which I know aren't always, or even ever, his."

Howard nodded. "And so, we thank God for his grace, for his unmerited favor, and for the gift of his son, that through his life, death, and resurrection we have forgiveness of sins and are co-heirs of the kingdom."

A stiff breeze off the Hudson rustled the tree leaves.

"And, of course, as you say, Mr. Pelham, we can't seem to stop sinning, can we? We live in a world of sin, constantly tempted by Satan and subject daily to trials and temptations. Which begs the question— is this person, Satan, still alive today?"

"Alive and well," Kirby said.

"An example?"

"The existence of slavery, sir," Upton said without hesitation.

"Slavery is the work of Satan?" pressed Howard. Though an abolitionist himself, he was silent on the subject.

"Absolutely. I believe Satan begets this worst of evils."

"Are we in agreement?" asked Howard, anticipating a response from one of the cotton state cadets.

Charlie Ball replied, his tone piqued, "We are not, sir. And to suggest it is, is unbiblical and condemning of the South, if not the whole world. Slavery existed before, during, and after the time of Christ. And to my knowledge Christ never said, 'Thou shalt not have slaves.' He did say we are all slaves—to sin. Slavery is a condition of society, sir, and foundational to the Union, certainly to the South." Ball eyed Upton, whose head was again bowed. "Whatever it is, it is man's doing in this broken world and, yes, kindled by Satan. But were it not to exist, how many unsaved blacks would have been butchered or enslaved in Africa?"

"So, the end justifies the means?" Howard said, letting his question hang in the air.

Pelham took up the defense. "In the South, sir, slavery is a fact of life. There, they at least have Christ. In that, there is no distinction between them and their masters. Their souls are saved for eternity."

Howard looked for a response from Upton, who remained silent.

"Well then, let's widen the scope. What other tactics does the enemy use against the faithful and the undecided? What else confounds our faith and seeks to separate us from the love and peace of God?"

Henry Farley, a hot-headed South Carolinian and Third Classman in Pelham's company, raised his hand. "He pits us against one another, sir, just as now demonstrated. And … it has troubled me greatly since last year, sir, when we studied world history, when we learned how Protestants and Catholics for centuries have killed each other in the name of Christ. How does God deal with that?"

"Now that's the question, isn't it? And I'm afraid I don't have the answer any more than you do. But it is, indeed, one of Satan's chief tactics, to take us from grace and truth into his realm of legalism, which ferments all manner of self-righteous pride as to what religion should look like, trivializing the all-important 'who' and 'why' of faith."

Howard placed a finger on his Bible. "Is there any mention in this book of the people we call Protestants or Catholics? Is there any mention of Lutherans, Presbyterians, Baptists, or Methodists?"

They all shook their heads.

"It is man's doing, isn't it? With encouragement from our one true enemy, and it divides us, divides his universal church."

Howard glanced at his watch.

"Our time is up. Let us pray to the God of the universe. Let us ask him for wisdom to discern that which is of his kingdom and that which is of the world. Let us pray for grace, that while we live in the world we would follow kingdom rules, and that we would allow the Holy Spirit to work through us and make us salt and light to the lost. Mr. Kirby, if you would start us, I will conclude. And as we depart, Mr. Pelham, please lead us in singing of the first two verses of 'Amazing Grace.'"

In the stillness of the morning, after each person had offered prayer, the group departed, Pelham singing, "Amazing grace, how sweet the sound . . ." They continued singing as they made their way up to the Plain.

After the hymn, Emory Upton came alongside Pelham. "I don't know about your Charlie Ball."

"Charlie's fine, Emory. He just doesn't think like you."

"You are both Alabamians, John, but so different.

"How do you mean?"

"Your heart is not behind slavery. You told me so yourself."

"Emory, your hearing is selective. I agree that it is a most unfortunate institution and very likely a grievous sin, but that doesn't change its reality. I don't see it ending in our lifetime."

"John, save for pigment, Negroes are no different from you or me. Slavery is the sum of all evils, worse than stealing, the same as killing. Rendering children of God hopeless and helpless."

Pelham knew better than to argue. "Emory, there are fruits of the spirit, aren't there?"

"Of course."

"Is one of them patience?"

Upton didn't respond.

"You've got to allow time for change, Emory. Your zeal is a two-edged sword. If you're not less judgmental, no one will listen to you or take you seriously. And what is this beef with du Pont?"

The question surprised Upton. "That's between Henry and me, John."

"Henry is a prince, Emory, the best of men. And he works like a dog for our class and the Corps. Attacking him does you no good."

Upton looked at Pelham but said nothing. Instead, he quick-timed up the hill.

Kirby took Upton's place. "It truly amazes me how you and Upton get along."

"The man means well, Ned."

Pelham and Kirby continued up the hill, unaware they were being watched from the third floor of the hotel.

At the window, Clara stood in a sleeping gown. Ellie was in the bed they shared.

"For the last time, Clara, what's going on out there?"

Hearing the singing, she had opened the window and was watching Pelham, Upton, Kirby, and the others walking up the hill.

"John was leading the hymn. Wasn't it beautiful?"

"Did you see Henry?"

"I don't think so," Clara said, returning to bed and crawling in next to Ellie. "Ellie, we've just one more night. And then we're gone." Her tone was morose, but only for a moment. "Hasn't it been grand, Ellie, and everything we could have hoped for?"

"Much more," Ellie allowed dreamily. "I may one day visit Delaware. Henry has invited me to his home. How about you? Does John know how you really feel?"

The setting on the Plain was unlike any Pelham had seen before. He had given Williams permission to run the course the second hour of the morning. The entire Second Class had turned out to support him, lining both sides of the obstacle course. Custer had escorted Williams from the stable.

"How do you feel, Ron?" Pelham asked.

"Scared."

"Nothing wrong with that. Take a warm-up lap and let me know how you feel. We're not going to do this unless you're ready."

"I just want to get it over with, sir."

"No sirs today."

William forced a smile and kicked his horse to a trot and then a gallop.

Rosser joined Custer and Pelham. "He should still be in the hospital. He's as white as milk. I'd be surprised if he makes one decent run."

Custer surveyed the crowd. "And all this attention doesn't help."

Upon his return, Williams said he was ready, and Pelham dispatched Rosser to the midpoint of the course and Custer to the finish line.

"You're sure, Ron?"

Williams nodded, beads of sweat on his forehead.

"Look around, Ron. These guys are going to kick your ass if you let them down."

Pelham signaled to Custer, who raised his hand.

When Custer dropped his hand, Williams kicked up a cloud of dust and was quickly at a gallop. He easily cleared the first jump, his form good, and was soon upon the second jump. Pelham held his breath as Williams's horse pushed off his back legs into the air. The sound of the horse's hind legs hitting the crossbar echoed across the Plain, and with it came the collective groans of a hundred spectators. Williams returned to the starting point, his eyes locked on Pelham.

"I'm done, John. I just can't make the four-foot jump. I think I'm going to throw up."

Rosser and Custer joined them.

"Fannie, tell your classmates not to go anywhere. I'm taking Williams on a trot."

"Gotcha, boss," Custer said, rendering a casual salute.

Pelham led Williams into a stand of trees at the eastern perimeter of the encampment. Five minutes later, they reemerged.

Upon their return, the number of spectators along the course had increased. Pelham directed Rosser and Custer back to their stations.

Custer again dropped his arm, and Williams began his second run, clearing the first jump in perfect alignment for the second. As the horse's front legs left the ground for the second jump, it was as if the whole of West Point had stopped breathing, every eye on the crossbar. When the front legs and then the back legs of the horse touched the ground and the bar was still in place, the Plain shook with cheers. Again at a gallop, Williams easily cleared the third jump and drew his saber. He leaned forward over the horse's mane and delivered a death blow to the hapless dummy and sprinted past Custer and the finish line.

Every eye was on Custer, whose thumb shot up in the air, triggering jubilation across the Plain.

Pelham was quickly to Williams's side. "You did it, Ron!"

The Second Classman returned a disoriented expression and slid off his horse to one knee.

"Drink this, Ron." Pelham gave Williams his canteen.

Barely had Williams taken a few swallows when he was swarmed by his classmates and hoisted on shoulders.

"Well done, Ron! Damn fine work," Custer shouted. "Thanks to you, I am now a poor man, but a small price to pay for a miracle."

Custer ceremoniously tossed his five-dollar gold piece in the air, which Pelham caught with an appreciative nod.

Rosser slapped Custer on the back, nearly unseating him.

Pelham drew his saber and held it high for attention. "To the Class of 1862, I salute you. You are indeed a proud bunch, with reason to be. Ron Williams is but an example! You are now all fair game for the fall jump masters. Good luck to you."

With that, he, Rosser, and Custer headed for the stables.

"So, what happened with you and Williams?" Custer asked. "He was a different man that second run."

"Same man," said Pelham. "Different horse."

"You switched mounts?"

"I told Williams that Old Red had never touched a crossbar, and that's why I rode him. I told him to sit back and let Old Red do the work."

"Is it true?" Custer asked.

Pelham winked." Of course not."

When Rosser stopped laughing, he confronted Custer. "So, Fannie, are you going to the hop tonight?"

"Hell, why not? The way I'm hiding in my tent, guys are starting to talk."

"Indeed, Fannie. We've all missed your dashing presence," said Pelham.

"I'll ask Carol Hill if she'll toss you a crumb," Rosser said. "Though, frankly, she has better taste."

"Done!" Custer announced, his spirits improved. "And you, John, may I expect a crumb from your table—a twirl with your Clara?"

"If she isn't already promised, for she doesn't lack suitors."

"So, I've heard," Custer said, kicking his horse to a gallop.

Chapter Twenty-Eight

Ten minutes before the final hop of the week, Clara waited for Pelham on the hotel veranda. She saw him coming from the encampment and met him at the foot of the stairs.

"Do you mind if we walk for a while?" she said, taking his arm.

"How was your day?" Pelham asked.

"Fine. I took Ellie down to the river, to Flirtation Walk. We broke your regulations," she said with a defiant look. "Henry was going to take her, but your commandant gave him a job. I showed her Kissing Rock. She so wanted to see it. Henry missed his chance."

"I'll have to tell him."

"Don't you dare!"

"Maybe he can make up for it."

"I think he should."

Pelham led her to the rear of the hotel, behind a flowered trellis that afforded a measure of privacy.

He sniffed the air. "Your perfume is different."

"It's Eva Taylor's. Do you like it?"

"Indeed." He squeezed her hand. "My lady, until now you have had free rein to kiss my cheek. I wondered if such license extended both ways."

Clara couldn't suppress a giggle. "It might."

He leaned forward and brushed her cheek with his lips, and she turned her other cheek.

"Umm. That was very nice," said Clara, a dreaminess in her eyes. "But I think I'm better at it." She stood on tiptoes and delicately kissed him on both cheeks, finishing with a feathery kiss on the lips.

Pelham smiled. "Infinitely better."

Clara removed her shawl, revealing bare shoulders and for the first time a hint of cleavage. "Do you like my dress?"

Pelham struggled not to stare. "Indeed, though I fear you will attract much attention."

She took his arm. "I suppose we had better make an appearance."

When they reached the hotel steps, Clara stopped. "John, I have had the most wonderful week, the best week of my life in fact. And I know tomorrow is coming. I will miss you, John. I will miss my dearest knight. But tonight, let us have the most incredible time."

"We shall, Clara," Pelham promised.

She opened her hop card. "I've saved all the waltzes for us."

"Have you a free dance for a friend? George Custer?"

"Of course." She penciled in Custer. "And, John, I hope we will have some time to ourselves tonight."

"Block out the last three dances."

"Done," she said, pointing an accusing finger. "You watch out for that Becky Thompson. She definitely has eyes for you."

After ringing the dance bell, Charlie Hazlett set the stage for the evening by announcing the obvious, that it was the last hop of the week and that everyone should make the most of it, since nearly all the ladies would be leaving the next day. Spotting Pelham, he winked.

During the first dance, always a waltz, Pelham and Clara glided across the floor as though lifelong partners. There wasn't a couple on the floor that didn't envy the grace of the cadet from Alabama and the girl from Philadelphia. After the dance, Pelham handed Clara off to Emory Upton.

Clara's third dance was with Nate Chambliss. Chas Patterson had the fourth, and her partner for the fifth dance was an animated Ron Williams who later met Pelham at the punch bowl.

Pelham gave Williams a playful thump on the chest. "You think just because you can ride a horse, you can steal my girl?"

Williams smiled. "I want to thank you again, John."

"Nonsense. And by the way, you look good on the dance floor."

"Miss Bolton made me so."

The band was in rare form and high spirits, and it was not until they had taken a short break that Custer got his turn with Clara.

After the dance, Custer confronted Pelham. "Did you tell Clara I bite?"

Pelham grinned. "She had to know, Fannie."

Custer was unamused. "How can I be dashing when I am so thoroughly dashed."

When the music for the next dance started, Pelham escorted Eva Taylor to the floor, informing her that she had captured Walter's heart.

"And he mine. Though sadly, I must break one in Kentucky." Pelham smiled. "I feel sorry for the man."

"Excuse my boldness," said Eva. "But I think you are making a big mistake with Clara."

"How so?"

"You should be more than friends," she said with a discerning look. "At least, that's my opinion."

"You have talked to her?" "Not in so many words."

"Clara and I are close," Pelham said, hoping to draw more out of her.

"That may be well and good, and if you are happy being … friends, so be it. And if you are, I know the girl for you."

"You know me that well?"

"I have eyes, John."

"And are a matchmaker?"

Eva cocked her head as though sizing him up. "You, John Pelham, are an uncommon spirit. You need a kindred spirit, one with comparable energy."

Pelham wanted to say that Clara Bolton fitted that mold perfectly but settled for a nod.

"My friend is at least your equal," Eva said as the dance came to an end. "She and I roomed together two years at William and Mary." Eva smiled over Pelham's shoulder at Clara and Adelbert Ames who joined them on the dance floor.

"Clara, Adelbert." Eva extended her gloved hand to Ames who pressed it to his lips and then left in search of Rebecca Astor.

"Clara, you are the queen of the ball," Eva said. "And I must have that dress. I was telling John about a friend of mine, that he would like her. I know he would, and she's more than pretty. Her name is Sallie Dandridge of the Virginia Dandridges."

Clara's face showed no emotion. "And how would you propose John meet this girl?"

"Just leave that to me, Clara. I know that Sallie and John would have chemistry. I am quite sure of it. They would be more than friends, or nothing at all."

"You are too kind, Eva," Clara said, her tone gracious. "I'm sure John will want to take you up on the offer."

Pelham avoided eye contact with either of them.

"I should first write Sallie," said Eva, "and make sure she is not otherwise engaged."

Walter Kingsbury came up behind Eva and tapped her on the shoulder. "My rose. Shall we?"

As Eva turned to join Kingsbury, she said, "I'll send you her address. That is, if Sallie's not engaged."

As the evening progressed, Hazlett heighten everyone's sense of urgency, announcing the declining number of dances. When he announced but three left, Pelham caught Clara's eye, and the two met at the refreshment table. Pelham poured Clara a cup of punch.

"I see the chaperones have switched posts. Frampton is at the hall door."

Clara, expressionless, said nothing.

"You are unusually quiet, my lady."

Clara took a sip of punch and let the cup linger on her lips. "It is almost over, John. Our time together."

Pelham was about to reply when his jaw dropped. "I don't believe it."

"But it is, John."

"No. I mean, look! Miss Frampton. She's smiling."

Clara turned, and indeed the assistant dean was smiling. Clara waved at Frampton, and Frampton waved back. "My, what can that be about?"

"Maybe she's nipping on something?" Pelham suggested.

"Follow me." Clara led the two of them unmolested past Frampton, who nearly floored Pelham with a cordial nod.

Moments later, they were on the rear veranda, gazing at another starry sky, the moon dancing off the Hudson.

Clara squeezed Pelham's hand. "A penny for your thoughts."

"It will cost you more than that, my lady."

She slipped something into his hand. "Just put it in your pocket. Don't look at it until later."

Pelham did, and before he could say anything, Clara placed a finger on his lips. "Don't say a word." After a few seconds, she took both of his hands. "John?"

"My lady?"

"I want you to kiss me."

"Of course." Pelham leaned forward to kiss Clara's cheek, but she pushed him away.

"No, John. Not like that. I want you to kiss me . . . as if . . ."

"As if what?"

"As if we were ... more than friends. As if you found me attractive."

"Attractive?"

Clara tilted her head.

"You are sure?"

When Clara didn't respond, Pelham took her in his arms and drew her tight against himself. He sensed her softness against his chest. Her breath tickled his nose. He lifted her chin. In the dark, he explored the margins of her mouth, tasting its sweetness, scarcely pausing for breath. Clara's tongue greeted his, and the two played at hide and seek.

"Oh, John. Don't stop."

Pelham didn't, until he heard the sound of boots on the veranda.

"Attention, soldier!"

Pelham prayed for a prankster. But the voice was too deep, too commanding, and too familiar.

A man's face appeared in the moonlight.

"Sir!" Pelham stood apart from Clara and snapped to attention.

Lieutenant Colonel Hardee emerged fully from the shadows. "Is that you, Mr. Pelham?"

Pelham fumbled for a response.

"Mr. Pelham, are you in the habit of not saluting a superior officer?"

"No, sir." Pelham rendered a sharp salute.

Hardee returned the salute. "Would you mind following me, Mr. Pelham?"

Clara caught Pelham's ashen face as he turned to follow the commandant.

Around the corner of the hotel, Clara heard muffled voices, footsteps, and then nothing. Seconds later, she heard footsteps again. A man in uniform appeared and identified himself as the aide to the commandant.

"Ma'am, I am truly sorry. But Cadet Pelham will not be able to accompany you for the balance of the evening."

Chapter Twenty-Nine

Saturday morning, Pelham awoke to the humiliation of the night before, his malaise heightened by the certainty of discipline. A thick fog covered the Hudson and the Plain. Rosser did his best to steer free of Pelham's transgression and said not a word of it through reveille and the march to the mess hall.

At breakfast, word of Pelham's fall from grace quickly spread through the Corps. In addition to Rosser's attempts at consolation, du Pont, Chambliss, Ames, Patterson, Upton, and Custer took turns attempting to lift Pelham's spirits. Chambliss offered to intercede with the commandant, but Pelham declined, insisting that he not receive special treatment. The only other person in the Corps more distraught than Pelham was Walter Kingsbury, whose lamentations over Eva Taylor's departure that day would render him incapable of being consoled or giving consolation.

After breakfast, Rosser returned to the encampment to find Kirby emerging from his tent.

"What's it to be, Ned?"

"The formal charge is gross public display of affection. Thankfully, Hardee chose not to report him for failure to render respect to a superior officer. He gets confinement to quarters until the end of encampment and reduction to the grade of cadet private."

"That's a tough one," said Rosser." But like you say, for disrespect he could have been dismissed from the Academy. How did he take it?"

"Hard to say."

"When does it start?"

"Immediately."

Rosser raised the tent flap and found Pelham sitting on his footlocker. "Ned filled me in."

Pelham cradled something in his hand.

"What's that?" Rosser asked.

Pelham handed Rosser a locket attached to a delicate gold chain.

He opened the locket to find a photograph of Clara inside. "My friend, she is truly beautiful."

For fifteen minutes, he and Pelham scurried about the tent in silence preparing for Saturday inspection later that morning, the most rigorous inspection of the week, which would be conducted by both Lieutenant Colonel Hardee and Lieutenant Lee.

Rosser suddenly tossed his hands in the air. "John, I can't believe I forgot. I've got to take care of something. Look after my side."

Before Pelham could object, Rosser was gone.

Rosser sprinted up the tree-lined path to the hotel, taking the hotel steps three at a time. He found a young bellboy in the lobby. "You have a guest here, a Miss Clara Bolton—do you know her?"

Joseph snapped to attention. "Oh, yes, sir."

"Would you tell her John Pelham is waiting for her in the parlor? It's urgent."

"Yes, sir, Mr. Pelham." Joseph bolted up the stairs.

Two minutes later, Clara appeared, her face radiant. "Hello, Tom." She glanced about. "Where's John?"

"He's not here, Clara. Let's go inside the parlor."

"I don't understand," Clara said, wringing her hands.

Rosser led her to a settee.

"It's about John, Clara."

"He is all right, Tom?"

"He's fine, Clara, but he's confined to quarters until the end of encampment."

"Oh, Tom, that's so dreadful, and it's all my fault." She shook her head despondently. "It's all my fault."

"Don't blame yourself. And trust me, he'll survive."

Clara gave Rosser a pleading look. "He'll still be able to see me off at the dock, won't he?"

"I'm sorry, Clara. That won't be possible."

"Oh, Tom, what have I done?"

"I wish there was something I could say," Rosser offered weakly.

"I can't leave without seeing him. I must see him, Tom."

"Clara, I understand. But it's just not possible. He can't leave the encampment. If he attempts anything else … you'll be able to see him all you want."

"Oh, Tom, this is awful."

"I can take him a note, though. He would like that. But it must be short. I have to get back before inspection."

Clara's expression turned stern. "Tom, I will see him, if only for a minute."

"Clara, you don't understand."

"No, Tom. You don't understand." Clara stood up, her hands on her hips. "You must take me to him, Tom."

"Me?"

"Yes . . . you." Clara's voice was sharp as glass.

"You can't be serious. The encampment is under guard. There is no way to get in or out unless you're a cadet or an officer."

"I will see him, Tom," Clara said. "With or without your help. Just tell me which tent he's in."

"God in heaven, you can't be serious, Clara. You can't just waltz into the cadet encampment."

Clara crossed her arms. "I will see him, Tom."

Rosser glanced out the parlor window, the encampment still obscured by fog. "You're going to do this?"

"With or without your help."

"No matter what I say?"

"I can't leave without seeing him, Tom."

"What?"

Rosser stifled an expletive. "Stand up… Now, turn."

"What?"

"Let me see your profile."

Clara turned.

"You're five-four?"

"Five-five."

"This is insane, Clara. No, worse. Crazy, brainless, stupid, stupid—really stupid." Rosser's mind raced. "Though, when I was a plebe, a First Classman snuck a girl into the barracks. But that was during graduation week."

"Yes, Tom." Clara couldn't hide her excitement.

"And it was at night. This would be in daylight in front of God and country."

"I'm willing, Tom. Anything."

"There is the fog. And it might last."

"Yes. Yes, anything!"

"If it persists, I'll be back in forty minutes, after inspection. We can only do this if the fog persists. Can you be very uncomfortable for an hour?"

"How do you mean?"

"No time to explain. The bellboy. Do you trust him?"

"With my life."

"I'll come to the rear of the hotel. Have him meet me."

"I will." Clara hugged Rosser. "God bless you, Tom."

"Clara, this is absolutely insane. You need to know that. The chances are better that I'll join John in confinement than you seeing John. Do you understand?"

"I do. And I thank you, Tom."

Pelham and Rosser survived inspection with only a demerit apiece, due in no small part to the confounding fog that still enveloped the encampment. Pelham wasn't surprised that nothing in Lieutenant Colonel Hardee's demeanor or actions reflected his indiscretion the night before. He had broken regulations and would serve his punishment, and that would be the end of it.

After inspection, Rosser abandoned Pelham in search of Doug Woodridge, the smallest man in the class. Minutes later he was en route to the hotel with a carpetbag. He found Joseph waiting on the back steps. Ten minutes later, Joseph appeared with Clara dressed in a cadet uniform—white trousers tight across her hips, gray dress coat with gold buttons tight across her chest, and a forage cap that sat high on her head.

She descended the stairs and crossed the lawn in a pair of black shoes, attempting to walk like a man.

Rosser couldn't help grinning. "Well, just look at you." He reached inside his pocket and produced a nickel for the bellboy. But Joseph shook his head.

"Oh, no thank you, sir. I do this freely and with the highest regard for Miss Bolton." Joseph turned to Clara. "Good luck, ma'am."

The cadet impersonator kissed the boy on the forehead and ruffled his hair. "Thank you, Joe. If only you were a little older."

The boy beamed and was gone.

"Cadet Bolton, reporting for duty, sir," Clara said gruffly.

Rosser pressed the forage cap down on her head. "You know, this just might work. The fog is still thick. But we've no time to waste."

Rosser led Clara to the northwest corner of the Fort Clinton parapet, and then south along its west side. Nearing the southwest corner of the fort, he warned her of the sentry they would encounter and pulled her behind an elm tree. From the corner parapet, they could almost make out the nearest of the A Company tents.

"When the guard passes, we move. Once in camp, look like you own the place. Understand?"

Clara nodded as she peered into the thick fog, ready to move despite the blisters forming on her feet.

"Are you wearing perfume?"

Clara dropped her eyes. "Sorry."

"We'll make our way between the tents and across each company street until we get to D Company." Rosser detected fear in Clara's eyes. "Are you okay?"

She returned a weak smile.

"You're doing fine."

The sentry came and went, and Rosser made his move.

The two crossed the encampment perimeter to the first row of A Company tents. They walked at an even pace, Rosser carrying on an inane conversation. He kept an eye on Clara, impressed with her relaxed manner and acquired swagger. Together, they sauntered through the heart of the encampment, the fog still holding.

Clara suddenly clutched Rosser's arm and shielded her eyes. "Tom, that man is … relieving himself."

Rosser chuckled.

Half a minute later they reached the first row of D Company tents.

"That's us," Rosser said, pointing.

"He knows I'm coming?"

"No, Clara. He doesn't."

"You didn't tell him?"

"I didn't think we'd make it."

"Bless you, Tom." Clara kissed Rosser on the cheek.

A moment later, she slipped soundlessly under the flap of a tent and found Pelham sitting on a locker in white trousers and an undershirt, reading a book.

"Care for some company?"

Pelham whirled about to see Clara trembling, tears streaming down her cheeks.

Pelham gawked as she raised a pitiful salute. And in the next instant was upon her with kisses. "God, this can't be happening. Please, lord, don't let me wake up."

Rosser cleared his throat at the entrance to the tent. "Two minutes, you two. Then it's back to the hotel."

"You listen to me, John Pelham," Clara said. "I love you."

Pelham eyes grew moist, and he squeezed Clara tight. He lifted her off the ground, swung her side to side, and shook the forage cap from her head, revealing hair tightly braided and pinned.

"You did this for me?"

Clara flashed a sheepish grin. "John, I'm so sorry." The buttons on her coat dug into his chest. "I've ruined it for you. For both of us."

"You have no idea what you've done," Pelham announced joyfully. "You've resurrected my life, given me a memory to feed on forever. You are my incredible lady!"

"Hold it down in there," growled Rosser.

Pelham shook his head. "I can't believe it. You're here."

"I wouldn't be, if weren't for your amazing friend."

Pelham kissed Clara a dozen times more, until she drew back. "John." Her tone was deadly serious. "You are not to listen to Eva

Taylor. I don't know who this Sallie Dandridge is, but I don't want you with her or anyone else."

"Is that so, my lady?" said Pelham.

"And I don't want to be your friend—or even your best friend. I don't know what I was thinking." Clara framed his face in her hands and smothered him with kisses. "John, I want to be your girlfriend, your only girlfriend, the way God intended me to be."

"Hey, Romeo." Rosser's voice was abrupt. "Wrap it up."

"Tom," Pelham replied. "There most certainly is a God, and you, blessed brother, are his divine instrument. A moment more."

He turned to Clara. "Truly, this is answered prayer." He kissed the tip of her nose, then the full of her mouth, all the while his hand exploring her uniform.

"John, my heart beats only for you." She took his hand and pressed it to her breast.

Pelham pulled her hard against himself. "God, you are so very beautiful."

Clara smiled an impish smile.

"Time's up, John." Rosser's tone was insistent.

"Dr. Bolton." Pelham kissed Clara's ear. "You have changed my life and stolen my heart."

The delight in Clara's face melted to apprehension. "John, what are we to do?"

"Whatever we must," Pelham said. "Our timing couldn't be worse, and it won't be easy. We'll have to discover each other through letters, and through them know each other fully. I will live for yours and you for mine. I'll pray for you and you for me. Each night I'll dream of you and you of me, of this day, and of a day that will be."

"And when will that day be, John? How long?"

"I'm afraid it will be a long time from now."

"When?"

"Graduation."

"But that's next June!"

"I know."

"John, that's nine months."

"We have no choice. Will you come to graduation?"

"I will live for it."

Rosser kicked the tent post. "Dammit, John, the sun is burning through."

"I do love you, John Pelham from Alabama, and I'm not asking you to say you love me. Not until you are ready."

Pelham smiled. "You do know me, don't you?" He fitted the forage cap on her head.

"John, let me write the first letter. Will you do that? As soon as I get to Clermont, I shall write you my heart."

"If that is your wish."

Chapter Thirty

Shortly after noon, the steamer for New York harbor pulled away from the North Dock. Pressed against the stern railing on the top deck were Clara Bolton, Ellie Lawson, Eva Taylor, Carol Hill, Jessica Danford, Alice Paine, and Rebecca Astor. They shouted and waved at Henry du Pont, Walter Kingsbury, Tom Rosser, Nate Chambliss, Chas Patterson, and Adelbert Ames, who stood on the dock until the steamer disappeared.

From the confines of his tent, Pelham heard the steamer's shrill whistle as it approached Gee's Point. He smiled as he snipped the threads that attached the three gold chevrons to his dress coat. If only for a few months, he had been a cadet officer. When he was done, he put the chevrons and the red satin sash, his dress sword, and accoutrements in his valise, and carried them to the cadet quartermaster store. Afterwards, he reported to the armory to pick up a musket, bayonet, and cartridge box.

After the midday meal, Pelham was told of the arrival of the northbound steamer that deposited the final group of starry-eyed girls to witness the end of summer encampment.

Late that afternoon, Kirby stuck his head inside Pelham's tent. "Lieutenant Lee wants to see you."

"What about?"

"He didn't say."

Pelham marked the page of a worn James Fennimore Cooper novel.

At the entrance to Lee's tent, Pelham saluted. "Sir, Cadet Pelham reporting as ordered."

Lee returned the salute. "Come in, Mr. Pelham. Confinement suiting you?"

Pelham sensed a smile behind Lee's beard. "I'm into a good book, sir, and intend to reread Nolan's book on cavalry next. He has much to say on the use of field artillery and horses."

"He does. Something the French have been experimenting with—horse artillery—but it takes a great number of horses."

"Yes, sir."

"I've news," Lee said, "that we are to receive twenty fresh mounts early this week, and they're likely to need breaking. I was hoping I might be able to enlist you, Rosser, and Custer again."

Pelham resisted a smile. "Anything to get out of confinement, sir. They'll be pleased to know."

"By the way, despite your … error in timing with the young lady, I want to commend you on your work with the Second Classmen. Not only did they all pass the course, but I understand they thoroughly enjoyed your instruction."

"Thank you, sir. I'll pass it on to Rosser and Custer."

"One last thing. Mathias Henry checked into the hospital this morning with a bug. He's in a bad way, and D company's going to need a replacement lead gunner for the artillery competition. Had you not been an officer, you would have been my choice for the competition. The position is yours if you want it."

"Yes, sir. Again, anything to escape confinement."

"Good." Lee stood up. "I'll let you know when the horses come in."

When Pelham returned to the tent, he found Rosser cleaning his musket and filled him in.

"Hot damn," Rosser declared. "It's been ages since I broke a horse." He pointed to Pelham's musket with a grin. "You better get with it, John. Ned's got us on guard detail in the morning."

"That didn't take long." Pelham hung his coat up and rooted around for his cleaning rod. "You and Carol Hill seem to have it going pretty well."

"Aye, my luck may be changing, and we had a fine send-off at the boat. A good thing Hardee wasn't around. But I'm to write first, John. And you know what that means. She's hoping for a letter this week. You'll help me?"

"Of course," Pelham said. "Just remember that less is more, until you know where she stands. And you won't know that until her first letter."

Rosser nodded. "I don't understand it, John. Face to face, I'm great with the ladies. But put a pen in my hand and I panic."

Pelham smiled. "Your encampment flairs do seem to fizzle in the mail."

An hour later, while Rosser was off to the confectionary, du Pont knocked once on the tent pole and entered. He found Pelham reclining on his footlocker.

"You got dealt some bad cards, brother," du Pont said, noticing the locket in his hand. "What do you have there?"

Pelham handed du Pont the locket.

"She is indeed a plum. I spoke with her on the dock—she even hugged me. You've made her a very happy woman."

"She's made me a very happy man."

"It was a sweet time on the dock, not a few tears."

"And you and Ellie?"

"We'd be as tight as you and Clara, had we made it to Flirty. I intend to write her this evening." Du Pont produced an envelope. "Clara asked me to give you this."

Pelham waited for du Pont to leave before opening the envelope. Inside a delicately formed bow of red and white ribbon, enclosed a note in Clara's hand. *You gave me a button. I give you a bow. Expect my letter soon. Love, your lady, Clara.*

At supper, except for Rosser and du Pont, there was universal curiosity over Pelham's ebullient mood. Kingsbury, on the other hand, was so beside himself that Chambliss had to ask du Pont to make the announcements.

After leaving the mess hall, Pelham caught up with Patterson. "So, how goes it with you and Alice Paine?"

"I fear the woman has misled me."

"Pray tell."

"Ellie Lawson told me that Alice has been courted by a lawyer on Long Island for more than two years. It's been an on and off thing, and apparently, it is in the off stage for now. At any rate, Alice said she would write, so—we'll see."

"A taste of your own dessert, eh?" Pelham quipped.

The remaining week of summer encampment passed quickly, with alternating days of rain and shine. Throughout the week, coveys of Third Classmen returned from their two-and-a-half-month furloughs, bringing the Corps to its full complement. Although Pelham had to start over with Rosser's first letter to Carol Hill, Rosser still managed to post the letter in Monday's mail. Tuesday morning came with word from Lee that the shipment of horses was in, and Wednesday morning, Pelham, Rosser, and Custer reported to Lee at the stables.

"Notice anything unusual?" Lee asked, as the three got their initial look at the new mounts.

"Hard to miss, sir." Pelham pointed to a white steed in a corral of nineteen sorrels.

"He would make a fine target on the battlefield," said Custer.

"But here at West Point, just another mount," Lee said. "Who wants him?"

"I'll take him, sir," said Pelham.

The four of them inspected the mounts and spent the better part of Wednesday, Thursday, and Friday mornings breaking the horses to the point they wouldn't break cadets. By the time the job was done, they had named all of the horses, Pelham naming the white horse, Cotton.

Friday after the midday meal, the Corps, the Academy staff, and a great number of visitors assembled in the area south of the cadet encampment to witness the Corps' end of encampment field artillery competition. The competition was the culmination of summer training and involved four of the Academy's six bronze field artillery pieces, the muzzles of the cannons sparkling gold on the Plain.

A crew of five serviced each gun: a horse-mounted gun captain, the gunner and a cannoneer at the trails of the cannon, and two cannoneers at the muzzle. For the competition, the captain was more or less for show, since the gunner at the trails would set the primer and firing lanyard and maneuver the weapon into position. The men at the muzzle would load and ram the powder bag and ammunition. After the gunner fired the cannon, they would sponge the barrel, so that the whole process could begin again.

For the competition, each of the four cadet companies proffered its most proficient gunnery team. Pelham entered the competition, having worked with the D Company crew an hour in the afternoon Monday and Tuesday, and half an hour late Thursday.

"I'll wager a dollar on D Company," Rosser announced loudly to no one in particular.

Adelbert Ames responded. "Against the field, Tom?"

"Why not?"

"Care to make it two?"

"Why not five?"

The two shook hands.

Cheers exploded across the Plain as the teams formed around their field pieces and continued until Lieutenant Colonel Hardee raised a hand for silence.

"Welcome to today's annual field artillery gunnery competition," Hardee said, recognizing special guests and explaining the nature of the competition, that the winner would be the gun crew that fired first and most accurately at the assigned target. For the many visitors in attendance, he assured them that no live projectiles would be used, and that the good people on the other side of the Hudson had nothing to worry about.

The four company commanders served as gun captains. Ames, on horseback, positioned himself behind the B Company gun crew, and Kirby behind the D Company crew.

"Give 'em hell, Alabama," Custer shouted at Pelham.

Hardee announced, "On my signal," and raised his arm. At the drop of his hand, the four gunnery crews flew into action.

Pelham and the three other competing gunners shouted the commands, "Load," "Ram," and "Heave—Halt," commands that readied the gun and moved them forward the required ten yards. Then he and the other gunners shouted adjusting commands to aim their pieces.

Satisfied, Pelham bellowed "Fire," followed by, "Swab."

The stillness of the valley reverberated with the retorts of the four cannons.

Rosser wasn't sure. Pelham's gun and a second gun had advanced to the firing line at the same time and had fired at nearly the same instant. Though, he thought the other gun might have had the edge.

As the Corps and the crowd argued the winner, Hardee, Lee, and the other company tactical officers trooped the line and independently sighted down the muzzle of each cannon. The group then caucused at the podium.

Ames dismounted next to Rosser. "I'll be taking your fiver, Tom. My company was first. I'm sure of it."

Rosser said nothing, his eye on Hardee who approached the podium.

"Ladies and Gentlemen and men of the Corps, this year's winner of the gunnery competition is the gunnery team from D Company."

Loud cheers and boos erupted from the Corps and the crowd.

"While second to fire," Hardee explained, "D Company's gun was accurately aimed at the target, unlike the piece that discharged first. D Company and its cannoneers are to be congratulated."

Rosser presented Ames with a gratuitous smile and open palm.

Leaving the mess hall that evening, Ames cornered Pelham. "How did you do it, John? You had your crew only days and the rest of us all summer. And you busted horses for three days. We fired first, but only by a split second."

"I posed a question to my crew, Adelbert" Pelham whispered what it was in Ames' ear.

"You asked if they wanted to die?"

"I said there are no second-place ribbons on the battlefield, that accuracy was first and speed second, and to imagine the other guns firing at us and to act accordingly."

Saturday night, the last night of encampment, featured the summer's finale, Camp Illumination. Amid final preparations, Pelham remained in confinement in his tent. Four hundred candles inside sanded bags were placed around the perimeter of the parade field, and beyond the lights, several hundred spectators waited for the spectacle. From his tent, Pelham could see the glow over the parade ground.

At eight o'clock, a single pistol shot signaled the beginning of festivities. Entering the parade ground through an opening in the perimeter of spectators and lights, cadets dressed as everything ridiculous—from military caricatures to ghosts, girls, Indians, and animals—paraded forth. Trailing them, and similarly attired, were a dozen cadets playing fiddles, banjos, harmonicas, and beating makeshift drums.

Bawdy exchanges between paraders and sideline spectators attended the procession. After it had circled the parade ground twice, and there had been a time for stag dancing on the parade ground, another pistol shot declared the affair over. Spectators dispersed as candles were snuffed out, and the procession retired to company streets.

Throughout the whole, Pelham lay on his pallet, contemplating the year ahead and the prospect of Clara in his life. As the final note of raucous music died, a verse of a Corps favorite, "Army Blue," brought a thought to mind and struck him with the sobering reality. He would never again greet "… *the ladies who come up in June.*"

CHAPTER THIRTY-ONE

Reveille the next morning came at the usual five o'clock, announced by the lone cannon, the inveterate Bentz, and the pitiless drummers. Pelham stumbled from his tent, lamenting an interrupted dream and blindly following Rosser to the first formation of the day. In the morning chill, he stood his place in ranks awaiting dismissal.

"Report," Paddy O'Rorke ordered in his morning voice. Receiving reports from D Company's three platoons, he executed an about-face and rendered an "all present" to Ned Kirby.

Kirby returned the salute and then announced in a loud voice, "All right, gentlemen, summer encampment is over. Let's hear it for Mr. Pelham who is once again a free man!"

The sacrosanct quietness of the hour was shattered by hoots, hollers, and whistles from every man in D Company, the noise escalated by the rest of the Corps. The uproar cascaded across the Hudson.

Pelham blinked hard.

After breakfast, what took a day to erect was, in ritualistic fashion, brought down in three hours. By noon the only evidence of the encampment was the graveled grid of company streets and naked wooden skeletal posts. The morning saw a steady stream of horse-drawn wagons loaded with footlockers, uniforms, bedding, washbowls, tents, and tent poles. Each cadet carried his own weapons.

The migration's destination was the large cinder-covered expanse known as Central Area, measuring three hundred by five hundred feet and defined by the cadet barracks to the north and west, the academic building to the east, and the commandant's office, boiler house, and shower facilities to the south.

Constructed principally of sandstone block, the massive four-story barracks consisted of eight divisions. The First Division was at the east end of the barracks, nearest the academic building, and each division extended the width of the building, with entrances from the front and back of the building. Each division had a central stairwell with four cadet rooms on each of four floors. The exception was the first floor, where one room served as the company orderly room.

On the Central Area side of the building, seven stone stairs led up to a broad covered stoop that accessed the first floor. The basement of the barracks housed mechanical equipment and miscellaneous storage and was interconnected between divisions by a narrow passageway.

Nate Chambliss, his battalion staff, and part of A Company quartered in the First Division; the balance of A Company quartered in the Second Division. B Company quartered in the Third and Fourth Divisions, C Company in the Fifth and Sixth Divisions, and D Company in the Seventh and Eighth Divisions at the extreme west end of the barracks. With the exception of the more spacious quarters of the battalion staff, where on the second floor Nate Chambliss enjoyed a two-room suite reserved for the first captain, every cadet room was the same.

"I am ready for a real bed," Rosser declared as he and Pelham carried their weapons to the Eighth Division.

"Aye, but remember what comes with it," Pelham warned.

They climbed the three flights of iron stairs with varnished wood handrails and handsome iron scrollwork to reach the fourth floor of the Eighth Division. Turning left, they entered an empty room, the same room they had vacated two and half months earlier. Pelham and Rosser had chosen the room the previous year for the privacy it afforded.

The room measured twenty feet by twenty feet and had a twelve-foot ceiling. The space was divided into a ten-foot by twenty-foot common area on the right, and the same size area on the left for sleeping. The sleeping area was partitioned into two separate alcoves. Against the outer wall of each alcove was a simple metal-spring bed with a rolled-up thin mattress. In front of the partition wall was a wooden stand with towel racks, a washbasin, and two slop buckets.

Centered on the right wall of the common area was a large leaded-glass window. On either side of the window, shelves and pegboards held muskets, sabers, swords, and accoutrements. The floor was old pine plank, stained a light gray. The walls were plaster, painted an off- white. The high baseboard and the window trim, as well as the wooden shelves and pegs on which uniforms, hats, duffel bags, and miscellaneous were stored, were painted blue. Printed curtains fronted the two alcoves, affording a measure of privacy and drawn back as required during the day.

Opposite the door was a small brick fireplace with a metal floor grate and firebox, and a metal hearth set flush with the floor and extending twelve inches from the fireplace. The fireplace was trimmed in wood and capped with a six-inch mantel, and both the wood and brick of the fireplace were painted black. To the right of the fireplace stood a five-shelf bookcase. The bookcase was painted beige and fronted with blue curtains. On the shelves, Pelham and Rosser would precisely arrange their clothing, extra linens, and personal items. The top shelf was reserved for academic books arranged by height and in specific order.

To the left of the door, along the interior wall, was a long wooden desk with two chairs. A gas light was mounted on the wall above it.

Pelham opened Clara's locket and hung it from the gas lamp.

"Sir," a plebe announced from the bottom of the division stairwell. "Class assignments have been posted in the sally port!"

"Like I said, Tom, the other shoe drops," Pelham said, retrieving a pad and pencil.

"Most merciful God," mumbled Rosser as they descended the staircase. "Protect me from Professor Mahan."

Arriving at the first floor, Pelham inspected himself in the full-length wall mirror. At the same time, Rosser checked the company bulletin board, bare except for the stick figure cartoon he had drawn before encampment, showing an upperclassman towering over a plebe.

Behind the bulletin board was the orderly room, the company's command-and-control center and mail drop.

Pelham stuck his head inside. "Welcome back, Jim."

James Wright, a Third Classman serving as charge-of-quarters, looked up. "Hey, John."

"Any mail yet?"

"Nope, not yet."

When Pelham and Rosser arrived at the sally port, it was a sea of bodies, cadets scribbling down class assignments posted in square framed class-covered bulletin boards that lined the walls. These same boards would post weekly class grades in the coming year.

"Yo, Pelham," Chas Patterson shouted from the end of the sally port. "Check this out."

Pelham answered the call and found himself in front of the demerit list. His name was at the top, his total half again the next offender.

"Over here, John," Rosser shouted. "We're in the same civil engineering section."

Within five minutes, Pelham and Rosser had journaled their class assignments and, in the process, crossed paths with du Pont, Upton, and Chambliss.

Back in their room, Pelham and Rosser unpacked their footlockers and prepared in advance for Sunday morning inspection, since during the academic year, inspections were on Sundays rather than Saturdays.

Rosser brooded over his class schedule. "I have a bad feeling, John."

"You say that every year."

"But this year we have Mahan."

"Tom, he's just another professor."

"No. He's Mahan."

"I'm going to see if the mail's come in," Pelham said.

He descended the three flights of stairs and queried the charge- of-quarters again.

"Just delivered," John. "I gave it to the plebe mail carrier. But I don't recall anything for you."

Pelham suddenly realized that it was only Friday. How could there be a letter? Had Clara written the day she left, her letter could not have been posted before Monday. He bounded up the stairs in high spirits.

"Alabama," shouted Custer from the room across the hall from Pelham and Rosser's. He appeared in the doorway with a musket and cleaning rod. "Can you spare some cleaning oil?"

"Sure. You know where it is."

Custer followed Pelham into his room, found the cleaning oil, and departed. Pelham sat at his desk and transcribed his notes into a coherent class schedule. When he finished, he weighed the semester workload and sensed he might actually have to apply himself.

Chapter Thirty-Two

Saturday, after the midday meal, McElheny knocked once upon the open door to Pelham and Rosser's room.

"Sir, mail for Mr. Pelham and Mr. Rosser."

"Well, well, well, beanhead," Rosser said, riding from his chair. "You've a letter for old Tom?"

"Yes, sir. As ordered, sir."

Rosser ripped open the envelope and removed the single sheet of vellum. After reading it, he glared at McElheny. "You find this amusing, Mr. McElheny?"

McElheny stood stoic, his eyes fixed on the wall behind Rosser. "No, sir."

Rosser handed the letter to Pelham, and he read it out aloud.

Dear Tom,

My feelings for you are beyond words. I cannot wait to see you again, to have you hold me the way you do, and until then I must nurse a broken heart. Take care, my gallant one, and know that I miss you more than life itself, and if you would, please be nice to the plebes, especially Mr. McElheny.

Love, Carol

It was nearly a minute before Pelham regained his composure. He gave McElheny a knowing wink and handed him an outgoing letter.

"I want you back in this room after taps," growled Rosser. "You understand me, beanhead? After taps!"

McElheny acknowledged he understood and crossed the hall to Custer's room.

The supper meal came and went, and Pelham ate little for reasons other than the food. Returning to his room, he opened the letter McElheny had delivered. It was from Clara, and he had yet to read it.

Rosser, in a stupor at the other end of the desk, cursed unintelligibly as he flipped the pages of one of a dozen textbooks he had picked up from the bookstore. "How the hell am I supposed to know what's in all of these books?" He closed the book and opened another.

Pelham sniffed the three scented pages of vellum from Clara. At the upper left-hand corner of each sheet, she had artfully drawn and colored a small flower, a different flower on each page. The date on her letter was August 27, 1860, and the subscript to the date was "Clermont College, Long Island, New York." As he read, he could hear her voice.

My dearest knight,

You will not believe the trip home and how we six jabbered on and on, each convinced we had a better time than the others. I, of course, know the truth, for you made it so! Ellie is nearly done with her letter to Henry, and the other girls are writing "thank-yous" to Chas, Nate, Tom, and Adelbert. They are all expecting replies! I quite marvel at the clever matches you made. Eva Taylor and I talked all the way back to New York City, and I think your Walter Kingsbury is a very lucky boy. You may find it curious, but I did not tell Eva about us, or about my visiting you in your camp. Thus, don't be surprised if she follows up on her friend, Sallie Dandridge. If she does, I will trust your feelings towards me.

I feel I should warn you on behalf of Chas Patterson that Alice Paine has not been entirely open with him, which is as I suspected. On the boat, she admitted her fondness for him, but also the uncertainty of her allegiance. She has been dating a local boy for some time—a rather timid man by your standards—but the two have history. While she is for now taken by your man from Arkansas, as time passes, I fear she will lean toward the "bird in the hand."

Pelham read on as Clara shared her first semester courses and her chagrin at not having been placed in the anatomy laboratory course she had requested. Her letter concluded with:

After receiving your return letter and knowing you have not changed in feelings towards me, I shall write Father to tell him of you, and to insist upon his blessing. I will also ask his support for the lab course and for channeling my applications to medical colleges. He is indeed "old school," but he is my father and loves me (so he says). With his influence, I can succeed, though I am not altogether optimistic and am prepared for rejection. Still, I shan't give up until every way is exhausted.

Miss Frampton has been somewhat encouraging, though still wanting me to pursue nursing.

In closing, dearest knight, I know God's providential hand is upon us for good. How else could one week mean so much and have so changed my life, and I pray yours. We can and will survive our separation, if we will it so, and you must know I do. Be careful, my love. There, I've said it with my pen. Know that my heart awaits your reply.

Your lady, Clara
P.S. I still grieve at the punishment you received on my account and pray for your forgiveness.

Pelham read Clara's letter a second time, this time with her locket in hand. He then withdrew from the desk drawer a sheet of embossed Academy vellum and dipped a quill pen in the inkwell. He wrote carefully, thoughtfully, not wanting to be anywhere other than where she needed him to be in this first letter. When he was finished, several wadded sheets on the floor testified to revisions. He blew on the last page, blotted the ink, and read what he had written.

September 1, 1860
West Point, New York

My Lady and Dearest Clara,

You need no forgiveness I assure you, and indeed had events not transpired as they did, I cannot know how we would be in the wondrous place we are. What you have prayed for has indeed occurred regarding my feelings, and in no way have they been diminished since your departure. Which is to say, my lady, you may be assured of my deepest affection and faithfulness. I appreciate your indulgence as I grow accustomed to the word you so bravely use, and which gives me such joy. For now, it seems to stick not only in my throat but in my pen.

Regarding Clara's medical pursuits, Pelham counseled against depending wholly upon her father and suggested she attempt contact with the practicing female doctor she had mentioned. She might even consider a face-to-face visit.

He was surprised by the call for lights out and folded the sheets of vellum and inserted them in an envelope. He then applied a hot wax seal. By the time Bentz sounded tattoo, both he and Rosser were in bed; and when the charge-of-quarters made his rounds, he was relieved to find Pelham and Rosser in bed.

Minutes later, there was a whisper at the door as McElheny reported to Rosser. Rosser slipped from his bed and proceeded to supervise McElheny's swim to Newburgh, the euphemism for lying on one's stomach and executing the crawl stroke until collapsing from fatigue.

CHAPTER THIRTY-THREE

PIEDMONT STATION, VIRGINIA
FRIDAY, JULY 19, 1861
TWO DAYS BEFORE THE FIRST BATTLE OF BULL RUN

Pelham was exhausted. The forced march from Winchester across the Shenandoah River, over the Blue Ridge Mountains, and south to Piedmont Station had taken thirty hours, and he had been in the saddle all but four of them. Behind General Jackson's brigade, Pelham's Alburtis battery was tucked between two regiments of Colonel Bartow's brigade. The brigades of General Bee and General Smith followed Bartow. When the long column headed southeast from Winchester, Pelham heard the retorts of small arms and Union artillery, assuming Colonel Stuart's cavalry was putting on a show for General Patterson's army. He prayed Patterson wouldn't be a factor in the ensuing battle.

The journey had begun on a sour note. For security reasons, General Johnston had instructed commanders at all levels not to divulge their true destination until well clear of Winchester. As a result, Pelham's men expressed displeasure at retreating in the face of Patterson's army. Their spirits did not improve until Pelham finally informed them that they would be reinforcing General Beauregard at Manassas Junction to repulse a much larger Union army pushing for Richmond.

For Pelham and the Alburtis battery, the first leg of the trip from Winchester had been the most grueling, crossing the Shenandoah River and climbing the Blue Ridge Mountains. Half a dozen wagon wheels had to be changed out, and he had been forced to put down three horses that gave out from muscling wagons and guns up the deeply rutted road.

During the brief stop in Paris after cresting the Blue Ridge, Stuart invited Pelham to share a smoke. The two talked of West Point and Benny Havens.

That morning, descending the eastern slope of the Blue Ridge and facing the sun, the heat, humidity, and parched earth tormented the long snake of humanity. While horse and wagon traveled easily enough, every soldier's nose and mouth were covered, eyes squinting into the unending dust.

On the final leg to Piedmont Station, Stuart rode for a time alongside Pelham, emphasizing the row they were in for and the importance of the Alburtis battery setting the example. Pelham's response had been direct—his men were ready and would do their duty.

Now at six o'clock the sun low on the horizon. Pelham sat slumped in the saddle watching the rail hands at Piedmont Station detach one locomotive from the string of Manassas Gap boxcars. The train had just returned from Manassas Junction after off-loading General Jackson and half of his brigade. As the locomotive took a spur to the other end of rolling stock to recouple and face the other direction, fifteen hundred troops advanced on the empty boxcars. When the cars were full, others climbed on top. After the train pulled away, more than seven thousand Confederates still awaited transport at Piedmont Station to Manassas.

The train, lunging forward and straining for speed, would average only four miles an hour, making the trip to Manassas Junction an eight-hour ordeal. Pelham wondered at the wisdom of putting infantry on trains that had a tendency to accidents and delays. He shared a further apprehension with most Southern troops: that the railroads held Northern sympathies. But none of that was his concern. Along with the cavalry, the guns would travel by road to Manassas Junction.

"Lieutenant, sir," Sergeant Miles told Pelham. "The horses are watered and the men ready."

Pelham returned the man's salute. "Very well, sergeant."

"Damn hot evening, sir," said the sergeant, passing a salt-encrusted handkerchief across his brow.

"Be glad you're not in one of those boxcars."

"Cannons, Lieutenant?" said the gunner, of the distant thunder.

"Possibly," Pelham said, knowing it was.

"We're going to us a have us a real battle. Aren't we, sir?"

"We are, Sergeant."

When the limbered battery and caissons took to the Manassas Road, they found its macadam surface eroded over long stretches, rattling the teeth of all not seated in a saddle. From time to time, Pelham trooped the length of the battery, making light and encouraging the men that soon they would be putting their talents to good use.

In the monotony of the journey, Pelham found himself reflecting on the reality of what was coming and wondering how his former roommate and other classmates were faring at Bull Run. He was told Rosser was with Ewell's brigade, commanding the First Company of Washington Artillery, a battery from New Orleans. He assumed Charlie Ball and Henry Farley, too, were commanding other artillery pieces somewhere along Bull Run.

Chapter Thirty-Four

Ten Months Earlier
West Point, New York
First Semester, 1860

Monday morning, September 3, Pelham awoke to the sound of reveille and rain pinging against the window, thankful for a warm bed and an uninterrupted night's sleep. Rosser announced himself with a moan from the next alcove. The two sat up in bed, their feet touching the floor at the same time. As room orderly for the week, Pelham got up and lit the gas lamp.

The two donned uniforms, rain capes, and caps, and joined the rumble of feet down the stairs, across the stoops, and out onto the dark, wet quadrangle of Central Area.

"Our last first day, Tom," Pelham whispered to Rosser as water dripped off the bill of his forage cap.

Breakfast in the mess hall was quiet, the mood of the Corps sullen in anticipation of academics. Rosser buttered a biscuit, drenched it with Sammy, and ate it quietly, absorbed in his thoughts.

Pelham sipped black coffee and considered his roommate, who was neither dumb nor slow. In fact, Rosser was a quick study of whatever was placed in front of him. Pelham couldn't understand why Rosser didn't bury the trauma of arriving at West Point with only four years of formal education. He had done the right thing, arriving six months earlier than anyone else to get tutored for the entrance examinations, and the investment had paid off. He had passed and was a member of the class. Yet the self-esteem so evident in every other aspect of Rosser's life did not extend to academics. In Rosser's mind, every new academic year would be his last, and every September he prepared for dismissal. Yet come every June, he was still around. At the end of the previous year, he had climbed from the bottom of the class to forty-second out of fifty.

Pelham, thirty-fourth in the class, waited patiently for what he knew would come from Rosser.

"John, just shoot me," Rosser said, his elbows on the table, his head in his hands.

"Cheer up. We have Mahan class first. You'll be at your sharpest." When they returned to the barracks, the rain was heavier, and the slapping wind sent it pinging against the window. It occurred to Pelham that it had rained the first day of every academic year. It had ushered in plebe year's algebra, geometry, trigonometry, English, literature, fundamental tactics, and fencing. It had announced Fourth Class year and more math, differential and integral calculus, more English, more literature, first-year French, artillery and infantry tactics, use of small arms, and more fencing. Third Class year, it had served up physics, astronomy, the final year of French, the only year of Spanish, the first year of drawing, more artillery and cavalry tactics, equitation, and still more fencing. And last year, in a deluge that lasted a week, it announced chemistry, the final year of drawing, philosophy and ethics, advanced cavalry, artillery and infantry tactics, advanced equitation, frontier outpost service, and, as always, more fencing.

Pelham failed to notice that the rain was only a drizzle when he made his way to the academic building and Professor Mahan's classroom, which on Mondays, Wednesdays, and Fridays would be filled with the concepts and formulas of civil engineering, and on Tuesdays and Thursdays with instruction in military science and the art of warfare.

Bentz's bugle call announced five minutes until class, and Pelham took a seat in the back row, where Rosser soon joined him. The two of them watched the clock on the wall, and at precisely eight o'clock the tiny form of Professor Mahan, his chin decorated with a white goatee, marched through the door to the front of the class.

Mahan opened his briefcase. "Attendance report, please."

Chas Patterson, the section leader, reported that all were present. "Welcome, gentlemen, to civil engineering. I know you are excited to be here, to have made it this far." Mahan's attempt at humor was lost on Rosser. "This course will be the crowning accomplishment of your academic education, and I wish all of you the wisdom and commitment necessary to arrive safely at its end." The dean's eyes narrowed. "For I assure you, luck will have nothing to do with it."

Rosser nudged Pelham. "I'm dead."

Mahan picked up a reference book. "Open your text, *Moseley's Mechanics of Engineering,* to the table of contents."

Pelham's attempts to console Rosser on the way to the ordnance laboratory below the north end of the Plain fell on deaf ears.

"Gentlemen, may I join you?" Captain James Benton, the ordnance instructor, asked, catching up with them.

"Certainly, sir," said Pelham.

"The sun's out, boys," Benton said. "An omen?"

Rosser seemed buoyed by the thought, and as Benton briefly described what they could expect in his class, Rosser's spirits improved. Ordnance, he could get his arms around. He confided to Benton that he was eager to learn what was needed to produce the various kinds of munitions for soldiering, and to improve his skill with the array of coastal guns that comprised the Academy's shore battery.

The midday meal was followed by mineralogy and geology, taught by Professor Henry Kendrick, popularly known as "Old Hank." Kendrick had knack for engaging a class and bringing the inanimate to life.

In the hallway after Kendrick's class, Pelham encountered Robert Weir, the Academy's drawing professor, and was greeted by him.

"Good day to you, Mr. Pelham." Weir put a fatherly hand on Pelham's shoulder. "Your final year, young man, and I believe you will survive despite my efforts."

Pelham laughed. "I continue to sketch, sir. What you teach is important, and I will endeavor to improve."

"To your credit, Mr. Pelham, your drawings have always been accurate. It was your technique that I took issue with. Seems I want all of you to be fine artists. But we all have our own style, don't we? And you have yours."

From Kendrick's classroom, Pelham walked the length of the second-floor hall to the tactics classroom for the first in a sequence of classes on advanced cavalry tactics taught by Lieutenant Lee.

The next day Pelham and Rosser again sat on the back row in Professor Mahan's classroom. For his military science class, the otherwise dour Mahan displayed an entirely different persona, his eyes fairly twinkling. "Gentlemen, what is the Academy if not a crucible for shaping military leaders? You have come a long way through a maze of training that has brought you to this day. Beginning today, you will venture outside your own time in history. We will look back at the great captains of the past. Learn from them and examine their victories and defeats. You will be challenged to enter the minds of these great men and to suffer with them through their campaigns, to judge them on how well they assessed situations, the enemy, and the terrain so that you might carry their strengths with you when you leave this cloistered nest."

Pelham looked forward to the class. Indeed, every First Classman did. Even Rosser. Mahan promised that the class, which he had come to call Military Art, would connect the seemingly disjointed military experiences of the past four years into a seamless whole.

"You have a legacy to follow, don't you?" said Mahan. "Graduates of West Point distinguished themselves most handsomely in the war with Mexico. Whether it was justified or not—that being a different and political thing. What was it that Winfield Scott said, which Robert E. Lee required every plebe to memorize, and which is still required of plebes today?"

Pelham was surprised to see Rosser's hand shoot up in the air.

"In the back, there," said Mahan.

"Sir, that would be General Winfield Scott's Fixed Opinion. He said, 'I give it as my fixed opinion, that but for our graduated cadets, the war between the United States and Mexico might, and probably would have lasted some four or five years, with, in its first half, more defeats than victories falling to our share; whereas, in less than two campaigns, we conquered a great country and a peace, without the loss of a single battle or skirmish.'"

Rosser's flawless recitation drew disingenuous approbation from his classmates.

"You, sir," Professor Mahan said, "are either very sharp or were a plebe the upperclassmen picked on quite regularly."

The room rocked with laughter.

The next class was the popular practical military engineering class taught by First Lieutenant James Duane, in which earthworks, pontoon bridging, and military defenses would be studied. The class was followed by the midday meal, and in turn by a curiously combined class entitled "Law and Literature," taught by Professor and Reverend John French. Pelham struggled to stay awake as French introduced notes on the rules and articles of war and the text by DeHart on courts-martial.

The day concluded with what Pelham considered a crucially important study. A tactics class taught by Lieutenant Colonel Hardee, in which he introduced the combined use of arms—infantry, cavalry, and artillery—in what he called "modern warfare." Pelham, like the rest of the Corps, would miss Hardee, and wondered about his replacement, Lieutenant Colonel John Reynolds, who was to succeed him in a week.

Saturday morning from eight until ten o'clock was more practical military engineering with Captain Duane, followed by fencing, a two-hour course that involved the entire First Class and taught in the expansive basement of the academic building. Pelham and the rest of the class arrived with their fencing foils and cavalry straight sabers, and were greeted by Mr. Antoni Lorentz, the Academy's long-time master of the sword. The slim, gaunt-faced man, fully sixty years old, wore fencing pads and directed the cadets to carts that held fencing pads and masks.

Properly protected, the cadets configured themselves in long rows, with ample room between each of them. They faced Lorentz, who slapped his foil against an open hand and commanded, "Starting position!"

Each cadet assumed the *en garde* position, and for ten minutes responded to well-known fencing commands, their individual performances criticized and corrected by Lorentz.

"That will have to do for now," Lorentz said with more than a hint of disappointment. "To your seats, please."

The class took to a set of bleachers along the wall.

Lorentz eyed the class, his hands behind his back. "Your final year, yes?" His thick Italian accent seemed to drip from his tongue. "And have we not spent many enjoyable hours together these past four years?"

Pelham thought otherwise.

"This year, we should be better with the blade. Don't you agree?"

No one cared to speculate.

"Mr. Pelham, you are the best swordsman in your class. Will you please join me?"

Lorentz's question was not a request, and this was not the first time Pelham found himself the object lesson. Seated on the top row, he dropped down from the bleachers.

"Let us see what we remember, Mr. Pelham."

Lorentz began slowly, parrying Pelham's thrusts and allowing Pelham to easily parry his.

After a minute, in a voice all could hear, Lorentz asked Pelham, "Have you ever stuck or cut a man with a blade, Mr. Pelham?"

Pelham awkwardly parried a move he had not seen before. "No, sir."

"It is different than anything you might expect." Lorentz glanced at the class as he said this. And in that instant Pelham lunged for the instructor's heart. Without even looking, Lorentz flicked Pelham's blade aside with his own, and against Pelham's momentum blunted the tip of his blade into the padding over Pelham's heart.

The class emitted a collective gasp.

The point of the blade, though blunt, sharply stung Pelham's chest.

Lorentz recovered his foil and nodded to Pelham. "One more time, please."

As before, the match had the appearance of parity, until Lorentz again turned his attention from Pelham to the class. "Gentlemen, can a headless enemy continue to fight?"

Before anyone could answer, Lorentz executed a combination of moves that culminated in a horizontal slash that spanked the padding around Pelham's neck.

The class was no less stunned than before.

"Thank you, Mr. Pelham. You may take your seat."

Pelham removed his mask, and Chambliss and Kirby made room for him on the front row.

"Private Norris," Lorentz called out, "if you please!" A blue-uniformed soldier pushed a tall canvass-covered cart through a set of double doors. He rolled the cart across the fencing room to a point in front of the bleachers.

"What is that smell?" Rosser said, making a face.

"Gentlemen," Lorentz began, "to date you have thrust your blunted blades into the air, tickled each other's padding, and stuck your sabers into sawdust dummies. I suggest that in war there are no dummies.

Your adversary, your enemy, young or old, will be no different than you. He will be keenly aware of your intent since it will be his own. With every fiber of his being he will endeavor to run you through with his own brand of steel. With these long knives"—Lorentz lovingly brandished his saber— "you will fight as men have fought since the dawn of time. You will stab and slash human flesh and bone until it is no longer a threat to you, or else be so stabbed and slashed that you are no longer a threat."

Lorentz nodded to the soldier to remove the canvas cover.

"Holy moly—" Rosser gasped.

From atop a seven-foot-tall tripod, hooks embedded in the flesh of its shoulders, the carcass of an enormous hog, the height of a man, hung—its pink eyes staring blankly at a world it no longer graced.

Lorentz allowed the image to set in.

"Have you ever wondered what it would feel like to really use your saber? To pierce flesh?" A faint smile crossed his face. "Well, this is your chance to find out. A volunteer, please."

No one volunteered.

"Come now. This is your chance," teased Lorentz.

Pelham stood up and, without a word, retrieved his dragoon saber. He glanced at Lorentz, who gestured to the carcass. Pelham approached the carcass, set his feet, and ran his saber through the hog's chest, the blade crunching through bone, the tip appearing out the backside of the animal.

Lorentz smiled. "Pretending it was me, Mr. Pelham?"

Chapter Thirty-Five

On September 10, following the Monday afternoon parade in honor of Lieutenant Colonel Hardee's departure and the arrival of Lieutenant Colonel John Reynolds, and after another disappointing supper, Pelham headed for the First-Class Club. The passage of an entire week of academics had removed the uncertainty of what the first semester courses would impose. It was no more than he had expected and would not overburden the time he wanted for himself. That he was stripped of his officer rank had the benefit that he was no longer responsible for the discipline and academic performance of a platoon of twenty-four men.

Earlier in the day, he had rejoiced with Rosser over a letter from Carol Hill. While the girl had not expressed quite the sentiment McElheny had, Rosser had reason to feel whole and confident in his game. The others too had received letters: du Pont from Ellie Lawson, Chambliss from Jessica Danford, Ames from Rebecca Astor, and Patterson from Alice Paine. Knowing what he did, Pelham asked Patterson about Alice Paine, and Patterson replied candidly, saying that she still seemed to be in his camp, which suited him, since he had no better pursuits. A letter from Eva Taylor to Walter Kingsbury had mended the broken man to such a degree that Pelham and the others found it hard to pass more than a few minutes with him.

When Pelham bounded up the steps to the First-Class Club, he was buoyed by the expectation of another letter from Clara. Inside the First-Class Club, there was lively discussion in response to the news at supper that congressional elections for both Maine and Rhode Island had gone Republican. The first person he encountered was Emory Upton.

"Gloating?" Pelham asked.

"Not necessary," said Upton.

Chambliss, Patterson, and du Pont stood looking at a map of the nation.

"There are a total of three hundred and three electoral votes at stake in the election," Chambliss said. "Maine and Rhode Island together account for only ten votes. It's Pennsylvania with twenty-seven votes and Indiana with thirteen that we'll need, and they vote in two weeks."

Patterson shook his head. "Even so, Pennsylvania and Indiana won't help if we can't settle on a compromise candidate."

"True enough," admitted du Pont with a shrug, "but which one do you pick—John Breckinridge, Stephen Douglas, or John Bell?"

"Douglas has to step down," Patterson insisted. "He's the bane of the South. And if he does, Bell might. And he should because he doesn't have a chance. That would leave Breckinridge, who, as Buchanan's vice president, at least has name recognition. He could win."

"I don't see it happening, Chas," Adelbert Ames said, drawn to the discussion. "Even if Douglas steps down, Missouri won't go with Breckinridge because of his slavery stance. Same for Delaware."

Du Pont wasn't so sure about Delaware but remained silent.

Ames turned to Upton. "Emory, you must be feeling rather cocky about now."

Upton's response surprised Pelham. "The people will vote what they know or think they know. And the sad thing is that they'll vote emotions fired by party-line half-truths, not really understanding the issues."

"I have to echo Emory," du Pont said. "A lot of gnashing of teeth, but little constructive dialogue. In the South, fire-eaters have the platform they want. In the North, abolitionists headline the papers."

Pelham remained silent on the subject and returned to the barracks to find Rosser penning a letter.

"Carol?"

"Nope—Sam Houston."

"The Texas governor?"

"He got me my appointment, John. I might as well get his take on what to do if Texas secedes."

Chapter Thirty-Six

By the third week of September, the Corps was fully immersed in academics, and the election had taken a back seat. Every day all were graded in every subject, a legacy of Sylvanus Thayer. Grades were on a three-point scale, with 3.0 a perfect grade and 2.0 a minimum passing grade. Every Friday afternoon Pelham, Rosser, and the rest of the Corps made the pilgrimage to the sally port to see the postings of the latest grades.

Rosser, who had started out better than he had expected in Mahan's civil engineering class and had earned a 2.2 grade point after two weeks, was devastated by the grades of the past week. He'd been reduced to a deficient 1.9 grade point. His cheerful disposition and sense of humor were the casualties of the lost three-tenths. Compounding his anxiety, a second letter from Carol Hill, fully ten pages long, suggested a real relationship, a thing he had hoped for and often discussed with Pelham. But that she was proving such a prolific writer presented a problem. It forced him to make a decision that surprised even Pelham. He presented Pelham with a one-page return letter. In it, he stated simply that he thought it best, in light of his academic difficulties, not to pursue an ongoing correspondence until he could get a handle on his grades. It was of little consolation to Rosser that Pelham found not a single thing in the letter to edit.

Wednesday, September 19th, Rosser and Pelham fell into formation for the midday meal, waiting on Paddy O'Rorke's attendance reports.

"Hey, Tom, did you hear the one about the mess hall cook?" Custer said in ranks, wanting to raise Rosser's spirits.

Rosser didn't answer.

"Seems a cadet told the cook that his soup was terrible. So, the cook says, 'Look, soldier, I cooked for Winfield Scott throughout the

Mexican War and was wounded three times.' The cadet comes back and says, 'Hell, I'm surprised he didn't kill you.'"

The cadet in front of Custer nearly doubled over with laughter.

Rosser growled, "Is that you, McElheny?"

The cadet stopped laughing. "Yes, sir."

"About-face, McElheny."

McElheny turned about.

"You think Mr. Custer's joke was funny?"

"Yes, sir."

"Are plebes permitted to laugh in ranks?"

"No, sir."

"Come to my room after taps."

"Yes, sir."

That night after taps, McElheny reported as ordered to Rosser, and Rosser closed the door behind him. The gas lamp dimly lit the room, and the window drapes were pinned to hide the light from the outside.

Rosser rubbed his chin. "Mr. McElheny, are we in agreement that you have a laughing problem?"

"Yes, sir," said McElheny.

"Then you'll be pleased to know there is a cure for it."

McElheny said nothing.

Rosser positioned his chair in the middle of the room.

"Stand up on the chair, McElheny."

McElheny complied.

"Are you comfortable?"

"Yes, sir."

Rosser handed McElheny a duffel bag. "Put the bag over your head, McElheny."

"Sir?"

"The duffel bag—put it over your head."

McElheny complied.

"Still comfortable?"

"Yes, sir."

"Dark in there?"

"Yes, sir."

"I want you to repeat after me, ha-ha, ho-ho, hee-hee; ha-ha, ho-ho, hee-hee. And I don't want you to stop until I tell you to stop. Is that understood?"

"Yes, sir."

In a surprisingly strong baritone voice and easy meter, McElheny repeated the words over and over. "Ha-ha, ho-ho, hee-hee. Ha-ha, ho-ho, hee-hee." Pelham passively observing the proceedings from his chair.

After a few minutes, Rosser said, "All right, McElheny. Now I want you to begin double-timing in place on the chair."

McElheny complied, initially with difficulty, lifting and dropping his feet on the chair and barking, "Ha-ha, ho-ho, hee-hee."

"McElheny, I'm going to assume that you enjoy a good cigar," Rosser said, having already puffed one to a good burn.

Smoke soon filled the bag that covered McElheny's head, as McElheny continued to double-time and repeat, "Ha-ha, ho-ho, hee-hee."

McElheny's delivery began to weaken.

"I can't hear you, Mr. McElheny," growled Rosser.

McElheny started coughing. He teetered on the chair but righted himself.

Suddenly, the duffel bag listed to an unrecoverable angle, and Pelham was on his feet in time to help Rosser catch the plebe.

Rosser removed the duffel bag and sat McElheny on the chair.

"You okay, McElheny?" Rosser asked.

McElheny coughed and gasped for air, then nodded.

"Feeling better?"

After regaining his composure, McElheny asked, "Sir, should I put the bag back on?"

Pelham had to bite his lip.

"Well, it depends, Mr. McElheny." Rosser circled the plebe. "Do you still feel like laughing?"

McElheny, his face wet with perspiration and his eyes blood shot, said, "No, sir."

"Then hallelujah and praise God, McElheny. You're cured!"

Chapter Thirty-Seven

The next day, Pelham finally received the letter he had been expecting from his father in response to the one he had sent a month earlier. His father apologized for his tardiness, explaining that he had wanted to observe the overseer, Butch Jansonne, to see if he was, in fact, stepping out of line. He suspected Jansonne got wind of his intentions, for the man was nearly angelic for almost three weeks. But returning home from a house call, the senior Pelham caught the overseer in the act of culling out the man Amos from the picking line and whipping him beyond any sense of necessity. Pelham's temper flared as he read on. *I called Jansonne to account and gave him strict notice that if I ever caught him abusing one of the blacks, I would discharge him on the spot.*

The warning enraged Pelham, for the overseer had but to carefully pick his times for brutality. The man held absolute power over the slaves, and unless he was actually caught in a condemning act by a responsible white, the overseer's word in a court of law would take precedence over the testimony of any slave.

Late that night, Pelham prayed for the slave family, for Willie and Samuel specifically. He prayed that Jansonne would be found out and discharged before anyone was seriously injured—or worse. After his petitions, he thanked God for the one piece of very good news in his father's letter. Samuel and fifteen-year-old Ora were to be a couple.

After class that day, Pelham noticed Rosser lifting the ash grate from the fireplace. He removed a tin cigar box and removed the lid. He then extracted something from his pocket and put it in the box.

"What's that all about?" Pelham asked Rosser.

Rosser crossed the room and let Pelham look inside the box.

"A rat?" said Pelham.

"Not a rat, John. A mouse. There's a difference." Rosser retrieved the tiny creature and stroked the animal's fur as it sniffed at his thumb. "This morning when I swept the room, he was in the corner looking up at me. He didn't run—just stared me down."

Rosser crumbled a sliver of stale bread in his fingers, producing a small pile of crumbs in the tin box. He returned the creature to the box, which he had fitted with tiny air holes.

Pelham watched the creature sniff the bread, eat a crumb, then another, and then the entire pile.

"He's got a good appetite," Rosser said with pride.

"Has he a name?"

Rosser considered and said, "Mouse."

"Just Mouse?"

Rosser reconsidered. "No. Mr. Mouse. Yes, that's his name. Mr. Mouse. And see, John, he looks like you and me."

"Like us?"

"Yeah. All gray." Rosser returned mouse and box to the fireplace.

The following Monday after supper, Pelham listened passively to members of the Dialectic Society debate the debate. A small faction wanted to steer clear of politics, but the majority were in favor of some sort of relevant issue. What it might be ranged from debating the right of women to vote, to party platforms, to adopting what Pelham had suggested in the previous meeting. It was Adelbert Ames who made the argument that debating party platforms was futile as there were four parties, the Northern Democrats, Southern Democrats, Republicans, and Constitutional Union. With Pelham's topic, Ames reasoned, there at least was clear relevance and two sides to the argument. A state either had a right to secede or didn't. Ames eventually prevailed on the group with a motion for Pelham's topic, and it carried by the needed majority, whether women should be given the right to vote adopted as a fallback topic.

Choosing the debate topic proved easier than choosing the debaters. At one point there were six names under consideration, including Pelham's, which he immediately withdrew since he intended to be the moderator. The chief obstacle to agreement was the complaint that the prospective debaters held views that were too similar. The resulting debate would be skewed to one side; specifically, the side of a state having the right to secede.

Henry du Pont finally offered an opinion that surprised Pelham. "I think our best choice for debating that a state does not have the right to secede is Emory Upton."

The mere mention of Upton's name seemed to drop the temperature in the room, but Ames immediately supported du Pont. "Henry's right. Emory is nearest to a true Republican and an independent thinker."

If Ames expected an "amen," he didn't receive it. Still, no one argued the point.

"Providing," Ames continued, "that the man doesn't go to meddling, which I sense he won't. Am I right, Emory?"

Upton nodded.

"And," Ames said, "if I may be so bold as to offer up his opponent, who better to espouse the opposing position than our own Henry du Pont?"

Du Pont could not have been more surprised or in disagreement. "Me?" His name hadn't even come up in discussion. "No, not me. I am a Democrat, but I am not a secessionist."

"I didn't say you were," said Ames. "But you are Upton's equal as an advocate in considering an issue and defending it." Ames addressed the broader group. "If we were to offer up a fire-eater, and I mean them no offense, John wouldn't stand a snowball's chance of getting the superintendent to go along with us."

Pelham gave Ames a nod of thanks and turned to Upton. "Are you agreeable, Emory?"

Upton said he was.

"Henry?"

Clearly ill at ease, du Pont acquiesced.

"Don't panic, Henry, there is still the vote." Pelham recapped the situation. "We now have du Pont and Upton in the mix with the others. Are there any other names we should consider?"

There were rumblings, but no additional names were mentioned.

"We'll do a secret ballot, each man writing down his choice of debaters for and against secession, including write-ins."

O'Rorke distributed small slips of paper to each member of the society, gave the members time to make their choices, and then collected the slips. He excused himself to a corner of the room and tallied the votes. He returned to the group, his face unreadable, and announced, "To debate that a state has the right to secede from the Union, we have by large majority, decided for Henry du Pont."

Of little consolation to du Pont, he was roundly applauded.

"To debate that a state does not have the right to secede from the Union," O'Rorke said, "We have decided on Emory Upton by a margin of one vote."

A short ponderous silence overshadowed the room until Pelham started clapping, joined by Ames.

"Now that wasn't so hard, was it?" Pelham said. "And now that we have our debaters, it is up to me to earn my keep. I will sugar this as best I can and present it to the superintendent tomorrow, assuming I can get in to see him, and then report back to you. If he doesn't agree with our first choice, I'll offer up universal suffrage, and we'll pick new debaters."

The group agreed unanimously.

"Whatever Delafield's decision," Pelham added, "we'll want to get the word out and give our debaters at least two weeks to prepare." He glanced at a calendar on the wall. "Shall we strike for October 27, a Saturday, and request the academic building lecture hall as the venue for debate?"

Chapter Thirty-Eight

On Friday morning, after Professor Mahan's class on Alexander the Great, Pelham visited post headquarters and made an appointment to meet with the superintendent following Lieutenant Colonel Reynolds' afternoon tactics class.

Shortly after five o'clock, he returned to the superintendent's office.

"I'll let the colonel know you are here, Mr. Pelham," said the superintendent's aide.

A minute later Pelham stood inside the superintendent's office. "Sir, Cadet Pelham reporting."

Colonel Delafield, in apparent good humor, returned Pelham's salute and gestured for him to take a seat. "What brings you to my office, Mr. Pelham?"

Pelham began the pitch he had rehearsed a dozen times. "Sir, as president of the Dialectic Society, I wanted to share with you the main program we have decided upon for the fall semester."

Delafield nodded.

"Sir, we want to host a debate that is timely to the upcoming presidential election."

"A political debate?" The colonel's tone was less than encouraging.

"Exactly, sir."

"Mr. Pelham, you should know my policy that, for good reason, I believe it best to avoid public discussion of political issues within the Corps."

"Yes, sir, I am aware of your position on political matters. But if I may ... I don't understand why?"

Delafield eyed Pelham. He could have easily dismissed him without an explanation. "Mr. Pelham, you are conscious of the delicate nature of the national scene, and I trust you appreciate the need to safeguard an environment in which we can accomplish our mission to train and educate our country's leaders. I cannot sanction anything that would fuel more rancor or aggression than is already evident in the Corps."

"Understood, sir, and I agree that quite vocal camps have formed, as I suspect they have in your academic and tactical departments."

Surprised by Pelham's observation, Delafield nodded in agreement. "So, doesn't that go to my point?"

"Sir, if I may, I think it profits little for us to ignore what is happening around us. We of the Corps are mature men in a course of instruction and a profession of arms that demands that we use the gift between our ears."

"You are being trained to follow orders and lead, Mr. Pelham." Delafield's tone was terse.

"Of course, sir, but how are we to lead without independent thought? Our intention with the debate is only to inform those in attendance about an important issue, so that all might better see the opposing viewpoints, sift fact from fiction, and decide for themselves."

"What is it you want to debate, Mr. Pelham?" Delafield asked.

Pelham responded without hesitation, "Sir, whether a state has the right to secede from the Union."

Delafield was certain he had misheard. "Come, again."

Pelham repeated himself.

"Mr. Pelham, are you purposely trying my patience? Do you actually think I would sanction talk of secession, even in the guise of a dialectic debate?"

"Sir, the point of the debate would not be to argue whether states should secede, but whether there is a legitimate basis in law for their doing so. We believe, sir, that there is a difference."

Delafield pressed the tips of his fingers together. "I see no difference, young man."

"Sir, sectionalist talk is already rampant behind closed doors and in cliques that undermine our unity. The debate, at the very least, will place the arguments squarely on the table."

"To what benefit?" Delafield asked.

"Sir, to the end we have what the founders fought for, free speech and expression of opinion. The debate might even quench some of the anarchical fires already ablaze."

Delafield drew in a deep breath and rapped his desk with a pen. "You know full well, it's about slavery. There'd be no talk of secession if slavery were allowed in the territories."

"I don't doubt that sir," Pelham conceded. "Yet I don't see how it is healthy to ignore an argument that goes to the broader question of states' rights."

"Ah!" Delafield wagged his finger. "That's the debate, isn't it? States' rights."

Pelham repressed an urge to smile. "Sir, why not give opportunity for reasoned debate so that both camps, Unionists and states' rights advocates, can hear what the other has to say? I don't see how an even-handed debate, and I assure you it will be so, will do harm. Rather, I think it might take much of the sting out of the air."

Delafield pulled at his whiskers.

"Sir," Pelham said, "if you agree, the debate will be held in the academic building lecture hall on Saturday, October 27. It would be open to the Corps and anyone else who might want to attend."

"I suspect it would be well attended," Delafield said. "And your debaters?"

"Henry du Pont, for a state's right to secede."

Pelham perceived a slight nod from Delafield.

"And for the opposing argument—Emory Upton." Pelham chastised himself for hesitating.

The superintendent's eyes narrowed. "The dueling abolitionist?"

"He's an excellent debater, sir," Pelham said in Upton's defense. "I admit the man has personal views beyond the issue, but he has assured me that he will not stray beyond the bounds of the debate. He understands that to do so would cost him the debate and an otherwise improved standing within the Corps."

Delafield continued to pull at his whiskers. "What assurance do I have the debate won't become something ugly?"

Pelham straightened himself. "I will be its moderator, sir."

That evening at supper Pelham informed members of the Dialectic Society that the debate was on and that he would call a meeting to consider how best to publicize the event. With one exception, the news was well received. Henry du Pont, convinced more than ever that he was miscast, appealed to be replaced, but to no avail. Pelham's ear was deaf to altering anything that had formed the basis upon which Delafield had granted approval.

Returning to the barracks, Pelham found Rosser humming "Three Blind Mice." He removed the grate from the fireplace and retrieved his pet. It had been nearly two weeks since the arrival of Mr. Mouse, and the creature had become a celebrity, receiving numerous visitors bearing morsels of cheese or crumbs of bread. Rosser had placed McElheny in charge of D Company's plebes to ensure that the tin box was kept clean and Mr. Mouse's water was changed on a daily basis.

"Mr. Mouse," Rosser said, his voice shrill and squeaky. "I've an edible for you." He removed the box lid and dropped a tiny piece of cheddar cheese inside and inquired how Mr. Mouse's day was.

Pelham found Rosser's communications with Mr. Mouse irritating but said nothing.

"C'mon little fella, it's your favorite." Rosser prodded the creature with his finger. "Up and at 'em, little buddy. Time to wake up."

Pelham flipped another page in Kendrick's geology text.

"John!" Rosser placed the tin box in front of Pelham and prodded the creature. "I think Mr. Mouse is—"

Pelham finished the sentence.

Rosser nudged the creature. "But I don't understand."

In truth, Pelham could see that the mouse, while tiny by most standards, was enormous for its size, and for several days had moved about on its stomach. That it had eaten itself to death was not what Rosser needed to hear, so in sympathy Pelham offered, "Critters like these have very short life spans, Tom. He likely died of old age."

"You think?"

Rosser seemed much relieved.

A knock at the door was followed by the appearance of McElheny. "Sir, a letter for Mr. Pelham."

"A bit late for mail, isn't it, Mr. McElheny?"

"Sir, Mr. Wiggins got yours by mistake, and he asked that I run it up."

"Then, I thank you," said Pelham, noticing that the letter was from Clara. "Thank you very much, indeed."

Before McElheny could retreat, Rosser blocked the door. "Mr. McElheny?"

"Sir?" McElheny stood erect, numbing himself to whatever was to follow.

"You remember Mr. Mouse, don't you?" Rosser showed McElheny the tin box.

"Yes, sir."

"Mr. Mouse is no longer with us."

"Yes, sir," McElheny said, eyeing the deceased. "I'm sorry, sir. My condolences."

"Yes. Thank you, McElheny. That means a lot to me."

McElheny waited in silence. "Sir … is there something else?"

The plebe's voice seemed to steady Rosser.

"Yes … yes, there is."

McElheny waited to hear it, but Rosser's mind seemed elsewhere. "Mr. Rosser, sir?"

Rosser put the lid on the tin box. "Sorry, McElheny. I was just … Do you mind if I impose on you?"

"Sir?"

"Would you make the final arrangements for Mr. Mouse?"

McElheny blinked in silence.

"And, if you would, maybe some appropriate remarks on his behalf—about the deceased?"

Pelham was about to split.

Betraying no emotion, McElheny said, "Certainly, sir. I'll see to it straightaway and let you know the particulars as soon as they are known."

Chapter Thirty-Nine

Friday, October 5, a dark cloud descended over a majority of the Corps. The results were in for Pennsylvania and Indiana. Both had gone Republican, and a cursory examination of the Electoral College showed that Lincoln had more than enough votes to secure the presidency. Nothing could change the outcome, not even the adoption of a compromise candidate by the Democrats. Knowing this, Pelham was even more convinced of the need for the debate. That evening he called a meeting of the society, at which it was agreed that an announcement of the debate would be prepared and posted on each company bulletin board, as well as distributed to the tactical and academic departments.

That evening, before he cracked a book, Pelham opened Clara's fifth letter in as many weeks, to find her flowered illustrations larger and more colorful. She had been admitted to the human anatomy course at Columbia University, despite the fact that she had missed the first four classes. Additionally, she had written to Dr. Elizabeth Blackwell and had received a warm reply from the country's first female doctor. Dr. Blackwell was encouraging in her letter, and informed Clara that she was not the only one attempting the hard climb. The doctor added that she would both welcome a visit and do whatever she could to help Clara secure acceptance to a reputable college. On her father's front, Clara had written him about her intention to become a doctor and to curry his support, but she had not yet broached the subject of the man from Alabama. She suggested that her father might choke on more than one pill at a time. Pelham smiled. For her to have done otherwise would have been foolish.

Her next paragraph, a short one, was for the benefit of Chas Patterson, whose Alice Paine was wavering. The previous Saturday and

Sunday, she had been observed in the company of her erstwhile lawyer friend.

The last of Clara's letter was a confession that, were she able to vote, she would vote for Lincoln. Her defense was the desire for change that she believed Lincoln represented. While not detailing the change she expected, she said that Lincoln was an independent mind, not tainted by the games in Washington and might bring a needed freshness and energy to the country.

Despite a paper due the next day in Professor French's law class, Pelham spent the best part of the evening replying to Clara's letter, urging her to visit Dr. Blackwell as soon as she could, supporting her decision to remain mum about their relationship until her father had digested his first pill, promising to soften the blow for Patterson, and honoring her right to vote as she saw fit—were she able to vote. He also wrote that she could rest easy, that Eva Taylor had communicated through Kingsbury the news that another man was presently courting Sallie Dandridge.

Chapter Forty

News of the funeral for Mr. Mouse spread throughout the Corps, and on Sunday, October 7, after the midday meal, nearly all of D Company, a number of other upperclassmen, and all of McElheny's classmates showed up at the riding hall in full dress gray to pay their final respects. The arrangements were orchestrated by McElheny, and the scene in the riding hall was one of somber reverence. In the middle of the enormous hall, fifty chairs were arranged in five rows. In front of the chairs was a lectern, and to the right of the lectern, a flat waist-high dolly curtained with black crepe.

McElheny stood where he could greet those who arrived and direct them to their seats. His demeanor of deference and piety was contagious and adopted by all in attendance. Upper classmen were ushered to seats, and those of the plebe class stood in a horseshoe around the upper classes.

By the time Rosser and Pelham arrived, all but the two chairs reserved for them had been taken.

"A sad day, Mr. McElheny," Pelham observed, as McElheny ushered them to the front row.

"Sir, perhaps you and Mr. Rosser would care to put on one of these." McElheny offered them each a black armband.

"Of course." Pelham's tone was reverent.

All seated, the silence and mood of the proceeding would have honored the passing of a head of state.

McElheny, with hands folded in front of his chest, approached the lectern, looked upon his audience, and cleared his throat.

Pelham fought for composure.

"My dear friends, it occurs to me that before we begin the service, I should ask Mr. Mouse's guardian, Mr. Thomas Rosser, if he would like to have a viewing of the open casket following the service."

Rosser, who himself was struggling for composure, whispered to Pelham, "What casket?"

"Mr. Rosser, sir?" McElheny repeated.

Rosser looked up. "Well, sure. I think we'd all like to see Mr. Mouse one last time."

"Very good, sir." McElheny nodded solemnly.

On cue, a door at the side of the riding hall opened, and through it walked eight of McElheny's D Company classmates, four on either side of a full-size casket, each plebe wearing a black armband. The funeral procession moved slowly and in lockstep across the hall. With synchronized movements the pallbearers placed the closed casket on the dolly, and then assumed a position of parade rest behind the casket.

"And, Mr. Rosser," McElheny said, "I understand that you have requested that Mr. Mouse be cremated after this service, and his ashes scattered over the Hudson."

Rosser didn't recall saying so, but said, "Yes. He would have liked that."

McElheny nodded perfunctorily, again cleared his throat, and faced the assembled mourners. "We are here to say farewell to one who in the short time he was with us spread great joy, lightened the burden of our days, and never once had a regard for himself. Selfless, is a word that personifies the departed …"

McElheny continued for twenty minutes, his eulogy straining the gut of every man present. Yet, remarkably, the decorum of the proceeding remained respectful.

"And so," McElheny finished, "we take heart, knowing that in heaven, we are united with the Lord and our loved ones, and hope that God in his infinite mercy has a place for the tiniest of his creatures, even our beloved Mr. Mouse. Amen."

Pelham glanced at Rosser whose eyes were glistening.

Responding to a nod from McElheny, two of the pallbearers removed the lid to the casket.

"My friends," McElheny said, "if we could proceed from right to left. Mr. Rosser, Mr. Pelham, if you would care to be first …"

Pelham put a hand on Rosser's shoulder, the muscles of his diaphragm aching. "Come, Tom. It's time."

Pelham was the first to view the casket and had to bite his lip. In the center of the padded, silk-lined casket was the tiny gray form of Mr. Mouse, his body somehow straightened, his forelegs crossed. A small swatch of black felt discreetly covered his lower half. Pelham consoled an emotional Rosser and stepped to the side, where the two of them received words of sympathy from those that followed.

In minutes, the viewing was over and the riding hall empty except for Rosser, Pelham, and McElheny. The pall bearers and the rest of McElheny's classmates had closed and removed the casket, the chairs, the lectern, and the dolly, and had readied the hall for its intended use.

"Mr. McElheny!" Rosser's voice boomed across the riding hall. "Front—and—center!"

Immediately, McElheny, stripped of persona, stood at attention at Rosser's feet.

"Mr. McElheny!" Rosser's voice echoed off the walls of the riding hall.

"Yes, sir."

"What is your name, beanhead?" Rosser asked in a tone even more intimidating.

"McElheny, sir."

"Your full name, beanhead!"

"Sir, John Daniel McElheny."

Rosser leaned forward, his nose nearly touching McElheny's. "What do your friends call you, beanhead?"

"Dan, sir."

"Then that will be your name from henceforth!" Rosser's menacing glare unscrewed to an enormous grin, his right hand extended.

Speechless, but unhesitating, McElheny grabbed Rosser's hand. He understood full well what was happening. He was being "recognized," the cadet term for acceptance of a plebe by an upperclassman as an equal, which before the end of plebe year was a rare occurrence, and a practice strictly prohibited within the same company.

Rosser and Pelham enjoyed a long laugh before Rosser grasped McElheny by the shoulders. "An incredible piece of work, Dan. Absolutely incredible. From now on, you call me Tom."

"Thank you, sir. Thank you very much, sir."

"Tom," repeated Rosser.

"Yes, sir."

"Dan, the name is Tom."

"Yes, Tom, thank you … Tom."

"Highly irregular, this is. You know that, Dan?"

"I do, sir. I mean, Tom. And I'll not abuse it. None will know from me that you are anything but the same bastard you've always been."

Both Rosser and Pelham guffawed.

"And with one of us, you get both, Dan." Pelham extended his hand.

As they left the riding hall, Rosser shook his head at McElheny. "Where the hell did you get the casket?"

Chapter Forty-One

At breakfast the next morning, Adelbert Ames informed Pelham that he was visiting Rebecca Astor in the City the next weekend and was there a message he might deliver to Clara. Concealing his envy, Pelham said there wasn't, but to have a wonderful time.

Before first hour class, Pelham was finishing his civil engineering homework when Rosser flew into the room, livid. The fluency of his profanity flawless.

Rosser collapsed in his chair. "We win the war. Hell, we won both, and are still made to suffer their boot!"

"What are you talking about?" Pelham asked.

"The bleeding British!"

"What do you mean?"

"They're coming, John! The bonny Prince of Wales is coming to West Point."

"Who told you that?"

"Kingsbury and du Pont. Reynolds briefed the battalion staff after breakfast. First ever heir to the British throne to visit North America."

Pelham loosed his own, albeit slightly less oiled, brand of profanity. "Seems somebody's always rocking the boat. And he wants to come here?

"He and his contingent are set to leave Canada. They'll bunk at the White House next, then a big parade in New York City, and last of all us."

"Bless his limey little heart," said Pelham. "We'll be drilling until he arrives. When is the show?"

"In a week. They come midday Monday and leave the next day."

An oddly satisfying thought occurred to Pelham. Adelbert Ames would not be seeing Rebecca Astor that weekend.

On his way back to the barracks after the midday meal, fellow Alabamian, Charlie Ball, cornered Pelham.

"John, I can't believe it." Ball was beside himself.

"I know," Pelham said. "We've enough on our plate without the royals."

"Not the royals," exclaimed Ball. "What were you thinking, putting Upton in the debate? The man's nuts!"

"Calm down, Charlie. He's not nuts. He's an abolitionist. He'll behave himself. I promise."

"We're talking Upton!"

"Listen, Charlie, Lincoln has the votes, right? He's going to be the next president of the United States. Right?"

Ball nodded.

"The debate will give the issue, secession, a fair forum. Henry will fairly represent what the South believes, and the North deserves equal billing. The debate is meaningless without competent advocates."

"There was no one else you could think of?" Ball pressed.

"Charlie, you're my only negative response. Listen, any forum to argue states' rights is a forum for all of us."

"You obviously haven't heard from the South Carolinians. Henry Farley in your own company is incensed. It's not the debate—it's Upton!"

"Upton can do no harm. Do me a favor and talk to the naysayers. Trust me, this is a good thing."

Tuesday afternoon, Lee summoned Pelham to his office in the commandant's building and wasted no words. "General Scott is coming for the royals. He wants a demonstration for them, a display of horsemanship for the visiting prince."

"Yes, sir," Pelham said, wondering at Lee's point.

"Our visitors will debark at South Dock and arrive on the Plain via omnibus. They'll troop the Corps on foot in front of the barracks and then proceed to the superintendent's quarters for the parade review. After the review is where you come in."

"Me, sir?"

"Set up a series of jumps, different heights, different types, behind the parade area. Make it interesting."

"I'm volunteering, sir?"

Lee smiled. "You are."

"The prince, sir. Do you know his age?"

"Twenty, I think. About yours."

Before supper, Patterson informed Pelham that he was no longer in the life of Alice Paine, that her lawyer beau had formally proposed, and she had formally accepted. Pelham expressed insincere condolences.

After supper, Kingsbury caught up with Pelham on the way to the barracks. "It's done, John!"

"What?"

"I'm engaged! Eva and I are to marry."

"You're kidding! When did this happen? We talked last night and you said nothing—"

"All by telegram. I decided at breakfast and sent Eva a telegram asking for her hand. By noon, I had her telegram and her hand."

Pelham smiled.

"Then I sent her father a telegram asking for his blessing, and just before supper I have it. Can you believe it—in a matter of ten hours, over and done?"

"And the big day?"

"Right after graduation."

Chapter Forty-Two

Sunday, October 14, the Corps, less Pelham, drilled for two hours on the Plain for the sixth day in a row, passing in review time and again, Reynolds and Hardee critical of the Corps' marching, alignment, and manual of arms, Hardee still lodging at the West Point Hotel awaiting passage to Savannah. The day before, General Winfield Scott, affectionally known as Old Fuss and Feathers, arrived to join in the critique. By virtue of his size, the general, weighing more than three hundred pounds, proved quite a challenge for James and the other attendants of the superintendent's quarters, where the Delafields hosted the Scotts. Left to his own devices, Pelham experimented with various configurations for the obstacle course. When he finished each configuration, he tested it, but always when the Corps couldn't see him.

The next morning at breakfast, word quickly spread that the British contingent would arrive on the federal revenue cutter *Harriett Lane* at the South Dock shortly after noon. It was also reported that the previous day half a million people lined Broadway in New York City for a glimpse of the heir apparent.

The British landed at one o'clock, greeted by Delafield and Reynolds and a squadron of blue uniformed cavalry. Since the royals declined the omnibus ride up to the Plain, preferring to walk, Delafield and Reynolds dismounted and led the royals up the bluff road on foot to the level of the Plain. There, a brilliant backdrop of fall color beneath a crisp blue sky greeted them, along with a national salute thundered by the West Point battery. The West Point band struck up "God Save the Queen," followed by "The Flower of Edinburgh." General Bruce, Duke of Newcastle, the principal spokesman for Crown Prince Albert Edward and his consort walked on one side of Delafield, the prince on the other.

By the time the prince and his contingent began to troop the Corps, the Corps had been standing in formation on Jefferson Road for over an hour. During the inspection, a plebe passed out and had to be taken to the hospital. At the lead of the reviewing party, the prince was of medium height, slim, and blond, with engaging blue eyes. The young royal passed within feet of the first rank of cadets in each company. When he reached D Company and the west end of the Corps formation, Pelham whispered to Rosser, "Looks a lot like Adelbert, but with a mustache."

"He's impressive," Rosser admitted.

The young royal sported a regal uniform with gleaming medals and a sash across his chest that suggested a seasoned warrior, which was not the case.

When the contingent passed D Company, Pelham took his leave and retreated through the sally port into Central Area, where a flustered enlisted man was struggling to control Cotton. Pelham approached the immaculately groomed horse, rubbed its nose, and stepped lightly into the saddle. "Easy, boy. We'll get our chance."

The royal contingent continued beyond the throng of spectators to the superintendent's quarters, where refreshments were taken, and General Scott was introduced to the crown prince. Delafield then announced it was time for the review, and he, Scott, and Reynolds led the visiting contingent to the reviewing stand.

The silhouette of six jumps and well-dressed target dummy were visible beyond the portion of the field reserved for the parade review and captured the attention of the six thousand spectators.

A single drum broke the relative silence, beating a cadence that set the Corps in motion. The commands of Chambliss were echoed by company commanders and platoon leaders. The crowd, four deep within the tree line along Jefferson Road, turned their heads in anticipation. As Chambliss and the battalion staff led A Company onto the Plain, the fife and drum section of the West Point band struck up the British march, "Garry Owen." The brisk lightness of the unfamiliar music delighted the Corps, especially George Custer.

Later, at the supper meal, in reference to the Corps' performance on the Plain, General Bruce would tell Reynolds that his British Palace Guard could not have marched as well as the Corps of Cadets had that afternoon.

After the Corps passed in review and marched off the field, they joined the array of onlookers to watch Pelham execute his run. Colonel Delafield explained to the guests what was to happen next, and Reynolds raised his hat—the signal for Pelham to begin his run. Until then, Pelham had been positioned near the east corner of the barracks, inside the tree line bordering Jefferson Road.

"All right, Cotton, time to dance." Pelham pressured Cotton's white flanks and galloped directly for the reviewing stand. To the delight of all in attendance, he reared Cotton in front of the reviewing stand and made eye contact with the prince. The two exchanged smiles. After a salute to the reviewing party, which included a bow by Cotton, Pelham kicked the horse to a gallop and sped north to the end of the obstacle course. He cleared the first jump with ease, as he did each succeeding and increasingly higher jump. Clearing the final jump, he drew his saber and decapitated the target dummy to the roar of the crowd.

The tumult continued as Pelham initiated the unexpected. Instead of returning to Jefferson Road and the stables, he proceeded at a full gallop toward the reviewing stand. As he approached, the roar of the crowd evaporated, accenting the sound of Cotton's pounding hoofs. Rosser told Pelham later that Scott, Delafield, and Reynolds could not have been more confused, and that the royal party had visibly shuffled to the rear of the stand. From a full gallop and less than fifteen yards from the reviewing party, Pelham abruptly drew Cotton to a stop, instantly dismounting and pulling the horse down by the bit onto his flank. Kneeling, with Cotton between him and the reviewing stand, he drew his pistol and brandished it high in the air.

The six thousand spectators remained stunned until the Corps of Cadets gave Pelham a rousing cheer. Reynolds explained, to the great delight of the visitors, that Pelham had just demonstrated the final tactic of a mounted trooper on the frontier defending himself against an Indian attack, a tactic taught in the second semester of the Second Class year.

Pelham then sprang to his feet and holstered his pistol, Cotton bouncing easily to his feet. Surprising all on the Plain, the Crown Prince descended from the reviewing stand and greeted Pelham with an extended hand.

"Bravo, young man. Bravo," the prince said.

"Thank you, your highness," Pelham said, shaking the royal's hand.

The prince rubbed Cotton's neck. "Yours is a most magnificent animal."

Pelham touched the bill of his cap in acknowledgment, his face dirty and streaked with sweat.

"And you, sir," the prince said, "have great skill. Do all in the Corps possess such skill?"

"Your Highness, you could pick anyone from the First Class, and they could do the same."

As the crowd dispersed, the Corps was dismissed to the barracks, and the young royal and his contingent were escorted to the hotel. It had been rumored about the Corps that there would be a grand celebration ball for all upper classes to honor the prince.

To the Corps' immense disappointment, especially after another supper of mutton, the rumor of a grand ball at the hotel proved false. General Bruce informed Delafield that the prince needed his rest, again not really the case.

An evening that would have been a total loss was softened by an invitation from Custer for Pelham and Rosser to join him for a fine hash, the aroma of which preceded the invitation. Custer had configured a cooking plate above the gas light in his room, and a pot simmered on it. He was whistling the "Garry Owen" march as Pelham and Rosser entered the room.

"Evening, Jim," Pelham greeted James Parker, Custer's roommate. "What's cooking?"

"The king's eggs, some bacon, and a few potatoes."

Parker served up the feast with his usual flair.

With full cheeks, Pelham said, "Tom, you and I are going to miss Fannie's cooking."

"Nope. I intend to take him with us," Rosser said, presenting Parker with an empty plate and a plea for seconds. "John, can you believe that royal brat? He could have given us a royal time, and instead we get the royal shaft."

"I don't believe for a second it was his doing." Pelham said, defending the prince. "In fact, I understand he's quite a social creature. I suspect his nurse man had instructions from the queen to keep the boy toned down. Can't have a royal making a spectacle of himself or having a good time."

"You think?"

"The lad's got fire in his eyes. And he's no different from you or me, except for a thousand rules to follow. You think we have it tough? Try being king."

Nate Chambliss appeared in the doorway with an expectant look. "Fannie, the smell of your hash wafted across the area."

Custer returned an apologetic look. "Sorry, Nate. Afraid the pot's empty."

"So, how is it with you and Jessica Danford?" Pelham asked Chambliss.

"Very well, I think. I'm invited to her house for a day or two over Christmas."

At two o'clock the next day, the prince met with members of the First Class, visited various academic classes, the riding hall, and the mess hall, and witnessed a second well-attended review in which Pelham marched as a nondescript private with a musket on his shoulder. Then the prince led his entourage down South Dock Road and departed on the *Harriett Lane*, but not before granting amnesty as a visiting head of state to all cadets who had tours to walk or confinements to sit, including Pelham, Rosser, and Custer … garnering thunderous approval from the Corps.

The letter from Clara that arrived on Friday, October 19, contained only good news. Her father admitted to being the force behind her entry into the human anatomy laboratory class, and while she had missed the first month and a half of classes, she had been well received by her male colleagues, who seemed to enjoy her response to a male cadaver. She also reported that she was to visit Geneva Medical College as the guest of Dr. Elizabeth Blackwell the third weekend in November.

The next day, after the midday meal, while Adelbert Ames was visiting Rebecca Astor in New York City, an official piece of mail greeted Rosser upon his return to the barracks. The letter bore the seal of the State of Texas.

"John," exclaimed Rosser, "it has to be from Governor Houston." Rosser tore open the letter, and as he read it the color drained from his face.

"What is it, Tom?" Pelham asked.

Rosser handed him the letter.

Pelham read it and whistled. "Not what you expected."

"Can you believe it? Houston wants me to stay and graduate."

"And if I read it right, even if Texas secedes?"

Rosser was incredulous. "The man is a … a bleeding Unionist!"

CHAPTER FORTY-THREE

At breakfast, Monday, October 22, Pelham cornered Adelbert Ames with a knowing wink. "So, tell me. A great time with Rebecca?"

Ames shook his head. "I now know the meaning of entrapment."

"How do you mean?"

"Rebecca is from Concord, Rhode Island. Not exactly across the street from New York City. When I get to Clermont, she has a surprise for me. Scarcely have we kissed, and that was one of only two the entire weekend, she introduces me to her mother, who just happens to be visiting from the city. I have never before been so scrutinized or interrogated in my life. Are your intentions honorable, sir? Do you intend to make the army a career? You wouldn't take my daughter to the frontier, would you? Rebecca wouldn't do well around Indians."

Pelham couldn't stop laughing.

"The old woman had me constantly on the defensive, and Rebecca wasn't herself around her mother—and I fear her mother will always be around. We had but five minutes to ourselves the whole weekend."

"Your intentions?"

"To flee."

Later, at the midday meal, Charlie Ball asked Walter Kingsbury to announce that he would be taking a straw poll for the presidential election at the supper meal, and ballots would be picked up on the way out of the mess hall. Kingsbury made the announcement, which roused little discussion in the mess hall.

That afternoon, Colonel Delafield received a lengthy telegram from General Scott, who had returned to New York City, to the effect that matters were rapidly heating up in Charleston, South Carolina. The message read:

> *Colonel John Gardner, in charge of federal installations in Charleston Harbor, is grossly undermanned to defend the installations should an initiative be taken by South Carolina to control them.*

Scott went on to express frustration with President Buchanan's secretary of war, John Floyd, who had dismissed out of hand the suggestion to reinforce federal forts and arsenals in the South, saying that such maneuvers would send inflammatory signals.

At the supper meal, Charlie Ball hand counted the ballots in the voting box and asked Kingsbury to announce that two hundred and forty-eight votes had been cast in the straw poll, or about 90 percent of the Corps, and that he would have the results in the morning.

"Other than Upton, I'd be surprised if there are a dozen votes for the Republican," Rosser told Pelham.

Pelham shook his head. "I think there could easily be as many as thirty. Remember, Lincoln is in favor of tariffs, which benefit the North."

"A dollar says you're wrong," Rosser countered. "Twenty-five or less and I win."

The two struck hands.

The next morning, the normally sedate Corps was abuzz in anticipation of the election results. Before the Corps took seats, Pelham saw Charlie Ball heading his direction.

"John," Ball whispered with an expression of disbelief. "I can't believe it. There were sixty-four Republican votes."

Pelham raised an eyebrow. "Hmm. That is surprising."

"I know."

"Have you told Walter?"

"Not yet."

"You've got to."

"I can't, John."

"Then I will." Pelham took Ball's tally and delivered it to Kingsbury who called for silence and read it immediately.

"The straw poll for the presidency has one hundred and eighty-four votes for the Democrats and sixty-four votes for the Republicans."

Except for an expletive from Rosser, the response from the Corps was passive.

After breakfast, Ball caught up with Pelham. "I'm sorry, John. I just wasn't prepared for the results."

"Don't worry about it."

"John, we're as conservative a group as you'll find in the entire country. Think how the masses will vote."

"You did well to call for the vote. We know Lincoln will win. But you showed me and the rest of the Corps that three out of four of us are not Republican. Which is not a bad thing."

CHAPTER FORTY-FOUR

Saturday afternoon, October 27, the air in the over-packed academic building lecture hall was electric with confrontation. The editor of the Cornwall weekly and a reporter from Newburgh were in attendance, and both sought comment from Colonel Delafield, who respectfully declined.

Taking a position at the lectern, Pelham raised a hand for quiet. The night before, he had slept fitfully, questioning his initiative. But by morning was convinced more than ever of the rightness of what was to take place.

"Thank you all for your attendance today," he began. "The topic for debate is whether a state has the right to secede from the Union, and I know that Mr. Henry du Pont and Mr. Emory Upton have thoroughly prepared themselves to advocate their assigned positions. Henry du Pont will argue that a state has the right, and Emory Upton will argue that it does not. The intent of the debate is to lay the issues before us, not to declare a winner." Pelham resisted the temptation to add that the winner would be decided soon enough.

"Before we begin, I would like to acknowledge the presence of Colonel Delafield and his wife, Lieutenant Colonel Reynolds and his wife, the balance of the tactical department, and, it appears, all of the other academic departments."

Professor Mahan nodded perfunctorily, while Professor Weir offered a genuine smile.

Pelham wasted no time explaining rules specially modified for the debate, which allowed each debater twenty minutes for his primary construction and ten minutes for rebuttal. He made it clear that the scope of the debate was not to be extended, and that no new arguments could be advanced in rebuttal. His remarks concluded; he retrieved a coin from his pocket.

"Mr. du Pont, by academic rank, will you please call the toss."

Pelham flipped the coin, and du Pont called heads. Pelham opened his fist. "Tails." He turned to the audience. "Mr. Upton will be first to argue the issue."

Upton approached the lectern with his briefcase. From it, he retrieved notes and several documents. He glanced at the wall clock, and then at Pelham for the signal to begin.

Receiving a nod from Pelham, Upton began. "I have in my hand a copy of the Constitution of the United States of America. With the signing of this compact, every member state inextricably assigned its right of sovereignty to the resulting Union we call the United States of America. What was previously a confederacy, and which embodied the sovereignty of individual states, ceased to exist."

"The premise for the United States being a perpetual union that cannot be dissolved lies in the process for its ratification. The people of each state accomplished ratification of the Union, not the individual governments of each state. In that one act, 'We the people,' not 'We the states,' became the Union. Governance of geographical boundaries and interests within the Union were rightly assigned to state governments, but only to the extent that such governments abided by and within the constraints of the Constitution and the amendments thereto."

Upton proceeded to support his argument with examples of precedence for the subservience of state governments to the federal government. His chief example was President Andrew Jackson, who in 1828 threatened to send troops to South Carolina in response to their threat to nullify a federal tariff law that was deemed not in the best interest of South Carolina.

At Pelham's one-minute signal, Upton summarized his argument, and when his time was up, collected his materials and took his seat.

The lecture hall, respectful throughout Upton's remarks, buzzed in anticipation of what du Pont had to say.

"We will now hear the opposing viewpoint from Henry du Pont." Pelham motioned to du Pont, who approached the lectern with his own materials.

"A paradox," du Pont began upon Pelham's nod, "is what we have. For I too hold up a copy of the Constitution. The same one that Mr. Upton showed you. There is nothing in this document that strips a state of its sovereignty in any matter not specifically vested in the federal government. Getting right to the point, neither the Constitution nor its amendments, beginning with what we call the Bill of Rights, give the federal government the power to prevent secession by a state. Further and unequivocally, the Tenth Amendment to the Constitution gives to the states and their people all rights not otherwise vested in the federal government. Ergo, a state has the right to secede, because there is no law or provision preventing it."

Du Pont paused.

"I could stop right here, and probably should. To say more would water down this primal point, which cannot be contested, at least not legally or by the Constitution. But I've nineteen minutes to go."

Light laughter eased tensions in the room.

"We'll have order, please," Pelham said, his tone respectful.

Du Pont used the rest of his time to defend with historical precedents the rights of individual states, taking head-on President Jackson's actions against South Carolina as unconstitutional, saying that while Jackson got his way, that did not make his actions lawful. He argued that a state had the right to ignore a federal law that went against the laws and interests of the state; and that when the compact between a sovereign state and the federal government was breached, it was null and void unless reparable to both parties. Du Pont then elevated the argument to the "pursuit of happiness" contained in the preamble of the Declaration of Independence, and the "promotion of the general welfare" contained in the preamble to the Constitution. The unhappiness of the people of a state and their view that the welfare they sought has not been promoted by a federal government are legitimate bases for redress. When redress is not satisfactorily served, the extreme measure of secession is a viable remedy.

Pelham kept an eye on Colonel Delafield throughout the debate, relieved to see him following the arguments intently and not once pulling at his whiskers. Despite his personal leanings, Pelham was impressed by the evenhanded treatment given by Upton for his side of the issue.

On Pelham's signal, du Pont took his seat.

"Mr. Upton will now have ten minutes to rebut Mr. du Pont's argument."

Upton approached the lectern. "Indeed, we do have a paradox," he conceded. "The letter of the Constitution and letter of its amendments may appear ambiguous, but their intent is not. The founding fathers envisioned a perpetual union of its member people. Furthermore, Article VI of the Constitution requires by oath or affirmation that federal and state legislators, executive officers, and judicial officers support the Constitution of the United States of America. Ours is the most solemn and permanent of marriages. Support of the Constitution is not an option. It is a sacred trust."

Upton again argued that "the people," not the states, formed the country, that majority rule was the cornerstone of democracy, and that the vast majority of the "the people" comprising the country would entirely oppose any thought of secession.

Upton sat down and du Pont again stood up.

In du Pont's rebuttal, he quickly seized upon Upton's metaphor of marriage, remarking that marriages that did not work out resulted in divorces, and that secession was no more, nor less, the result of a failed marriage. He then returned to the central issue, the absence of any provision in the Constitution or its amendments that would preclude a state from seceding. Lastly, du Pont constructed the argument that there was no provision to prevent a state from undoing what it had done to join the Union, suggesting that the people of a state, by public referendum, could decide because of their collective grievances to vote themselves out of the Union.

Bearing a sour expression, du Pont sat down.

The debate over, Pelham approached the lectern. He eyed the audience that seemed to him in authentic reflection. He was pleased with what had taken place. Neither debater had made any connection with the divisive issue of slavery, and both had gone to the Constitution and its amendments for their constructs.

"Let's express our appreciation to Mr. du Pont and Mr. Upton for a fine debate."

Du Pont and Upton received a sincere, though muted round of applause from all in attendance.

After the room emptied, du Pont and Upton waited for Pelham in the hall.

"So, what did you think, John?" du Pont asked.

"What do you think, Henry?" Pelham countered with a smile.

"For my part, I expected more of a response," Upton said, visibly disappointed.

"Don't confuse what you didn't hear with the import of the message. You both did well. You served up what has frustrated both Unionists and states' rights advocates for eighty years. You presented the paradox."

Pelham and du Pont returned to the barracks together, and during the short walk du Pont made clear that he wished he'd played no part in the debate, that personally he believed secession was wrong, even unconscionable. While he had voted Democrat in the straw poll, he abhorred the thought of a divided nation. Pelham heard him out and applauded his suppression of personal opinion. He told du Pont he well represented a large faction of the country and had impartially defended its position, and now that the debate was over he should let it go.

Later that afternoon, Pelham reported as ordered to the superintendent's quarters, where Delafield soberly congratulated him on the debate, making the observation that the defensibility of the opposing arguments did not bode well for the country.

When Pelham returned to the barracks, he found a letter from his father on his desk. The letter conveyed the news that Butch Jansonne had been sacked the last week of picking season when Charles, Pelham's oldest brother, found him whipping two of the blacks. The final straw had been a visit the same week by the county sheriff, who delivered a lawsuit brought by the neighboring Watson family. The lawsuit accused Jansonne of destruction of property, to wit the death of the runaway slave Charlie Watson, and named the Pelham family co-defendants by virtue of supervising responsibility. The lawsuit alleged that the slave ran off due to excessive maltreatment—the Watson overseer swearing the idea came from Butch Jansonne. Pelham was relieved to read in the next sentence that the lawsuit was dismissed a week later.

In the balance of the letter, his father provided an update on the family and plantation matters, chief of which was the agreement he had made with Samuel, that if Samuel could get the plantation work done without an overseer, he would serve as the new overseer and receive one quarter of the salary paid a white overseer.

Chapter Forty-Five

While discussions in the barracks, between classes, and in the mess hall continued to center on the debate and the issue of secession, Henry du Pont and Emory Upton sought cover from the bombardment of supporters and detractors.

The following Monday, with the temperature dipping well below freezing, Pelham went to the library between classes to check out Charles Dickens's *American Notes*, finally giving in to Clara's urging that he read it. He was on his way back to the barracks when du Pont approached him.

"Can we talk, John?" Du Pont's expression suggested a serious matter.

"Sure, Henry. What is it?"

"Not here." Du Pont led Pelham around the corner to the side of the barracks. "I need a favor—a big favor."

"Anything, so long as it's not money," Pelham said with a smirk.

"I need a second for a pugilistic match."

"You're fighting someone?"

Du Pont nodded.

"Who?"

Du Pont hesitated before saying, "Upton."

"Emory? You're kidding?"

Du Pont shook his head.

"But that makes no sense."

"He's convinced I called him a liar."

Pelham eyed du Pont. "Did you?"

"You know better than that. Somebody got to Emory, John. And Emory won't say who."

Pelham couldn't help grinning. "And you two were doing so well."

"For a whole week."

"What was it you were supposed to have lied about?"

"That too is a mystery. He wouldn't tell me."

"Vintage Upton. When is it to be?"

"Day after tomorrow, below Fort Clinton."

"That soon?"

"Anyway, I was hoping you would—"

Pelham interrupted. "You know Emory and I are friends. But if that's what you want, I'll stand by you."

Du Pont clasped Pelham's hand. "I need more than that, John. I need coaching. You did a first-rate job on that sadistic First Classman plebe year. I'll take any tips you can give me."

After class, Pelham met du Pont in the fencing gymnasium and fitted him with boxing gloves. He then gave him tips on stance, footwork, balance, breathing, and how to maximize power behind punches. Then he talked about Upton, pointing out the obvious, that Upton had a two-inch longer reach, so there would be a zone that he needed to be either inside of or outside of. Otherwise, Upton could pop him at will.

"The important thing," Pelham said, "is to stay centered on your feet, just like fencing, and parry the incoming blows. Move in only when you see an opening, and then strike and retreat. Breathe deep and often. The less you breathe, the faster you fatigue."

Pelham donned gloves and demonstrated two punch combinations: two left jabs and a right cross, and two left jabs and an uppercut. "Okay, now you try it."

The response from du Pont was less than inspiring, and Pelham forced a straight face. "Not bad. Watch me again."

By supper, everyone in the Corps knew of the fight and few cared why, only that there would be one. Rosser was in that camp, putting his entrepreneurial spirit to good use.

CHAPTER FORTY-SIX

Tuesday, October 30, a letter from Clara brought sunshine to an otherwise gray day. After classes, Pelham reclined on his bed and slit open the scented envelope with a penknife. The letter was unlike any of her others, save for the final paragraph in which she again affirmed her willingness to suffer all for the chance to be with him again.

Her focus was on an autobiographical book she had read, *Twelve Years a Slave*, written by Solomon Northup. Northup had been a free Negro who had been kidnapped, brutalized, and sold into slavery while conducting business in Washington DC, leaving a wife and three children. He was shipped by captors to Louisiana, where he was purchased by the owner of a cotton plantation. Every year seeking an opportunity to escape, in his twelfth year of captivity, Northup successfully secreted a letter to a politically connected friend who launched an investigation that resulted in his rescue.

Clara asked Pelham if he had read the book, and if the things described in the book really happened. Pelham wrote back that he had never heard of the book and that he was not personally aware of any free blacks who had been sold into slavery, but that he couldn't deny it could happen. He again expressed hope that one day she would see Alabama for herself, see that the treatment of a vast majority of blacks was humane, that humankind, not slavery itself, was the evil. He admitted to abhorring the institution himself, but that its sheer weight was beyond his or anyone's intervention, save God himself.

By supper, Rosser had taken more than fifty bets on the outcome of the du Pont-Upton fight. The vast majority favoring Upton, the taller and wirier fighter, who at least had experience dueling with blades. Word of the skewed betting somehow got to du Pont, with predictable effect, and Pelham found himself not only a boxing coach but the steward of du Pont's confidence.

News of the fight had also reached Lieutenant Lee, who chose to keep it to himself, it not being uncommon for tactical staff to look the other way when cadets settled disputes.

In the thirty minutes of free time after supper, Pelham and du Pont again met in the basement of the academic building.

"Take your stance, Henry," Pelham said, immediately moving parts of du Pont's body. "Left shoulder forward, chin down, hands in front, left hand up and forward, thumbs up, more bend at the waist." Pelham stepped back. "How do you feel?"

"Like a pretzel!"

"The important thing is to keep your guard up, Henry. Keep moving and bide your time. Don't be in a hurry."

A few minutes after taps, Pelham was still at his desk when he heard a knock at the door. The South Carolinian, Henry Farley, stood in the doorway, a guilty expression on his face.

"What brings you out, Henry, risking a skin?" Pelham asked.

Farley motioned Pelham into the hallway. Rosser's head was in an engineering book.

"What is it, Henry?"

"Du Pont and Upton."

"The fight?"

"It was just in jest, John."

They both heard the door open three floors below. Pelham peered over the banister to see a cadet returning from the showers.

"What was?"

"I just came from du Pont's room. I tried to explain to him that it was never supposed to get this far."

"You're the one who framed him?"

Farley smiled weakly. "I may have stretched a point."

"What did you tell Upton?"

"That du Pont thought him equivocal in the debate."

"Equivocal?" said Pelham.

"It was just a rib. And you and I both know Upton's a flaming abolitionist. If he'd really been honest, he'd have come across much different. Anyway, some of us were talking that it was a shame to see the two of them getting along so well. I suggested it wouldn't last. Paddy

O'Rorke said it would. That led to a bet, and I—wanted to hedge my bet."

Pelham repressed a smile. "You dog."

"But du Pont is still going through with it!"

"Why?"

"He said the whole Corps is expecting it, and how would it look if it got out that the two of them had been duped by a sham? Worse… by me."

Pelham grinned. "There's some logic to that."

"He made me promise to keep quiet. Just let it happen."

"Then I suggest you do just that, Henry. Bide your tongue and get back to your room."

Chapter Forty-Seven

The next day, Delafield was oblivious to the stream of cadets moving across the Plain toward old Fort Clinton. He had just received another troubling telegram from General Scott.

James detected the tension in the colonel's face. "Sir, I made some fresh coffee."

"James," Delafield said. "John Floyd, our slippery secretary of war, has ordered eleven 32-pounders and a hundred and ten Columbiad cannons to be made and sent to Ship Island, Mississippi, and Galveston, Texas. Do you have any idea how much firepower that is?"

"No, sir."

"Do you know what that is?"

"No, sir."

"It's treason, James. That's what it is. Boldfaced, served-up-hot, treason by a Virginian who's arming the South." Delafield sipped his coffee. "Here we are a week short of the election and the cotton states have declared from the treetops their intention to secede once Lincoln is elected. Why in God's great creation would we fortify the shores of two states that will no longer belong to us?"

James cut the superintendent a slice of pound cake.

"Buchanan isn't paying attention, James. Three of his cabinet are avowed fire-eaters. Along with Floyd, you have Howell Cobb of Georgia, his secretary of the treasury, and Jacob Thompson of Mississippi, his secretary of interior. Those three won't let the Washington sun set on their traitorous rumps the day their states secede." Delafield looked skyward. "God, please grant Buchanan some wisdom."

Below and east of old Fort Clinton, the crowd of gray uniforms grew to witness the fight between du Pont and Upton. A number of cadets huddled around Rosser who was taking last minute bets. Despite the chill, du Pont and Upton were attired in riding pants and long-sleeved undershirts, both fitted with eight-ounce boxing gloves.

Pelham massaged du Pont's shoulders. "How do you feel, champ?"

Du Pont mumbled something unintelligible.

Pelham glanced across the small opening in the crowd at John Rodgers, Upton's roommate and second. They exchanged nods.

"Let's do this, Henry." Pelham slapped du Pont on the back.

The crowd of nearly a hundred and fifty cheered as Upton and du Pont faced off, Walter Kingsbury standing between them as referee.

"There will be no rounds," Kingsbury announced. "Simply a fight that continues until one of you concedes or is down for the count of ten. There will be no hitting below the waist, no kicking, no biting, and no head butting. Anyone doing so will be declared the loser."

Du Pont and Upton nodded.

"Touch gloves and may the best man win."

"This is stupid, Emory," du Pont whispered as they touched gloves.

"I know, Henry. Farley told me everything, and I agree with you—but do we have a choice?"

Upton hadn't finished his sentence when he stung du Pont with a left jab to the chin, snapping his head back.

Dazed, du Pont absorbed a second jab, followed by a right to the stomach. Barely ten seconds into the fight, du Pont dropped to one knee, gasping for air and tasting blood.

"You okay, Henry?" Kingsbury asked.

Du Pont spat blood and got to his feet.

"Give it up, Henry," Upton urged. "You don't need this."

Du Pont took a roundhouse swing at Upton, missing and losing his balance.

Upton answered with another jab, followed by an uppercut, both landing squarely on du Pont's jaw. Du Pont stumbled backward, blood trickling from his mouth. Shaking his head, he lunged at Upton, locking him in a clinch.

The crowd responded with boos, and Kingsbury stepped in. "Break it up, Henry."

Pelham shouted instructions to du Pont. "Guard up, Henry. Keep moving!"

Du Pont was clearly dazed, and the crowd sensed an all too short fight. Some shouted for Upton to finish the job, others urged du Pont to make it a fight.

The two separated, and after absorbing another head shot, du Pont clinched again. The pattern continued, and after two minutes du Pont had yet to land a punch.

"Dammit, Henry, give it up," growled Upton. "I don't want to hurt you."

Du Pont wiped his nose with the back of his glove, and in the process painted his face red.

"It's your choice, Henry," Upton said, popping the right side of du Pont's head with a hook that made his ear ring.

Du Pont clinched again, his upper lip fat and his left eye already swollen. All the while, in du Pont's corner, Pelham coolly repeated the same instructions, "Guard up, Henry. Move around. Breathe, Henry. Back off."

Du Pont seemed finally to hear Pelham when he saw him moving his hands apart and repeating the gesture. He backed away from Upton and took a deep breath. He began waving his arms and shuffling his feet just inches beyond Upton's reach.

Upton's next three punches, two jabs and a hook, fell short.

Du Pont began jutting his chin at Upton like a barnyard chicken, drawing laughter from the crowd.

"Henry, you can't hide, and you're hurt. Give it up," Upton said, lunging at du Pont with a jab, followed by a hook, either of which, had they hit their mark, would have been the talk of the barracks. But neither did, and Upton found himself for the first time off balance.

Du Pont didn't hesitate. He pummeled Upton's face and midsection with a series of rights and lefts, the blows more surprising than effective. Before Upton could collect himself, du Pont delivered a punch that audibly popped Upton's jaw, snapping his head back.

The crowd reveled in the action. They had a fight.

For the first time, du Pont found himself the aggressor, and Upton clinching and suffering the boos.

The two continued to fight without a break for nearly twenty minutes, the crowd cheering the ebb and flow of fortunes. The longer-armed Upton at one point regained the advantage, putting du Pont down a second and third time. But du Pont kept getting up, and as the fight wore on, exhaustion overtook the abolitionist. The scar from the duel with Gibbes opened on his right cheek, and each time he attempted to wipe his eyes, du Pont popped him with a jab. Upton's face grew ashen, his breathing irregular. Du Pont, no less exhausted, at least remained in balance, his lips swollen and one eye all but shut.

A lackluster right hook from du Pont to the side of Upton's nose finally put him face down in the dirt. The crowd shouted for him to get up.

"One—two—three—four—five—," counted Kingsbury.

Upton struggled to his feet on the count of nine. He swayed on rubbery legs, blood streaming from his nose.

The crowd sensed the end and swung in favor of du Pont, whose right hand was poised behind his ear as Upton's arms hung listless.

Rodgers shouted for Upton to get his hands up.

"Defend yourself, Emory," du Pont said, spitting blood.

Upton was unable to lift his arms.

Du Pont circled his fist.

"Do it, Henry," cried someone in the crowd. "Put him on the ground!"

Du Pont glanced at Pelham, and then the crowd, and then at Upton's bloody face. He let his right hand drop to his side.

A hush fell over the crowd.

Du Point attempted a grin. Upton blinked hard and attempted the same.

The two touched gloves, and Kingsbury stepped in. "I declare this match a draw!"

Chapter Forty-Eight

The day after the fight, the attention of every First Classman was on Professor Mahan's midterm civil engineering exam to be administered the next day. Rosser, whose grade point in the course had again slipped under 2.0, didn't know whether to study or pack his bags.

"Think of it this way, Tom," Pelham told Rosser after supper, himself immersed in the course notes. "You can get it all back on this one test."

"And just how am I supposed to suddenly comprehend everything that's flown over my head? I tell you, John, you'll be rooming by yourself."

"You could try Henry."

"Henry? I … I don't think so."

"How is Henry not a good idea?"

"I don't think he's happy with me."

Pelham expressed confusion.

"And why is that?"

"He found out I bet on Upton."

Pelham grinned. "Burned the wrong bridge?"

Rosser shrugged.

"Still, talk to him, Tom," Pelham pressed. "Plead for mercy. Grovel if you must. What do you have to lose?"

"You know, you're right." Rosser gathered up his notes and the course text and slinked down the stairwell, out the back door, and over to the First Division. He knocked on du Pont's door and without pretense bared his soul.

Du Pont, expressionless, allowed Rosser to ramble on with his apology, that the bet wasn't personal, and how he couldn't face being drummed out of the Corps.

After Rosser exhausted his plea and du Pont gave no reaction, he turned to leave.

"Why did you wait until tonight?" asked du Pont, who turned to his Virginia roommate, Llewellyn Hoxton. "Lew, do you mind if I work with Tom a bit?"

Hoxton was already collecting his study materials. "Take my chair, Tom. I'll study in bed."

For five hours, three hours after lights out—Pelham made up a dummy that got Rosser past bed check—Rosser hung on every word du Pont said. Long after Hoxton was asleep, du Pont talked engineering terms, concepts, and formulas, and drilled Rosser on definitions and engineering design processes, and made him work problem after problem. Together, they reviewed Rosser's answers and the steps he had taken to get them. If Rosser made a mistake, du Pont made him work the same problem again until he got the right answer.

When du Pont finally released Rosser, he wondered if the man would make it back to the Eighth Division.

Chapter Forty-Nine

The next morning, Friday, November 2, was cold and wet. Pelham and Rosser hung their long overcoats outside the civil engineering classroom, the last in the section to be seated. Rosser's head was shiny with perspiration, his pallor pasty, and his eyes vacant.

"Section, attention!" ordered Pelham, section leader, as Professor Mahan entered the room. "Sir, the section is all present!"

Mahan returned Pelham's salute with a wave of the hand. "Take seats." Mahan surveyed the class, his gaze momentarily resting on Rosser, whose head hung so low it nearly touched his desk. "You'll have the rest of the class period to complete the midterm examination, and as usual, the use of any notes or texts is strictly forbidden." He gestured for Pelham to pass out the test papers, and when Pelham had, gave the order to commence work.

For nearly an hour and a half, there was stark silence except for the sounds of pencils scratching, erasers erasing, and papers shuffling.

Periodically, Mahan glanced about the room over his spectacles.

As time ticked, one by one members of the class got up, turned in their tests, and left the room. Fifteen minutes before the end of the class period, Pelham departed, leaving Rosser and one other man still at work.

Ten minutes later, Rosser was on his fourth pencil, his test paper a smudge of erasures. He had done everything that du Pont had said. He had read every problem before beginning the test, worked the easiest problems first. He had numbered his steps and showed all his work so he could get partial credit if he made a mistake. Du Pont had been right about what would be on the test, but as Rosser worked the problems, he began to question his memory and judgment. Was he using the right formula, had he memorized it correctly, had he made errors with his slide rule? The familiar panic of a brain gone dead undid him.

"Cease work," Mahan announced without mercy.

Rosser, the only one in the room with Mahan, put down his pencil. With shaky hands, he assembled his test papers and set them on Mahan's desk.

Pelham didn't have a chance to talk to Rosser until the midday meal.

"So—how did it go, roommate?"

Rosser casually buttered his bread. "You're gonna miss me."

Nearly three hundred miles to the south of West Point, South Carolina Representative William Porcher Miles followed Texas Senator Louis Trezevant Wigfall and a host of other members of the Senate and House into a seldom used committee room in the United States Capitol. Every face expressed elation and anticipation as they assembled around the room's large conference table.

"Gentlemen of the South," Wigfall began, seated at one end of the table, "we've the weekend, a Monday, and then election day, and there is more solidarity for our cause now than we could have ever hoped for. May the power of heaven remain on our side."

Miles stood up. "Each state will follow the process we agreed upon. That is, have a public referendum to renounce membership in the Union. A majority vote of the people in that direction will free them to enter whatever new compact they might view in their best interest."

At a recess later that day, Wigfall asked Miles whether he regretted not being able to make his annual pilgrimage to West Point. Miles' response surprised him. "On the contrary, Louis, the timing for a trip to West Point could not be better."

Chapter Fifty

On Monday, November 5, cold and fog embraced West Point, although the fog lifted mid-morning. After the midday meal, a plebe delivered Pelham another perfumed letter from Clara.

"Have a heart, John," Rosser protested as he entered the room. "I could smell Clara's letter from the bottom floor up."

Pelham ignored Rosser and read the letter in the light of the window, four sheets of vellum with Clara's fine handwriting and signature flowers. She reported that life at Clermont centered on the election and that, except for Carol Hill, all her friends would vote Republican, had they the right to vote. For the first time, she wrote at length about what in Lincoln's platform appealed to her, and again asked for his forgiveness that she should think this way. She went on to describe rather graphically an autopsy that her anatomy class had witnessed the day before, observing, "How kind God was to put a layer of skin over all that forms us, that it might be quite hard to love one another otherwise."

But the most surprising news concerned her father. Of him, she wrote, *I had wanted to tell Father face to face about you, how wonderful you are, what a gentleman you are, and how much I dearly love you. But he still hadn't come to visit. In fact, I haven't seen him since mid-summer, the claims of the university so great—he says. Anyway, two weeks ago, I wrote him about us and today received his response.*

Pelham's heart pounded in his chest.

I wish I could report that he was thrilled for me, for us. But that would be an untruth. However, he did not contest my love for you. Which is to say I can go to work on him, the way only a daughter can.

Pelham finished the letter, satisfied, as Clara was, that they were no longer in the closet. He almost felt sorry for the man, knowing what

Clara was capable of. He slipped the letter in a drawer nearly full of her letters and turned to Rosser. "Carol Hill sends her best."

That afternoon after class, Pelham found Rosser stretched out on the bed, staring at the ceiling.

"Have you been to the sally port?" Pelham asked. "I heard the midterm test grades are posted."

"I can't make myself do it." Rosser spoke as one condemned.

"You are pathetic. I'll be right back."

When Pelham returned from the sally port, he found Rosser's position in bed unchanged, his eyes closed. He stood at the front of Rosser's bed, his arms crossed. "Aren't you even going to ask?"

Rosser didn't bother to open his eyes.

Pelham kicked the bed. "Tom, your execution is stayed!"

Rosser opened one eye.

"Dog, you got a 2.3! Your new grade point is 2.15."

Rosser fairly levitated above the bed. "The hell you say."

"The hell I say! I only got a 2.2."

"For true?"

"For true, my friend! Apparently, Henry knows his stuff."

Rosser let out a howl that carried across the quadrangle. Hugging Pelham, he danced around the room, hugged Pelham again, and then ran as fast as his legs could carry him to the First Division.

At supper, in the joy of the moment, Pelham and Rosser determined that they must celebrate. If ever there was reason to visit Benny Havens, they had one. Chas Patterson, nursing a cold, allowed he couldn't join them this time, and neither Pelham nor Rosser wanted to jeopardize Ned Kirby's position as company commander.

Fifteen minutes after call to quarters and bed check, Pelham and Rosser slipped down the Eighth Division stairwell in their socks, shoes in hand, and out the back door. They sat on the steps to put on their shoes when a voice rang out from the darkness.

"Going somewhere?"

Pelham recognized the voice. So did Rosser. As one, they snapped to attention in their socks and saluted Lieutenant Lee, standing in the lamplight.

Before either of them could speak, Lee held up a hand. "Not a word. You'll only incriminate yourself, and then I won't have a choice."

Pelham and Rosser dropped their salutes.

"I suggest you return to your room. If you do, this goes no further."

Pelham and Rosser nodded.

"And Mr. Rosser. Nice work on the exam."

CHAPTER FIFTY-ONE

Tuesday, November 6, Election Day, classes should have been suspended for lack of interest, not only for cadets, but for faculty as well. The previous day, Colonel Delafield had informed the Corps that it would be kept abreast of election results as they came in. As in the election of 1856, telegraph dispatches communicated state results with blinding speed. The election of Abraham Lincoln was decided by early evening. At the midday meal on Wednesday, the final tallies were in. Lincoln had been elected president with 40 percent of the popular vote and 59 percent of the electoral vote. He had taken every Northern state, and California and Oregon as well. The Northern Democrat, Stephen Douglas, managed a respectable 29.5 percent of the popular vote, but a paltry 4 percent of the electoral vote, comprised of Missouri and three of the seven votes from New Jersey. By contrast, the Southern Democrat, John Breckinridge, garnered only 18 percent of the popular vote, but 24 percent of the electoral vote, including all of the Deep South. John Bell of the Constitutional Union rounded out the election with 12.5 percent of the popular vote and 13 percent of the electoral vote, all from Kentucky, Tennessee, and Virginia.

In the span of a single day, the incessant rhetoric of political campaigning ceased. The reign of the Democratic Party was over. Now the Republican Party would scramble to set its agenda and fill its appointments.

That evening in the First-Class Club, Pelham, du Pont, and Upton sat at a card table discussing the election.

"The fact that Breckinridge took all of the cotton states, is telling." Pelham said, not in the least surprised by the election results.

"What surprises me," du Pont observed, "is that he took my state and Maryland as well."

Pelham turned to Upton. "Your man is in, Emory."

"And a good one, I assure you. He'll serve us well, given half a chance."

"Will he?" said Charlie Ball, Rosser's guest at the adjacent table. "When all of us is only half of us? I'll be surprised if John and I aren't back in Alabama within the month."

"I pray you're wrong, Charlie," Upton said. "You deserve to graduate."

Upton spoke Pelham's heart, and Ball's directness soured him, knowing he was right. If Alabama seceded, he'd have no choice.

"And, of course," Ball added, "there are many on the fence in the border states. If Delaware secedes, I wouldn't think Henry would stay."

"Delaware's not going anywhere," du Pont said. "And the South shouldn't either."

Ball let it drop.

"Still, Charlie's point can't be ignored," Pelham said. "A man's allegiance is to his family, home, and state—before country. Besides, once a state secedes, those from it probably won't be allowed to stay. I mean, what would be the point?"

"It will be interesting to see how the regular officers react," said Ball. "Lieutenant Lee is a Virginian; Lieutenant Colonel Hardee is from Georgia. If Virginia and Georgia bolt, I don't see them serving the Union."

Du Pont stood up. "It hasn't been twenty-four hours since the election, and neither Breckinridge nor Douglas, and certainly not Bell, have talked secession. Let's not overreact."

"More to the point," Upton said, "wouldn't it be lunacy not to give Lincoln a fair chance. Give him time to compromise. I think he'll do what he must to keep the Union whole."

"Trust me, Emory," Ball said, almost under his breath. "It's not up to Lincoln."

Chapter Fifty-Two

On Thursday, with a night's sleep making little difference, Pelham wrestled with an endless sequence of scenarios. He believed, as Ball and other Southern cadets did, that secessions would come. And there was an undeniable magnetism and energy to the prospect. As a consequence of the distractions, he moved through morning classes unprepared, his recitations weak. That his grades would suffer concerned him little. As soon as it was clear that Alabama would secede, he would write his father and ask for permission to resign.

After the midday meal and upon his return to Central Area, Pelham saw Lieutenant Lee in the company of two gentlemen in three-piece suits and long overcoats. As they walked towards him, one of the two recognized Pelham. It was the congressman on the train, William Porcher Miles of South Carolina.

With Lee on his heels, Miles approached Pelham.

"Lieutenant Lee, I met this this young man when traveling the train to Washington this past August." Miles hesitated. "John Pelham, isn't it?"

"Yes, sir. It's kind of you to remember," Pelham said.

"You're a man not easily forgotten, and as I recall, one with a healthy appetite." Miles smiled. "Lieutenant Lee, might I have a private word with Mr. Pelham?"

"By all means, sir. I'll be in my office."

Miles put an arm around Pelham's shoulders. "Let's walk, John. It is indeed good fortune that I run into you. I am here to speak with my South Carolina cadets. Something I do every year, but particularly useful this year. This evening, I am hosting a dinner at the hotel, and I would be most pleased if you would join us."

Pelham beamed. "Sir, I'd be honored."

"Excellent. Seven o'clock, if that's convenient."

"Quite convenient, sir."

At the West Point Hotel, in a room reserved for the South Carolina contingent and closed off except for food service, Pelham found himself seated next to Miles at a large round table with eight South Carolina cadets, including Henry Farley.

Miles wasted no time getting to the point. "Gentlemen, I am here for just the night and will be returning south on tomorrow's boat, and I mean to Charleston, not Washington."

He reached for his wine glass, the only such glass on the table, and raised it. "Gentlemen, I propose a toast to the great State of South Carolina."

The South Carolinians and Pelham raised their water glasses. "To the great State of South Carolina."

Miles nodded at Pelham. "I trust you all know Mr. Pelham?"

The question brought cheers from the other cadets and a catcall from Farley. Pelham waved off the attention.

Miles made a second toast, this time to the State of Alabama, and while the main course was being served, engaged Pelham. "We are in a most interesting time, Mr. Pelham."

"Indeed, sir," said Pelham.

"And you wear the right colors here."

"I'm sorry?" Pelham said.

Miles declined to explain, since the hotel's waiting staff had begun serving supper. Once all were served, he asked Farley to close the door.

"Gentlemen, nothing said in this room leaves this room. Are we agreed?"

Everyone, including Pelham, agreed.

Miles drew himself up to the table. "The die is thoroughly cast, my young friends. The Black Republican and his party can have the Union, but not South Carolina. The state of South Carolina will resume her place among the nations of the world, with all the attendant powers and opportunities that have been for so long denied it."

The pronouncement was electric, and the euphoria palpable around the table.

"The experiment of the United States has failed us, the result of a constitution betrayed by states of the North not caring a whit for the states of the South. The basic tenets of the constitution no longer apply to *we the people*, but to *they the people of the* North. And so be it. The construct of the Union has changed so dramatically that its dismemberment or even death will be a blessing to all concerned." Miles eyed each man at the table. "North and South have evolved so differently that they have become two entirely different animals, one preying wantonly upon the other."

Pelham was taken by the effect Miles had on the South Carolinians. Farley's flushed cheeks matched his red hair.

"I am very pleased to hear that the question of secession has already been debated here at the Academy." Miles gave Pelham a knowing wink. "And that convincing argument for the right to secede has already been voiced. I am here to announce that South Carolina will be the first to do so, believing most assuredly it will not be the last. Soon the states of the South will form a new and glorious union whose values are one."

Farley led a cheer that Pelham feared could be heard throughout the hotel.

"We are all of us cotton states. South Carolina, Alabama, Mississippi, Georgia, Florida, and Texas. We are pledged to secede from the Union as soon as public elections can be held. Our hope is that we can accomplish the process before Lincoln takes office. Buchanan is not inclined to interfere with us, and there is time enough." Miles spoke as though he had the keys to heaven, and the sons of his state reacted as if they couldn't wait to get in.

"Mark my words. More than the cotton states will follow. Look for North Carolina, Virginia, Tennessee, Kentucky, Arkansas, Maryland, Missouri, and Delaware to follow our lead. Ours will be the grandest of nations, exceeding what the United States could ever be, and we shall call ourselves the Confederate States of America."

The reaction of South Carolina cadets was provocative, and Pelham found it hard not to join in the jubilation.

"So, what say you, Mr. Pelham?" asked Miles as the others cheered.

"Is there no room for compromise, sir?"

Miles returned a placid smile. "Compromise has no place in God's chosen course for us, John."

Farley stood on his chair, his eyes flashing, his face flushed with passion. "I pledge my sword and my life to South Carolina!"

Pelham didn't doubt Farley's conviction, and one by one, the other South Carolinians pledged the same, their eyes shiny with tears.

Miles wrapped his arm around Pelham's shoulder. "This is just the beginning, John. We will be a country of millions. You are about to witness an incredible chapter in history."

The next day, Congressman Miles departed on the noon steamer, Pelham briefing Rosser on the evening before. The Texan's reaction was not his own. Rosser was ready to walk away from West Point and not look back. Around campus, wherever two or more cadets were gathered, the topic was secession. How many states would secede? Would the North acquiesce? Would there be compromise—slavery allowed in the new territories? Would Lincoln comprehend the thin thread that held his country together?

That evening, after lights out and bed check, Pelham heard a tap on the door. He slipped from his bed to find Henry Farley in the hall.

"I wanted you to be the first to know, John."

Pelham joined Farley in the hall, closing the door behind him.

"I have your confidence?"

"Of course."

"I'm resigning."

Pelham feigned surprise.

"I want to be first, John. South Carolina is holding its convention later this month. Miles told me so."

"But why now?"

"Like I said. I want to be first. Only one of us can be first, and why not me? Once it begins, there will be an exodus."

Pelham didn't doubt it. "Your resignation. You should craft it carefully."

Farley nodded. "I know. I've already written it and have permission from my father. I'm simply saying that I'm needed at home."

"Needed at home." Turning the reason over in his mind, Pelham smiled. "I like it." He put a hand on Farley's shoulder. "You're sure about this?"

"Dead sure."

Chapter Fifty-Three

On Saturday, November 10, the South Carolina General Assembly called for a convention to draw up an ordinance of secession. Two days later, Henry Farley submitted his resignation to Lieutenant Lee, despite Lee's attempt to persuade him to delay until South Carolina actually seceded. Lee submitted Farley's resignation to Lieutenant Colonel Reynolds, who passed it up the chain to Colonel Delafield. Farley informed Pelham and Rosser at the midday meal that he had done the deed and that he had informed his fellow South Carolinians. Farley's resignation took a week to process. During that time, he settled accounts with the Corps quartermaster, du Pont, who added his chastisement, as did others.

On the day of Farley's departure, November 19, South Carolina had still not convened to draw up its ordinance of secession, prompting many to question his decision. But remaining resolute, after the midday meal Farley bade his friends farewell. The last man he approached was Pelham, who pulled him aside. "You have your wish, Henry. Make the most of it."

"I intend to, John. God bless you and all will follow me."

Farley's departure was a clarion call that had many speculating who would be next. Sunday evening in the mess hall, a heated exchange broke out between three South Carolinians and half a dozen Northern cadets. Charlie Ball of Alabama quickly sided with the South Carolinians and flicked a spoon of peas at the most vocal of the Northerners. The volley was incendiary. Before Ball could reload, the dining hall erupted in a food fight. As the battle wore on, none was unmarked, and the deadliest combatant proved to be George Custer, who had mastered rapid-fire launching of brussel sprouts with a spoon.

Frenetic, Chambliss tried to restore order.

"Enough, Fannie!" Pelham shouted. "Tom, you, too!"

"Just one more, John." Rosser tossed a water-soaked wad of bread at Emory Upton.

Kirby, Ames, and du Pont joined in the attempt to curb the carnage. For a third time Kingsbury hollered, "Battalion, attention!" Finally, the worst of the offenders were collared, and a ceasefire achieved. When order was restored, the ravages of war were everywhere—on uniforms, tables, chairs, walls, windows, floor, and even the high ceiling.

Glancing at Custer, Rosser burst out laughing. Custer's hair was thick with bread pudding.

"Look at your dress coat, Tom," Custer shot back. Rosser had taken a hit in the chest with gravied mashed potatoes.

Chambliss fumed as he stood on a table in the center of the dining hall. "Dammit to hell, people, do you not understand what you have done! You'll be walking Central Area until graduation." He ordered every man back to the barracks to change into utility uniform and return for work detail.

Pelham could only grin. If there was ever a time he was glad to be a private, it was then. He knew what Chambliss faced as first captain. He would be held responsible for the entire incident. Yet the flare-up had served a purpose. By the time the Corps had scrubbed every surface of the dining hall and returned to the barracks near midnight, the tension in the air seemed to have evaporated. Tempers had cooled, and a measure of good humor was restored.

Chapter Fifty-Four

When the United States Congress convened on Monday, December 3, the two senators from South Carolina were absent, having both resigned. However, at the urging of the South Carolina governor, the state representatives, including William Porcher Miles, remain seated, though they would do so only until preparations for the state's secession convention were finalized. Before Miles headed home, he co-authored and delivered a letter to President Buchanan, the subject of the letter being South Carolina's position on Union forts in Charleston Harbor.

That same Sunday, the Corps awoke to a hard freeze and a long sermon from Reverend French on the perils of trusting in the things of this world.

Late that afternoon at the superintendent's quarters, Colonel Delafield welcomed Lieutenant Colonel Reynolds into his study.

"James, we are not to be disturbed."

James closed the door behind them.

"A brandy, John?"

"No, thank you, sir."

Delafield poured himself two fingers. "Read this dispatch from Scott." As Reynolds read, Delafield downed a finger of the brandy.

Reynolds returned the telegram. "Incredibly presumptuous."

"Criminal is the word I would have used. You have a commission from South Carolina acting as if their state no longer belongs to the Union, presenting the president of the United States a letter of truce on Forts Moultrie, Castle Pinckney, and Sumter in Charleston Harbor. The unmitigated gall of it, saying they intend no action against the installations as long as they are not reinforced, and allowing that they'll pay a fair, but not unreasonable, price for them."

"What about the federal arsenal in Charleston?" Reynolds asked. "The telegram doesn't speak to it."

"I know. Major Anderson has his arms around a beehive."

"You mean Colonel Gardner, don't you? I believe he has charge of Charleston."

Delafield shook his head. "Did. Major Anderson replaced him a few weeks ago. The work of our seditious secretary of war. A month back Gardner attempted to remove arms from the arsenal to better supply his installations. Floyd berated him for the action and had him reassigned. And the devil knew what he was doing when he brought in Anderson."

"Why would you say that, sir?" Reynolds said.

"You trust Anderson?"

"With my life, sir."

Delafield returned a jaundiced look. "Anderson is from Kentucky, his wife is from Georgia, and he's pro-slavery. Doesn't that make you a little uncomfortable?"

"Sir, Bob Anderson is a patriot and the finest sort of man. He was my artillery instructor here at the Academy, and we served together in the Mexican War. He served brilliantly for General Scott and was severely wounded at Molino del Rey. The man has fight. He'll do his duty."

Delafield pulled at his whiskers. "Um. Maybe he can walk the fence better than anyone else. Still, this premature cat and mouse game bodes ill. Nothing good will come of it."

"In truth, sir," Reynolds said. "I doubt Anderson has a hundred regulars to man the three forts, let alone the arsenal. He can't initiate a fight, and I suspect that when South Carolina jumps, the Union will take the money for the forts and run."

"I suppose. Buchanan is the lamest of ducks. He's all but abdicated being commander in chief."

"Sir, in fairness to him, what would you do in his position? How do you force the South to accept the election?"

"That's just it. They do accept the election! They've taken it as their mandate to form a slave union, and unless Buchanan makes some sort of deal on slavery, we'll be half the country we were."

"I think slavery is only part of it, sir. But I agree with you. We're treading on eggshells, and there is likely nothing Buchanan can say or do to appease the South that the Republicans won't unsay or undo."

"The shame of it," said Delafield in a defeated tone. "South Carolina is the one fueling the fire. I say let the brigands go and good riddance."

At supper, Monday, December 10, Chambliss informed Pelham that he and Jessica Danford agreed to end their relationship. Her father, initially warm to an Academy man, had cooled to the thought of the man being from a seceded state, since he believes Tennessee would be just that.

"But she's from Virginia," Pelham said.

"Northwestern Virginia, the Clarksburg area. Her father is a committed Unionist and said he'd move the family across the border if Virginia chose the wrong side."

"I'm sorry to know it, Nate. I thought you two so well matched."

"We're not totally done. If Tennessee doesn't secede, we've pledged to pick up where we left off."

"You think they won't?"

"I hope they don't."

"Nate, Tennessee is a slave state."

"But also a border state."

That night, Pelham wrote two letters, neither to Clara. In light of South Carolina's intention to hold a secession convention on December 17, his first letter was to his father asking for immediate permission to resign. Especially since Alabama had already declared its intent to secede. He strengthened his argument with the fact that most of the cotton state men had already written home for permission to resign.

His second letter was to Judge Walker. It was short and to the point, requesting guidance on how best to make himself useful to the state of Alabama.

Chapter Fifty-Five

Monday, December 18, Pelham ran nearly all the way to the Ordnance Compound for coastal gunnery class. Despite gray skies, the gloom of academics, and the uncertain status of the nation, having read Clara's latest letter three times, he was thoroughly in the Christmas spirit. He marveled at her writing, upbeat and full of wit and mirth. Her descriptions of seasonal transformations at Clermont more real than a landscape painting.

She wrote that she was doing famously in her anatomy course and per his request would provide no further details. But her most unexpected news was from her father. The good doctor was finally warming to the notion that a cadet, even from Alabama, was perhaps not such a bad thing. She quoted him saying, *I have heard that gentlemen of the South are often beyond reproach, and such a man is my desire for you.* That he had expressed to her the same concern that Jessica Danford's father had about Chambliss, seemed a small thing to Pelham. To his mind, the Confederacy could be fully established in six months, and ties with the United States would be restored for the benefit of both not many months after. Unquestionably, the North needed the South's cotton, and the South needed the North's textile mills. It would be but a matter of time before her father came around.

At the midday meal on Friday, December 21, the Corps learned that the previous evening South Carolina had formally voted to secede from the United States of America, declaring itself a sovereign commonwealth. Representatives at the South Carolina secession convention had voted one hundred and sixty-nine in favor of session—none opposed. That evening at supper, talk of South Carolina's secession spread as if an intoxicating mist over the Southern faction of the Corps. Catching Pelham's eye across the dining hall, Charlie Ball raised a toast with his water glass.

The next afternoon, Delafield called a joint meeting of the Tactical Department and Academic Department. He addressed the realities of what they faced and delineated the actions that should be followed with respect to the Corps, assuming that other states would follow South Carolina's lead. The discussion that followed anticipated a stream of cadet resignations, as well as circumstances that would undoubtedly impact academic classes and cadet performance. He also recognized that Southern members of the two departments might follow their states. Delafield made it clear that any decisions to leave the Academy or the army would be honored and requested that Professor Mahan direct his department heads to adjust expectations for cadet performance until such time as normalcy was restored.

The last issue discussed was how best to expedite voluntary separations to minimize disruption at the Academy. Lieutenant Colonel Reynolds said he would address the Corps at the supper meal and would inform the four cadet company tactical officers do the same in meetings after the meal. He would assign Lieutenant Lee the First Class Club as the venue for D Company's meeting.

When Walter Kingsbury finished his announcements at the supper meal, he introduced Lieutenant Colonel Reynolds.

"Take seats, men," Reynolds said, his tone easy, reassuring.

Pelham liked and respected Reynolds. He had proven the equal of Hardee and inspired as easily.

"As you know," Reynolds said, "South Carolina has announced its departure from the Union. And other states have announced similar intentions. Whether they do or not and how this will all play out, we don't know. Regardless, the Academy is faced with the challenge of maintaining order and discipline and continuing its mission to educate and train the Corps of Cadets."

Pelham and Rosser exchanged glances.

"We are nearly upon Christmas break," Reynolds continued. "A time to remember and reflect, and to appreciate who we are and the bond we share. As some of us depart and go our separate ways, let those who stay respect their choices and harbor neither ill will nor disdain, considering that if they were in Southern shoes, they would likely do the same."

Reynolds talked about the importance of maintaining the daily regimen, focusing on academics, preserving order and discipline, and moving through the Christmas holiday with a positive, thankful attitude. He then spoke to the administration of resignations. At this, Pelham noticed du Pont at the battalion head table squirm in his seat. It would be his duty to out-process every departing cadet.

"Immediately following supper, your company tactical officer will meet with you," Reynolds said, afterwards introducing the company tactical officers, each officer then announcing where his company meeting would take place.

"Let me conclude," Reynolds said, "by assuring you, as in the past, that you will be informed of all matters that affect your lives. It is no less than you deserve. Either I or your company tactical officers will communicate developments on the national scene as they become known."

Reynolds surveyed the room of more than two hundred and seventy sober-faced cadets. "In this uncertain time, may God bless our country and watch over each and every one of you. You are dismissed."

In the First-Class Club, chairs were stacked in a corner to accommodate the whole of D Company. Pelham, Rosser, Kirby, and Custer were shoulder to shoulder against a wall.

At the approach of Lieutenant Lee, Paddy O'Rorke at the door stood straight as a pine. "Company, attention!"

"At ease, gentlemen," Lee said, crossing the room and taking a position at the end of the conference table.

"I've been thinking of what to say," Lee began, meeting the eye of every man in the room. "How I might soften the harshness of what lies ahead. But I find there is no benefit in sugarcoating the reality of what we face. I will be brief, for there is not much I can add to what the commandant has already said. Suffice to say, we cannot undo what has been done. When you return to your rooms, you must put aside the obvious burden of what you have heard or may hear from this day forward, and how it will play upon you and your families, and even the friendships you've formed here at the Academy. You must do your duty despite the distractions. As you would on the battlefield, you must accept what is and go on with the business at hand, conducting yourselves as disciplined soldiers and completing your academic assignments to the best of your ability."

Pelham noticed Lee glancing repeatedly at the Stars and Stripes that hung in the corner of the room.

"I have a concern," Lee continued, "and I will say it only once, that some of you may have the tendency to see others differently as events unfold. I insist that this not occur in D Company, and I will not stand for it. As the commandant said, we will treat one another with the respect we ask in return. Certainly, no member of the Corps has wished for what is upon us. Rather it is the doing of political processes over which we have no control. Our lot at West Point is to live in harmony and draw no lines in the sand. I promise to deal harshly with any evidence of dissension or malicious gossip. I trust I am clear on this point."

Lee spoke for another five minutes, describing the process by which he would keep them informed, and the procedure for a member of the company to exercise his option to leave the Academy.

"Lastly, before any man makes the decision to resign from the Academy, I want to seem personally."

Rosser raised his hand. "Sir, what will you do if Virginia secedes?"

Lee stared at Rosser. "Probably no different than you, Mr. Rosser."

Chapter Fifty-Six

Monday, December 24, the Corps celebrated its first day off for the Christmas holiday. By mid-morning, Pelham, Kingsbury, Ames, Rosser, and half a dozen underclassmen, all wearing long overcoats, frolicked on skates on the ice-covered Hudson beneath a brilliant sun, the wind chill below freezing.

"Stay more centered over your feet, John," Kingsbury shouted to Pelham. His personal goal for three years had been to teach the Alabamian how to ice skate, and he was pleased with what he saw.

At noon, Ames and Rosser, the latter happy to be off the ice after a series of hard falls, headed back to the barracks for the midday meal. Pelham and Kingsbury, in possession of passes to Garrison's Landing across the Hudson, readied for the trip Kingsbury had promised. It would be Pelham's first long-range skate, and his first trip to Garrison. His pass Lieutenant Lee's reward for moderating the debate.

Kingsbury skated up to Pelham. "Ready, John?"

Pelham massaged his gloved hands for warmth. "Don't worry about me. Just keep looking over your shoulder to see if I'm vertical."

"You'll do fine. Remember, eyes out front, not between your feet. And as an incentive, if you cross the river without falling, I'll buy the first round."

"Lay on, MacDuff," Pelham said, getting the jump on Kingsbury.

The two crossed the Hudson in a matter of minutes, and on the far side removed their skates, slinging them over their shoulders.

"Just up ahead," Kingsbury said, pointing to a pub with the name Van Winkle's.

"Greetings, lads," said the man behind the bar flashing a grin. "Just drop your skates by the door."

Pelham and Kingsbury hung their overcoats and forage caps on wall hooks and made for the fireplace, where an Irish terrier was curled up by the hearth. On the mantle evergreen clippings arranged with holly gave off a wintergreen scent. Seasonal decorations and patrons enjoying themselves promoted a festive atmosphere.

Kingsbury approached the bar. "Merry Christmas to you, sir."

The bartender extended his hand. "And to you, young man. And you can call me Rip. And, no, it's not my real name. You're my first Academy customers this fine day before Christmas. What might I serve you?"

"Two pints of ale, sir!" shouted Pelham from across the room. "And put it on his tab."

Van Winkle smiled at Kingsbury. "And something to eat?"

"What have you?"

"The special. A plate of bratwurst with sauerkraut, mustard, hard rolls, and butter. Quite nice, actually."

"Anything else?" Pelham asked, never having had bratwurst.

"Nope. Just the special."

"Then two of your fine specials," declared Kingsbury.

"Anything for two Academy lads who have obviously braved the river. The ice cannot be so thick yet," said the bartender, giving Kingsbury a look.

"Trust me, sir, it's hard as rock," said Pelham, taking the stool next to Kingsbury.

"Aye. But 'tis good to remember ice is still water."

The door opened, ushering in a gust of freezing air and two locals bundled in layers and topped with Dutch hats. Stripping their layers, they took stools next to Pelham. The one next to Pelham was short, the other stocky and tall, both in their late fifties, their faces weathered.

"Whatever you're serving for food, Rip, and a pint," the tall man said in a raspy voice.

The short man smiled at Pelham. "From across the river?"

"We are, sir. And a Merry Christmas to you."

The tall man's eyes narrowed on Pelham. "From your accent, I take you to be a Southerner?"

Pelham ignored the man's tone and offered his hand. "I am, sir. From Alabama. John Pelham's my name."

The tall man made no move to take Pelham's hand. After an awkward silence, the short man took it. "Please to meet you, John Pelham. Peter Duncan's my name. That's quite a uniform you're wearing there."

The tall man eyed Pelham. "I suppose you, too, will be gone soon?"

"If Alabama leaves the Union? Yes, sir, I will return home, if that is your question."

"Of course, you will, after we pay to put you nose-in-the-air Southerners through the nation's school."

"It ain't the boy's doing, Jack," the short man said. "Leave him be."

He turned to Pelham. "Don't mind Jack, son."

Kingsbury nudged Pelham. "Let's take our meal by the window."

"A pleasure, Mr. Duncan," Pelham said with a warm smile.

The short man nodded respectfully, while the tall man growled into his beer.

Pelham and Kingsbury crossed the pub and sat next to a frost-lined window, framing a Currier and Ives landscape of the Hudson and West Point on the distant bluff. When the meal was served, Pelham found bratwurst very much to his liking. He ordered another round of ale, and it wasn't until three o'clock that the two of them left the pub.

By the time they crossed the river, trekked up the bluff road, and entered Central Area, the highlight of the afternoon was already in progress. The tradition started by Superintendent Robert E. Lee was likely intended to exhaust cadets to the point they couldn't pursue unworthy recreation. It was the annual chasing of the greased pig, and a crowd of nearly two hundred formed a tight circle, cheering and laughing at what was happening inside the circle.

"John!" Rosser shouted. "You and Walter are missing a good one."

Pelham pushed his way into the crowd. Paddy O'Rorke was chasing a pig lathered with axle grease inside the circle. He would have the allotted one minute to catch the pig. O'Rorke feinted right, feinted left, and deftly maneuvered the pig against the legs of the crowd, where it would have seemed a simple matter to reach down and grab the animal and earn the rights to a fine pork dinner with friends. O'Rorke, indeed, got his hands on the pig, but after a grunt and a squeal, it wriggled free and darted between his legs, upsetting his balance, and landing him in the quagmire.

"All hail the first sergeant," shouted a grinning Pelham.

"This one can't be got!" Rosser insisted, himself covered with mud. "You give him a go, John!"

Pelham might have considered it, but for his uniform. As a Third Classman he had caught the pig, and Rosser had shared the culinary award.

Another man stepped inside the circle, and after him another, and still another; the Golden Fleece eluding them all.

Then McElheny, the first plebe to risk it, jumped inside the circle.

Rosser elbowed Pelham. "This should be good."

Instantly in a whir of motion, McElheny chased the pig in a circle at a pace none of the others had. When his time was nearly up, like O'Rorke, he skillfully backed the much-fatigued animal against the crowd. Unlike O'Rorke, when he reached down, instead of trying to grasp the pig, he pushed it down into the mud and sat on it. Despite accusations of cheating and unsportsman conduct, McElheny was declared the winner, delighting all the plebes. He selected nine of his D Company classmates to share a Christmas feast at a table that would be reserved for them in the dining hall.

After supper, John French, in his role as spiritual leader, conducted a Christmas Eve service in the chapel. His message was one of peace, tolerance, and dependence upon an all-powerful God to heal all things, including the recent wound to the nation. Pelham left the chapel wondering at the reverend's choice of words. As previously planned, he joined five other cadets in a caroling group at the superintendent's quarters, singing, *It Came Upon a Midnight Clear; Oh, Little Town of Bethlehem;* and *Away in a Manger.*

Awaking to the stillness of Christmas Day, Pelham and the rest of the Corps found everything bathed in glorious light. Central Area, the commandant's office, the academic building, the quarters along Jefferson Road, the Plain, the distant West Point Hotel, and everything man-made and otherwise were blanketed with six inches of bright white, pristine snow.

There were no formations that day, and at midday, a sumptuous Christmas meal was served in the mess hall. The artfully done menu boasted oysters, roast beef, roasted turnips and potatoes, candied yams, yeast rolls, and mincemeat pie. McElheny and his friends enjoyed these and succulent roast pork to the extreme.

After the meal, Pelham walked the Plain, enchanted by the white landscape and the thought that he would never again see so much snow. His eyes were alive to everything, his mind captive to four years of memories. As he walked, the largest flakes he had ever seen began to fall. Upon his return to the barracks, he bounded up the stairs, intent on penning a thought that had played in his mind during his walk. After revising and re-revising what he had written, he started a letter to Clara, describing the beauty of the snow- clad campus, the joy of the day, and the plans he had for the two of them once sanity was restored to the universe. At the end of the letter, he added, *My lady and love, this is not a perfect world. What we are facing makes me all the more sure of, and thankful for, an all-powerful God who controls all things. I pray you will enjoy the following, which speaks my heart, that grace is indeed key.* And at this, he wrote what he had drafted earlier and entitled Grace and Snow.

Have you ever thought or cared to know
How grace so much is like the snow?
That swirls and streams from far above,
So white and light, and pure as love,
Covering all that lies below.

Or think you this—it isn't so.
That grace so different is from snow,
Which only hides and cannot clean
The sin of life and all that's mean.
That grace alone defeats the foe.

Pelham sealed the letter and took it to the orderly room. From there, he went to the library to check out Nolan's book on cavalry tactics and the use of artillery for the third time.

CHAPTER FIFTY-SEVEN

December 26 passed with little fanfare, and it was not until the next day that Colonel Delafield received General Scott's telegram relating the events of the night before. Major Anderson had shown his mettle. He had moved his command from Fort Moultrie on the mainland to Fort Sumter, an unfinished fortification situated on a two-hundred-acre island at the mouth of Charleston Harbor. The cannons at Fort Moultrie were spiked and the gun carriages burned.

The families of the officers and enlisted men were sent to unfortified Fort Johnson across the harbor. Anderson and his command of nine officers, seventy-four enlisted men, and forty-three civilian construction workers would hold out where the odds favored them most. Captain Abner Doubleday, Anderson's second in command, gave orders to limit construction activities to those that would best enable Sumter's defense against bombardment and amphibious assault.

In the same telegram, Scott informed Delafield that he was moving to Washington to have more immediate access to the president.

Saturday morning, December 29, Charlie Ball intercepted Pelham outside the mess hall. His face radiant, his hand extended. "I've done it, John—submitted my resignation. Reynolds should have it this afternoon."

Pelham shook Ball's hand. "So, it doesn't matter that Alabama hasn't yet seceded?"

"The convention is planned. It will happen."

"Somehow, I knew you'd be first."

"I tell you, brother, it's exciting—damn exciting. And I know you'll be right behind me."

That afternoon, General Scott reported an unusual exchange in the longest dispatch Delafield had yet received. Senator Jefferson Davis of Mississippi, a senator from Virginia, and a former senator from South Carolina, who until South Carolina's secession had been assistant secretary of state for Buchanan, were to meet with the president on December 27 to discuss the gravity of any future federal initiatives in the South. Having been informed by former senator Louis Wigfall of the events the night before in Charleston Harbor, Davis and his associates confronted the president with the Sumter charade. They considered it a provocative breach of an earlier accord made with the three South Carolina commissioners. The meeting concluded amicably enough, with a tentative agreement that the status quo be maintained until terms could be adopted to turn the federal installations over to South Carolina.

However, a day later, the South Carolina commissioners acted independently and precipitously. They declared to the president that the breach in their agreement was irrevocable and demanded that he do the only honorable thing—order Anderson and his troops to leave Charleston immediately. Indignant, Buchanan summarily dismissed their demand.

In the same dispatch, Scott informed Delafield that Secretary Floyd had chosen Louisianan Pierre Gustave Toutant Beauregard to be West Point's next superintendent, and that he would arrive at the Academy in late January. He went on to say that Beauregard was a good man by every measure and had served on his staff during the Mexican War, twice wounded and brevetted for gallantry. While ecstatic over the prospect of turning over the reins and pleased that his wife was finally taking to the idea, Delafield was struck by the selection.

In the days following Christmas, Pelham and the rest of the Corps were briefed daily on dispatches received by Academy leadership. On their own, they read newspaper accounts chronicling South Carolina's indignation over Anderson's nocturnal maneuver to Sumter and South Carolina's subsequent bloodless seizure of Forts Moultrie and Castle Pinckney and the Charleston arsenal.

On the last day of the year, Pelham spent the morning in the library, finding the day's newspaper unusually thick. It contained reprints of two documents prepared by South Carolina lawmakers. The first was entitled, "Declaration of the Immediate Causes which Induce and Justify the Secession of South Carolina from the Federal Union." The second was entitled, "An Address to the People of the Slave-Holding States of the United States." Pelham read the two documents with a growing sense of resignation. The crafters of the documents had more than achieved their aim. No Southerner reading the documents could respond other than he had. For the first time, he was wholly convinced that the intent and benefits of the United States' Constitution no longer served the South.

Returning to the barracks, Pelham wished that the Christmas break was over, that he could again be immersed in academics with no time to stew over Southern grievances.

That night, in a conciliatory gesture, Lieutenant Colonel Reynolds granted the First Class the privilege of assembling in their club to bring in the New Year, even sanctioning the use of tobacco products.

"Can I get you another punch?" Patterson asked Pelham, a thin thread of smoke rising from his pipe.

Pelham exhaled and flicked cigar ashes into a tin cup. "Can you make that a flip?"

"Soon enough, John. And I, for one, would like Benny's take on all this."

The evening was alternately gay and solemn, the gaiety a function of bawdy anecdotes, songs, and reminiscences, especially about plebe year. The solemnity a function of political argument and planned departures by Southern classmates once their home states seceded.

At ten minutes before midnight, Pelham clapped his hands loudly and mounted a chair. Raising his punch glass, he shouted, "My friends, in minutes we will enter the year of our class, and in honor of our class and our bond as brothers, I propose a toast to West Point!"

The room echoed the toast.

Hardly had the toast been made, when Pelham began singing the second verse of "Benny Havens, Oh."

To our kind old Alma Mater, our rockbound highland home,
We'll cast back many a fond regret, as o'er life's sea we roam.
Until on our last battlefield the light of heaven shall glow,
We'll never fail to drink to her and Benny Havens, Oh!

Oh! Benny Havens, Oh!—Oh! Benny Havens, Oh!
We'll sing our reminiscences of Benny Havens, Oh!

Pelham had expected the others to join in but was instead given the floor. When he finished, the room erupted with bravos and the stomping of feet. Pelham returned a weak smile, stood down, and glanced at Chambliss.

Chambliss raised his glass. "In less than a minute, brothers, we'll ring in our last New Year as cadets and clearly the most uncertain year of our lives. Let us bring it in loud and strong."

When the minute hand struck midnight, the class of 1861 responded with solemn sentiment.

Should auld acquaintance be forgot
And never brought to mind?
Should auld acquaintance be forgot
And auld lang syne?

For auld lang syne, my dear,
For auld lang syne.
We'll take a cup of kindness yet,
For auld lang syne.

CHAPTER FIFTY-EIGHT

MANASSAS JUNCTION, VIRGINIA
SATURDAY, JULY 20, 1861
The DAY BEFORE THE FIRST BATTLE OF BULL RUN

After leaving Piedmont Station and pausing for a few hours for sleep around midnight, Pelham and the Alburtis battery arrived at Manassas Junction mid-morning, July 20. He was curious, traveling within earshot of the railroad, not to have heard a train passing. He later learned that railroad engineers and crews had refused to operate the trains the previous evening, complaining they had been without sleep for twenty-four hours. Confederate commanders were furious when the railroad men didn't return to work until daybreak.

Pelham was greeted near Manassas by one of Beauregard's general staff officers and an attendant sergeant.

"Alburtis battery?" the officer asked.

"Yes, sir. Lieutenant Pelham, battery commander."

"You made exceptional time, Lieutenant. Your entire column did. I'm Major Whitman, and this is Sergeant Cramer. He'll see to your men and horses."

Pelham shook the dust from his scarf. "Where do you want my guns, sir?"

"Just pull them off the road for now. Except for harassing artillery and picket fire, the Union hasn't tried anything since Blackburn's Ford. Rather odd, we're all thinking. Though answered prayer."

The officer motioned for Pelham to follow him. "I'll take you to headquarters."

"Lieutenant Findley!" Pelham shouted over his shoulder. "Do whatever the sergeant tells you."

Minutes later, Pelham was ushered into a marquee tent filled with generals and those of near rank. He recognized Beauregard and Johnston hovering over a map table. The officers surrounding them included Jackson and Johnston's other brigade commanders, less General Kirby Smith, whose brigade was still at Piedmont Station. Jackson caught Pelham's eye and offered a faint smile.

A hand grasped Pelham's shoulder. He turned to see Tom Rosser sporting a nearly full beard. "Brother Tom," Pelham exclaimed. "Damn, if you don't look the soldier. And what's this?" Pelham fingered the captain's epaulet on Rosser's shoulder.

"Just got 'em, roommate."

Pelham returned a smile. "They look good on you. But don't expect me to salute."

Rosser grinned, the strain of the past few days etched in his face. "You've been at it, then?"

"All but melted our barrels, John. Trying to make the Yankees think we've twice the artillery."

Pelham nodded. "And I bring more. With Johnston's other batteries, we bring twenty-four guns."

A man approached them. "Well, if it's not my two nemeses!"

Pelham and Rosser turned to see Fitzhugh Lee with major's epaulettes.

"Good to see the two of you together again," Lee said. "Though, I'm jealous that you'll be commanding guns tomorrow while I run around as a staffer."

"For General Ewell," Rosser said. "And don't kid yourself, sir. You'll have a brigade of cavalry within a month."

"I hope the thing won't last that long."

A plumed hat approached from the other side of the tent. "Fitz Lee? Is that you?" Jeb Stuart wrapped his arms around the smaller man. "How long has it been, Fitz?" Stuart cocked his head. "I thought you'd been killed by Indians."

They all laughed.

"If we can make it happen," Stuart said, "let's the four of us get together tonight. I'll drop by Ewell's headquarters after dark."

An aide to General Johnston suddenly shouted above the din of the tent. "Attention, Gentlemen. Your attention, please!"

Johnston, senior to Beauregard, stood beside him in front of a war map, held aloft by two orderlies. "Gentlemen, lest there be any confusion, I have given General Beauregard, who fully understands the situation here and the lay of the land, command of the field and the authority to implement his operational plan. Give the general your undivided attention."

Beauregard nodded to Johnston and scanned the faces of Johnston's brigade commanders. "First of all, we here cannot thank the Army of the Shenandoah enough for coming as quickly as you have."

Beauregard's commanders in the Army of the Potomac raised a rousing cheer.

"As a result, we have parity," Beauregard said, "and unless my classmate, Irvin McDowell, preempts us, we are going to take the battle to him at first light, turn his left flank at Centreville, and cut his line of communication back to Alexandria. We'll make Professor Mahan proud."

Those who understood chuckled.

"In our distinct favor is the circus forming about the Union forces. Spectators by the hundreds from Washington and surroundings are quite literally gumming up the roads. All coming, I suppose, to witness the demise of the Union Army."

More laughter filled the tent.

"If we succeed, my friends, we can hope to end the North's aggression, for we will have their capital in our sights, and I suspect a rather large number of prisoners with which to bargain."

Beauregard proceeded to describe the locations and strengths of the Union and Confederate forces, and to detail his plan for the divisions of Longstreet and Early to lead a morning attack from Blackburn's Ford and Mitchell's Ford.

Later that evening, Pelham, whose battery was to be held in reserve, as was much of Johnston's army, found Lee and Rosser in Ewell's camp seated on a log before a fire. Rosser offered Pelham a cigar and some burnt coffee.

Pelham tasted the coffee and dumped it. "Think of it, Tom. Three months ago, we were at Benny's."

"I could really enjoy a flip about now," Lee said, surprising them both.

His face animated in the fire, Rosser said, "And strike me dead if I wouldn't take the worst of the mess hall food with no complaint."

Pelham glanced across Bull Run at the countless Union fires on the east side. "I wonder if we'll see some of our mates tomorrow?"

"I pray not," Rosser said. "I'd hate to make that decision. Yet, we know they're there, every one of them. Our class graduated a month early in May, and Custer's class made such a stink, they graduated in June. And both classes were sent straight to Washington. All that was in a letter I got from Lew Hoxton, du Pont's roommate. Poor Lew. Henry mentally beat the Virginian into graduating, but once Lew put on the blue uniform, he realized his mistake and resigned his commission. I understand he's somewhere out west commanding a battery for our old commandant, Hardee."

"Hoxton's a good man," Lee said. "The decision was tough for a lot of us Virginians."

When Stuart had yet to make an appearance, Pelham stood up and stretched. "I've got to get back." He clasped hands with Lee and Rosser. "May we celebrate a glorious victory tomorrow."

"And toast with some old Kentucky bourbon," said Rosser.

Late that night, after two trains returned to Piedmont Station to load General Kirby Smith's troops, an incident occurred. On the trip back to Manassas Junction, one of the trains derailed, resulting in a delay of many hours. A summary investigation suggested the problem was caused by either poor tracks, a collision with something on the track, or an outright act of sabotage. Strong suspicion of the latter and extremely hot tempers resulted in a swift trial and execution of the train's conductor.

CHAPTER FIFTY-NINE

Seven Months Earlier
West Point, New York
Second Semester, 1861

The first days of the New Year were a tonic to the Corps, with perspectives narrowed from what would happen to the country to what would happen in Professor Mahan's class. By the close of Friday's classes, Rosser despaired of losing his entire cushion of "tenths."

Thursday evening, January 3, Nate Chambliss invited Charlie Ball to address the Corps on the eve of his departure. The dining hall was uncharacteristically hushed in anticipation of the popular Alabamian.

The man who would have been first captain of his class stood at the lectern. "My friends—and you are my friends, whether of Northern or Southern persuasion, tomorrow I depart for home. To my classmates, I say that we have come a long way since our plebe days. Along the way, you have helped make me the man I otherwise would never have been, and for that I thank you. I count the past three and half years as the best years of my life. What a privilege to have been a part of the Corps, and for the Corps to have become a part of me." Ball fought for composure. "I … I count myself blessed and bid you farewell."

The dining hall erupted in cheers that shook the building windows. As Pelham applauded, he found himself envious of the man who would be able to pick any position he wanted with the Alabama state militia.

The next morning, Ball stood in Central Area ready to leave, enshrouded by his classmates and others in a gray cocoon. He was not a little surprised given it was an academic day. A lesser number escorted him to the South Dock, where he boarded the ferry to Garrison, and waved a final time to those on the dock, which included Pelham and Rosser.

The following day, Saturday, began as another cold, gray day, but by early afternoon was transformed by sun, blue skies, and rising temperatures. After the midday meal, Pelham and Rosser returned to their room. Rosser picked up a novel, and Pelham had started a letter to Clara when the door suddenly opened to Dan McElheny wearing a Cheshire grin.

"What's got you so happy, Dan?" Pelham asked.

"John, I have a note … it's from the author of your letters." Rosser's head spun around, and Pelham gawked at McElheny. "Joseph," McElheny said, winded, "the boy works summers and holidays at the hotel. He said you would remember him. He asked me to deliver it. It's definitely from Miss Bolton. I know her handwriting and perfume better than you do."

Pelham looked to Rosser, who shrugged ignorance, and then back at McElheny. "Don't be playing with me, Dan."

"I wouldn't! Not about this." McElheny's grin widened as he handed Pelham the note.

The message bore a single line. *Dear knight, I am at the hotel. Your lady.*

"Let me see that," Rosser demanded, and after he had, jumped to his feet and dragged Pelham from his chair. "Damn, John, if this ain't the best come-lately Christmas present a man ever had! Take his other hand, Dan."

Rosser proceeded to lead the three of them around the room in an awful jig and after two turns said, "I suppose you'll be breaking some rules, roommate?"

"Every one of them," Pelham bellowed.

Dawning his long overcoat, he squeezed the breath from McElheny and plunged down the stairwell.

Daring anyone to stop him, but encountering no one, Pelham ran to the hotel. When he reached it, he saw Clara waving in the parlor window. He sped past the desk clerk and found her still at the window. In a red and green velvet dress, her shoulders covered with a white wool shawl, her face was radiant. Even at a distance, he could tell she had been crying. He advanced toward her and she toward him, meeting in the middle of the room. For a long moment they said nothing, but only gazed at each other. He retrieved a handkerchief and dabbed her cheeks, and then drew her to him, compressing her body hard against his. Framing her face in his hands, he kissed both cheeks and then her parted lips.

"God, don't let this be a dream."

"It isn't, my knight."

Pelham led her to a love seat, and after countless passionate kisses apologized. "I meant to shave this morning."

She ran her finger across his stubble. "I don't mind." She nestled in the crook of his shoulder.

"Why didn't you … How did?" Pelham wasn't sure where to start.

Clara took two mints from a glass jar on the coffee table and offered him one. "My dear knight, this is such an awful world, and I had to do something." She peppered him with airy kisses and in a giddy tone announced, "You can thank Ellie that I'm here. In fact, she almost joined me."

"I thought she and Henry were over."

"They are. Not that she's found anyone else. It's just, the separation—and she still has feelings for Henry." Clara gazed at the floor. "What's going to happen to us, John?"

"Only good, I promise."

"I love you so very much," Clara said. "I think, too much. But I know God has a plan for us. He must. And I know that I have never been happier in my life—with you in it."

Pelham wanted desperately to say something clever, romantic, but could only manage, "Me, too."

"Let's go to Canada, John. Let's get away from all this."

"Let me just look at you."

"Not here," Clara said, lowering her eyes. "I'm upstairs in room 208 at the end of the hall. It has an incredible view of the river. Give me five minutes. I'll leave the door unlocked."

"Are you sure?"

Clara smiled and was gone.

Five minutes later, after pacing the hall and passing again and again the same etchings of the Hudson Valley, the Academy, and cadets and soldiers in various uniforms, Pelham knocked softly on the door to room 208. Hearing nothing, he turned the knob and entered.

Clara lay in bed under a comforter drawn up to her chin. A small blaze crackled in the room's fireplace, and the air had the smell of lilac.

Pelham tossed his overcoat on the vanity chair and stood awkwardly. "You, my lady, are the most precious of imps. Why didn't you tell me you were coming?"

"I wanted to surprise you. And I didn't finally decide until the day before yesterday, when Ellie said, 'Clara, just do it.'" She pointed to the window. "Look outside. Isn't it beautiful?"

"Maybe later."

Clara patted the bed and extended her hand. "I do love you, John Pelham. My knight in shining armor."

Pelham sat beside her. "I believe you do."

"Will you hold me?"

Pelham circled his arms around Clara's bare shoulders and kissed her. "My lady, you are warm as toast."

"Hmm. I wonder why?" She closed her eyes.

Pelham explored and caressed her through the comforter, his eyes suddenly wide. "You're naked."

Clara opened one eye. "Maybe."

Passion denied him for five long months surged through Pelham as he slipped his hand beneath the comforter.

"Ooh!" Clara squealed. "You are cold as ice."

Pelham stripped himself of shoes, dress coat, and trousers, and slipped under the covers.

"Damn, these buttons," he said, fumbling with his long underwear beneath the comforter.

Clara giggled. "Is someone in a hurry?"

When he finally pressed against her, she made another squeaking sound.

"You're sure?"

Clara searched Pelham's eyes and nodded.

What followed was more than Pelham had ever dreamed of. And there had been many dreams. He and Clara kissed, explored, and loved deeply and completely, and after they were exhausted and wet with perspiration, lay limp beside one another.

"Did I hurt you?" Pelham asked, concern in his voice.

Clara rose up and gazed down at him. "You truly are my sensitive knight, aren't you? No, you didn't hurt me. It's just that …"

"What?"

She shrugged.

"You mean …?

She put a finger to his lips. "Not anymore."

He grinned and glanced at the vanity clock. "It's barely three o'clock. Next time will be better."

"I'm sure it will." Her smile lit up the room.

"We just need to talk a bit."

"And kiss?" She wrapped her arms around his neck. "John, we are going to survive this, I know it. Do you know it, too?"

"We are, my lady. But we must be as wise as serpents. Let me tell you what I was writing when blessed McElheny delivered your note."

She beamed. "Oh, yes, do."

"We also need patience. The country is split, and I feel certain it will become two nations. Until that happens, there will be a time—possibly months, maybe as long as a year, possibly more, when we'll have to suffer the counsel of fathers, family, and friends that we forget each other and move on. If we are strong and can bide our time, meet as often as we can, as deliciously as we are now, the world will regain its axis and we will survive. But to be clear, my lady, you must know that our future must be in Alabama, with you the mistress of a fine plantation."

"You'll not be a soldier?"

"I pray not," he said, sitting up with his back against the headboard.

Clara sat up beside him, pulling the comforter across her chest.

"This very day, Alabama is having a referendum to decide the question of secession. The majority of the people will vote for it, and within the week we'll separate from the Union."

"I've been praying against it," Clara said. "But it is all over the papers. So many states say they are leaving."

"Don't despair, for it will be a good thing, and feathers ruffled will unruffle soon enough."

She nestled in the crook of his arm. "So, you will leave the Academy?"

Pelham told her he had yet to receive his father's permission, but that it would come, and when it did, he would resign. "If Alabama does not need my services in the militia, I hope to help Pa with the cotton. Anyway, I think you would very much like your new home in Alabama. And I know with certainty that the Pelham family would adore you."

"John, I love all you've told me about your home, about Alabama, and especially your family. I'll love everything, even the summers, for I can learn to perspire."

"And with dignity. But there is the dream of your being a doctor. If you think the North unaccepting, you'll find the South even more closed-minded."

Clara kissed him. "Right now, I'm thinking only about you being my husband, about having your babies, and you being their father." She kissed him again. "I was crazy to think of being a doctor."

"Don't say that. Times have changed, and you should be a part of it. And you are gifted the way a doctor should be. I won't let you abandon your dream."

Clara kissed him for saying so. "There actually is a medical school considering me, but it's far from settled. Anyway, about slavery, I will trust you to show me how it is not such a bad thing, that your Negroes are God's creatures like you and me and are treated well."

"You will see for yourself. Now tell me about life at Clermont."

"I wish you hadn't asked. Carol Hill's gone back to Mississippi. Her father ordered her home. She left after Christmas, and I do dearly miss her. We all do."

"I assure you the exodus is in full vigor here as well."

"May I ask you a question, John?"

"Anything."

"Your slave friend, Samuel. What is it that you haven't told me?"

"You want to know it all, don't you?" Pelham obliged her curiosity with as much detail as he could remember about the day in the cotton field, about the game he had forced Samuel to play, about his father, about Willie's salt and pepper talk, and about what remained unresolved with Samuel.

"That must have been so hard losing your best friend, and then growing up so fast."

He shrugged. "It was a lesson I had to learn."

"But what is it that isn't resolved between you and Samuel?"

"I can see I'll have to watch my tongue." He told her about the year before he came to West Point, about getting the acreage from his father to clear and plant, and about Samuel and the other blacks who worked for him, how they had been on their own for almost nine months and had brought in a crop. "And through it all," he said, "Samuel worked the hardest. We were together again, almost like before. And he was such a thinker. He would come to me, not as a friend, but as someone who saw a problem and how to solve it and suggesting this or that. I would see right away that he was right. We'd do it, whatever it was, his way."

"Sounds like a wonderful man."

"He is, and that's the problem. After we broke the land and before I left for West Point, I promised him that I would set him free when I had the power to do so. I wanted Samuel to have all that I had."

Clara beamed. "You are a truly good and noble man, John."

Pelham shook his head. "You don't understand, Clara. I can't do that."

"Of course not. You're here at West Point."

"No, I mean, even if I was back home."

"Why not?"

"It's complicated."

"Tell me."

"As much as I hate slavery and how it dehumanizes people, I can't change it, not in Alabama … not in the South. No one can the way things are now. And what about Samuel? I realize he knows no other life. His family is the plantation."

"Tell me more," Clara said, locking her hands behind her head, and in the process exposing one of her breasts.

"Maybe later."

Chapter Sixty

That evening, Pelham arrived at the barracks just as the Corps was returning from supper. The look on Rosser's face communicated all he needed to know. He would pay for his pudding. That night, he told Rosser about Carol Hill's return to Mississippi, and Rosser allowed she had made the right decision, and that maybe one day he might try to revive their relationship.

The next morning, Kirby informed Pelham that Lieutenant Lee wanted to see him—immediately.

Pelham made his way across Central Area and climbed the stairs to the suite of offices on the second floor reserved for company tactical officers.

He knocked on Lee's door. "You wanted to see me, sir?"

Lee's eyes narrowed. "I hope it was worth it, Pelham."

Pelham had determined to say nothing.

"How is it that you miss not only a required formation, but an entire meal?"

Pelham eyed the painting over Lee's desk, a western scene portraying a remnant of cavalry crouched behind dead horses in the face of a massive Indian charge. "No excuse, sir."

"You think I like coming in on Sunday?"

"No, sir."

"Mr. Pelham, I had intended on making you a lieutenant for the second semester, but then you so something like this. How does someone with your potential so often put his brain on leave?"

"Again, sir, no excuse."

"Is not burdening me with an excuse some sort of consolation for you?"

"No, sir."

"And, of course, now you give me no choice. Do you?"

Pelham's gazed at the painting, anticipating his punishment.

"Since confinement obviously makes no impression on you, you'll walk the area for the next month. And I'm letting you off easy. You could easily be dismissed or walking the area until graduation."

That afternoon after chapel and the midday meal, Pelham fell into formation in full dress uniform under arms with seven underclassmen with tours to walk. They stood for inspection by the officer of the guard. Three demerits later, Pelham began a three-hour tour marching back and forth across Central Area.

Wednesday, January 9, Colonel Delafield received a telegram from General Scott, informing him that the Union merchant ship *Star of the West* had been fired upon as it approached Charleston Harbor to land supplies and reinforcements at Fort Sumter. Fortunately, a subsequent telegram stated that there had been no injury to persons or damage to the ship. Despite pressuring by Governor Francis Pickens of South Carolina for immediate surrender of Fort Sumter, the uneasy truce held. As a concession from the self-proclaimed Commonwealth of South Carolina, Major Anderson was permitted to provision his men with vegetables and meat from the Charleston markets, with the clear understanding that the garrison of Fort Sumter was not to be reinforced. Additionally, the garrison's women and children at Fort Johnson would be afforded passage to New York City.

At the supper meal, the Corps was informed by Lieutenant Colonel Reynolds that Mississippi had seceded from the Union. On January 10, Florida seceded. A day later, Alabama did, and all eyes fell upon Pelham, who said nothing, having not yet received permission from his father to resign.

On January 19, Georgia seceded, uniting much of the Cotton Belt. In the mess hall that evening, news of Georgia's departure had the Corps speculating on whether former commandant Hardee would resign. Two days later, they learned that he had.

On Monday, January 21, a flustered Delafield ushered Reynolds into his office. "I'm inclined to another shot of whiskey, John. The country's unraveling."

"Only if we recognize secession, sir."

Delafield shook his head. "We, the Union, can do or not do whatever the hell we want. But the simple fact is, Buchanan hasn't raised a finger to stop a single state from announcing it and doing it. Until he does, for which I hold out no hope, there will be no stopping those that have the notion."

"In fairness to him, sir, he's struggled with the Constitution, whether he has the legal right to take action, let alone forceful action."

"I know, and I find it ridiculous. In one breath he says unequivocally that a state cannot secede, and in the next says that the federal government is powerless to prevent it. It makes no sense!"

"No, sir."

"By my count, the seceded states have taken three more arsenals, Augusta, Baton Rouge, and Mount Vernon, and nearly a dozen fortifications along the Southern coast. Hell, with the exception of Fort Sumter and Fort Pickens off Pensacola, the South controls everything."

"There is still Texas, sir."

"For how long?"

Reynolds shrugged.

"Not a day goes by, I don't hear from Scott," Delafield said. "Today, he says he's never seen the stoic Lincoln so riled over Buchanan's inaction. That once he's in office, he'll be out-the-gate bold to undo what's been done. He told Scott to ready for action—that any surrendered federal installations will be retaken, and any installations still garrisoned will be reinforced."

"That will bring conflict, sir."

"Indeed. But Lincoln's a shrewd one. He knows he cannot be the aggressor, that federal installations in the South are his ace in the hole. South Carolina is not about to hand over the forts in Charleston harbor, let alone the arsenal."

"A Pandora's box."

"Yes. Still, even with Lincoln ready to fall on his sword to preserve the Union, something sane could happen before the inauguration."

"In any event, sir, the Corps seems to be handling the chaos better than I expected."

"Which is a true blessing. Where do we stand now?"

Reynolds retrieved and unfolded a sheet of paper from a folder in his briefcase. "Fewer than forty have resigned for reason of state affiliation."

"There will be more. Not all the states have jumped," Delafield muttered under his breath. "Just two more days and this will be Beauregard's problem."

That same morning, in the chambers of the United States Senate, two weeks after his home state of Mississippi had seceded, an emotional Jefferson Davis bid farewell to his senate colleagues. Later in the day, before Beauregard made his initial appearance at West Point, Delafield defended Davis to Reynolds.

"You don't know the man," he said. "Jeff Davis is a states' rights man, not a secessionist. But what could he do? Mississippi has already made him a major general in charge of their militia, and I pray it stops there. I would hate to see him commanding an army of Southerners."

"He won't hesitate to fight if ordered to, sir," Reynolds replied. "And the man can rally the dead."

"He'll do his duty, no doubt, and be a worthy foe if it comes to that. But he wants peace as much as we do. He's seen enough of war."

That evening, at the encouragement of his wife, Delafield asked James to join him on the veranda. They both stood in the darkness after a day that had been wet, cold, and gray.

"James, I expect you've had as much of West Point winters as I have," Delafield said as he looked across the Plain.

"A warm coat fixes that, sir."

"You can come with us, James," Delafield said, his tone hopeful. "My position in charge of the New York Harbor provides for paid house service, and, of course, that would include room and board. Mrs. Delafield and I would be obliged. We're much attached to you."

The black man, too, gazed across the Plain. "You are kind to offer, sir."

"We would be in your debt if you came with us, James."

"I thank you, sir. Your offer is most gracious, but the healing in my life has been here. The strange thing, sir, when I leave, even for a holiday—go to the city—the past comes back to me ... and with it the pain."

Delafield rested a consoling hand on the black man's arm.

On Wednesday, January 23, Major P. G. T. Beauregard assumed command of West Point—its twelfth superintendent. A parade review scheduled for that afternoon to honor the occasion was canceled due to rain, the announcement bringing a thunderous roar from the barracks. The next day, Delafield and his wife, having shipped their household goods to quarters on Governors Island, departed the Academy without fanfare.

That evening, Beauregard addressed the Corps at the supper meal, his words stirring and void of politics. The fit and impeccably dressed officer, fully twenty years younger than his predecessor, impressed all in attendance, including Pelham.

On the way back to the barracks, Pelham and du Pont talked. "How long before he leaves?" du Pont asked.

"Not long. His being here makes no sense."

"And more's the pity. I like him."

On Friday, January 25, Lieutenant Charles Fields, the tactical officer for Cadet Company C, submitted his resignation, the first regular army officer at West Point to do so. News of the resignation was a great disappointment to a company composed predominately of Northern cadets. That evening, in the First-Class Club, Pelham learned from Emory Upton that Reynolds had denied Fields the opportunity to say farewell to his company.

"Things have changed," Upton said. "There is a possibility, though a small one I think, of armed conflict. That, of course, would change everything."

On Monday, five days after assuming the superintendency, Beauregard, brevetted a colonel, sent for Reynolds. Upon Reynolds' arrival, Beauregard closed the door behind them.

"Is there a problem, sir?" Reynolds asked.

Beauregard handed him a telegram. "I just received this."

Reynolds read it. "As we both expected, Louisiana, too, sir."

"By the end of the day, it will be official."

"Your intentions, sir?"

"Do I have choice, John?"

Chapter Sixty-One

Before supper Monday evening, du Pont bounded up the Eighth Division stairwell to the fourth floor, finding Pelham and Rosser at their desk. "Old Bory's gone—left on the afternoon steamer!"

Rosser glanced over his shoulder. "They won't even need to change the sheets."

"The three Louisiana boys are leaving too."

Pelham slammed his fist on the desk, ink spilling from the inkwell.

"Whoa, roommate, what's gotten into your craw?" Rosser said.

"It's not right me being here. I should be gone too!"

"What's your hurry, John," du Pont said. "What's so urgent in Alabama?"

Rosser rose from his chair and yawned. "Well, I don't need permission. I can leave any damn time I want, and now is as good a time as any. Mahan can shove his text up his ass!"

"You stupid rock!" exclaimed du Pont. "Texas hasn't seceded."

"You forget, I'm from Virginia too."

"So what? Virginia hasn't seceded either."

"It will," Rosser countered. "They both will."

"I don't understand you, Henry," said Pelham, confronting du Pont. "Delaware is a slave state, no different from ours. Why are you in Tom's face?"

"I'm not in his face, and he and you can go for all I care. But Delaware is no cotton state. We won't secede over slavery or anything else."

During the supper meal, the dining hall was a hive of thread-worn rhetoric and voices that had begun to take on belligerent tones. The mess hall officer alerted the waiters to remove food platters at the first sign of a food fight.

But there was not to be another scene. Before the meal was over, Walter Kingsbury called the Corps to attention, and Nate Chambliss rapped the lectern with a gavel. At the same time, Lieutenant Colonel Reynolds, Lieutenant Lee, and the remaining two tactical officers appeared from the faculty mess at the opposite end of the dining hall. The dining hall was silent as Reynolds made his way to the lectern.

Lee and the other two officers spaced themselves around the perimeter of the dining hall.

Reynolds gestured for Chambliss and Kingsbury to take their seats.

"What more can the man say?" Rosser whispered to Pelham.

Pelham, his arms crossed. "Damage control, I suppose."

"Gentlemen, please continue eating." Reynolds fixed his hands on the corners of the lectern and managed a smile. "It seems that hardly a day passes that we aren't served up a major development, and today is no different." His delivery was slow and measured. "Yet our response, even to this development, the departure of a superintendent, should be no different than we've talked about before. We are an institution funded federally and by individual states. We cannot contest a student's right to leave or stay in light of his motivations, political or otherwise, and we can't contest the decision made by those in the regular army faced with similar choices. That Colonel Beauregard has seen fit to return to his home state of Louisiana is neither surprising nor wrong. It just is. Life here at the Academy need not, and will not, change because of it. Tomorrow, Colonel Delafield will return as acting superintendent, to serve until a successor is chosen."

Reynolds paused.

"The conclusion to what is happening is far from predictable, and there are many initiatives being tried to resolve differences at the national level and to achieve a peaceful end. My counsel to each of you is that you do your duty in the classroom to the best of your ability. Let's allow those in Washington, knowing circumstances and facts we cannot know, to pursue what is best for the nation. Finally ..." Pelham sensed that Reynolds was looking directly at him. "There are some in this room from states that have already seceded. Most are awaiting permission from families to leave, and that is their desire and right. I adjure all of you to respect and honor these men who must be in the most uncomfortable of positions."

Reynolds's words achieved their aim of calming the Corps. That evening, even Rosser backed off from his commitment to resign, saying he would wait for Texas to announce its independence. But regardless of the commandant's remarks, Beauregard's departure solidified the commitment by Pelham and Rosser to leave as soon as they could. Knowing this could be any time, they busied themselves on the way back from the mess hall with soliciting interest for a final trip to visit Benny Havens.

The next morning, Tuesday, January 29, both Pelham and Rosser were summoned to Lieutenant Lee's office.

"Have a seat," Lee said, closing the door behind them. "I won't take much of your time, but given your circumstances, I wanted you to know that I am very close to making my own decision." He lowered his voice. "I will very likely resign my commission and offer my sword to Virginia. Unless I see real evidence that Virginia will not secede, that will be my decision. My hope was to finish out the academic year, so that D Company would not suffer unneeded transition. But that's four months down the road, and I don't know that it is possible."

"What are the odds, sir, that Virginia will stay with the Union?" Pelham asked.

Lee stroked his beard. "I should think nil, and I say this for the simple reason that we border two sides of the nation's capital. Any Union movement against the South, South Carolina in particular, will cross Virginia's soil, and Virginia won't abide it. At best, we would be neutral on secession, but our hand would be forced if the Union intended harm to a Southern neighbor."

"Is there any realistic chance of reconciliation, sir?" Rosser asked.

"Between North and South?" said Lee.

"Yes, sir."

Lee gestured equivocally. "Neither wants war. I'm certain of that. The rub is that neither is willing to concede nor compromise. It's a rather irrational game we're playing."

"Sir, do you see the Union taking unilateral action?" Pelham asked.

"Even with Confederate seizure of federal installations in the South, no. At least not on Buchanan's watch."

Lee glanced out the window.

"I'm convinced the worst is down the road. Do yourselves and your states a favor. Hang in here as long as you can. There is much in the second semester that might benefit you later."

CHAPTER SIXTY-TWO

Tuesday night, a snowstorm pounded the Hudson Valley and sorely tested all who ventured to Benny Havens' Landing. When Rosser, Kirby, and Patterson finally arrived, with Chambliss and du Pont in tow, they were surprised to find Custer already sitting on the hearth sipping an ale and smoking a cigar, his feet propped up on a chair.

"Dicey night," Havens boomed from behind the bar. "I'll fix you boys right up!"

Custer tipped his tankard to Rosser. "About time you got here."

"How the hell did you beat us, Fannie?" demanded Rosser. "We left the barracks the same time you did and wasted no time in coming."

Custer nodded at a pair of skates hanging on the wall.

"You didn't!"

"Why not?"

"You're not sane, Fannie!"

"Nothing to it. From the South Dock, head south, and it's the first tavern on your right."

"You're worse than Pelham," Chambliss said, looking around for the man.

Custer anticipated him. "He's not here yet."

"Needn't worry about John," Patterson said, shedding his overcoat and gloves. "He'll appear when the flip does."

"Master Patterson is right, lads." Havens set a tray of ales on the table. After eyeing Chambliss and du Pont, he extended a hand. "Don't believe I've had the pleasure."

Patterson made the introductions. "Nate Chambliss is our top dog, Benny—first captain of the Corps. And Henry du Pont is our class president. You are in august company, Benny."

The others snickered.

"Nate will have a flip, Benny," said Patterson. "But I'm not sure about Henry. He's more into sherry."

Rosser nearly choked on his ale.

"What's wrong with sherry," du Pont said indignantly. "But recognizing these are unusual times, maybe I will try what you lads have talked about all these years."

"Just so," said Havens with a generous smile. "I'll get straight to it."

Pelham's cloaked figure moved through the dark shadows of the snowstorm, the pungent smell of wet wool strong in his nose. He was beyond the South Gate and less than a half mile from the landing. He chastised himself for finishing a letter to Clara that could easily have waited until morning. The short delay allowed the storm to fully wax.

At the approach of a wagon, he ducked behind a frozen elm, drawing his overcoat tighter and leaning into the blowing snow. His shoes and socks were soaked, and his feet numb. Only a sixth sense guided him past the granite precipice that had cost Jefferson Davis a fractured leg.

Then, as quickly as it had blown in, the storm slacked, as though God had said, "Enough!" A half-moon soon appeared in a patch of starry sky, casting shadows on the fresh snow. Pelham saw the faint glow of the landing below and began his descent, slipping on the icy steps, clutching tree trunks and rocks with numbed fingers.

Finally, Pelham pounded on the tavern door.

When Rosser opened it, he saw Pelham swaying side to side, his eyes nearly shut.

"Damn, roommate, looks like you got the whole of it!" Rosser said, catching Pelham as he collapsed.

Custer stripped Pelham of his overcoat, gloves, and hat, and helped him to the fireplace. "You're a drowned rat, John. I'll take your shoes."

"About time, Master Pelham," Havens bellowed from the bar. "These friends of yours were about to run it back to the barracks."

The others laughed.

"You'll be wanting the usual?"

Pelham shuddered, his face colorless. "If not, Benny, I'll die from exposure."

"Nope. Can't be having that. Nobody dies in my tavern."

The conviviality of the gathering was a stimulant to all present, and when Benny rang the bell and delivered seven steaming tankards of flip the celebration of brotherhood was instantly taken to a higher level.

"Here's your cure, boys," said Havens.

"Y-you're a G-godsend … Benny," Pelham stammered, wrapping partially thawed fingers around a hot tankard. After a couple of swallows, he began to breathe easier, and for the first time noticed du Pont. "What? Are my eyes deceiving me? Henry? Nate?"

Du Pont nodded, almost sheepishly, a tankard of flip untouched in front of him.

"Damn, Henry," Pelham exclaimed. "Just look at you. You're at Benny Havens' Landing and haven't gone straight to hell."

Du Pont ignored Pelham. "I have yet to imbibe."

"Then do it, Henry. Your salvation is not at stake here."

"You all seem to worship what I can take or leave."

"Don't be a prig, Henry," teased Kirby. "Take it."

"A prig, am I?" Du Pont sniffed the tankard and took a sip. Then another and smacked his lips. He eyed the beverage with curiosity.

"Careful, Henry. Flip can sneak up on you," Pelham said, standing up to make a toast. "To Henry and Nate's first visit!"

Rosser seconded the toast.

"Fannie's been here a few times," Pelham said, winking at Custer.

"You could have picked a better night," du Pont said, after another sip of flip.

"True enough, Henry."

The seven friends caught up on the day and the latest mental flogging administered by Professor Mahan on poor Rosser, who once again hung tenuously to the bottom rung. No one broached the subject of parting, preferring topics of merry making, until Pelham suddenly drew himself up in front of the hearth. "My friends, Tom and I thank you for coming, an expression of no mean account to us, especially in this weather." He forced a smile.

"So, this is it?" Patterson said, refilling his pipe. "You and Tom are next?"

Pelham eyed Patterson and the others who had fought the storm to be there, and then stepped forward. He offered a hand to Kirby. Kirby took it and shook it firmly.

"We are friends, aren't we, Ned?" Pelham said, blinking back the moisture in his eyes. "And I believe our souls are bound together in God's grace."

Now it was Kirby's eyes that shined.

Pelham turned to du Pont. "Henry, same question."

"Of course, John. Best friends. Since plebe year."

"Hear, hear," said Chambliss, raising his tankard, as did the others.

Pelham's face reddened from the heat of the fire. "Where do you see this going, Henry?" Pelham asked du Pont.

Du Pont took a generous sip of his flip before answering, and not altogether distinctly. "I admit we are in a sad state. But some hope remains that we can work something out. We always have. Right?"

"You really think so?"

Du Pont shook his head. "No. Not really."

"My friends," Pelham said, "despite what you've seen and heard from me since Alabama made its decision, I've had a real time of it. This is a foul business, me being here when I should be home with Charlie Ball."

"Not your doing," protested Custer. "We all know that."

"You'll get your permission," Kirby said.

"Permission or not," Pelham continued, "how do I just hang around as if nothing is happening, when I know full well what I might be called to do?"

"And pray tell, what is that?" Du Pont said, standing up, his face flushed with flip. "I suppose if we met on the field of battle, you'd just run me through?"

Du Pont's remark tickled Pelham. "Henry, haven't I done that in just about every fencing class?"

The tavern filled with laughter.

"Aye, John. Well said," toasted Patterson. "Brevity is the soul of wit, and you are the soul of brevity."

"John," said Chambliss, taking the floor, "you take yourself too seriously. No one doubts your motives. Least of all me, and you know how we all feel about you. While I may be leading the Corps, you, my friend, are its favorite and always have been."

"True words," said Kirby. "Nate's right."

"Face it, John," Chambliss said. "You could have been first captain if you had cared a whit for playing the game."

"I think not," said Pelham. "But, clearly, I'm now on the outside. Both Tom and me. I seem to breathe in order and exhale chaos."

Du Pont gave Pelham a puzzled look. "What the hell does that mean?" After an extended belch, he suggested another round of flip.

Pelham eyed du Pont with a smile. "I'll join you Henry, but someone has to help me carry you home!"

"Me?" Du Pont glanced around the room, a pasty grin on his face. "I'm fine, John. Really … fine."

The order placed, Havens set back to work, while the cadets passed the evening recounting anecdotes that defined nearly five years of shared life. Fifteen minutes before midnight, Havens, unusually quiet all evening, announced, "Tis time you boys were getting back."

"Benny's right," said Pelham, already on his feet. "My friends, the six of us have been through the best and worst of times, and we've always been there for each other. Tonight, you are here for Tom and me, and you have helped me make sense of something."

A blurry-eyed du Pont stared at Pelham. "Huh? Of what?"

"Honor, Henry. Make sense of honor."

"Honor?" du Pont repeated, slurring the word. "What about it?"

"I felt I was betraying it, Henry. That being here, I was being unfaithful, both to Alabama and the Union."

At this, Rosser rose to his feet. "Now wait a damn minute, John. What the blazes does honor have to do with it? What's wrong with finishing what we started? I for one have invested more of my body and brain in this place than anyone else to quit now on conscience."

With a finger on Rosser's chest, du Pont reminded him that he had been ready to resign a week before.

"So? That was … then," declared Rosser awkwardly.

Kirby stood up. "Here it is, John. You, Tom, and all our Southern mates, you've been put squarely in a place not of your choosing. And the rest of us know it. In your place, I would think and feel the same. But the fact is both of you have the same rights as the rest of us. You were picked to be here the same as Nate, Henry, Chas, Fannie, and me. So long as we're not in armed conflict, I see no problem with you staying through graduation. I would—and see no taint on my honor."

"There it is," Rosser said, as if he had said it himself.

Kirby smiled. "Besides, if you do stay you just might see the error in your thinking."

"You bastard!" exclaimed Rosser, his response smothered by laughter.

"Although…" Kirby eyed Chambliss. "Maybe we should secure their weapons. What say you, Nate?"

"One more matter," Du Pont said, attempting to put a right-handed glove on his left hand and speaking as though with borrowed lips. "We get our rings—class rings in two weeks. John, you and Tom—you still want your rings, don't you?"

Rosser responded vehemently, "Hell, yes, after what I've been through!"

"And you, John?"

Mention of the ring caught Pelham off guard. "Really? You would be okay with us wearing our rings?"

"Of course," Kirby exclaimed, slapping Pelham on the back. "We're brothers, John. You and Tom are as much a part of the class as I am, and always will be."

Chapter Sixty-Three

Saturday, February 2, Pelham was sitting at his desk when Rosser's size thirteen shoes pounded up the stairs. Pelham turned to see the huge grin on Rosser's face.

"Professor Mahan's dead?"

"Better!" Rosser exclaimed. "Texas has joined the Confederacy. The delegates voted yesterday. One hundred and sixty-six to eight."

"So, you're gone?"

"It has to be ratified by public referendum on the twenty-third, a popular vote. But it will happen, and when it does, yes, I'm gone."

Pelham embraced Rosser's jubilance as his own. "We'll go arm in arm, Tom. I'm certain to have permission by then."

"Let's do it, John. You and me on the ferry, waving goodbye to our Yankee friends."

The next Friday, Pelham received two letters: the permission he had asked for from his father, and a letter from Judge Walker. The letter from his father contained a separate sheet of vellum with the precise wording needed for his resignation. But Pelham's exhilaration was short-lived. In the second letter, the judge, who had earlier insisted he catch the next train home, now admonished him to stay put, to finish the course of instruction, and in so doing best equip himself to serve his state and new country. Pelham desperately wanted to argue the point by return letter, until the strength of the judge's counsel was further weighted by a concluding remark in his letter: *And this is not only my opinion, but that of Jefferson Davis.* As frustrated as he was, Pelham couldn't deny the value of what he would learn in the balance of military art, engineering, ordnance, and artillery and cavalry tactics. The judge's advice took seed with Rosser as well, who, too, resolved to stay despite an intense desire to distance himself from Professor Mahan.

Again superintendent, Delafield had come to the point where the sight of a telegram from Scott made him physically ill. And such was the effect of Scott's most recent dispatch, dated February 17. The telegram reported that seventy-year-old Brigadier General Twiggs, commander of the Texas Department of the Army, had surrendered without a fight his command to the newly formed Confederate State of Texas, and thereafter resigned his commission to serve the Confederacy. In his place, Colonel Robert E. Lee took command of the Texas department, and he and twenty-six hundred federal troops garrisoned in forts along the Texas frontier left the state, but bearing only their individual weapons, personal effects, and limited supplies.

After sharing the telegram with Reynolds, Delafield lamented Governor Houston's predicament. Having advocated so strongly for the Union, Houston had alienated himself from the state's fire-eaters, vehemently led by ex-senator Louis Wigfall.

On Tuesday, February 19, Lieutenant Colonel Reynolds strode at an accelerated pace across Central Area, a courier having made it clear that the superintendent needed to see him right away.

Delafield handed Reynolds the briefest of Scott's more recent telegrams. *Jeff Davis took oath of office yesterday and is now the provisional president of the Confederate States of America.*

"I didn't think Davis wanted the job," Reynolds said.

"Of course, he didn't. He's a soldier, better suited for command. But I understand he had no choice. They elected him in absentia. Still, it may be to our gain—as I think he still remains hopeful for peace." Delafield held up another dispatch. "Scott says that Davis is sending a formal commission to meet with Buchanan, and if need be, Lincoln. But Davis has made it clear to the commission that their authority is limited to paying for federal installations on Southern soil, including Sumter and Pickens, and paying the Southern share of the Union national debt. Under no circumstances are they to discuss terms for reuniting with the Union."

Reynolds considered. "Having Davis as president, instead of a fire-eater, certainly does the least harm, but soon we will march not to Buchanan's orders, but Lincoln's."

"Yes, and I fear that Lincoln is not averse to using force. Not if it will keep the Union whole."

Reynolds nodded. "So, there it is. Davis must make his deal on Buchanan's watch."

That evening in the mess hall, what Pelham had dreaded surfaced. Two classmates confronted him and Rosser in harsh terms, one holding a newspaper article that specifically named the two as having been conferred appointments as first lieutenants in the Confederate Army.

Rosser responded with righteous indignation. Pelham took a softer approach.

"You know us well enough," Pelham said to both of them. "We would never accept a position in the Confederacy while in the employ of the Union as cadets. You can believe what you want, but neither of us has been contacted by anyone about such a commission, and neither of us has initiated anything from our end."

The issue was resolved when du Pont and Upton came to their defense.

Friday night, after the Corps had entered the mess hall, news came that the Cozzen's Hotel in Buttermilk Falls was on fire. Chambliss immediately formed the four cadet companies and led them to the scene. Flames, whipped by strong winds, spewed from the main building. There was no saving the building or some of the nearby cottages, but before the roof of the main building collapsed, the Corps managed to recover most of the hotel's furniture and furnishings. On the march back, Custer observed ruefully that the loss of the Cozzen's Hotel meant fewer ladies for next year's summer hops.

On Saturday, the six guns of the West Point battery were ordered to Washington DC, and Delafield communicated to Reynolds a thwarted plot to assassinate Lincoln in Baltimore. The next day, a one-line dispatch from Washington reported that Texas, by public referendum, had voted forty-four thousand in favor of secession; thirteen thousand opposed.

On Wednesday, February 27, outside the mess hall, Pelham again had to defend his presence at the Academy. When he returned to the barracks, he vented on Rosser.

"It's your call, John," Rosser said. "I'm only too ready to leave."

Pelham shook his head. "No. President Davis has made the call. Though, I will write him about what we face."

"It will be two weeks before you hear back, John. Hell, if we time this thing wrong, we'll be locked in irons in a Union prison."

It took Pelham less than fifteen minutes to pen Davis an explanation of their dilemma.

The next day, Pelham and the rest of the class received class rings, the cost of which was twenty-five dollars. Pelham read the inscription inside his shiny ring, *John Pelham, Graduating Class of 1861*. On one side of the ring's gold setting were insignias of the Corps of Engineers, Cavalry, and Ordnance Corps: on the other side, insignias of the Infantry, Artillery, and Judge Advocate General's Office. The class crest, a sword behind a shield, was engraved on the polished signet stone, and bore the class motto, *Faithful to Death*.

At supper, the First Classmen, Pelham and Rosser included, were obnoxious with their rings, allowing underclassmen to ogle them.

"I'm using my seal tonight," Patterson told Pelham as they left the mess hall.

"Anyone in particular?"

Patterson smiled. "A girl I met before you returned from furlough. She has potential."

Pelham intended to use his seal responding to the letter he had just received from Clara.

After a feeble attempt at studying, Pelham reread Clara's last letter, the eighth since their intimacy, the memory of which had not faded. Pelham dipped his pen in the inkwell. *My lady, the seal on the envelope was made with my class ring, received this very day, which I shall wear and use for the rest of my life.*

The letter finished, Pelham heated and dripped hot sealing wax across the flap of the envelope, let it cool, and applied his signet ring.

CHAPTER SIXTY-FOUR

On Friday, March 1, Colonel Delafield once again said good-bye to James and the other house domestics and made his way to South Dock to catch the steamer to New York City and his wife. The day previous, the sky a brilliant blue, the Corps conducted a grand review honoring his departure and the arrival of his replacement, Colonel Alexander Bowman, Class of 1825.

Friday afternoon, Colonel Bowman's enlisted aide entered the superintendent's office. "Sir, would the Colonel care for some coffee?"

"Make that two, please—the commandant is joining me."

Minutes later, Reynolds was seated in Bowman's office.

"Let's pick up where we left off, John," Bowman said, referring to the briefing that Reynolds had started the day before on what Bowman needed to know regarding the tactical department and Corps of Cadets. Earlier in the day, Professor Mahan had briefed him on the academic program. The whole sequence of being selected superintendent, transferring to someone else the duties of his prior assignment, and moving to West Point had taken less than a week, and Bowman was scrambling to catch up.

When Reynolds finished, Bowman asked, "The Southern cadets from seceded states, they are all gone?"

"We still have a few, sir. In the First Class, only two, John Pelham from Alabama and Thomas Rosser from Texas."

"They intend to stay with the Union?"

"I wish, sir. But no. Actually, short of hostilities, they have expressed a desire to graduate before they go home. They are good men and not troublemakers, and the Corps seems amenable to their presence."

"Yes. I suppose five years is a long time to come up empty-handed."

"Colonel Delafield briefed you on how General Scott keeps us informed?" Reynolds asked.

"He did, and I've already received and responded to the first of his dispatches. I've also heard from William Seward, a good friend. He'll soon be Lincoln's secretary of state. I visited with him before coming here. He told me that on February 25th, Jefferson Davis sent a three-man Confederate commission to negotiate surrender of the two still-occupied federal installations in the South."

"Colonel Delafield informed me, sir," said Reynolds.

"Excellent. Did you also know that because the Union doesn't recognize the existence of the Confederacy, the commissioners have no direct access? They are communicating with Seward through Justice John Campbell."

"That I did not know. And I see it as a problem, both in lost time and meanings confused in translation."

"As do I. Seward is an honorable man, but I think he has climbed too far out on a limb. He is allowing the commissioners to think what they want, believing he can work out the details. The problem is, while Seward has the president's ear, he is not the president. Lincoln has proven to be his own man. I don't see him giving up his kindling."

On Saturday, March 2nd, Texas formally joined the Confederacy. On March 4th, Abraham Lincoln and James Buchanan left the Willard Hotel, near the White House, for the east portico of the unfinished capitol building, where Chief Justice Roger Taney swore in Lincoln as the sixteenth president of the United States.

The following day, a synopsis of Lincoln's acceptance speech was printed and distributed to the Corps. In the synopsis, Pelham read the impassioned appeal by Lincoln to preserve the Union and for compromises that would heal strife between North and South. He handed the flyer to Rosser, who, upon reading it, expressed surprise that Lincoln promised not to use force to maintain the Union or to interfere with slavery where it existed. If true, Rosser thought, a shooting war might be avoided. Pelham was more pessimistic, believing Lincoln would not give up Fort Sumter and Fort Pickens.

In the days and weeks that followed, Pelham and Rosser pursued their studies as though they were exchange students, as if the inauguration and attendant events concerned another country. With so few Southerners remaining, the mess hall, First Class Club, and barracks were forums for discussing Republican agendas and saving the Union. Whenever Pelham or Rosser were in the mix, such topics were avoided. However, the need for concession was minimal since Pelham and Rosser generally kept to themselves, self-exiled in their barracks quarters.

During this time, Pelham witnessed a subtle change in his friends. Those who had articulated and defended the rights of individual states and the basic themes of the Democratic Party, most notably Henry du Pont, were now ardent for the Union and its perpetuation. Even the lighthearted Custer was inclined to Lincoln's defense. But Pelham understood and begrudged no one their political stance. And he believed a person deciding the issue of secession would naturally gravitate from the fence to one side or the other. He certainly had. Wasn't he more convinced than ever of the rightness of Southern states to form their own union of like-minded people?

After chapel on Sunday, March 17th, Pelham sat at a desk in the library reading the March 16th edition of *Harpers Weekly*. It contained the full text of President Lincoln's inauguration speech. A deeper interest in the man who might be an adversary spurred Pelham to read the entire speech. After doing so, he saw Lincoln differently, though no more favorably. He saw Lincoln as neither the man painted by Judge Walker, Senator Wigfall, Congressman Miles, nor as a malleable duck like Buchanan. There was backbone and fight in the man and an eloquence that would draw respect. His homespun appearance and selflessness could well attract blind allegiance.

Pelham reread parts of Lincoln's speech, reflecting on the issue debated by Upton and du Pont. Lincoln maintained that perpetuity, as applied to the Union, was implied in the fundamental law of national governments. Accordingly, no state could lawfully secede on its own volition. The Union must be maintained, unless by due process and by the people it was dissolved. The majority must rule in a democracy. But hadn't public referendums in states of the South done just that—voted overwhelmingly to dissolve ties with the Union? How was due process somehow lacking? In his mind, Pelham found Lincoln guilty of double-talk.

Yet, as Rosser observed, Lincoln affirmed that the issue of armed conflict rested entirely in the hands of the South, that the North would not be the aggressor. If Lincoln's word was his bond, why couldn't the Confederacy have its way? What did it matter that the Union didn't recognize the Confederacy? And if Sumter and Pickens remained in federal hands, couldn't the Confederacy abide the insult, at least long enough to gain its strength?

That evening, Pelham tossed in bed unable to sleep. Statements by Lincoln in his speech rolled about in his head— *Plainly, the central idea of secession is the essence of anarchy.* How did that make any sense? Hadn't the thirteen colonies seceded from Great Britain? Was that anarchy? Hadn't history been nothing if not a continuum of seceding factions forming succeeding governments?

Chapter Sixty-Five

Monday, March 18, Lieutenant Colonel Reynolds joined Colonel Bowman for breakfast on the veranda of the superintendent's quarters. James appeared with a pot of steaming coffee, a platter of scrambled eggs, ham, and fried potatoes, and a basket of hot biscuits.

"Will there be anything else, sir?"

"No. Thank you, James."

Once they were alone, Bowman spoke freely. "We nearly had us an incident, John." Bowman informed Reynolds that the day before, one of General Beauregard's cannons had nicked a corner of the Fort Sumter parapet with a purported training round.

"It may have simply been tit for tat, sir," said Reynolds. "In response to one of Anderson's gun crews lobbing a wayward round near downtown Charleston."

"If so, both suggest neither side is quite ready for war."

Reynolds smiled at Bowman's observation.

"That there were no injuries," said Bowman, "makes white flags, inquiries, and apologies the easier."

"Gives me the shivers to think what Anderson is up against," Reynolds said. "Bob is quite literally sitting on a powder keg. Any word on the Confederate commission, sir?"

"Still in Washington, last I heard. Seward's last telegram indicated that the possibility remains for Sumter and Pickens to be handed over to the Confederates. Now that he's in office, Lincoln's under great pressure from moderates concerned about the economy not to antagonize the Confederates. Although, there are as many who would decry him as treasonous if he turned over the forts. I for one don't see Lincoln backing down. And I'm convinced he can shovel this crap."

"I understand General Scott insists on reinforcing Pickens and Sumter," Reynolds said, buttering a biscuit.

"More accurately, I think, his position is that if we intend to defend them, then we should be serious about it. He says that Anderson is wholly dependent upon Charleston for food and has been denied permission to release construction workers who consume nearly half his rations."

"Interesting, Scott's position—given he's a Virginian."

"But staunch against slavery," Bowman said. "Which, I suppose, is what cost him the presidency against Fillmore."

"No question he's a brilliant military mind. But at seventy-three and the size of both of us, he's barely able to cross the street. We need a true field general."

"And Scott knows it," Bowman said. "I understand he's keen on Bob Lee."

Reynolds's countenance brightened. "Aren't we all?"

That afternoon after class, Pelham found three letters in his room. Two on his side of the shared desk and one on Rosser's. He opened the letter from Clara first. It was short and expressed growing anticipation over graduation, just three months off. She surprised him with the news that her father thought he might attend graduation, having never seen West Point.

The second letter, from his father, wished he was home, but supported his decision to finish as much of the year as possible. *All we hear at the courthouse is the call for militia to defend ourselves against Northern aggression. Some anticipate pillaging, which I find patently absurd. Your mother and I pray there is no substance to the possibility of actual war—that men of reason can arrive at a peaceful compromise.* His father went on to praise Samuel's initiative in early planting and weeding; and then relayed the sad but not unexpected news that Reverend Smith had gone to be with his maker, and that Reverend Knox had delivered an inspiring eulogy.

Rosser's letter was the second from Sam Houston, an impassioned plea not to follow as one of many sheep the pathway to destruction adopted by a state that Houston had so long and faithfully served, but had inserted itself to the mire of rebellion and uncertain fate. Houston speculated that by the time Rosser received his letter, he would have been stripped of his governorship.

The next day, having checked dispatches and newspapers kept by the Academy curator, Pelham learned that Houston, the multi-term congressman from Tennessee, seventh governor of Tennessee, first and third president of the Republic of Texas, multi-term senator from Texas, and seventh governor of the state of Texas was out—*persona non grata*. Edward Clark was now governor of the new Confederate State of Texas.

On April 4, Colonel Bowman received a decoded telegram from General Scott—all official dispatches now encrypted. After reading the message, Bowman sent a runner for Reynolds. Five minutes later, the two were behind closed doors. Reynolds read the message, *Lincoln has directed Sumter be resupplied, by force if necessary.*

Reynolds shook his head. "His line in the sand."

Bowman shrugged. "Yesterday, the schooner *Boston* waltzed into Charleston Harbor by mistake and took a round through the mainsail. The damn thing was carrying ice for God's sake! There's no telling what will happen to a resupply ship."

"Everyone's on edge," Reynolds said. "Expecting the worst."

"Me included," said Bowman. "I just bit Professor Mahan's head off. He tells me this morning that cadet grades are falling. And I tell him, to hell with grades—these kids are going to war!"

Scott continued to feed Bowman coded telegrams twice daily about Fort Sumter and the resupply effort. Over the next seven days, the telegrams described a scenario of Lincoln's own design. He would resupply the fort with bread and salt pork. Additional troops would not be landed unless the resupply effort was opposed. It would be the Confederacy and not the Union to cast the first stone.

On April 5, Lincoln selected Captain Gustavus Fox, an Annapolis graduate turned merchantman, to resupply Fort Sumter. Governor Pickens of South Carolina was informed of the resupply effort and that no troops would be landed if the provisions were delivered unopposed. He was also informed that three Union warships and a revenue cutter would be posted off the sandbar in front of Charleston Harbor to escort the resupply ship in the event it comes under fire.

As late as April 7, Seward, through Justice Campbell, was still assuring the Confederate commissioners in Washington that Fort Sumter would be surrendered. For his part, Seward was not intentionally misleading the commissioners, as Lincoln had indicated that he was agreeable to exchanging Sumter for the allegiance of Virginia to the Union. However, the afternoon of April 7 that prospect dissolved when Lincoln learned that Virginia was in session to consider an ordinance of secession.

Captain Fox sailed south from New York Harbor on April 9, and on April 10, President Davis directed General Beauregard, former Academy superintendent, to demand surrender of Fort Sumter. If it wasn't surrendered, General Beauregard was to reduce it as he saw fit. On April 11, as Captain Fox steamed south through a rough Atlantic, Beauregard prepared a formal demand for the surrender of Fort Sumter. Shortly after noon, three military aides under white flag carried the demand to Major Anderson. Anderson received the demand and requested time to caucus with his staff. After an hour's deliberation, Anderson returned a written response to his former West Point artillery student—that he could not and would not surrender the federal installation. He did, however, say orally that in a few days he would be starved out and forced to surrender. Both the written and oral responses were communicated to Beauregard, and in turn to President Davis. Davis instructed Beauregard to obtain written confirmation of Anderson's oral response, expressing distrust not of Anderson, but of the Union in general given perceived fabrications by Seward and others.

At midnight, the Confederate aides returned to Fort Sumter with the demand that Anderson put in writing what he had said orally. Anderson did so, saying that he would evacuate the fort at noon on April 15th. However, he added a caveat—unless otherwise resupplied before then. The senior Confederate aide, knowing of the approach of the Union resupply ship and its escorts and understanding Beauregard's position, penned a short response to Anderson, writing that Confederate batteries would open fire in one hour. Anderson accepted the reply and shook hands with the Confederate aides, saying that if they never met again in this world, he prayed they would meet in the next. It was 3:20 AM, April 12, 1861.

CHAPTER SIXTY-SIX

At 4:30 AM, April 12th, while John Pelham and Tom Rosser were asleep, Confederate Lieutenant Henry Farley pulled the lanyard that fired the first shot of what would be called by many the American Civil War. It was a signal shot over Fort Sumter. Colonel Bowman learned of the bombardment at 7:00 AM. He summoned Reynolds, and they decided it was best not to inform the Corps until they received further word from General Scott. Neither was convinced that the firing on Sumter would be the catalyst for war, but rather an incident calling for measured response.

After thirty-four hours of bombardment and the miracle of no casualties, a Confederate shell started a fire, threatening Sumter's main magazine. Major Anderson then agreed to surrender the fort, provided he could conduct a one-hundred-gun salute to the Union flag before it was taken down. Shortly after noon on April 14th, the surrender ceremony took place. During the artillery salute, a pile of cartridges was sparked, exploding, and killing one man and mortally wounding a second. After the ceremony, Anderson and his command boarded a Union vessel and steamed north.

After Bowman received Scott's telegram the afternoon of April 14th, he determined to address the Corps. At the supper meal, his remarks about the incident were brief and factual.

After the meal, Pelham joined Kirby, Upton, and others who regularly attended the bi-weekly prayer meetings held at the foot of the altar in the cadet chapel. Lieutenant Howard noticed Tom Rosser arriving with Pelham.

He extended his hand. "Good of you to join us, Mr. Rosser."

"I'm not sure I had a choice, sir," Rosser said.

"That may be. But this is indeed a time for prayer."

"Yes, sir."

"Come sit by me, Tom," said Upton.

When all were seated, Lieutenant Howard bowed his head. "Father God, we come before you with humble and heavy hearts and a desire to know your will. As our nation faces its gravest hour, we pray wisdom and grace for our Union and Confederate leaders. We do not know what is coming, except that soon most of us will leave this place to do our duty in the light of serving you. We pray for strength, compassion, and honorable conduct. We pray that we might do our duty well. Father, we know that in all things, through the worst that this world can offer, you intend good to those who know and love you. Bless our time together and our fellowship. In Christ's name we pray, Amen."

In a departure from his usual bible-based message followed by discussion and prayer, Howard asked a question. "What is on your heart right now?"

A long silence followed, unexpectedly broken by Rosser, who stood up and made eye contact with all in the chapel. "Except for John and me, the rest of you will be fighting for the North, if it comes to that. And I want you to know that I have no desire to harm or kill any of you. And I hope you feel the same about John and me."

Rosser's remark not only eased the tension in the chapel but started a dialogue that questioned how men of faith live out war, and more pointedly, a war between brothers.

Howard read scripture that encouraged prayer for one's enemies, offering interpretation without reference to the immediate situation. He concluded with a prayer thanking God for the survival of those at Fort Sumter and asking for divine blessing upon all in attendance and upon a divided Union.

After the prayer meeting, Howard asked Pelham if he might have a word with him.

"Am I going to see you at our next prayer meeting?" Howard asked.

"Sir, I think by then I will be a great distance from the Academy."

"Of course. I will pray for you, John. And knowing you are a praying man gives me joy. It is essential that you remain so."

Pelham hadn't missed that Howard addressed him by his first name. "Yes, sir, and thank you for tonight. Your question has given me much to think about. Something much larger than us is going on here."

At the supper meal on Monday, April 15th, Lieutenant Colonel Reynolds approached the lectern, his face drained of color. "Men, this has been a time that changes history as we might have wanted it. It is my sad duty to inform you that a state of war now exists between the United States of America and the Confederate States of America."

The silence that followed numbed Pelham.

"President Lincoln has called for the conscription of seventy-five thousand militia from states loyal to the Union to repress what he has termed a Southern Rebellion."

Pelham stared at his plate.

"In light of the circumstances, it is unlikely that the Class of 1861 will have its one month of graduation leave. I will have more on that in the days to come."

Without looking at Pelham or Rosser, Reynolds said, "There are those of the South still with us. As before, they are to be afforded every courtesy. They are not to be confronted with what others have done. They are still your brothers."

That night Pelham and Rosser resolved to submit their resignations the next day. Rosser paced the floor as Pelham finished his letter of resignation and blew on the ink. He handed it to Rosser to read.

> *West Point, N.Y., April 15, 1861.*
>
> *Sir, I have the honor to tender the resignation of my appointment as a cadet in the service of the United States. I have accepted no place or appointment from any state or government.*
>
> *I am, sir, very respectfully your obedient servant, John Pelham, Cadet, USMA.*

Rosser nodded his approval and returned the letter to Pelham, who inserted the letter along with his father's permission in an envelope.

On Tuesday, April 16th, Pelham and Rosser submitted their resignations to Lieutenant Lee after breakfast. Lee read them without comment, except to say he would forward them through channels.

"What about you, sir?" Rosser asked.

"I, too, will be leaving," Lee said without elaboration.

"Sir, I don't know that it's possible," Pelham said, "but I would be honored to serve under your command if there is a way you can make that happen."

"Me too, sir," said Rosser.

Lee didn't respond to their request, but only wished them the best of luck.

Together, Pelham and Rosser visited Henry du Pont, informing him of their decision and asking that he expedite the process. Du Pont said he would, his demeanor surprisingly distant.

Late in the morning, Colonel Bowman received a dispatch from General Scott stating that President Lincoln would be offering command of the Union Army to Robert E. Lee, now at his Arlington House in Virginia.

At the midday meal, Pelham and Rosser informed their friends that they would be gone within the week. As with du Pont, their responses were less than warm. Pelham accepted that even close friends like Kirby and Patterson would greet their departure with reticence, given the current nature of things. What stunned Pelham was Emory Upton—who exhibited genuine kindheartedness.

The next day, Scott telegraphed Bowman that Colonel Lee had declined command of the Union Army, citing his reluctance to take part in an invasion of Southern states. A second dispatch, late that afternoon, reported that Virginia had seceded, and Lee had resigned his commission.

On Thursday, Pelham returned to his room after the last academic class to find a letter from his father. The letter expressed heartfelt regret over the demise of the Union, ardent concern for the future of Alabama, and the strongest desire that Alabama distant itself from South Carolina, whose actions he believed would precipitate war. It was belief that President Davis would not have ordered Beauregard to bombard Fort Sumter had he not known that South Carolina would have done so on its own.

We are elated, his father wrote on a positive note, *that you will be returning home very soon, and will have fatted calf and anything else you desire waiting.* But it was what followed that gave Pelham the greatest joy. *While I'm at a loss as to what he means, Samuel wanted me to relate that he no longer desires what you promised. He offered no explanation, so I leave it up to you to interpret his meaning. Anyway, I am glad to report that he and young Ora are now a couple, and she expecting. Samuel says he would like a large family and I believe Ora will make a wonderful mother.*

Pelham couldn't wait to share the news with Clara.

You will also want to know, his father wrote, *that Samuel has done a great service to the family and the plantation, and I have no reservations about his overseeing the planting and harvesting. Moreover, he commands the respect of the blacks as did our dear Willie, who I'm very sad to say has finally slowed and has the cough I so greatly dread. That he spends most evenings with Samuel, wanting to leave things in good order, is a such a blessing. We shall all dearly miss him."*

In the days that followed, Pelham made a point of being the last to enter a classroom and the first to leave and avoiding contact with everyone but Rosser. Rosser, on the other hand, had for all purposes ceased to be a cadet. He attended no formations or classes and arrived at the mess hall on his own recognizance to take meals with Pelham.

Saturday's mail call included a letter from Clara. Pelham opened it with trepidation, not knowing if it had been written pre- or post-Sumter. By its date, it was post-Sumter, yet no reference was made to the conflict or to Lincoln's declaration of war. Rather, Clara wrote of things pleasant and of their life together when all the craziness was over.

Saturday afternoon after classes, Pelham heard a knock on the door.

Ned Kirby poked his head inside. "How is it going, John?"

"I won't lie, Ned. It's been tough," Pelham said, his head in a book. "Where's Tom?"

"Selling his uniforms. You know him—never misses a trick."

Kirby nodded. "I'm here, John, because some of the boys … we want to give you a proper send-off."

Pelham expressed confusion.

"We were thinking maybe a final run to Benny's—tomorrow night."

For the first time in weeks, Pelham smiled. "That would be amazing, Ned. Who's coming?"

"You'll see."

Chapter Sixty-Seven

Sunday night, those running it to Benny Havens' Landing snuck away from the barracks under moonlight in twos and threes, and most made their way in silence. Passing Cozzen's Hotel, Pelham was surprised to see a new roof on the main structure and stacks of construction materials about the grounds. He followed Rosser for the last time down the stone steps to the landing, his thoughts a thousand miles away. He had learned from the *Charleston Mercury* sent by Henry Farley that it was the senator he had met on the train, Louis Wigfall, now a Confederate colonel, who had rowed to Fort Sumter during the bombardment to convince Major Anderson to surrender.

Inside the tavern, Havens greeted more cadets than he had seen in many years. Letitia was fully employed taking food orders and preparing flip. "We need more rum, husband," she shouted, as she disappeared up the stairs to the locker where the liquors were kept.

By the time Pelham and Rosser arrived, Havens bore a panicked expression. "Tell me there are no more of you."

Pelham surveyed the room. At one table sat du Pont, Chambliss, Patterson, Kirby, and Ames. At another Kingsbury, Custer, Upton, and O'Rorke.

"No, Benny. I think Tom and I are the last."

"Thanks be to God. Not that I'm beyond the company. It's just that if we're raided, the country will be out half its officer corps."

Haven's wit set a genial mood in the tavern.

"A flip for me, Benny," Rosser said.

"You have to tell me that?" Havens said, pretending offense. "And it's on your friends, for the both of you. So, you best drink up!"

Pelham and Rosser visited and joked with their friends as in bygone days. Presently all had a hand on a steaming tankard of flip, save Upton, who would sooner dance with the devil than allow alcohol to pass his lips.

Pelham rose from his chair, struggling with his emotions. "God bless you all for this night. And Walter, Emory, and Paddy—you do Tom and me the greatest honor by coming, no doubt fearful that you've done so." Pelham raised his tankard high. "To the dearest of friends."

"Hear, hear," shouted du Pont beneath a mustache of flip.

Rosser rose. "Let those of the North take no offense that those of the South have no desire for marriage, and let those of the South take no offence that Lincoln has no desire for divorce."

"And that wars, in like fashion, could be settled in a court of law," Kirby added, though without conviction.

"And with no loss of blood," said Ames.

Upton stood up, irritatingly sober, a tin of black coffee in his hand. "God ordains governments to rule, and those in authority to exercise power, which is, of course, what separates us from monkeys. But authority granted or taken comes with its peril—"

Rosser pushed Upton down in his chair to the delight of the others. "On behalf of whatever Upton just said, I propose a toast to the unsurpassed Class of 1861!"

Hurrahs echoed through the tavern.

Patterson, who had been pensively stirring his flip, took the floor. "In the words of the Bard, *'Double, double toil and trouble; fire burn, and cauldron bubble. When shall we*—'" Patterson paused to count noses. "—eleven *meet again? In thunder, lightning, or in rain?*"

"Clever man," said Kingsbury. "How about when North and South are done and one?"

Kingsbury's Union brothers laughed heartily, Rosser holding his tongue in the presence of so vast an enemy. As a diversion, Pelham suggested a second round of flip.

"If you gentlemen will excuse me," Letitia Havens said, bowing with her hands in prayerful pose. "You have worn out this old lady. And I'll be wishing all of you a good evening. But before I do—" She crossed the room, fighting back tears, and hugged the necks of Pelham and Rosser.

As the woman started up the staircase, Rosser shouted, "To Mrs. H! The love of my life." All rose in response and cheered the woman until she disappeared from view.

"She's a good woman, her," Benny said. "Sometimes a little emotional."

"How many years, Benny?" Patterson asked.

"Joined at the hip these forty-five years, we are. Each year better than the last."

"We see it, Benny," Pelham said. "May we be as lucky."

For the next two hours, emboldened by elixir, the gray-clad friends made light of things others would never have voiced, until, to the surprise of all, Benny Havens interrupted them. "Lads! If you will pardon me—and it's not my place …"

Puzzled, Pelham looked at Havens, who stood in front of the hearth. "What is it, Benny?"

"Master Pelham, I struggle to keep my peace …"

Havens looked warmer than Pelham had ever seen him. "Why should you keep your peace, Benny? If anyone has a right to speak, it is you."

The old man wrung his hands. "Aye … well. First, a mighty thanks to all of you for coming, for filling my coffers—but what is undoing me is the business that brings you here. You men—and I call you men, for you are—but when I first laid eyes on you, some of you anyway, you were boys. Just boys." He slapped his thigh, a thing he often did when he was about to ask a question. "Do any of you come from families that didn't fight in the Revolution?"

The silence in the room suggested otherwise.

"No, of course not. Your families, as did mine, shed blood—British blood if they could, but likely their own as well. And because of it, because of their sacrifice, you and me are heirs of something no people in history have ever had. Liberty, blessed freedom, each man the equal of the next."

Rosser shifted in his chair.

"Our country may not be perfect." Havens' eyes sparkled. "I'll grant you that. And things are crazy mixed up now. But I'm telling you— we've got a damn sight better place to live than any other on this big ball of dirt."

Upton raised his coffee tin. "Amen, Mr. Havens."

"Tell me," Havens continued, his eyes on Pelham and Rosser, "how a South Carolina, or an Alabama, or a Texas, or any other state, is going to be better off as its own little kingdom, or holding hands with other such kingdoms, than it is right now? The Union works because we are different and contribute differently. It works because we have sound government, and not too much of it, and because we have a leader whose tenure is short and at the will of the people." Havens wrung his hands again. "Again, the country's not perfect, and we don't always see eye to eye, or love the man on top. I for one didn't vote for Lincoln. But he's my president for the next four years, and I'll get through it, and don't know why we all can't."

Pelham poured Havens a glass of ale.

Havens took a long draft. "Thank you, Master Pelham." He reached in his pocket and extracted a pouch of pipe tobacco and sniffed it. "Don't you see how we need each other? This here tobacco, of which I am quite fond, comes from North Carolina, which I'm told is likely to flee the nest. But, dang, if it ain't the best tobacco I ever piped. And those big Baldwin locomotives that move trade throughout your Southland," Havens stared directly at Pelham, "where do they come from? Why from Philadelphia—that's where."

"Don't think just because I fix your drink and the missus cooks your meal that I'm not aware of what goes on. And don't think I don't have a stand on it. Because I do. But it's not political, lads. It's heartbreaking personal. All these years, I've watched you, and those who came before you. Some of you make it, some of you don't. But damn if I'm not proud of every one of you!"

Havens' countenance turned morose. "I see something ugly, fully brewed and boiling over. I see my lads pitted against each other, facing off in the hell of battle, friend against friend—and it is madness, I tell you!"

Havens hung his head.

"There. I've said too much. And I'm sorry. You'll decide your own minds, as rightly you should. It's just that—"

"Just what, Benny?" Pelham asked, joining the tavern keeper at the hearth.

"It's just that I hate to see the dream end."

Pelham put his arm around Havens. "Benny, you are truly the dearest, kindest soul on earth, and you must never think that we don't understand your meaning. You express it only too well. But what is to be done about it?"

Pelham glanced at his friends, and back at Havens.

"Benny, can you not see the thing from our side—where Tom and I are? It is not a matter of issues of rightness or wrongness. We're sons and brothers of families that love us and that we love. We left homes to come here. To go to school, to become soldiers. But isn't it natural that we go home? Would it be natural if we didn't? We can no more separate ourselves from what makes us who we are, than change the color of our skin."

Pelham's eyes danced about the room.

"I know you can't see it, Benny. But perhaps—just maybe—the dream you speak of isn't gone. Maybe it isn't over. Maybe it's just changed. Evolved differently than you expected."

Pelham put a hand on Havens' shoulder and turned to the others. "Brothers, shall I surprise you?" He retrieved a piece of paper from dress coat. "Benny, our class has yet to pen a verse to you, to add to all that have been penned before. And our time is almost done. With the permission of my classmates …"

"Yes, John! Let us hear it," exclaimed Chambliss. Kirby, du Point, and the others urged the same.

Pelham proceeded to sing the refrain to "Benny Havens, Oh," and then a verse that none of them had heard before.

Go we now our separate way, boys, fate's not to us been just
We know not what the future holds, the lifeblood poured from us.
But when all is done and all is past, we pray God heals our pain
And brings us back to Benny's place, to toast our bond again.

Custer sprang to his feet, as did the others, singing:
Oh! Benny Havens, Oh!—Oh! Benny Havens, Oh!
We'll sing our reminiscences of Benny Havens, Oh!

Chambliss slipped the handwritten verse from Pelham's fingers and led the group a second time through the new verse, while Pelham looked on in silence, his eyes shining.

When they had finished, there wasn't a dry eye in the tavern.

"Bravo, John," Rosser shouted, his voice cracking. "Bravo, my dear, best friend!"

Du Pont blew his nose, "A cheer for Alabama!"

Havens' hand was suddenly in the air, and Rosser bellowed, "Another word from Benny!"

"Master Pelham, Master Rosser—I am so proud of you. So proud of all of you. You are truly without choice, and you're a testament to all that is noble. Forgive a foolish old man for saying what he ought not. Further, I am so sorry, lads, for the hand you've been dealt. 'Tis the devil's work. But you'll play it your best, I know you will. And you'll make me proud."

Pelham embraced the old man. "Thank you, Benny, and God bless you and all your family."

"To Benny Havens," shouted Rosser.

"To Benny Havens," echoed the others.

Pelham bounded for the front door. "Away boys, tomorrow is here."

As his friends filed out singing another verse to the tavern keeper, Pelham flashed a final smile at Benny Havens and entered the night.

Chapter Sixty-Eight

Two hours later, on April 22nd, Mike Hood, the charge-of-quarters, cracked the door to Pelham's room and found him at his desk, the gas lamp still on. Returning at 3:00 AM, he found Pelham still at his desk. While duty bound to report a man out of bed after taps, a two- demerit offense for each infraction, what was the point?

"Try and get some sleep, John."

Pelham turned, his face drawn and colorless. "Thanks, Mike, I need it." A nest of wadded vellum surrounded his chair. He leaned back, stretched his arms, and read his last effort.

April 22, 1861, West Point, New York

My dearest Clara,

When you receive this, I will be several days gone from the Academy. Forgive me, my lady, for not writing sooner, an unpardonable sin against my true love, for which my only excuse is the realization that the dream we have fought so hard to preserve cannot be. It is fantasy for me, for us, to think we can survive the war and that you would be happy in Alabama for the rest of your life.

That we should not come together as one, not raise a family of the most beautiful children, and not grow old and more devoted to one another with each season, is more than my heart can bear or my pen admit. But I am not God and am powerless to affect what charts our course. Yet I do love you, my lady, and always will, and on another canvas our love would have been a masterpiece, a story for the ages.

And so, my lady, I reluctantly return to you your heart, which I have cherished more than my own for these eight glorious months. I free you to give it to another with my blessing and the full blessing of almighty God.

With this parting, my lady, I ask that you pray for me as I will for you, and know that as I leave West Point this very morning, and henceforth attempt to do my duty as God grants me vision and strength, that if the worst befall me, I shall await you in heaven.

Your faithful knight,
John

He was no more pleased with this effort than his earlier drafts, but he ached for sleep. He folded and inserted the two sheets of vellum in an envelope, waxed, and sealed it, and crawled into bed. He slept fitfully for the short time before Bentz and his drummers did their worst. For the last time, he played the game, standing reveille formation as though nothing had changed.

When he returned to the room, Rosser was sitting on the edge of his bed. "We're the last to leave, John. How do you think it will go?"

Pelham shrugged and headed downstairs to the orderly room to drop the letter in the mailbox—unable to do it.

Breakfast was as solemn a time as Pelham could remember but passed without incident. He ate little and declined Kingsbury's invitation to address the Corps. He felt that enough had been heard from departing Southerners. Rosser likewise passed on the offer.

After the meal, Chambliss cornered Pelham outside the mess hall, his face grave. "I didn't say anything yesterday, John, because I hoped it would come to nothing. But I heard from my brother what is happening in Nashville."

"Oh?"

"He thinks Tennessee will secede—that the Union response to Fort Sumter was too much."

Pelham nodded. "You're not the only one. On the way back from Benny's, Chas told me Arkansas was likely to leave, though he thinks he can still graduate." Pelham put a hand on Chambliss's shoulder. "For one of us, your news is good news. I'd much rather have you with me than against me."

"You know my heart is not with the Confederacy."

"Fair enough, Nate. But you'll go home if Tennessee secedes."

"I won't have a choice."

"None of us do."

After breakfast, the barracks divisions were quiet and Central Area deserted, with everyone but Pelham and Rosser in class.

"With three hours before we leave," Rosser said, "I'm taking a nap."

Pelham chose to a walk, his first walk on Academy grounds in civilian clothes. The sky was clear, and the campus renewed by spring. Crossing Jefferson Road, he skirted past the library, around the perimeter of the Plain, and north along the river bluff. The green of spring was in the grass on the Plain, and it would remain so until the tramplings of summer encampment. Near Fort Clinton, he sat for nearly an hour at the foot of Kosciusko's monument, gazing across the river at the distant Highland Hills. Proceeding past the hotel, he found gardeners busy weeding and planting and men distributing cinders from a large horse-drawn wagon on the path to the summer encampment.

The scent of spring was strong in the air, the temperature mild. The elms and maples of Trophy Point were in full leaf, and the shadblow and dogwoods bloomed their best.

Passing the artifact cannons of earlier wars, he descended the bluff to North Dock and Flirtation Walk, which he followed as far as Kissing Rock before retracing his steps to the Plain, the commandant's quarters, the superintendent's quarters, and finally the barracks.

It was nearly twelve o'clock when he returned to Central Area. A quartermaster wagon stood in front of the Eighth Division stoops. Rosser was talking to a young, enlisted man, his effects already in the wagon. The prospect of an immediate departure lifted Pelham's spirits.

"Give me a minute, young man," Pelham shouted to the driver.

The driver jumped down from his seat. "Sir, please let me help. I'm Private Kinnard. I'm new here and work the stables. I've heard a lot about you and Mr. Rosser. You're almost legends."

Pelham couldn't resist a smile. On the fourth floor, he picked up his valise and pointed to a steamer trunk. "Are you sure?"

With effort, Bowers hoisted the trunk onto his back. After loading the wagon, he climbed up onto the driver's seat. "You can both ride up here with me, if you like."

"I think I'll walk. But thank you," Pelham said.

Rosser said the same.

The private made a clucking sound, and the four-horse team lurched forward, crossing Central Area in front of the commandant's office. As the team rounded the First Division, what Pelham and Rosser saw stunned them. What seemed to be the entire Corps of Cadets blocked their passage. In front was Nate Chambliss. Behind him, Henry du Pont, Ned Kirby, Walter Kingsbury, Emory Upton, Adelbert Ames, Chas Patterson, Charlie Hazlett, George Custer, and Paddy O'Rorke. Chambliss stepped forward and shouted over his shoulder, "How do we say good-bye to a brother?"

The mass of gray erupted in hurrahs and whistles and descended upon Pelham and Rosser, hoisting them on their shoulders.

Pelham was speechless.

"You two don't deserve this," shouted Custer with a grin. "You're damn traitors. I'll be keeping an eye on you."

"You do that, Fannie," Rosser shouted back. "And you won't have to look far, because we'll be at the front of it."

Du Pont pointed an accusing finger at Rosser. "So fast to slit a throat?"

"You Northerners can surrender anytime—no hard feelings."

Rosser's words drew a raucous retort.

"Good luck, boys," shouted Kirby. "Trust your flip to me!"

"A low blow, Ned," said Pelham.

"Tom," Patterson said, rubbing his chin, "you can now grow a beard. For *He that hath a beard is more than a youth, and he that hath no beard is less than a man.*"

Rosser grinned. "Where do you get that stuff?"

Upton, bearing a sober expression, extended a hand to Pelham. "God protect you from all the flaming arrows, John. You too, Tom."

The formation for the midday meal being half an hour off, the banter and cries did not diminish as the Corps carried the two Southerners past the chapel, the library and post headquarters, and down South Dock Road to catch the Garrison ferry.

At the dock, Pelham and Rosser shook hands, shed tears, and exchanged final embraces. Only after boarding the ferry did Pelham sense the peace he'd been seeking.

After Chambliss ordered the Corps back to the barracks and as the ferry sounded its horn to depart, a lone figure ran at breakneck speed down the road toward the doc.

Rosser squinted. "Who the hell is…?"

Pelham cupped his eyes. "It's Dan, Tom! He's got something in his hand."

By the time McElheny reached the end of the dock, the ferry had pulled away a few yards. McElheny stuffed what he was holding inside the band of his forage cap and sailed it onto the ferry deck.

"For you, John!" McElheny shouted over the roar of the ferry's engine.

Rosser grabbed the cap, removed a letter, and winged the cap back to McElheny, who grabbed it midair and raced back up the boardwalk.

"I believe this is yours," said Rosser, handing Pelham the letter.

Pelham tore it open.

"That's not Clara's handwriting," Rosser said, looking over Pelham's shoulder.

"No. It's from … Kingsbury's fiancée, Eva Taylor."

Pelham handed Rosser an enclosed photograph of a very attractive woman. On the back was the name Sallie Dandridge.

CHAPTER SIXTY-NINE

On the ferry to Garrison before catching the train to New York City, Pelham informed Rosser of his intention to visit Clara at Clermont College before heading south. His protestations to no avail, Rosser acceded to the detour.

Late that afternoon, Pelham found the Clermont campus exactly as Clara had described it. Meticulously landscaped. Mottled sunlight streaming through the crowns of Pin Oaks and Red Maples, highlighted a quadrangle of three-story redbrick buildings trimmed in white and connected by trellis-covered crosswalks.

Having learned from Miss Frampton where Clara would be and satisfying the woman that he was only going to simplify her life, Pelham surprised Clara as she emerged from a classroom. Seeing him, she flew into his arms and kissed him full on the lips in front of the other girls.

"This time you're the little sneak," she said.

Pelham grinned. "Discretion, my lady."

"Hang discretion. You don't know any of these girls." Clara pulled him inside the classroom.

Now the aggressor, Pelham embraced, kissed, and caressed Clara until they came up for air. "God, I have missed you, my lady."

Clara nuzzled his chin. "How can you be here?"

"Didn't I say that in January?"

"You are so clever to find me."

"Our friend, the troll."

"But … I don't understand. Where's your uniform?"

"Tom and I are headed home, Clara." Pelham wanted to tell her what he had come to say, but found himself saying meaningless, safe things, holding and kissing her as if nothing had changed. But after a few minutes, he found his nerve.

"My lady, can you bear to hear what I must say?"

Clara's eyes glistened with tears, as she nearly collapsed. "Dear God, why us?"

Pelham rocked her in his arms.

"It's—it's not fair, John."

He handed Clara his handkerchief, and she blew her nose. Recovering herself, she attempted a smile. "I guess we're not going to Canada."

Pelham smiled weakly.

"I'll never see you again. Will I?"

Pelham drew Clara tight, fighting his emotions. "My lady, I wish with every part of my being that I could say you will. But the conflict that is coming will be more than you or I could ever imagine. It will be ugly beyond what you could ever conceive. The South, for its part, will fight to the last, for we have everything at stake. And whatever the outcome, I fear you and I will be in much different places. You'll be a doctor—I'll be a farmer."

"A plantation owner." Clara corrected him, tears streaming down her cheeks. "John, you will forever be my knight."

Unable to hold back his tears, Pelham and Clara wept in each other's arms until no tears remained. Withdrawing, he kissed her softly on each cheek.

"You, my dearest, will always be my lady, and I will say to you now what you have so longed to hear, and that has been true since first we met. I love you, Clara Bolton, in every way that love is possible. I love you. I love you. I love you."

After Pelham and Rosser departed Clermont, Pelham tore up the letter he had written Clara. As best they could, they avoided New York City, where talk of the city seceding from the state had authorities throwing anyone suspicious into overfilled jails. In like fashion, they avoided Baltimore, where mobs controlled the streets. At Pelham's insistence, they headed west and eventually crossed the Ohio River at Maysville, Kentucky. The Maysville College superintendent informed Pelham that his sister Bettie had departed three weeks earlier.

CHAPTER SEVENTY

THE FIRST BATTLE OF BULL RUN
SUNDAY, JULY 21, 1861

The Confederate attack on McDowell's left flank, planned by Beauregard, approved by Johnston, and anticipated by Pelham and every commander west of Bull Run, did not take place. The previous afternoon, after two days of reconnoitering Confederate positions and points to cross Bull Run and reprovision troops, McDowell directed his aide, Lieutenant Walter Kingsbury, to assemble the division commanders. At First Division headquarters, Kingsbury exchanged a warm handshake with two other aide-de-camps: Lieutenants Emory Upton and Patrick O'Rorke. It had been Upton who directed Union artillery fire across Blackburn's Ford on the failed attempt of the eighteenth.

When the division commanders were assembled, McDowell spoke plainly. "Gentlemen, we launch the main attack at two- thirty in the morning." He pointed to the battle map prepared by his chief engineer. "Confederate strength is well south of Stone Bridge, still centered on Blackburn's Ford and Mitchell's Ford, and we've seen no evidence of significant redeployment. Bory's stretched himself thin over eight miles of Bull Run, and our intelligence is that his left flank is anchored with no more than two regiments at Stone Bridge. The opening is clear—"

There was a commotion at the entrance to the tent, and Kingsbury turned to see George Custer, covered with dust and heading his direction.

Kingsbury smiled. "What do you have, Fannie?"

Custer shook the dust from his forage cap. "Frankly, Walter, General Scott is at a loss why you haven't attacked the Rebs yet. He's getting political heat and doesn't like the fact that half of Washington has come out to see the show. He insists McDowell get on with it before the Confederates gain more strength."

"You're going to tell him this?"

"No. As Scott's aide, I'm going to give him this sealed letter that says the same thing."

Kingsbury grinned. "General Winfield Scott's courier, Fannie? How is it you always land on your feet? I heard you were about to be court-martialed at the Academy for some extracurriculars, until your class graduated early. And now you're, free and clear, and a lieutenant."

Custer smiled. "Destiny, Walter. It's all about destiny."

At two-thirty Sunday morning, July 21, McDowell set his plan in motion, which from the beginning suffered setbacks. The two divisions that were to make the main attack by flanking Stone Bridge to the north bottlenecked in Centreville. Then they waited on the Warrenton Turnpike for a bridge to be repaired. But the greatest drawback to the battle plan came from a simple math error, the miscalculation of the distance to be covered by the flanking divisions. Instead of the seven miles reported, they would have to cover thirteen miles.

At five o'clock, Pelham heard Union artillery open fire to the north around Stone Bridge. This was followed by artillery fire to the south at Blackburn's Ford. He mobilized his battery, ordering his troops to down a quick breakfast and prepare for a long day. Throughout the early morning hours, he was in meetings with Generals Jackson and Bee, and Colonel Bartow.

Shortly after eight o'clock, Colonel Bartow informed Pelham that his brigade and General Bee's brigade were to move posthaste to reinforce the Confederate left flank—that the Union was moving a large number of troops to the north. General Jackson's brigade was to follow in reserve.

The battle that was to unfold centered on an intersection a mile west of Stone Bridge, formed by the Warrenton Turnpike—oriented roughly east-west—and Sudley Springs Road—oriented roughly north-south. Key terrain features were Matthews Hill to the northeast, Dogan Ridge to the northwest, Chinn Ridge to the southwest, and Henry House Hill to the southeast. Young's Branch, a steeply sloped, narrow tributary to Bull Run, meandered south of Dogan Ridge and Matthews Hill, and north of Chinn Ridge and Henry House Hill.

The landscape featured a patchwork of farmland, pastures, and meadows, with scattered pines and patchy dense forests of oak—a pastoral scene, save for the transformation taking place. Tall grass, chest high corn, and a scattering of wood fences finished the landscape, providing dips and depressions that later would offer fleeting haven to infantry on both sides.

On the upslope of Matthews Hill, just shy of the crest, an original force of only nine hundred Confederates and two light cannons encountered the flanking Union force, which would eventually number twenty thousand. Incredibly, the Confederates resisted the onslaught for nearly an hour before being reinforced by the brigades of Bartow and Bee.

Pelham's Alburtis battery and a battery attached to Bee's brigade unlimbered behind a natural parapet northwest of Henry House Hill and fed a furious shelling on Union troops advancing along the Sudley Springs Road.

By mid-morning, six senators, at least ten congressmen, and hundreds of civilian notables oblivious to the reality of what was unfolding appeared on the east side of Bull Run, fully expecting to witness the end of Southern foolishness. However, their presence only added confusion to the movement of green Union troops, puzzled by the presence of women in Victorian attire spreading picnic blankets and arraying them with victuals and drink, while they marched into battle to kill or be killed.

Soon the Union attack was bolstered on Dogan Ridge by two regular army artillery batteries boasting heavier guns than those of the Confederate batteries. The batteries were commanded by Captain Charles Griffin and Captain James Ricketts. Lieutenants Adelbert Ames and Charlie Hazlett commanded two-gun sections in Griffin's battery. Lieutenant Ned Kirby commanded two guns in Ricketts' battery.

By eleven o'clock, the vastly outnumbered brigades of Bartow and Bee and the original Confederate force on Matthews Hill were forced to rapidly retreat a mile across the turnpike and Young's Branch to

Henry House Hill. Pelham's battery and other batteries covered the Confederate retreat and pounded the Union troops overrunning the abandoned Confederate positions.

An hour later, General Jackson deployed his nearly three thousand Virginians along a broad front on the southeast side of Henry House Hill, just below the crest. On his right flank were South Carolina troops and, on his left, Jeb Stuart's Black Horse Cavalry. Exhausted and wounded troops from Matthews Hill congregated at the rear of Jackson's brigade.

Jackson ordered Pelham's battery and two other batteries to fall back under the fusillade of the Union's long range rifled guns on Dogan Ridge. As Pelham limbered his guns to fall back, his horse took a minie ball, but managed to keep its footing. The last battery to withdraw, Pelham spotted a mass of blue uniforms appearing from the wood line along Bull Run, positioned to roll up Jackson's right flank. Instinctively, he unlimbered his guns and fired deadly canister point blank at the advancing bluecoats until they receded back into the woods. Relimbering his guns, he fell back and deployed them in a depression on Jackson's right flank.

For two hours, Jackson and the other units on Henry House Hill withstood withering fire from Union guns and the torrid pressure of repeated infantry assaults. All the while, Generals Johnston and Beauregard exhorted unengaged brigades to advance to the sound of the guns. Colonel Bartow, attempting to rally his beleaguered troops, was mortally wounded by a Union sniper. General Bee was likewise felled, but not before exclaiming, "Look at Jackson standing there like a stone wall! Rally behind the Virginians!"

On the Union side, regiment after regiment threatened the Confederate left flank, outnumbering the Confederates almost three to one. However, they failed to mass their attacks, choosing instead to attack piecemeal, regiment after regiment as Union artillery pounded Confederate positions.

Shortly after one o'clock, McDowell sent Lieutenant Kingsbury to Captains Griffin and Ricketts with orders that they move their batteries to the crest of Henry House Hill. Both commanders questioned the order of advancing artillery in front of heavy infantry. Nevertheless, they limbered their guns and proceeded forward, reaching the crest of

Henry House Hill at about two o'clock. They unlimbered their guns just south and east of what was known as the Widow Henry's house.

A thundering duel ensued between Union and Confederate batteries separated by three hundred yards across the flat expanse of Henry House Hill. Opposing infantry hugged the earth as jets of flame through smoke wreaths hurled destruction. Nevertheless, the less powerful smoothbore Confederate guns proved deadly accurate, and Confederate sharpshooters took a heavy toll. In Griffin's battery, Adelbert Ames was lifted off his feet and spun around by a minie ball in the thigh. Ordered rearward by Griffin, Ames wouldn't hear of it. Instead, with a tourniquet tied above the wound and positioned on a rock, he continued to direct his guns.

In the haze of black smoke, Griffin informed Hazlett that he was taking two guns to the south of Ricketts battery to pour enfilade fire on the Rebel guns. Griffin succeeded in moving his guns but was immediately faced with a large number of blue-uniformed soldiers in an open field on his right flank. He loaded canister and was about to cut them down when the Union chief of artillery ordered him not to fire, declaring, "They are friendly troops, Captain. Just look at the uniforms." Griffin hotly argued to the contrary. "They are not friendly! How could they be, coming from that direction?"

An instant later, the argument was settled. Jackson's blue-uniformed 33rd Virginia Regiment charged the Union guns. Their initial volley dropping most of the gun crews and all the horse teams in Griffin's battery. Ricketts' battery fared worse, himself felled by four minie balls, and his second in command killed instantly. Ned Kirby found himself in command of a battery that couldn't move and had suffered twenty-seven killed or wounded.

Seeing the exposed guns, Jeb Stuart's black-horse cavalry charged the Union batteries from the southwest, scattering the remaining gunners and Union infantry. Another of Jackson's regiments joined the charge and, despite a furious barrage from Union troops, overran and captured the Union guns. However, possession of the guns teetered back and forth until finally claimed by the Confederates.

Pelham watched the whole through binoculars. Across the plain lay the remnant of what remained of the two Union batteries. He spied an officer staring in his direction, his visage obscured with soot and blood, wholly unrecognizable. The man bent down to help a second man to his feet. The two headed for the reforming Union line.

For the next hour, the battle seesawed. More fresh Union troops, including the light brigade of Colonel Oliver Howard, extended the Union right flank over Chinn Ridge. Sixteen hours earlier, at the conclusion of McDowell's battle briefing, He had offered prayer for the Union army's victory.

Just before four o'clock, McDowell ordered an all-out assault on Jackson's brigade. Expecting the attack, Jackson directed Pelham and the other Confederate battery commanders to load canister and to wilt the barrels on his command. As Jackson trooped the line, Pelham heard him coolly encouraging his men. "Wait, boys, until they are fifty yards. Then fire and then give them the bayonet … and yell like furies."

The expected attack came, pressing the Confederate line once again. But again, the Confederate line held. Shortly after four o'clock, the Union found its own right flank exposed. General Kirby Smith of Johnston's army, having just arrived by rail, fell in next to Jubal Early's brigade and other Confederate regiments to quickly extend the Confederate left flank. In mass they initiated a turning movement that started rolling up the Union right flank.

The scent of victory was strong in the Confederate nose. Beauregard ordered a general advance along the entire Confederate line. Within minutes, the Union ranks broke, fell back, and withdrew to the turnpike. The retreat across Stone Bridge began orderly, with some of the Union troops crossing at fords to the north. Soon, however, the withdrawal turned into a rout. Retreating troops found the turnpike blocked with supply wagons waiting to cross Bull Run. Advancing Confederate artillery capsized a haul wagon on a second turnpike bridge, preventing all but foot traffic. Confederate cavalry, led by Stuart, stung the flanks of the retreating Union column all the way to Centreville. Union artillery pieces, individual weapons, supply wagons, and horses were abandoned in place. A thousand Union soldiers were captured.

The battle was over.

On Henry House Hill, convinced that the Union had abandoned its guns for good, Pelham directed a dozen of his men to follow him with six-horse teams and an additional wagon.

In the midst of Union dead and wounded, shattered wagons, artillery pieces, dead and dying horses, and munitions, Pelham shouted, "Boys, would you look at this!"

"Whatcha got, Lieutenant?" Sergeant Miles's face was animated with victory.

Pelham ran a reverential hand over a tarnished brass barrel. "I trained with these for almost five years at West Point. We've just captured the West Point battery."

Having already ordered a general check for survivors, Pelham heard a noise. "You hear that, Miles?"

"What's that, sir?"

Pelham cocked his head. "There it is again."

"Sir, I'm about deef with all this shootin'."

Pelham stepped gingerly over two mangled bodies and squatted beneath an artillery gun barrel. Half buried in the dirt was a man, his blue uniform soaked with blood.

"Somebody give me a canteen," Pelham shouted as he bent over the man, an officer with the epaulets of a captain. Pelham squatted close to the man's ear. "Can you hear me, sir?"

The man managed a low groan.

"Here you go, Lieutenant." One of Pelham's cannoneers handed him a Union canteen.

Pelham soaked his kerchief with hot water from the canteen and swabbed the man's forehead. As he did, he noticed the man's Academy ring.

"Sergeant Miles, get me medical supplies and a doc if you can find one. Do it quick. I mean now!"

Pelham leaned down and whispered in the man's ear, "Sir, I'm going to poke around a bit. You let me know what hurts."

Pelham made a cursory inspection, feeling around several wounds. Eliciting no response, he thought the man in shock.

"You've got some holes in you, sir, and that's a fact. You're lucky to be alive. Can you tell me your name?"

The man moved his lips, but there was no sound.

"Here, take some water. It's okay. You're not gut shot."

Pelham raised the man's head, and the man took water. One slow sip at a time.

"Sir, your name?" Pelham asked a second time.

"Ri ... Ricketts—" said the man.

"Easy, sir. You're in good hands."

"Obliged ..." the man managed in a whisper.

"Sir, if I may, a question? Do you have a man in your battery by the name of Kirby?"

The man opened one eye and stared at Pelham, and then nodded.

EPILOGUE

FORTIETH REUNION, CLASSES OF MAY AND JUNE 1861
NOVEMBER 1901
WEST POINT, NEW YORK

What started as a beautiful Saturday morning with a full-dress review by the 480-member Corps of Cadets; a West Point victory over Annapolis, 11 to 5, in the seventh year of the Army-Navy football game; and a trip to the West Point cemetery had been reduced to an overcast afternoon, everything taking on a shade of gray. The May and June Classes of 1861 were celebrating their fortieth-year reunion. Fewer than twenty members and former members of the two classes sat on folding chairs for a remembrance ceremony in a clearing west of the ivy-covered West Point Hotel now celebrating its seventy-fifth anniversary. A number of wives and other family members were also present, sitting on chairs set apart from the class members. The mostly somber gathering was seasoned with enough mirth to achieve a good end by Henry du Pont at the podium.

"Good words, Henry," Tom Rosser said, putting his arm around du Pont's shoulders as he sat down.

Rosser's own remarks had opened the program, a gesture of good will from his Union classmates, and had preceded du Pont's. Rosser's wife, seeing West Point for the first time, sat with Libbie Custer, the widow of Rosser's dear friend and Civil War nemesis. The Texan had weathered well enough over the years but carried a lean in his posture. Having been seriously wounded three times in the war, he should have shown more evidence of infirmity. That Rosser had finished the war a major general, would have amazed his former taskmaster, Professor

Mahan. Devoted to a girl he met in the war, and whom he married just hours before he and all the male wedding guests rode off for Gettysburg, Rosser had struggled for purpose and identity after the war, as had most Confederates. For a time, he served as the chief engineer for a railroad, and in the Spanish-American War as a brigadier general for the country he had fought against. Early in their marriage, his wife had given him seven children. They had named one of the sons John Pelham.

Henry du Pont had fared well, receiving the Congressional Medal of Honor at Cedar Creek, and concluding the war as chief of artillery for the Department of West Virginia. He too had married and fathered seven children, though only two lived to adulthood. For many years, he was president of the Wilmington and Northern Railroad. He was also instrumental in the family business, incorporated as E. I. du Pont de Nemours and Company. Earlier in the reunion, du Pont told Rosser that he was now inclined toward politics.

Rosser and du Pont waited for the remarks of Adelbert Ames. Like Rosser, Ames attained the rank of major general; and like du Pont, received the Congressional Medal of Honor, his at First Bull Run. After the war, he resigned his commission to enter politics, serving as U.S. senator from Mississippi, and then as Mississippi's governor. He had the distinction of being the last "carpetbag" governor of the South; and like Rosser, was commissioned a brigadier general in the Spanish-American War. He married and had six children. One graduated from West Point in the Class of 1894. Ames, too, was little changed, except for a goatee and whiteness of hair.

"My beloved friends," Ames began. "The visit to the cemetery was a clear reminder that we've not much longer here to stay."

Several of the assembled found the remark amusing, though at the cemetery there had not been a dry eye when du Pont read the roll call of deceased classmates.

Ames acknowledged the attendees and family members, and the remarks made by Rosser and du Pont, and suggested that it might be pleasant to review what had happened to those who had played such an important or amusing role in their lives as cadets.

"The bane of our existence, Old Bentz," he began, "continued to bugle for another fifteen years until forced to retire. He died in 1878, offering his horn to St. Gabriel. And, as we saw in the cemetery, received a very fine grave marker from the Corps of Cadets.

"Also buried at West Point is General Winfield Scott, who in 1863, after fifty years of remarkable service to the nation, retired to West Point, where he witnessed the end of the war, before passing into paradise in 1866 at the age of seventy-nine.

"And what about our superintendents? Colonel Delafield was promoted to major general, became chief of the Corps of Engineers, and after retiring from the army, served as regent for the Smithsonian Institute. Old Del died in 1873. Our last superintendent, Alexander Bowman, passed early in 1865—I'm not sure what got him."

"Our shortest-tenured superintendent, Beauregard ..." Ames glanced at Rosser. "Old Bory commanded Confederate armies throughout the war, and afterwards ran two railroad companies and became an inventor of some renown, with several patents to his name. It was in 1893 that he entered eternity.

"As for our commandants, William Hardee commanded Confederate corps throughout the war and survived to run a cotton plantation in Selma, Alabama. This being insufficient diversion, he also operated a warehouse, an insurance business, and presided over the Selma & Meridian Railroad. Hardee passed in 1873.

"John Reynolds, God rest his soul, was the Union's best corps commander. I personally know he was seriously considered by Lincoln to command the Army of the Potomac. Reynolds, of course, fell at Gettysburg. But we all know that—" Ames had to dry his eye on that one.

"After surviving Fort Sumter, Major Robert Anderson was promoted to major general, was a driving force in creating our Association of Graduates, and by and by picked Nice, France, as the place to depart the earth, which he did in 1871. As we saw, he too is interred in the West Point cemetery.

"After the war, Jeff Davis was charged but never convicted of treason, though he did spend two years in prison before Northern and Southern notables posted his bail. He was elected to the U.S. Senate again, but not allowed to serve, and completed two fine literary works on the Confederacy before he passed in 1889.

"And what of our lieutenants? Oliver Howard, our Bible-preaching math teacher?" Ames couldn't resist a chuckle. "Hell, he goes straight to the top, wearing all the stars allowed, commanding Union armies, and receiving the Congressional Medal of Honor in exchange for a right arm. But even with one arm he continued to soldier on the frontier, and in the early eighties returned to West Point as superintendent. To his considerable credit, he was a co-founder of Howard University in Washington DC, a nonsectarian institution for men and women, with no regard for race. And, of course, other institutions bear his mark. As far as I know, the man remains on this side of the grass." Ames smiled. "It appears to pay well to be in the Lord's camp."

"Fitzhugh Lee, one of my favorites—and Rosser's too—did what we would have expected. Made major general early in the war and commanded cavalry units throughout, and at the end—after Jeb Stuart was killed—very ably supported his uncle, Robert E. Lee. Following the war and after a hand at growing cotton and a family—he had five children—Fitz went on to serve as governor of Virginia. After that, like Rosser, he was called up as a major general for the Spanish-American War. Last I heard, he too is still kicking.

"Finally, what of our professors, those demigods who held our fates in their stoic little hands? They, of course, are all lecturing in heaven now. Professors Mahan and Agnel died in office in 1871. Professor Church died on his mathematics throne in 1878. Professor Weir not only lived to retire in 1876, after forty-two years at West Point, but lived to the ripe age of eighty-five, giving up the ghost in 1889. Professor Kendrick—I for one will never forget his peach brandy—retired in 1880 and departed for glory in 1891. He was eighty, and I understand there was quite a turnout for his funeral. Old Bartlett, he outlasted them all. After forty years, he retired in 1871, and didn't pass until 1893 at the age of eighty-eight.

"As for the Warner sisters, those dear angels of God. Some of us knelt this morning at Susan's grave, the plot donated by the Academy. And I daresay one day the earthly remains of her sister, Anna, will reside beside her."

As Ames continued, Rosser reflected on the roll call at the cemetery. He thought of Chas Patterson, Shakespeare incarnate, and the first to die in the war. He had been a lieutenant colonel, leading his infantry regiment at Shiloh in April 1862. Walter Kingsbury, whose voice ruled the Plain and the mess hall, was next in September 1862—leading his regiment into the hell storm of Antietam Creek near Sharpsburg on the bloodiest day of the war. When they carried his body away, it bore eight musket balls. In tragic irony, he was killed by men in the division commanded by his brother-in-law, Major General David Jones. Five months later, his beloved Eva delivered a son, Walter Kingsbury, Jr. Rosser understood that Eva never really recovered from Walter's death.

Rosser had to blink hard, thinking of Ned Kirby at Chancellorsville. He'd been seriously wounded, his leg shattered, but he wouldn't allow himself to be taken from the battlefield. He continued to inspire his men until he collapsed from loss of blood. After the battle, his leg was amputated, and for a time there was hope he would survive. But gangrene developed, and senior officers in the Army of the Potomac approached President Lincoln on Kirby's behalf. Lincoln immediately came to Kirby's bedside and promoted him to brigadier general an hour before he breathed his last.

Rosser's thoughts turned to Gettysburg, where for him and so many, the war had been lost. On the Union side, Paddy O'Rorke, first captain and favorite of the Class of June 1861, was killed rushing his regiment to the defense of Little Round Top. Hours later, Charlie Hazlett fell next to his guns on the same piece of smoking earth.

But for Rosser, he had a hard time remembering these and other things. The war seemed a lifetime ago. His reflections turned instead to George Custer, last in his class but its highest ranking and most decorated member during the war. He and Fannie, both commanding cavalry brigades, had chased each other up and down the Shenandoah Valley the last two years of the war, Fannie proving as fiercest a foe as he had been faithful a friend. But they had renewed their friendship after the war. And Custer was gone now and had been for many years. Thinking of the Little Big Horn, he glanced at Libbie Custer. The little woman, still pretty as a picture, would never remarry. She would be brave and proud for her man until the day she joined him.

He thought of Nate Chambliss, who had managed to graduate with the class. But when Tennessee announced secession and Chambliss submitted his resignation, rather than being allowed to resign like others of the South, he was dismissed for refusing to do battle with the Confederacy. Chas Patterson shared the same fate two weeks later when Arkansas seceded. In any event, Chambliss survived the war to marry the youngest daughter of former commandant William Hardee and run a cotton plantation, edit a newspaper, and teach mathematics at the University of Alabama. Much to his credit, Chambliss had been one of the first Confederates to renew ties with West Point and to join the post-war Association of Graduates. He had been a key planner for the fortieth reunion before dying at the age of sixty-two, missing the reunion by two years.

"So, that is about it from me," Ames said. "Let me end by saying I am deeply honored to be part of our class, and of our motto *Faithful to Death*, and even more so to be a member of the Long Gray Line. God bless you all—and may God grant us safe passage into his peace."

Ames received a standing ovation. As he returned to his seat, du Pont announced that everyone was on their own until supper in the hotel dining room.

"Let's the three of us walk," Ames said to Rosser and du Pont. "The cold has got to my bones. If I don't keep moving, I start to seize up in my leg."

Rosser nodded. "I know. Don't expect any of us is without at least one extra hole in him."

The three walked the short distance to the newly constructed Battle Monument, the most impressive edifice on the West Point campus. Upon a broad circular terrace, a five-foot diameter Roman Doric column of granite rose forty-six feet, supporting a winged statue of fame. Positioned at octagonal points around the terrace were eight square pedestals topped by large bronze-banded granite spheres flanked by miniature cannons. The monument had been designed to memorialize the officers and men of the regular army who had died in the Civil War, and its dedication four years earlier had been attended by du Pont, Ames, and Chambliss. The bronze bands around the granite spheres bore the names of two thousand and forty-two enlisted men. The base of the granite column bore the names of one hundred and eighty-eight officers. The three of them silently scanned the names at the base of the column.

Rosser suddenly fell to his knees and wept.

Ames was quick to understand.

Rosser's finger shook as it traced the name—*Daniel McElheny.*

"I know, Tom. I know," Ames said, no less affected, and placing a hand on Rosser's shoulder.

Du Pont place a hand on Rosser's other shoulder. "Oh, how the boy could make us laugh."

Rosser struggled to his feet, the three of them standing in silence, staring at the column.

Turning toward the Plain, Rosser swept his hand across the horizon silhouetted with distant structures. A behemoth building a hundred yards north of the library stood overlooking the Hudson. The structure had been named for General George Cullum and boasted a huge ballroom with a ceiling of three hundred and forty lights. "Except for Cullum Hall," Rosser said, "where the likes of us could have had some mighty fine parties, nothing's really changed."

"Forty years," Ames said, as if it wasn't possible.

"Yet there have been changes," said du Pont. "And Emory Upton must have enjoyed one of them very much."

"Emory?" Rosser expressed surprise.

"Henry O. Flipper, Class of 1877. He was our first Negro graduate and a cadet while Emory was commandant."

"But wasn't he … silenced by the Corps?" Ames asked, referring to the practice of members of the Corps not talking to one of their own except on official business.

"Indeed. All four years. And I suppose not surprising given the times. But the incredible thing is that Flipper took it all in stride, and upon graduation, to a man, the Corps roundly cheered him and took his hand in friendship. I'm told it was a very moving scene."

"I can imagine," Ames said. "For myself, I always thought Emory a different sort of duck. But he was more man than most of us."

"And not so different, really," said du Pont. "He and I became close after the war, both of us in positions to assist West Point. A remarkable man, and no more honorable and serving a heart has ever beat. And he certainly didn't deserve his end."

Rosser and Ames nodded. They all knew the story, that after the war, in which he attained the rank of major general, Upton had fallen hard for a young and very beautiful woman, who deeply loved him. Her effect upon him had been transforming. But just two years into the marriage she died, at about the time he learned he was to be commandant at West

Point. A few years later, at the age of forty-two, the class abolitionist had put a gun to his head. Some speculated it was grief over the loss of his wife, but du Pont and others knew the truth. He had suffered from intense headaches and the sensation of blood surging through his head. Toward the end, he thought himself going insane. After his death, an autopsy revealed that he had suffered a brain aneurysm and a probable brain tumor.

A silence followed, until Ames, his eyes suddenly moist, said, "How is it none of us speaks of John?"

Du Pont, who up to that moment had been a rock, could no longer hold back the tears.

Rosser, out of tears, drew the two of them to himself and attempted a laugh. He pinched his cheeks. "You know, I envy the boy. Think of it—he'll never grow old. I'm so wrinkled, I can't find my face."

Du Pont and Ames, cheeks as lined, welcomed the humor.

"Tell us, Tom," du Pont said. "Tell us about John."

"All right. But let's start walking again. I've got the same problem Adelbert has."

As they walked in a slow circle around the monument, Rosser related events as best he could recall them, from the time he and Pelham departed West Point on the steamer in April 1861.

"I saw a lot of John during the war, both of us serving in Virginia and in Jackson's army. Jeb Stuart loved John like a brother and kept him close. He wanted John's input on everything." Rosser hesitated, as if reflecting. "Remember the girl I snuck into camp for Pelham?"

Ames smiled. "Clara, wasn't it?"

"How could we forget?" du Pont said.

"Good memories," said Rosser. "The sweetest gal and obviously over the edge with our John. Anyway, the two of them survived our last year on letters and her visit after Christmas."

Du Pont shot Rosser a look. "She came back to West Point?"

"John never told you?"

"Not a peep," said Ames.

"I suppose I was the only one that knew—me and Dan McElheny." Rosser had to clear his throat again. "Anyway, after Sumter, they agreed to end it. Not that they had a choice." Rosser didn't mention the trip to Clermont. "But on the boat from West Point, John showed me a letter from Eva Taylor, who, of course, married our Walter. In the letter she said that a Miss Sallie Dandridge was no longer seeing anyone and would be pleased to have him call on her in Virginia at a place called the Bowery, near Martinsburg."

"And?" pressed du Pont.

"John did. Before Manassas, the Army of Virginia trained near where her family lived. I met Sallie a few times—quite a looker and a match for John—and she and John hit it off from the start. They saw a lot of each other between campaigns, because that was where the army rested and wintered as much as it could."

Rosser paused and adjusted his scarf against the wind.

"The last we talked, John announced he was going to marry the girl once there was time to do the deed. That was about the time he received a final letter from Clara Bolton. She was attending Smithfield Medical College and had a proposal of marriage from a recently graduated doctor, the two of them having courted for a while. She wanted John to know and to have his blessing, which he freely gave her. John was genuinely happy for her."

Rosser hesitated, as if catching his breath. "As for John the soldier, from the very beginning, at First Manassas, he proved himself the shining star of the South, all action and humble as dirt. He just had a knack for artillery, how to do battle, and getting his guns in and out of the most god-awful places. His men would do anything for him. Audacious—that's what he was. Damn, he was audacious!" Rosser wagged a finger at Ames. "After Manassas and what John did there, Jeb Stuart says, 'I want horse artillery,' and tells John to make it happen and be its chief. He wanted guns moving like the wind across the battlefield. And John delivered. It wasn't long before he had five batteries under him, and not a few times the artillery of other divisions. I daresay Pelham's horse artillery was one of the most unnerving weapons we had against you boys."

"Easily," admitted Ames.

"Yep, John's guns were everywhere at once," Rosser mused. "He could move, shoot, move, shoot, and never be in a place long enough for you guys to get a bead on him … just plain audacious."

Ames laughed. "Sharpsburg and Fredericksburg, that's where I remember him best—or worst."

Rosser smiled. "Damn straight. Especially Fredericksburg. That would have been December 1862. You bluecoats outmatched us in numbers—more than usual. We were in a pinch. That's when John told Jeb Stuart he could take two guns and get some enfilade fire on you bluecoats. A damn scary sight, you were. Your front stretched three miles. Three rows of infantry, fifty-five thousand strong, bayonets gleaming, coming straight at us. Anyway, what he did with those two artillery pieces was nothing short of a miracle."

Rosser seemed to revel in the memory.

"He pinned your left flank, the sixteen thousand troops of John Reynolds, our old commandant. And how does he do it? By moving his guns after every shot—that's how! There was no give-up in the man. After an hour, you guys got lucky and took out one of his guns." Rosser put a finger on du Pont's chest. "So then, what does he do? For another hour, he hops around with just the one gun, blazing away—Reynolds slowed down—a hundred of your guns trying to nail him." Rosser took a breath. "That was my roommate … and that was a good day— damn, that was a good day. All of us, from Lee down, knew what John had done. That's when General Lee singled John out, called him, 'the gallant Pelham.'" Said, "'It is glorious to see such courage in one so young.'"

Ames and du Pont couldn't help but share in Rosser's pride.

"What you say is true, Tom," du Pont said. "John would never retreat."

"Amen on that," said Ames.

Rosser drew himself up. "Did you know that John was in every engagement he could possibly have been in? More than sixty, and through them all, he lived the charmed life. Never sick, not even a scratch—though I can't say the same for his horse."

Ames and du Pont chuckled.

Rosser glanced up the river. "Our own Fannie, God rest his soul, in the middle of the war he sends John a telegram of congratulations!"

"Just what he'd do," Ames said with affection.

"It was Kelly's Ford where John went down, wasn't it, Tom?" du Pont said in a whisper.

Rosser's eyes dropped to the pavers around the monument. "Yeah. It was. March 1863."

Du Pont put a hand on Rosser's shoulder.

"The morning of Kelly's Ford, John and I were breakfasting with Stuart when a courier nearly runs his horse into the fire with news that large Union cavalry had engaged Fitz Lee's cavalry pickets. John didn't say a word. Just borrowed a horse and rode to the sound of the guns. He was everywhere in the early stage of the fight, exhorting the troops. The consummate officer high on his horse." Rosser's voice trailed off. "After the war, I talked to a man who was there, who witnessed it. Said there was an airburst, and John just slumped down from his horse. When they got to him, he was unconscious. At first, they couldn't find a wound, but then they found where a splinter of shrapnel had pierced the back of his skull. He never regained consciousness. Our John— who had never suffered a scratch—died the next morning."

Ames and du Pont had to turn their heads.

"Stuart, of course, was heartbroken. In John, he'd lost his right arm. Sallie Dandridge was devastated. Clara Bolton, thank God, never knew. John's body lay in state in Richmond— thousands paid their respects." Rosser's eyes glistened. "Our dear friend was mourned throughout the South and eventually taken home to be buried in Jacksonville, Alabama."

Du Pont wiped his eyes with the back of his hand. "I can just see him now—that grin of his."

"The irony," Rosser said. "I, too, went down at Kelly's Ford, not a quarter mile from John. Think of it. I survive and live out my life, and John dies thinking the South is winning its independence."

A gust of wind blew leaves across the terrace of the monument and between their feet.

Two cadets in dress gray, who had been watching the three alumni from a respectful distance, approached the monument. From the two chevrons on their dress coat cuffs, Rosser assumed they were Second Classmen.

One of the two addressed him. "Sir, we see from your arm bands that you are Class of May 1861."

The cadet extended his hand.

"We couldn't help noticing your connection with the monument."

"Indeed," said Rosser, shaking the cadet's hand. "The name is Tom Rosser, and don't be taking any pity on us. I'll have you know we were once as young as you. What's your name, son?"

"MacArthur, sir. Douglas MacArthur. And this is my classmate, Ulysses Grant."

Rosser's head snapped back. "Any kin to …?"

"My grandfather, sir."

Rosser forced a smile. "You know, your grandfather made life very unpleasant for us."

Rosser introduced Ames and du Pont.

"Sirs," MacArthur said, "I'm sure we'll come across your names next year when we study the Civil War."

"I think you mean the War between the States, young man," Rosser said, his dander up.

"Had you won the war, Tom," Ames said under his breath.

"I'm from Arkansas," MacArthur said, as if in conciliation. "Ulysses is from Illinois."

"Sir," Grant said, his tone respectful. "To my mind, this monument is as much yours as the Union's. I can't imagine what your class went through, and how you handled it."

"We all have our challenges," Rosser said evenly. "I daresay yours will too."

The two cadets held the three veterans captive, asking questions about what it was like to be a First Classman on the eve of the war, to serve in the war itself, to face friends in war, to learn of their deaths, and to reconcile after so much had been at stake. They especially grilled Rosser as one who had been on the losing side.

"Now, I think it's my turn, boys," said Rosser after he had been picked clean. Remembering the old days, the things he, Pelham, and Custer had done, he asked, "Tell me, do you play everything by the book here?"

"Actually, sir." Grant turned to MacArthur. "Can I tell him, Doug?"

"Why not. He might appreciate it more than you think," said MacArthur with a straight face.

"Sir, you see the reveille cannon over there?" Grant pointed to the small cannon next to the post flagpole.

"I do," said Rosser.

"It's fixed with bolts to a concrete pad," MacArthur said.

"One night last month," Grant said, "Doug and I, with a little help, put that cannon on top of the clock tower in Central Area." Grant beamed with pride. "All Doug's plan—pure genius. No one has a clue how it was done or who did it."

Rosser glanced at MacArthur, whose face bore a grin. "What say you, Henry? Adelbert? Does that qualify for the large testicle award?"

"Sir," MacArthur said, after they had all enjoyed a good laugh, "we've badgered you enough. But I've one last question—which you might think strange."

"Shoot," said Rosser, his arms crossed.

"Sir, next year we celebrate the centennial of the Academy. As you know, we have many traditions here. And some of us wonder how much is fact, and how much is fiction. For instance, we sing 'Benny Havens, Oh.' All those verses."

Rosser smiled. "Yes. A lot of verses."

"Sir—did the man really exist?"

Rosser looked at Ames and du Pont, the three guffawing. Prior to the reunion, he and Ames had visited Havens' gravesite in the Highland Union Cemetery south of Buttermilk Falls, learning that the town was now called Highland Falls. Buried beside Havens were Letitia and their three children. They had learned over a pint in a local pub that Havens had tired of the tavern business in the early years after the Civil War, and had begun to spend time in New York City, though still making the Landing his home. After his death in 1877 at the age of ninety, the tavern and home were razed to make way for a railroad, the same railroad whose trains passed beneath the Plain during the reunion.

"Young man, would you like to see where Benny's tavern used to be?"

IT IS FINISHED

While serving as the postmaster of Charlottesville, Virginia, Thomas Lafayette Rosser died on March 29, 1910, at the age of seventy-three, his wife at his side.

Having served two terms as United States senator from the State of Delaware and having proved himself a lifelong advocate of West Point, Henry Algernon du Pont died peacefully at his Delaware home (Winterthur) on December 31, 1926, at the age of eighty-eight.

A close friend and golfing partner of John D. Rockefeller, the last surviving member of the Class of May 1861, and the oldest living graduate of the Academy, Adelbert Ames died at his summer home in Ormond Beach, Florida, on April 13, 1933, at the age of ninety-seven.

ACKNOWLEDGEMENTS

The Parting could not have been written without continual reference to the nonfictional works of Mary Elizabeth (Betty) Sergent (1919- 2005), *They Lie Forgotten* and *An Unremaining Glory*; and her fictional work *Growing up in Alabama*. In aggregate, they chronicle the West Point Classes of May and June 1861 and the life of John Pelham. I was blessed to have known Mary Betty—a wonderful woman of faith and an amazing friend of West Point who "adopted' six West Point plebes as "nephews" over the years—and to have accepted her challenge to write this story.

I am most grateful to Elaine McConnell, Suzanne Christoff, Susan Lintelmann, Alicia Mauldin-Ware, Valerie Dutdut, and the many other extremely helpful members of the West Point Library Special Collections and Archives staffs who suffered me to nest in their quiet space, and who provided the photograph of Edmund (Ned) Kirby, the sketch map of West Point, and the photograph of cadets conducting artillery drill on the Plain pictured herein. Similarly, my thanks to Brett Bradshaw, president of the John Pelham Historical Association, for permission to use the photograph of John Pelham taken in his furlough uniform, and thanks as well to the association's treasurer, Bill Gilmore.

A very special thanks to Tom Petrie, my dear friend, classmate, and renowned collector of American art, for his permission to adapt the painting "Encampment on the Plain," by William Guy Wall, 1862, for inclusion in this book. As a member of the Gettysburg Foundation's board of directors and a man with a thorough knowledge of the Civil War and American history, his insights were most helpful to me.

Thanks also to Jon Malinowski, professor of geography, United States Military Academy, classmate Freed Lowrey, and Rich Barbuto (Class of 1971) for their review of period-specific descriptions of West Point and the times; to classmate Paul Haseman for his unswerving support; to Anne McNeil for her "horse sense;" and to the *many, many* friends who read the various drafts of my manuscript and gave me the feedback needed to make the story better.

Thanks also to the Squaw Valley Community of Writers family, who encouraged me and prodded my writing craft in a better direction, and to Elizabeth L. Barrett for her early line editing.

A very special thanks, also, to the West Point Class of 1961, who conceived, funded, and continue to maintain Reconciliation Plaza at West Point, and to its member, Colonel (Ret.) Ed Brown, who has been a true ally throughout the writing of this story.

And a very special thanks to the incredible instructors who served with me in administering the small-group race relations seminar training program throughout the 24th Engineer Group (Construction) in Germany from late 1973 to mid 1974 (Lieutenant Washington, Master Sergeant Justman, Staff Sergeant Cotto Perez, and Corporal Roundtree).

Finally, immeasurable gratitude to my loving family, to the Class of 1967, to our two African American classmates (Jimmy Fowler and Bobby Whaley) and to every man and woman of the Long Gray Line who for more than two centuries have stood in the gap for a grateful nation, and after the Civil War have played such an important role in its healing.

AUTHOR'S NOTE

Much of *The Parting* is based on facts derived from archival research and nonfiction publications; and seasoned by my experiences as a West Point cadet and graduate, and later, as an Academy adjunct assistant professor. Such form the basis for the story's period portrayal of West Point, the cadet class system, the regimen of summer encampment, the hops at the West Point Hotel, meals in the mess hall, the routine of barracks life, the regimen of academics, the "extracurricular" activities of cadets, and the inexorable unraveling of the country in 1860-1861.

The reader may wonder at the truth of whether Jefferson Davis actually chaired a federal commission to evaluate West Point in the summer of 1860; whether Major Robert Anderson (later commanding federal forces at Fort Sumter) was part of that commission; whether John Pelham was president of the Dialectic Society and could have encouraged the society to debate the right of a state to secede; whether Flirtation Walk was truly the venue for intimacy portrayed in the story; whether the first-ever visit by British royalty to North America included a stop at West Point; whether Benny Havens ever existed, with his lure of hot flip; whether a straw poll was taken within the Corps before the election of 1860; whether Henry du Pont actually fought a pugilistic contest with John Pelham as his second; whether cadets really skated across the Hudson to Garrison and at Christmastime chased a greased pig for the right to a feast; whether the antics of cadets (those future defenders of American and world liberty) could be as inane as portrayed in the story; whether academic life was as rigorous as described; whether Henry Farley of South Carolina, the first Southern cadet to resign in the face of secession, later pulled the lanyard that started the Civil War; and whether Douglas MacArthur and Ulysses S. Grant III were actually cadets in 1901. The reader may take heart that all these things and more are based in fact or the documented memory of those alive at the time. Additionally, the reader may take comfort that almost all the characters in the story (cadets, Academy military and academic leadership, and others) are real, and that their relationships to one another and their actions within the story are, with few exceptions, authentic.

Whether John Pelham actually had a love affair with Clara Bolton, I leave to the reader, but not the reality that he was caught by Lieutenant Colonel Hardee displaying his affection to a girl while attending a hop at the West Point Hotel, and for the offense was confined to quarters for the balance of the 1860 summer encampment. That Pelham met and fell in love with Sallie Dandridge in the fall of 1861, and that they were engaged to be married, is also much more fact than fiction.

The events of the three days leading up to and including the First Battle of Bull Run are similarly based in fact; and the likelihood is great that John Pelham and Ned Kirby indeed peered at each other across the crest of Henry House Hill during the decisive encounter that gave the Confederacy the first major victory of the Civil War.

The story's epilogue, the fortieth reunion, while apocryphal, could easily have taken place, and the fates of the story characters presented in the epilogue are true.

To my readers, I cannot urge strongly enough that if you have never visited West Point, that you do so; and that among all the historical attractions you can see, you allot sufficient time to experience the emotion and relevance of Reconciliation Plaza.

Lastly, you'll find on the following page my poem, *In Their Eyes*. My intent with the poem was to capture for returning graduates walking the Plain in the morning before a Saturday Alumni Review the emotions associated with fall and spring West Point class reunions, when graduates spanning more the sixty years return to the Academy to renew their bonds . . . men and women of *The Long Gray Line*.

In Their Eyes

Ere cloaking Hudson mist gives birth to pensive early dawn,
And warming sun imbues the day with color's magic wand,
Some walk the quiet of that time recalling what had been,
When younger then, they too were called, a country to defend.

So much the same, the sight and sound and scent upon the wind.
Roused memory of former times, sweet chapters deep within.
When first the Corps assembled there, uncertain what to be,
Til men of worth and men of faith saw clear its destiny.

Three hallowed words would cross their lips, a motto ever be.
The first was **DUTY**, selfless love, to serve a nation free.
Then **HONOR** next, a guarding shield against the tempter's sting.
And **COUNTRY** followed, sacred trust, of which they'd often sing.

The river's might, the circling hills, beneath God's brilliant arch,
Calls forth to mind those harried times when they, too, formed to march.
When shoes and brass were made to shine, and belts the purest white
Were donned on black trimmed coats of gray, beneath a dress hat bright.

Behind them lay so much of life since first they wore the gray.
When light their step and clear their eye, they savored each new day.
Those happy times of West Point years when bonds for life were made.
Til oaths were sworn and forth they went, their mettle to be weighed.

Still on they walk on legs grown old, with eyes that strain to see.
But gaining strength with every step, infused by history,
By classmates gone whose deeds on earth live on in mind and heart.
Remembered friends in marbled stone who bravely did their part.

What's that they hear upon the Plain, but sound of fife and drum,
As turn they all to join a class whose time to march has come,
And march they do with heads held high before the grateful throng.
And with them wait for freedom's band to call the new guard on.

The granite walls release their hold and free the waiting Corps,
Young men and women marching forth to martial music score.
They pass the Line, their span of years, as heads look right to see.
And in their eyes catch full a glimpse of who they'll one day be.

All sense a spirit in the air, a bond across the stage,
As eyes grow moist and hearts beat fast, uniting all in age.
The young march off and leave the plain, the stirring music dies.
But those who stay, inspired so, renew their lifelong ties.

God grant them mercy in your will, the Black and Gold and Gray.
To find a servant's resting place, when comes the final day.
With family, friends, The Long Gray Line, eternity to share;
Immortal life by heaven's grace with all who gather there.

ABOUT THE AUTHOR

Richard Barlow Adams (Rich), born to Colonel and Mrs. Ernest C. Adams, was the first of three sons to graduate from West Point. He received his appointment to join the Class of 1967 from Representative Homer Thornberry of the 10th Congressional District of Texas. Six months after graduation, he deployed to Vietnam as an artillery forward observer for D Company, 1/506th Infantry, 3rd Brigade, 101st Airborne Division. Upon returning to the States, he served as a basic training company commander, transferred to the Army Corps of Engineers, and became a fixed-wing aviator, serving a year-long flight tour in the middle east. After seven years in the military, culminating with a tour in Germany, he and his family returned to Austin, Texas, where he began a career as a consulting civil/environmental engineer. Later, moving to Baton Rouge, Louisiana, he formed, grew, and sold a civil/environmental engineering company. He is active in West Point alumni affairs and the many activities of his class and has served as an adjunct professor in the School of Engineering and Applied Science, Southern Methodist University, and as an adjunct assistant professor in the West Point Department of Geography and Environmental Engineering. He and his wife have two married children, five grandchildren, reside in Miramar Beach, Florida, and are active members of the Destin Methodist Church.

As Adams pursues his writing, he serves as the Chief Strategy Officer for Ion Power Group LLC, continues to serve as a consulting engineer, and enjoys speaking engagements, traveling, golfing, skiing (a former Vail Resorts ski instructor), and sharing his faith. Among his other works, Adams is the author of *Eben Kruge: How "A Christmas Carol" Came to be Written*, a story about Charles Dickens and what inspired him to write the Christmas classic; and *Charlie's Ashes: A Greatest Generation Story*, a fact-based narrative about five WWII veterans ranging in age from 93 to 101 in a Florida assisted living facility.

The Author

The Cadet

Story Characters

John Pelham, AL

Tom Rosser, TX

Ned Kirby, NY

Henry du Pont, DE

Nathaniel
Chambliss, TN

Emory Upton, NY

Walter Kingsbury, CT

Adelbert Ames, ME

Charles Patterson, AR

George A. Custer, OH

Patrick O'Rorke, NY

Al Mordecai, NC

COL/GEN Richard
Delafield, NY

LTC/GEN John
Reynolds, PA

LT/GEN Fitzhugh
Lee, VA

Professor Dennis
Mahan, NY

LT/GEN Oliver
O. Howard, ME

GEN Winfield
Scott, NY

GEN P.G.T.
Beauregard, LA

CPL Louis Bentz
and Hanzi

Senator Louis
Wigfall, TX

Congressman
William Miles, SC

Albert Edward
Prince of Wales

CPT/GEN James
Ricketts, NY

GEN Thomas
Jackson, VA

COL/GEN J.E.B.
Stuart, VA

Douglas MacArthur
Class of 1903, AR

Ulysses S. Grant III,
Class of 1903, IL

Benny Havens, NY
Tavern Keeper

Dr. Atkinson Pelham
(Pelham's father), AL

West Point Images, Circa 1860

1) Academy view to northeast, 2) Academy view to the east, 3) View to northeast of Central Area Barracks, 4) view east of entire Corps of Cadets in formation north of the barracks, 5) view west of the Academic building and barracks, 6) Academic Building view southwest, 7) interior of cadet mess hall, 8) Academy Riding Hall, 9) sketch of a riding class, 10) interior of cadet chapel, 11) the West Point Hotel, 12) Sketch of a cadet hop in the hotel, 13) visitors at the Summer Encampment Guest Tent, 14) artillery drill on the Plain, 15) cadets in formation by the barracks, 16) view of Benny Havens' Tavern, 1.5 miles south of the Academy on the west shore of the Hudson River, before it was razed in 1883.